THE APPRENTICE

THE APPRENTICE

A NOVEL

by

LESLIE GILLETT

LONDON
VICTOR GOLLANCZ LTD
1978

© Leslie Gillett 1978

ISBN 0 575 02357 0

Printed in Great Britain by Bristol Typesetting Co. Ltd,
Barton Manor, St Philips, Bristol

"Where once my careless childhood stray'd
A stranger yet to pain!"
GRAY

THE APPRENTICE

I

THE FIRST TIME I knowingly saw Marcus Daveney was on a
Monday evening when I was going to choir practice. He was
choosing biscuits in my father's shop, running his eye along the
square fronts of the big Huntley and Palmer tins and allowing my
father to pull them from their shelves for a free tasting. I remember
that he chose Osborne, though I could have told him that the
Garibaldi lasted longer. If you went at them slowly you could
dissolve away the biscuit and leave your mouth full of currants. The
biscuit tins, their labels printed with that splendid buckled-belt
device, had no secrets for me. I asked my father to give me a sixpence; we were clubbing together to buy a Christmas present for
Mr. Dyball, the choir master, and that night was the one ordained
by the head chorister for collection. Leaving his biscuits he went
round behind the counter, whispering to me behind a pile of tins,
"Marcus Daveney. Father's a Lord", slid the greasy till open and
clinked in the hollow wooden hemisphere that held the silver.
Marcus Daveney gave me an Osborne biscuit. If you look underneath an Osborne you can see the marks of the wire tray they bake
it on. But I didn't look for them that time; I was looking intently
at the face of Marcus Daveney.

We had choir practice on Mondays, Wednesdays and Fridays. At
half-past six on the first two, but at eight o'clock on Fridays, for
that was the night when the altos and tenors and basses came and
when Mr. Dyball, so patient with us on Mondays and Wednesdays,
could, if we missed a lead or shirked a treble entry, reduce us to
tearful shame. I remember once when we were practising Stanford's
Te Deum in B flat and I had to sing the treble solo, "We therefore
pray thee help thy servants . . .", I was so nervous that when that
tender little passage began, I was dumb. One of the tenors was
Mr. Webster, a master at my school. Mr. Dyball, taking his hands
from the keys, said, "Don't you teach your boys to count, Mr.
Webster?" An anguish of embarrassment choked me. Tears were

A*   9

drowning my eyes. Someone else had to sing my part. Even in my misery I supposed it was more cruel to Mr. Webster than to me, but I was not old enough to distinguish between gentle fun and calculated sarcasm in my elders. I remember that Mr. Webster didn't seem to mind. But the laughter of the men almost had me dashing from the vestry to hide my agony.

On that Monday we followed our usual practice: a quick correction of last Sunday's mistakes, the responses had been slack; we had sung "an' with they spiri' " instead of "and with thy spirit", a careful preparation of the Psalms for the coming Sunday, a few verses of the hymns (it was Advent; the Baptist's cry could be heard on Jordan's banks), a perfecting of the Tallis Sevenfold Amen for after the blessing, and a first look at the new anthem.

For the psalms we had a fat, comforting red-leather 'Cathedral Psalter' and a flimsy, floppy green cloth-bound chant book—the chants all copied into it by hand. (Whose hand? Mr. Dyball's? I never asked him.)

Anyhow, there we were, Cathedral Psalter in one hand, floppy chant-book in the other, watching out for when the chant changed or the second part had to be repeated because the psalm had an odd number of verses, hoping *Laetatus sum*, 'I was glad when they said unto me', or *Deus noster refugium*, 'God is our help and strength', would turn up, and fearful lest Sunday should fall on the twenty-fourth day of the month, because that meant Psalm 119 with its 176 verses.

That night it was 'Are your minds set upon righteousness . . .?', Psalm 58. It has the bit in it about the deaf adder that stoppeth its ears and refuseth to hear the voice of the charmer; it was one of Mr. Dyball's jokes to observe that the adder did this by laying one ear to the ground and putting the tip of its tail in the other. But funnily enough he didn't repeat it that night; instead, he got on as if his mind wasn't set upon righteousness at all, and after we had had a quick look at 'Oh come, Oh come, E-ma-a-an-u-el' he shut the lid of the faded grand firmly, hoisted a sleek bunch of keys from his left hand trouser-pocket by a chain long enough to moor a boat, chose a key with a complicated metal pattern at both ends, snapped the lock and had us gratefully out of the vestry almost before the piano wires were still.

Flat electric torches with clumsy egg-shaped lenses were the thing in those days. As soon as Mr. Dyball had faded into the gloom behind the North porch pencils of light dappled the upright tombstones round the vestry. Our natural assembly point for all extra-mural choir business was the tomb of Henry Rabjohn and his wife Hannah, who, a hundred years earlier, had been sorely missed by a lamenting parish. Henry and his wife were well served by the choir-boys; it is true that we often sat on the flat stone which was at comfortable table-height; we sometimes sharpened our pen-knives on it; we once chipped it outrageously—for had we not been told that if you poured vinegar on flakes of marble you could obtain a new kind of gas that would put out a fire; but at least we picked the moss out of the letters so that Henry, his wife and the lamenting parish were not entirely lost to the curious. Preparatory to the business of auditing the accounts and choosing the choirmaster's Christmas present we lit our winter-warmers—rags stuffed into cocoa-tins whose ends had been punctured to admit a draught when the tins, held in frozen hands, were swung to and fro.

In the smoke of burning rags, like pious incense from a censer old, and under the light of bull's-eye torches, our sixpences were placed on Henry Rabjohn's tomb for the inspection of Ernest Green, the head chorister. Greeny, who took most of the solos and might have gone as a chorister to Hereford but for an impediment which kindled his face and gripped his throat when he tried to speak, prodded the coins into place with a long forefinger, arranging them as the head chorister always did, one sixpence of each letter of Henry Rabjohn's last link with living—and reaching the Q of Esquire. There was the usual hush while our leader pondered—his seniority was meticulously observed—and the smoke rose pungently round the tomb, so that an observer might have suspected that we were demoniacally tampering with Henry Rabjohn's remains, then Greeny spoke. "I vote we buy him braces," he said. "Anything over on cigars." My father wore braces of fascinating mechanism which included clips and minute rollers. They were, I think, called 'Mikado' braces, though why a robe-wearing potentate should have inspired a manufacturer of braces, I have never found out. I shyly suggested that Mr. Dyball's Christmas braces should be 'Mikado' brand, and was gratified at the murmurs of assent. I spent the next year feeling as to Mr. Dyball's trousers as the distinguished lady must feel to a ship which she has named and launched.

My father, in truth, did not often wear braces. He favoured a leather belt with shining metal rings at the hips and a brass buckle

11

bearing the engraved words, 'Acme Clothing Co.'. No one worked harder than my father, and I suspect that his Mikado braces would have been unequal to the strains imposed by all the jobs he did in a day.

My father owned the sweet and grocery shop favoured by the College boys. He loved the shop and he loved the boys. Sometimes they played him up; sometimes they stole from him, but I never heard him complain or threaten. I believe that he considered himself so honoured that real gents should patronise him that he felt obscurely that to question what they did would be to challenge the whole structure of society. For me the College boys were beings from another planet. They had limitless supplies of money; they were subject to none of the laws that bound me and my little circle; they could do no wrong. I suppose I might have claimed some kinship with them: the day-school to which I went was said to be the old town grammar school which had given birth to the great boarding-establishment. But if it was, no one acted as if it was. Yes. Someone did. I did. Whenever I passed one of the College masters in the street I prepared myself for some rebuke—"Hook, your boots are dirty. Clean them." No rebuke ever came. The splendid figures in cap and gown had me in thrall, unquestioningly obedient to their sternest commands—had they but known it. They did not know it. How should they? True, once a year we were allowed to use the College cinder-track for our running races; we even received the magazines discarded by the great College library (and once a week it was my task to collect them). True, our coat-of-arms bore one tiny emblem to be found also on the fine College escutcheon, but the flourishing offspring of the old Grammar school never openly acknowledged its parent. I have noticed that a dog once parted from its dam never again seems to recognise her. Perhaps it is the same with schools; best to forget the old bitch!

My sister, Bell, who did typing for one of the College masters, told me that he had hardly heard of my school. I had to take a packet of papers to him once when she had a bad cold and my mother made her stay in bed. She used a typewriter called Oliver, and she did most of those papers sitting up in bed with the big machine on a tray on her lap. But my mother never knew that. She was always in the kitchen in our basement between four and six in the evenings, frying sausages for my father to sell in the shop, and that was when Bell turned up the gas and tapped away for Mr. Annesley and her independence.

I found Mr. Annesley's house all right. Perhaps I ought to give house a capital letter. Mr. Annesley's House. For it was one of the College boarding-houses, and called Annesley's. I found a great green door, pocked with ball-marks and hooked open. Then it was all stone corridors with gas-jets in cages, and stone steps with saucer treads winding up into darkness, and leather buckets full of sand hanging on great wooden arms, and a faint smell of mouldering cabbage, and doors with names on, and one of the names, Marcus Daveney. When I didn't know which way to turn I was found by a green baize apron surmounted at a great height by a shiny pink head who asked me what my business might be. When this green factory chimney was satisfied with my credentials and mollified by Bell's package it pressed a penny into my surprised hand before leading me nimbly up stone steps to a green baize door.

Then it was all shining green kamptulicon and glowing mahogany and Mr. Annesley with lustrous brown shoes saying he was sorry to hear that Miss Hook was sick (fancy calling Bell, who was only eighteen, Miss Hook! And fancy saying she was sick when she hadn't been sick at all!) and he hoped she would soon be well, and here was something for my trouble. Sixpence. And where did I go to school? Sixpence trebled my week's pocket money. I suppose I should have thought ahead and kept the sixpence to give to Greeny for Mr. Dyball's braces. But it was summer then. You couldn't very well have Mr. Dyball's Christmas present in mind when there were ice-cream cornets at Miss Parkin's shop and sherbert-dabs at Mr. Caxton's. I never thought of Miss Parkin and Mr. Caxton as being rivals to my father's establishment. No inner whisperings of treachery soiled my commerce with them. Besides, you could buy Colonial gums from Mr. Caxton, and nothing in my father's great glass jars yielded anything quite like Colonial gums.

Ernest Green, rounding up the sixpences carefully, declared that he personally would purchase the braces and cigars and that anyone letting on what we were going to buy had better look out and that anyone who thought of sucking cough-lozenges or Melloids during next Sunday's sermon had better share them round beforehand or he had better look out and that there was no passing-note between the two syllables of 'angels' in 'Oh come, all ye faithful' which we should be practising next week and that anyone who couldn't resist the temptation of putting one in had better look out, too. I noticed that when he was telling us about the cough-sweets and the braces he took ages to get it out and had to squeeze the corner of Henry Rabjohn's stone slab; but when he was telling us about 'born the King of angels' the words came out as smooth as Mr. Annesley's oil-cloth. Then he announced a short game of tombstones and no shouting.

'Tombstones' has a modern equivalent in a game that I think is called 'Sardines'. One of us had to make off into the darkness of the churchyard and hide behind a tombstone. As others found him so they hid with him, bursting with suppressed glee when one or two less-sharp explorers were left groping fruitlessly among eerie hiding-places. When there was only one left and he drew near the throbbing concealed mass he was rewarded by a howling groan no less terrifying for being anticipated.

It was a game I didn't like. Not only did the culmination frighten me terribly (and I had a way of always being among the stragglers) but I never got over the conviction that it was both wrong and dangerous to make free with gravestones. As we crouched sacrilegiously over the slabs I was always expecting the earth to yawn—which sometimes, thanks to moles, it did—to draw us down to some ghastly charnel heap.

That night it was my turn to hide. With my misgivings and my blind torch I dodged round the stones into the murk where damp elms dripping on forgotten graves helped to conceal the sexton's little tool-shed. Had I known then that the shed was not so small that it could not afford a temporary refuge for a coffin and its inmate, I don't suppose I should have scuttled towards it as I did. It leaned against a high wall of soft red brick on the other side of which was Mr. Annesley's House. It was made of pulpy planks coated in a greenish slime, windowless, with a roof of hostile corrugated iron from which nails rose like mushrooms—we knew this from more than one successful ascent of the slippery post at the back corner where crude iron spikes held the timbers to the wall. In front of the door was a little clearing with a threshold of flat gravestones which had somehow abandoned their first allotted task. There was one stone there which we always avoided. Cracked right across and worn almost smooth, its carving unmistakably depicted a skull. There were all sorts of stories about it. None of them pleasing to a benighted imagination.

In this angle of brick and timber some of the choir-boys would press themselves to smoke cigarettes—home-made with tea-leaves and coltsfoot, or the more sophisticated kind. That night there were no tell-tale smouldering points to show that the sexton's little niche had tenants. It was my intention to conceal myself in the corner and cleverly point out in due course that I was not cheating by being there, but that I was indeed hiding behind a gravestone— the one bearing the skull. I should have hopped over it (for nothing would induce me to put a foot on it) to merge into the dark shadows of hut and wall.

But someone had come before me, or, rather two had come before me to shelter in shadow; and as I stepped into the little clearing, with a gasp and a shuffle and a confusion of footsteps and a scurry they detached themselves from their corner to vanish among the sentinel tombstones.

When I got home that night my mother was put about because I was late. She had kept a plate of hot sausage-ends for me, and there was cocoa. There was also a remnant of homework to be done—to learn by heart the first three verses of *The Inchcape Rock* for Mr. Selby, the English master. I dare say I was not very communicative that Monday night. When I took my candle and stone hot water bottle up to my room I took up a heavy secret also. I kept awake as long as I could, listening for Bell to come up to her room. I heard no sound of her. I fell asleep wondering if she and Marcus Daveney had crept back to that shadowy corner in the churchyard from which I had so clumsily dislodged them.

II

I EXPECTED MY sister to be different next morning. But she wasn't. I watched her as closely as I could in my morning scramble to be ready for school. As I was finishing my breakfast, not altogether enjoying it because Sir Ralph the Rover and the Inchcape Bell stood between me and its pleasures, Bell came down, as serene as ever and certainly not burdened by any of the grave doubts that had kept me awake the night before. Or so I thought at the time. I had to wait until dinner-time—we always called it dinner-time, never lunch-time—before she unbent a little. She did deign to notice me, though, before I asked leave to get down from the breakfast table.

"Are you going to the College library today?"

She knew very well I wasn't. I never went on Tuesdays. It was on Fridays I collected the pile of last week's magazines to take back to the school.

"No. Why?"

"Nothing. I just wondered."

You have probably noticed that if anyone says he ' just wondered ' it always turns out that he is deeply concerned. Anyhow, she said nothing more beyond pointing out that my nails wanted scrubbing, and when I had put my books in my satchel, buttoned my blue overcoat over my scarf (a shawl-like stole, crossed over my chest in the way my mother insisted on) and carefully drawn on my cap from forehead to poll, I kissed my mother and ran out to catch up Willie Waites. I found him, as I usually did, dressed much the same as I was, drawing his ruler musically along the iron railings of Roper's Alley.

"Do you know it?" he said.

"Not the last verse."

"What did you get number two?"

"It would take three men three and a half days."

"Same here."

16

"Did you find out what 'Zenith' meant?"

"It's a motor-bike, I think."

"Same here."

We followed our usual ritual of avoiding certain man-hole covers and making sure that we trod on others, we gave a comprehensive stare at the windows of the One and All Stores, we hurried past Jimmy Leaper's house because we were afraid of Jimmy Leaper, we arrived at school in time to find that the pundits, to a man, had estimated that it would take three men seven days, and began our scholastic morning in a most un-advent-like way to 'Christian, dost thou see them on the holy ground' to that monotone first line that the critics are so disagreeable about. I have never discovered why 'the troops of Midian prowl and prowl around', but I have remained impressed by the sombre tune to which they did it. I think I was impressed by everything in that hymn-book—largely because it was called *The Public School Hymn Book*. I am sure we were acting rather above our station in using it. Probably our copies were cast-offs from the College.

I had a difficult morning. *The Inchcape Rock* rolled out smoothly, but that was my only success. Mr. Webster, who did arithmetic, was always patient with me (did we not sing in the same choir?'), but I tried him sorely that morning. Men pumping water from sinking ships, or grocers mixing coffee with chicory never failed to baffle me, and I think I baffled Mr. Webster. But it was really Bell and Marcus Daveney who occupied my mind. I was glad to get home for dinner. Tuesday afternoon lessons were ones I liked—drawing, reading, geometry; so Tuesday dinner-time was a good one, or could be—if one's sister was not up to something.

But whatever she was up to, it had yet to trouble her. She spent most of dinner-time telling me to be quiet and chew my food (I was only going through the afternoon's geometry to myself, to be ready for Mr. Webster's inevitable "Close your text-books and write out the proof"), while she looked over her plate of shepherd's pie at a propped-up copy of Pitman's *Shorthand for Advanced Students*.

My sister had, as I saw it, an ideal life. Every morning she did the books for my father in his little office. In the holidays I was allowed to watch her doing the books; I used to sit on a little green safe ('The Cerberus'. Guaranteed fire-proof), my head embowered in dusty receipts impaled on hooks and sometimes yielding uncancelled stamps, while she ran two fingers down columns of figures in a great ledger and deftly pencilled neat totals or clicked her tongue and dipped her long fingers into a pocket of concertina-like files on the floor by her side. Once a month she went off to do the same thing for my Uncle Hector who kept the Post Office and General Stores.

In the afternoons she practised her typing up in her room or clattered away professionally for anyone who needed manuscripts copying. Three evenings a week, Mondays, Wednesdays and Fridays, she went off with sharpened pencils and Pitman's manuals to the Polytechnic. An ideal life.

We saw little of my father at dinner-time. Somehow he was always busy elsewhere. And although my mother never failed to lay a place for him it was bread and cheese, standing up by the side-board, that had to suffice. What kept him from the dinner-table depended on the season of the year. In summer he was engaged in making ice-cream, a fascinating task involving the packing of ice and salt round a metal cylinder in a wooden tub and the turning of a crank-handle to churn metal paddles inside the ice-cream mixture. The scraping of the finished product from the paddles with a long knife made one of the most appetising sights and sounds I can remember. In winter my father's dinner-time was consumed by the carving of ham for sandwiches. His dexterity with the long knife, and the salty, spicy smell of the slices and slivers of pink ham was even more exciting than the ice-cream.

During the week we led a mole-like existence below street level. Stone steps led down to the kitchen from our back yard; from the kitchen you could reach shop level by going up dark stairs. To get to the scullery you went through a grotto-like coal-store, always damp. The scullery was under the shop, so that when business was good you could hear the swishing shoe-leather over your head, and through an iron-barred high narrow window over the sink see the lower third of customers on their way in and out. Under the stairs leading up to the shop was a dark cupboard, my own, where in candle light I worked and played with my set of carpenter's tools and my Hobbies fretwork outfit.

On that Tuesday when we were helping to wash up the dinner things I fancied that my sister was on edge. By custom she washed and I wiped; when she was in a dreamy mood singing quietly to herself I could never keep up with the flow of plates from her bowl, and on this day when she almost dashed them on to the draining-board I should have been quite lost had she not absent-mindedly begun to wash some of them twice. I did not point out to her that she was going round again.

"Are you sure you're not going to the College library today?"

"Of course I'm sure. Why?"

"Oh, nothing."

"What do you want?"

"Nothing."

"Supposing I said I was?"

"Well, are you?"

"I might."

"Are you, or not?"

"I could."

I couldn't really, and I don't know what made me say I could. I expect I made it sound as if I could pop in any time I liked, just to have a look round or a chat with Mr. Leaf who looked after the books. Mr. Leaf wasn't the librarian, he only looked after the books. Mr. Leaf had been a footman in the Headmaster's House, but now Mr. Leaf had to wear a truss (whatever that was, and I wondered if he ever heeded the advertisements which urged so sternly, 'Don't wear a truss') and he couldn't do heavy work. I liked him. When I called every Friday he always seemed glad to see me, always had the pile of magazines ready, with *Blackwood's* at the top and the thick orange-covered *London Mercury* at the bottom, always said, "You read 'em, every word of 'em. They can never take your education away from you. 'Tomorrow night', tell your Dad."

I always told my father that Mr. Leaf had said, 'Tomorrow night.' He always replied, "Oh. Ah." I never thought to ask who 'they' were—'they' who were powerless to take my education from me.

"Well, if you are, you can take a note for me."

"Who for? Mr. Leaf?"

"No. Mr. Annesley. It's on the way."

It wasn't on the way, but I was so relieved that I wasn't expected to go into the library, even with the safe-conduct of a note for Mr. Leaf—for in truth, though I dearly loved that quiet store-house of eloquent books, I was scared lest someone should ask me what I was doing there—I didn't say so to my sister.

" Why can't you take it?" I said.

"Because it's not convenient."

"Oh. All right, then."

"Well . . . actually, it's not for Mr. Annesley. . . ."

"Who's it for?"

"It's all on the envelope."

From her handbag which stood on the brick floor by her side she drew a shabby blue book, *Five Hundred Grammalogues for Secretaries,* and from between the leaves she slid a large, crisp, azure envelope. I was so certain that I knew the name her neat hand had inscribed, and so unwilling to become involved that I stuffed it into my jacket pocket without a glance and without drying my hands.

"There's no need to crease it up," said Bell.

"I wasn't creasing it up."

"Do you know where to take it?"

I only just avoided saying 'yes' and so landing myself into a slough of uncomfortable half-truths. As it was, I pulled out the envelope, tried to hide from her the damp stains on it, and read the name. It was not written in her neat hand. It was typed. That was the only surprise. The rest I knew. 'The Honourable M. Daveney. Mr. Annesley's House.'

"Leave it on the table in the hall," she said (she knew, then, that there was a table in the hall). "Or give it to Mr. Cater."

"Who's Mr. Cater?"

"The butler."

I stuffed the envelope back in my pocket. I thought about it a lot afterwards. Funny she couldn't bring herself to mouth the name 'Marcus Daveney'. Was she embarrassed? It it hard sometimes to bring out a name that opens the door to a secret garden. To say that name aloud to someone else makes you feel vulnerable. Funny she had her handbag with her in the scullery. Had she wanted to make sure that my father and mother did not witness the transaction?

I noticed that her washing-up rate fell sharply after that. She almost caressed the plates, humming dreamily to herself as she mopped them.

All that afternoon the envelope pulled at my pocket as the albatross must have pulled at the Mariner's neck. I took it out during Geometry when Mr. Webster was at the black-board proving that the angles at the base of an isosceles triangle are equal, held it up to the light, bent it. If it held secrets it did not reveal them. I had heard that you could open envelopes by steaming them with a kettle, but I wasn't sure how it was done, and I didn't like to ask anyone, even Willie Waites. Willie had once told me that glue was made from horses' hooves and so were the Colonial gums that Mr. Caxton sold. Willie was obviously an authority on glue. Even so I couldn't bring myself to ask this man of the world how you steam open an envelope.

After school we kicked a football about until it got dusk and our boots and trouser-legs were veneered with mud; then, slinging our satchels and holding our twelve-inch rulers *en garde* for a duel we made for home.

That evening (was it to avoid seeing Bell?) I didn't go straight home; I called in at the Post Office and General Stores to see Uncle Hector and Aunt May.

I did not love Uncle Hector nor Aunt May nor their son, Arnold; but I loved everything about their shop, even the two yards of counter, forbidden to me, devoted to Post Office business. I did not resent the ban; the Post Office territory, encased in a greenish brass wire mesh, housed a small rack of rubber stamps including one for the date, adjustable for every day of the year and designed to be of service until 1939, the daintiest little balance in lacquered brass, a cumbersome spring-balance with a bent pointer and three layers of gummed labels on its dial to show you how much Mr. Alston, the postman, would charge to carry your parcel, and an empty 'Bishop's Move' tobacco tin containing an assortment of foreign or spurious coins which somehow a callous public had foisted on Uncle Hector. All these things had been exhibited to me—indeed, I had been allowed to handle them—by my cousin Arnold in one of his rare expansive moments when he had been left to look after the shop. Arnold was some four years older than I. He had pimples, lots of money, a motor bike, a shot-gun and, like Bell, a place by night at the 'Tec' where he was studying machine-drawing. By day he worked for Boscastles, the printers, and was privy to all the gossip included in or excluded by the local paper, *The Observer*.

The rest of Uncle Hector's shop somehow managed to demonstrate what beauty there is in everyday things. You would have said that a bunch of flue-brushes hanging over a box of lamp-chimneys standing in a nest of galvanised baths surrounded by tea-pots of varying sizes was the epitome of ugliness. You might have thought that the odours of paraffin, balls of twine, carbide and coir mats went ill together. Uncle Hector's stock proved you wrong.

In fact, the pervading smells at Uncle Hector's were those of linseed oil and Aunt May's cooking. Uncle was a cricketer; he lived for cricket; he very nearly died for cricket. There was no department of the game that found him wanting; he was steeped in its history, he patronised its followers, he made his own bats, he scored more runs than any cricketer for miles around.

You would not say that Aunt May had such success in the kitchen; yet the kitchen was her natural habitat, and somehow it got round that she excelled there as Uncle Hector excelled on the cricket field. I loathed her cooking. There was no morsel of food served by her that I could enjoy. To me it always seemed that everything was underdone and smelt of the paraffin stove on which she cooked. Your jaws had to cleave the potatoes; cabbage wrapped itself stubbornly over your teeth. With her fork she would point out pieces of stringy meat which you had pushed to one side of your plate, demanding to know what was wrong with that bit, and that bit there, and that piece under the marrow. Didn't you like onion sauce? If you wanted to grow up you had better finish that dumpling.

I learned to obey her. To refuse, I found out, was to have her leaning over you from behind, to have your knife and fork taken from your hands and to have your meat cut up for you and held by her on your own fork in front of you until you craned forward and took it, cold and greasy, into your mouth.

I ought to remember with gratitude meals at Uncle Hector's. He and Aunt May were very generous though they did have a way of forcing food down your throat. I ought to remember that I never went into their house without being offered a wedge of jam tart, an apple, a piece of gingerbread or a mince-pie. I do remember it, and there rises in my mind the sickening noise that Uncle Hector made as he mashed his food in his great, white, clicking false teeth, and the stale stink of cold sweat that somehow emanated from him. I learned years later (I don't know how) that Aunt May was not unaware of this aura and used to make him wash his feet in permanganate of potash solution and put his socks outside the bedroom door every night. I might have found her meals more agreeable had she given them the same consideration.

When I called that night Uncle Hector was in the shop cashing up. Elsie Catcher, the assistant, had gone at five o'clock. As I pushed open the door I triggered off, in spite of the stiff spring, the great cup-shaped bell, above, announcing my arrival with a clanging 'stong' and making me feel guilty at disturbing him in his sums. He did not look up.

My uncle had a way when concentrating of putting out his tongue, drawing in his breath, holding it until you thought he must explode, and then letting it out in a sharp (and, to my young nostrils, smelly) hiss. "May! Sssss . . . Here's young Arthur. Give him a bite."

Without taking his eyes off the neat stacks of coins he reached out with his left hand, raised the heavy mahogany flap of the counter and lowered it gently when I had steamed safely into port. Aunt May's shadow darkened the rose-patterned glass panels of the door behind the counter and I was admitted to the parlour. As usual, there was a meal laid. From the kitchen came strong whiffs of simmering paraffin and simmering fish.

I got off lightly with a slice of cold apple pie and a glass of milk. I was glad that tea was not ready—the tea-pot, I could see, was still impaled on the spout of the kettle—for Aunt May's tea came out viscid and throat-catching, and even though I pre-posterously associated the milk intimately with Aunt May herself and had to fight down the notion that I was somehow being breast-fed, the splendid crust of the pie helped it down.

Aunt May, as usual, asked me what I had been doing.

"Nothing."

"You've been to school, haven't you?"

"Yes."

"Well what have they learnt you?"

"Oh, about triangles and things. And there was pertry and . . ."

"Arnold's top of his class at the Tec. You ought to see what he has to do. And it's all real useful things, too. Arnold'll have letters after his name when he's finished. Drink up your milk. Arnold'll be earning more than his teachers when he's got his diploma. He says there'll always be machines; more and more of 'em. He says Germany will have to buy our machines. He says they used to have a moponoly but now they'll have to buy from us. Do you want more pie?"

Uncle Hector came into the parlour carrying a heavy black cash-box.

"How's your Mum? And young Bell? Don't see much of her these days. Reckon she's playing a hard game."

"Now, Hector!" said Aunt May.

I said that Mum was all right (he never asked about my father's health) and that Bell was all right. Was she all right? What game was she playing? What was a hard game?

"Tell yer dad I had the Major in today. Wants me to play for the toffs against the boys next year. Told 'im I'd think about it." And he laughed in the heavy way he had. "Hur, hur, hur. Think about it! I'll think about it all right. I'll give 'em something to think about when I get out there with a bat in me hand. Tell yer dad."

I said I would tell my father.

Major Frank Birkitt, 'a real toff', lived at Great Lodge seven miles away. Like my uncle he was a devoted cricketer, and to the pretty ground of Great Lodge there came each summer week-end gay bands of cricketing Cantabs, dour professionals anxious or desperate to earn a few extra pounds, and a sprinkling of Lords, Colonels and Captains who had played a bit of cricket in their time. The match of the season was that against the College; to play in this match my uncle had been invited, and was now thinking about it.

Major Birkitt was better known to me as a collector of stamps; indeed, I had even been invited to Great Lodge to show him my modest set of over-printed Cameroons. His father was said to be at least an Earl, his wife was dead, his lady housekeeper was handsome, his daughter, Frances, was lovely in appearance and, I now know, beautiful in disposition. I somehow didn't see Uncle Hector mingling freely with the cricketing guests at Great Lodge. They came. They played. They did brilliant things on the cricket field or they failed on the cricket field. When one of them did well it was a source of infectious joy to all the others who somehow seemed to share the heady drink of success so that the whole of the little band was richer and gayer for it. When one of them failed, his failure seemed to be spread amongst them all so that it became lighter, a calamity shared, a subject for laughter, a joke.

Uncle Hector's cricket knew no such blessings. Failure to him meant a muttering return to the pavilion, the necessity of explaining to anyone who was polite enough to hear him out how ill-luck had foiled him, how, if he was on form, he would never allow himself to be bamboozled out of his wicket like that, how some chaps had all the luck. At the worst it meant the flinging of his red spiked batting-gloves before him as he returned to the pavilion, the crashing of his bat through the dressing-room door and the stout declaration that with his bloody luck he was going to bloody-well give up.

24

If he did well he was smiling, effusive and magnanimous; and when he was at the wicket with runs flowing sweetly and serenely off his home-made bat, the little knots of spectators would stand hushed and awe-struck as this paragon, this giant, showed the ample scope of his artistry.

I had no doubt that Uncle Hector would play for the Major. He shared my father's respect and admiration for the toffs, but, unlike my father, he saw no reason why he should not move freely with them, why they should not accept him.

They would hardly have accepted him at that moment. In a smooth, practised move he stepped out of his boots, shed his jacket, discarded his tie and celluloid collar, took up a buttered crust from the table and stood there in braces, brass collar-stud and stockinged feet methodically chewing.

"Tell Dad the Major brought a couple of pheasants," he said.

"All right."

"You like pheasant?"

"Don't know, Uncle."

"Course you don't. Course you don't. Tell Dad to come on Sunday. Dinner. We'll find out. What d'you say, May?"

May did not exactly commit herself; but, then, she seldom did.

"And you see that young Bell comes. Unless . . ." He paused with a cumbrous air of mystery. "Unless . . . hur, hur, hur, unless she's otherwise engaged. What d'you say, May?" And he winked heavily.

I couldn't go to sleep that night. Did Uncle Hector know all about Bell, or was he only indulging in his favourite indoor game of chaffing? And what was the hard game Bell was playing? What was a hard game? I would ask Mr. Bagnall. He would tell me.

Very late, Bell tiptoed into my room. With her candle she looked like Florence Nightingale. But I was not pleased to see her. When she leaned over my bed and whispered, "Did you take the note? Arthur! The note. Did you take it?" I closed my eyes more firmly and made a sound which may have sounded like, 'Yes'. At length she crept away, leaving me alone with my conscience.

She could have answered her own question easily enough. The note, undelivered and unopened, lay under my pillow.

III

"MR. BAGNALL," I said timidly. "Mr. Bagnall . . ." I didn't
know how to put it. "What's the age . . . how old must a girl be to
get married?"

Mr. Bagnall brought the curry-comb to a standstill, stretched
one arm over Dinah's shining back and leaning against her twitching
hind-quarters gave me as searching a look as his watery bloodshot
eyes could manage.

"You 'avn't been up to somethin'?"

What had I said? He looked unhappy? Did he know about the
note? Bell had said nothing to me. Had she told him?

"No, Mr. Bagnall, I don't think so."

His face relaxed to its usual genial softness. His warm, clicking
laugh clattered out. "Yuk, yuk, yuk. Thought for a moment you'd
blotted yer copy. Yuk, yuk, yuk. Yer just enquiring in the spirit of
learning; that it, eh?"

I said that was it.

"Well now, let me see, as the bishop said to the . . ." and with
lots of yuks he went into a rigmarole that I did not understand about
apples being ripe for plucking. He must have seen my perplexity
for he pulled himself up. "I can't say I rightly know when a gal
can commit holy deadlock," he said seriously. "I'll tell you what,
though; they do say the blushin' bride ought to be, what's it now—
'arf 'er 'ubby's hage plus height years. That any good?"

I tried to work it out but didn't make much of it. Mr. Bagnall,
who, over the years, had in his fashion answered scores of my
groping questions and (though I did not know it then) told me
hundreds of things I had not asked about, had for once failed me.
Perhaps it was because I did not really know what I was hoping to
find out.

I had had to wait four days before I was able to consult him.
They had been four uneasy days. I had watched Bell, and I fancy
she had watched me. I usually paid Mr. Bagnall a visit on Saturday

26

mornings, this being the time when he was for some reason not required by the travelling public and could polish his cab and groom his horses. This morning I had to wait for an audience because when I got to the stable Mr. Sands the blacksmith was shoeing Dinah. Like Uncle Hector, Mr. Sands hissed and put his tongue out. Mr. Sands, it seemed, dare not breathe while he had a job in hand. He was driving home the last of the great square-headed nails to hold the shoe, and I winced and held my breath too lest the long point should be thrust into the quick. Four metallic thuds, and Mr. Sands' imprisoned breath came out in a hissing plume. Dinah, given the use of her new shoes, slithered and clattered on stone. Mr. Bagnall took coins from a black tin without, it seemed to me, counting them, dropped them altogether into the blacksmith's open hand and said it was nice of him to come. Mr. Sands, denying this, spat, to my surprise, on the silver and slid it under his apron into his corduroy pocket.

Next to my father's shop there was a long archway, and next to that The Chequers public house. On one wall of the archway was painted in great brown blocked letters a notice which I did not understand—COMMIT NO NUISANCE. I had asked Mr. Bagnall about this, but hadn't had much satisfaction. Perhaps, I thought, he was too busy getting Dinah or Prince to draw the cab safely through the arch to notice anything else; I sometimes wondered if he couldn't read, for there had been times when he got me to read letters for him, or instructions on tins, or police notices, though I was never asked to perform this service before he had groped about himself clumsily for his 'lost gig-lamps'. He never found his spectacles on those occasions, nor did I ever see him wearing any.

He lived on the wooden floor above Dinah and Prince. There was no staircase, only a vertical ladder nailed to the tarred wooden wall. No one, so far as I know, apart from myself, had ever climbed those rungs except Mr. Bagnall. If you looked up through the square opening you could see only his whips and his hats—two long whips hanging over half cotton-reels nailed to the wall and three hats: a greenish bowler, a sinister bowler proofed with shining tar and a great, gloomy top-hat with a cockade curling at the edges. Mr. Bagnall told me that he wore the top-hat for 'seeing them home' and that it owed its lustre to Guinness. He seemed to assume I knew what he meant, and I didn't like to ask him.

He polished his cab with a thick liquid which he called Antimiraculus. This he made up himself, and whatever it was, it gave a splendid, rich gleam and caked itself in a resinous, amber collar round the neck of the beer bottle in which it was decanted. The cab I got to know intimately. I had swung on its axles, climbed on its roof, turned its stiff brass handles to get to its shining, buttoned leather seats—all spikey with horsehair and rich with the smell of horses, saddle-soap and tobacco.

"What do you want to know for?" said Mr. Bagnall.

"Nothing," I said.

"All right," he said, and with a thin, bent poker he lifted the iron disc on top of the little stove, spat thickly on to the glowing coals, added a slither of slack from a bucket and daintily dropped the top back. "All right. You were only asking." His silence became oppressive.

"Mr. Bagnall, what's a hard game?"

He didn't understand at first, and went on about skittles—there was a skittle-alley at the back of The Chequers.

"No, Mr. Bagnall," I said, desperate. " If a girl was playing a hard game what game would she be playing?"

"Ah," he said. "I reckon she'd be going in for a bit of pigtail-pulling. Yuk, yuk, yuk. That what you mean?"

This was no help to me. But Mr. Bagnall was not entirely blind to my struggles. "Reckon it would mean she was no better than she should be. Know what I mean?"

I didn't know. 'No better than she should be'. What kind of language was that?

"Not that Elsie Catcher, is it?" he asked.

I didn't really know much about Elsie Catcher. She was Uncle Hector's shop-assistant with special powers in the Post Office. She was quick at figures, didn't like getting her fingers sticky serving in the shop; she had a haughty face and she was thought by my circle to be going out with Arnold.

"What about Elsie Catcher?" I said.

"No good askin' me. Thought she might be the one."

"What one?"

"The one you keep on about. Thought it might be our Else."

"She wouldn't like to hear you calling her 'Else', Mr. Bagnall. She's very ladylike sometimes."

"Treat a hoo-er like a lady, and a lady like a hoo-er," said Mr. Bagnall mysteriously. "Well, if it ain't her ladyship, 'oo, pray, might it be?"

I said nothing. He took up the bent poker to prod at the flap at bottom of the stove. "Well, never mind, lad," he said. "It hain't none of my business. I'll tell yer wot: straight questions—straight answers. No fartin' about. 'Ow's that?"

"Mr. Bagnall," I said desperately, "please tell me. What's a hard game, and who plays it?"

"You're a bit green, young Arthur. You've got a sister, yer know."

My heart shot. Did he know already? Was I as obvious as all that? Was I so green? How did he know?

"You've got a sister, ain't you?"

"Yes, but . . ."

"And don't she tell you nothing? I mean, you aren't all that simple, are you? I mean, you know what . . ." He was becoming as uncomfortable as I was.

"What about Bell?" I said desperately.

"Nothing about Bell. I mean, she ain't told you nothing? You ain't seen nothing? She, or your mum, 'asn't let on about the stork, or the doctor's little black bag or the gusberry bush or anythin' like that?"

I expect I went red. "I know about the doctor's bag," I mumbled.

"You believe it?" Mr. Bagnall said.

"Yes."

"Squit," said Mr. Bagnall. "All squit."

He put a heavy hand on my shoulder. "Come over 'ere. See this lovely creature: wot's its name?"

"Dinah."

"Now come 'ere. Wot's this one called?"

"Prince."

"Right. Notice anything?"

I am not sure whether he told me all he meant to tell me or whether I understood all that I was meant to understand, but before we were interrupted by Maidment (no one called him anything else but Maidment—never Mr. Maidment or Roy Maidment, which was his name), we had as it were left Dinah and Prince far behind, and a lot of things that had been dark to me were clear, and a lot of things which had been clear were dark.

Maidment was Major Birkitt's manservant. No one, I think, liked him, though I had heard it said that he was the late Mrs. Birkitt's fancy man. I shouldn't like to guess his age. Somewhere between thirty and forty, I suppose. He had sandy hair above a podgy yet lean face. His boots were always brightly polished and he always wore a kind of waistcoat with narrow yellow and black stripes, brass buttons and black, casement-cloth sleeves—the kind of half-jacket that railway-porters wear. The most remarkable thing about him was his eyes which, somehow, like his hair, were sandy in colour. Mr. Bagnall once said they were like piss-holes in the snow.

"Major says can you take him to the junction for the three o'clock," said Maidment.

Mr. Bagnall did not answer at once. He turned to face the sheep's-head clock on the wooden wall. He stared at it so long that I wondered if he thought it had stopped, though I couldn't see why for the long pendulum was swinging sweetly. Then he drew from his pocket a length of string, got it the right way round, ran his fingers over its irregularly spaced knots and said that he reckoned he could oblige the Major.

"What's the matter with the motor, then?" he added.

"Oil."

"O-ah."

"This bloody weather. Too bloody cold," said Maidment.

"Oh-ah?"

"Won't bloody-well flow."

"Oh-ah. Tell you somethin' . . .?"

"What's that?" said Maidment.

"That clock. Know what it's oiled with? Gin. 'Ollands gin. Been goin' for years."

"The Major's got better things to put gin into than a bloody motor-car. Tell us another."

Maidment did not exactly sneer. He did not have to. He was probably right about the Major though I did not think it right of him to say so. There were all sorts of stories about Major Birkitt's drinking powers: he was a bottle-a-day man, he suffered from alcoholic remorse, he had hollow legs. He did not in fact use his legs much. On the cricket-field he always played wicket-keeper, so he didn't have to run at all. He was said to put raw beef-steaks inside his wicket-keeping gloves. His face looked like raw beef-steaks. He walked very little for he had a splendid motor-car, a Napier, with a great brass radiator and tall water-filler, and an expansive canvas hood with wooden struts. Maidment usually drove him, but at times the Major looked after himself—large leather gauntlets, motoring hat and ulster.

"I reckon I can oblige his nibs," said Mr. Bagnall. "Three half-crowns. Wot's 'e up to? On the gees?"

"Gees or fancy-bits," said Maidment. To me this last exchange would have been so much gibberish had not Maidment, vibrating the little finger of his right hand in his ear 'to shift the bloody wax,' added "He's playing a hard game, all right." I saw Mr. Bagnall slowly turning his watery eyes on me, but pretending to be consulting the clock I would not meet them.

Maidment stepped outside remarking that it was bloody cold. He was going to say something more about the severity of the weather but he was interrupted by Mr. Bagnall who solemnly declared, "Cold as an icicle, chilly and glum; cold as the fringe on a polar-bear's bum." And he laughed, Yuk, yuk, yuk.

I see now that when I left Mr. Bagnall that Saturday morning I should have wandered off alone to ponder on the momentous things I had learned from Dinah and Prince. As it was I went to my father, reminded him that it was Saturday and that my weekly pocket-money, sixpence, was payable.

He tried to put me off, as he always did, by saying "We'll see", and then, "Presently", and then by claiming he couldn't go to the safe in the office because he had a bone in his leg. He eventually took six coppers from the greasy till and added to them a bright new farthing which he swore was a half-sovereign.

A certain amount of husbandry had to be observed over the weekly sixpence. Willie Waites and I always pooled part of our resources to buy *The Magnet,* and *The Popular.* Harry Wharton and Co. were credible figures, for was not the College made up by their counterparts? Somehow, I could never fit Marcus Daveney into the Greyfriars scene; but whether that was because he was less real to me than Billy Bunter was, I don't know. It never, I think, occurred to me that if I got to know Marcus Daveney I might find that my fear of him, or rather, my fear of what might become of Bell through him, might vanish at a stroke. I think I do not know what I feared.

Saturdays were good days. There was my weekly visit to Mr. Bagnall. Pocket-money. The visit to Empson's, the paper shop, with Willie Waites. A call at Mr. Caxton's sweet-shop with the subsequent assessment of the merits of the contents of all the sweet-jars in the cheaper range. In winter we usually chose the tablets which by their colour should have tasted of orange but reeked in fact of paregoric. Rowntree's blackcurrant pastilles were really our choice but their price was beyond us. Mixed fruit-drops were popular with us, but the blue ones had to be thrown away because, as everyone knew, they contained arsenic. With coconut confections we would have nothing to do; we had once made ourselves sick on coconut-ice, and the memory lingered. Colonial gums were for the summer as were those triangular paper bags of sherbert which you emptied by sucking through a liquorice tube. Liquorice was gratifying at any time whether in ribbons, strips, rods or pipes with red hundreds-and-thousands over the mouth of the bowl. We used to warm our liquorice in our pockets to bring out the succulent juices, and if it reached out mouths gritty or fluffy I do not remember any discomfort.

Our Saturday afternoons were spent at The Cinema. It was not called The Regal or The Majestic or The Dominion. It was called The Cinema. The plush seats bled sawdust; there were said to be fleas; it smelt of gas and hot metal from the fitful EXIT signs, but though it could do little better than the magic lantern we had at school its sepulchral darkness generated a magic that lasted the whole week until we paid our threepences again. We ate our sweets during the travel film—on how many rivers did we float as we crunched our mixed fruit-drops and the pianist rippled that Schubert impromptu which purls and cascades in bright streams of liquid notes! To how many cities did we say good-bye as the sun set behind their pinnacles, and the pianist reached for the cup of tea which an armless hand unfailingly placed on top of the piano! But sweets were forgotten when the big picture came. Saturday afternoon was serial time. *Pirate's Gold* the serial. In the lingo of today, *Pirate's Gold* 'had everything'—train crashes, hold-ups, landslides, explosions, shipwrecks, fires and encounters between opponents of every kind—man and man, man and lion, airman and eagle, redskin and Mounty, train-driver and brigand, swimmer and shark, policeman and robber, and, never to be forgotten, a ghastly struggle between a cumbersome diver, his helmet streaming bubbles, and a nightmare squid shooting suckers and ink. With the outcome of every fight held over until the following week we would emerge frustrated but elated into the raw air of the winter for a meat tea which Willie Waites' mother had ready for us.

Some films coloured our lives for weeks at a time. Douglas Fairbanks turned us into Robin Hood and Little John or Zorro, carving with wooden swords the letter 'Z' on imaginary foreheads. With Willie in pursuit it was as Zorro that I first climbed the wooden ladder to Mr. Bagnall's room above the stable.

32

I respected Mr. Bagnall. I respected his room. I didn't mean to pry. It was the heat of the chase that had driven me up there, darting past a surprised Prince, baffling an unsuspecting Willie, to find myself across Mr. Bagnall's threshold.

There was an iron bed with grey blankets, a small table with a circular marble top and three cast-iron legs, a piece of mirror was nailed to a post, a mahogany chest-of-drawers with a serpentine front, an unemptied chamberpot and little else. From nails driven into the posts hung heavy blue serge garments and yellowing woollen under-clothes stained brown at various parts.

The wooden walls were decorated with faded pictures. These I inspected. With one exception they fell into two categories: faded sepia photographs curling at the edges and vanishing prints and cuttings from newspapers. Each was fastened up by one or more of the cruel nails of the kind which Mr. Sands used to secure Dinah's shoes. Each photograph was inscribed in tired ink— 'Yours, Lil'; 'Billy Boy from Lil'; 'Happy Christmas, dear, from Lil'; 'Good luck, Billy, from Lil'; 'Won't be long now dear, L'. The pictures cut from the newspapers were of racehorses mounted by a slim young jockey whom I thought I vaguely recognised. Match-box, W. Bagnall up; Snuff-box, W. Bagnall; Sailor's Girl, Willy Bagnall up; Springer, Bagnall.

Lil had her hair in a pile and with a twinkle in her eye smiled at you over a costume of spangles and tights. W. Bagnall sat very straight in the saddle, hands relaxed before him. The exception in the picture gallery did not wear spangles and tights, neither was her back straight, nor was she relaxed. She was a naked lady sitting on a swing being pushed by a bearded gentleman who wore evening dress and a top hat. The lady wasn't Lil. The gentleman wasn't Billy Boy. The caption said, 'The Swingers.'

IV

WHEN MR. LEAF said, "Tomorrow night, tell your Dad", he meant that he would be along for the usual Saturday evening game of cards. I cannot remember a Saturday night when there was no game. Our best upstairs room over the shop was used, even though that meant its having another dusting for occupation on the following day. A fire was lit early; the flaps of the table were raised and the whole covered with a rep cloth in a kind of prussian blue. I now never finger a playing card without hearing the patient tick of a long-case clock and the hiss and pop of gas mantles.

The company usually consisted of Uncle Hector and Aunt May, Mr. Leaf from the library, Mother and Father and sometimes Bell and myself, who, though we were no doubt not very sharp in the game of 'Newmarket' were said to be useful when it came to handing round plates; for my mother, though always declaring it was nothing at all and hardly worth stopping the game for, always insisted on providing a knife and fork supper.

Bell wasn't there that evening, so I had to be at the front door. Mr. Leaf arrived first. You knew him by the way he rang; the merest twitch on the bell-pull, the faintest rustle of the bell-wire, the apologetic shudder of the clapper. He greeted me as he always did, "Well, young Arthur! How are your book-studies, eh?" and as usual wiped his boots on a clean corner of the mat. Mr. Leaf was a great one for wiping his boots and washing his hands. I once asked Bell why Mr. Leaf had to wash his hands so often when he was only playing cards, and she said I'd know one day. He wiped his boots on his favourite corner of the mat, said he'd have a little wash and gave me a threepenny joey—as he always did.

My uncle Hector, as usual, nearly ripped the entire bell-system out through the wall, setting up a clangour which persisted throughout his noisy entry and almost until he was in the sitting-room upstairs. I think he resented finding the door locked against him and having to ring at all; he never observed formalities if the door was unlocked or the shop-door open. You would find him looking into cupboards or helping himself from the unlocked tantalus on the side-board. He never seemed to be put out in the slightest by the fact that one caught him reading the postcards set out on the mantelpiece or nosing into the pile of letters that somehow accumulated behind the biscuit-barrel. The former and the latter never failed to attract him, and while his teeth clicked and clattered with hideous scrunching sounds as he fed cheese biscuits into them (as my mother fed washing into the mangle) he would coyly peep into envelopes, holding them ajar with a great square thumb.

But that evening he had to wait until I unfastened the door for him. There was no doubt who had rung the bell for it jangled away until the stair carpet no longer showed his wet footprints and he had called down, "Come on up, Maidment; make yourself at home," and, "Come on, May, we weren't all born in a field."

Aunt May scuttled in bearing a wet paper bag. "Some sheep's brains for your mother, Arthur," and I found myself holding the bag. Worse was to come. There followed her on to the doormat a pair of boots, brightly polished still, as if the rain meant nothing to them. Their owner observed to me in passing, "Rain. Like bloody stair-rods," and took them unwiped up the stairs. Maidment had come.

Maidment was, I knew, not welcome in our house. I had heard my mother call him, "that man"—which was the extreme of her contempt; my father had once called him a whipper-snapper. Gingerly holding the bag of sheep's brains fearful lest the wet paper should split, I followed Maidment up the stairs to see my father order him out of the house.

What followed did not take long.

Uncle Hector said he'd brought Maidment along because he was a great one for a game of cards. Maidment said there was nothing he enjoyed better than a game of cards. Mr. Leaf said that cards on a Saturday night was a tonic. Maidment said he always said that cards took you out of yourself. My father said, "Let's begin then." So they began.

And they seemed to get on very well so that I felt somehow deceived.

In 'Newmarket' you try to get rid of your cards by following in sequence and suit what the previous player has laid down. Your hope is to hold and then shed one of the court cards whose duplicate in the centre of the table bears the random halfpennies of the gamblers. Not all the cards are dealt, so your run of success at discarding may come to a barren halt; but if you do relinquish all your cards en route not only may you collect the coppers heaped on the court cards but you win everything in the kitty.

It was our custom to call out together the value of the cards played as they promised to lead to a climax. And everyone would scream with glee or frustration, and cards were shuffled and dealt for the next round and fancies were backed, and the kitty, a shallow pewter dish with two ears, known as "the bleeding bowl", was replenished.

It was, I suppose, simple, homely fun, though on that particular Saturday night I was given reason to doubt. But that was not until after supper.

What did surprise me was Maidment's consideration for my mother. When the tall clock went 'stong' and jangled nine times my mother said, "One more round, Father, and then we'll have a bite. It will hardly be worth stopping the game for, I'm afraid . . ."

"Nonsense, Mrs. Hook," cried Maidment. "It's very nice of you to give us anything at all. Very nice."

The others looked rather taken aback at the presumption of a newcomer who on his first (and, as it turned out, his last) night praised what they for years had taken for granted. But they had to mumble agreement, and Aunt May could only salve her conscience by saying that she hoped the sheep's brains were acceptable.

Maidment insisted on helping with the plates while Uncle Hector was explaining how it was that Major Birkitt couldn't do without him for next year's cricket, and while Mr. Leaf was washing his hands and Aunt May was telling me how her Arnold bought his own clothes now and how he had the shop-assistants running round and how nothing but the best was good enough for him.

Maidment's readiness to help with the supper things may have sprung from the greedy urgings of his appetite, or even his hunger, for he polished off his first helping of ham and pickles almost before Mr. Leaf had adjusted his plate and his napkin and his knife and his fork and his chair (and his truss?) preparatory to beginning a mincing attack. Aunt May somehow managed to inspect both sides of everything she ate. I think she would have turned the grains of salt over for scrutiny had she taken salt. Uncle Hector breathed heavily and hissed while, like a general handling troops on a battlefield, he manoeuvred what was on his plate into lines and outposts and pickets before demolishing them in a methodical sequence. I noticed that the heavy redoubt of pickled onions was always the last line to be attacked. He never failed to point out that pickled onions repeated on him something chronic but he reckoned it was worth it. I cannot believe that anyone agreed with his evaluation; in any case, the noise of the crushing of the onions in his back teeth I found so revolting that I wondered that the whole company did not urge him to revise his views.

No one had mentioned Bell. She had gone off after tea 'to see a friend', she told me. I was at that age when grown-ups never considered that I had any right to know what they were doing. My mother, of course, always told me what she was going to do if she thought it would increase my general understanding of the way of the world—"I'm just going next door to borrow some bay-leaves to put in the casserole to make it more tasty"—but when my father left the house it was usually to see a man about a dog. Uncle Hector, embarking on otherwise unspecified missions, also had an interest in the animal world, declaring, much to the dismay of my aunt, that he was going out to find how tight a duck's arse was. I asked Mr. Bagnall about this and was surprised at the glee it caused him. "Yuk, yuk, yuk. I reckon it would have to be watertight or the little bugger would sink. Yuk, yuk, yuk." Mr. Bagnall was not one for concealing his intentions. "Here, Arthur, just you go on polishing this (plenty o' spit, mind) while I have a Jimmy Riddle."

Bell always went 'to see a friend' when she wanted to slip away. She had many friends, and might be anywhere. My mother and father did not, as far as I know, question her closely when she simply said she was 'going out', but I had always worried about her absence after dark. There had been the awful occasion when I alone did not know that she was spending the night with a friend. Night does not give rise to optimism, and there are few who do not know how spectre after spectre of apprehension creeps into the mind, growing in horrid stature to black doubt, to fear, to cold panic until every bright aspiration of the day is quenched in fearful despondency. On that night Bell suffered every imaginable disaster. Even daylight did not erase from my mind the heavy mark made by the sleepless hours of worry.

They would have to mention Bell sooner or later. Uncle Hector, when he had finished off the food so carefully deployed on his plate, was more than likely to enquire if young Bell was up to her tricks, pig-tail pulling, poodle-faking (I had never asked Mr. Bagnall what poodle-faking was), playing a hard game, getting her feet under someone's table or hanging her hat in someone's hall. Mr. Leaf in his innocent kindly way might observe that he had been surprised to see Bell as he passed Mr. Annesley's House. Maidment in his present mood of graciousness seemed unlikely to be so bold as to intrude on family matters.

Looking back, I cannot understand why I did not want Bell's whereabouts discussed. What I thought I knew was her secret. If the grown-ups started probing they might easily turn on me and I would have to say what I knew or tell lies, and I didn't want to do either of those things. And yet I wanted everything about Bell and Marcus Daveney ('everything'—whatever did I mean by 'every-thing'?) cleared up and made straightforward. And what did I mean by that? Did I mean everything dropped between them, or did I want Marcus Daveney to get his feet under our table, hang his hat up in our hall? At that time I had not read *Romeo and Juliet,* but even at that time I could not see the Daveneys and the Hooks united by Marcus and Bell.

These considerations did not impair my appetite. They say that however sick in mind you are you can always eat ham, just as you can listen to Schumann. After the ham there was trifle, with blanched almonds sticking out of it like filed teeth. Then there was cheese and cream crackers, and then, to my surprise, because Maidment was there, port wine.

Everyone became expansive. Even I was allowed a little port wine. I liked it in sips although it did not taste of all the fruits of the earth as I thought a wine should. We had had at school, a year earlier, a private competition, with a packet of Gold Flake cigar-ettes as first prize, to see who could eat the most acorns and drink the most ink in ten minutes. Reggie Tate won easily. We didn't like that because he was a loud-mouth, but it was all right in the end because as soon as he lit a Gold Flake it made him sick. Port wine reminded me a little of the ink. Maidment didn't drink it straight down but seemed to suck it through his teeth. He pro-nounced it a very good wood port, which gratified everyone. Uncle Hector lit a cigar after demonstrating that if you held it between your middle fingers it wouldn't fall out of your hand if you went to sleep; he left the band on, declaring that the makers put it there to afford you a better grip. When he had swilled his mouth with the last of his port wine Maidment, having apologetically asked my mother if she could bear a tobacco pipe in her best parlour, filled it magically by placing a heap of tobacco in the palm of his left hand, inverting the pipe-bowl over it and with a slow circular motion inducing the tobacco to fill the bowl. Even Mr. Leaf was moved to declare it 'very neat'.

Then the plates were cleared by Maidment and me, cards and coins produced and, when Mr. Leaf had returned from washing his hands, the game began again.

From that point everything seemed to go Maidment's way. Whenever the bleeding-bowl brimmed with copper Maidment slapped card after card out of his hand to claim the heap of pennies. And however often my uncle observed that if you didn't speculate you didn't accumulate, or Uncle Hector pleaded for the dog to be allowed to see the rabbit, it was Maidment who tipped the bleeding-bowl with a clatter and with curved hand dragged the coins to his front for counting and transfer to his jacket pocket. I was happy enough to play out the Jack of Hearts when he came my way and collect the few pence entrusted to him in the middle of the table. I never aspired to the bleeding-bowl so I did not share the real or pretended dismay of the others when Maidment cried, "Queen of Clubs. That's a stop. Queen of Spades, King of Spades, jolly old Ace of Spades, that's the Herbert! Out." And so he was. And everybody else groaned or gasped admiration in accordance with his own hopes of success.

Until I was allowed to stay up to play 'Newmarket' I had always been suspicious or scornful of authors who permitted their characters to 'cry' things. "Where is Sir Denver?" she cried. "Look, Sir, the black devils are closing in!" cried Paul. "I say, you fellows," cried Jim, "have you seen the new beak?" For me, crying meant tears; but now I had found that card-players in the rigour of the game did not 'say', they 'cried'.

We were approaching the stage in a hand when I was sure that Maidment was about to cry, "That's a stop! I've got the King. That's the Herbert! Anyone got the Ace? No? Here it is! Ace and out!" I myself had no further hopes of success after picking up a halfpenny from the Jack. Maidment was clearly, in his own assessment, on the last lap, ready to slap down his two remaining cards to win; the others were visibly united to frustrate him— when our front-door bell interrupted.

"Go and see who it is, Arthur," said my mother, for once fully intent on the game. I laid my cards on the table, was reprimanded for putting them face-up, and pushing back my chair went downstairs.

It was Madge Ingles at the door. I call her Madge Ingles because that is how we knew her. It wasn't until years afterwards that I learned that her name was Margaret Inglis. I liked Madge. At times I thought I loved her. She was older than me, of course, being one of Bell's friends, but she never treated me like a kid, and somehow her sparkling disposition made you think that she knew of a life which was all love and fun and laughter. She didn't have much fun or laughter. Her father. It was to speak of her father that she had called.

"Is Bell in, Arthur?"

"No. At least, I . . ."

"Tell her she'd better not call to-night. Dad's had one of his bad turns and I've got to go to Aunt Enid's so that Mum can use my bed."

"I'm sorry, Madge. Will you have a butter-ball?"

I had no right to offer her a butter-ball. To have given her one would have been to incur a larceny, but I knew where the jar was in the shop, and I was sure my father wouldn't have minded my giving a sweet to Jack Ingles' girl.

"No, thank you, Arthur, dear. I must fly."

And she smiled a smile that banished the rain and the night, and promised sun and happiness.

Jack Ingles had been wounded in the war. I think I can remember his coming home from hospital with crutches and a suit of vivid blue. Jack Ingles had lost a leg; but they had found him a wooden one. It wasn't really a wooden one, and I knew that, because I had seen it. There was a rumour that he had a wooden leg and kept his sock up with a tin-tack; but once when Bell and I were at the Ingles' for tea I had asked him. Everyone was silent except Mr. Ingles. He laughed.

"Help me up, lad," he had said; and he had fastened his hand on my shoulder like a claw. When he stood I saw he was without his leg, wooden or otherwise, and that the lower half of his trouser was folded and pinned up by his waist. On our three legs we shuffled and hopped, his steel hand guiding me, to the cupboard by the fireplace. He lifted the hook. The door obediently swung open. Leaning inside, a ghastly contraption of perforated aluminium and leather stood daintily poised on a metal toe.

"Not much wood about that, eh, boy?" said Mr. Ingles.

"Mr. Ingles likes to keep it warm for his stump," said Mrs. Ingles.

My imagination had stirred at the thought of that leather and metal bucket, nicely warmed, receiving Mr. Ingles' chilly stump, and I was afraid he might insist on showing me. I was torn, I remember, between two certainties—that I badly wanted to see Mr. Ingles' stump and that I would be sick if I did.

He had more than a stump, had Jack Ingles. He had a bullet in him somewhere and he had a weak chest. And even more. Because he had a weak chest he had a broad black beard to protect it from the cold. His bullet seemed to travel round his body like a jam-jar in a harbour. Sometimes it would turn up beneath his skin, and friends were invited to feel it. Sometimes it went off into the hinterland of his belly and he came over queer and took to his bed. The doctor who had advised him to grow a beard had also advised that the leaden fugitive should be given a free run of his body and would one day give itself up.

I somehow could not put from my mind the sight and sound of Jack Ingles' bullet popping out from the end of his warm stump and falling with a clatter into the hideous bucket of his artificial leg.

Sadly I locked the door behind Madge. I felt, the moment after parting, that I could have, or should have said more than I did. Just what it was that needed expression I did not know; and I have noticed many times since that farewells are most sad when it is too late to utter the thoughts that arise after the door has been shut or the train has drawn away. You would suppose that Madge was destined to disappear from my life that night, such was the intensity of my feelings towards her when she left. No such thing, though I have often wondered if the total of my happiness afterwards would have been greater had she done so, so great were my yearnings towards her.

No point in looking for Bell in the house. I was sure she was out; she was spending the evening with Madge.

I went upstairs again, uneasy about Bell but confident that I should be the centre of attention as bearer of news about Jack Ingles; for everyone took an interest in his ups and downs.

No one took any notice of me. Voices were raised. Maidment and Uncle Hector were standing. My father looked worried. My mother looked white and ill. I didn't notice Aunt May. Mr. Leaf was outside washing his hands.

"I saw it with my own eyes," said Uncle Hector.

"Well, look again," replied Maidment.

"You've moved it."

"How could I?"

"Leave it, Hector, leave it," said my father.

"I saw it with my own eyes. He said the ten of clubs was a stop—and he had the Jack in his hand. I saw it."

"Well, you shouldn't have seen it," said Maidment. "That's cheating."

"Cheating! Look who's talking! You needn't think I haven't had my eye on you all the evening. Cheating! Of course it's bloody-well cheating! And it's you that's doing it!"

"Leave it," said my father. "Shuffle the cards, Hector, and let's have another round."

"I'm not touching the bloody cards," stormed Uncle Hector; "not if he's going to play again. I'm not touching 'em."

Mr. Leaf came back, and they all turned to him as to an infallible adjudicator.

"Hey, Leaf," raved Uncle Hector, "you saw what he did, didn't you! Been doing it all the evening; saying it was a stop when it wasn't, so's he could get his best cards out. You saw it. You saw the Jack o' clubs in his hand—didn't you?"

Mr. Leaf was pathetically ill at ease. The silence could only be broken by him. No one else was going to speak.

At length he spoke. Timidly the words came out. "Well, I must confess . . ." he began. "I must confess I . . ."

He never made his confession. There was a slithering crash as my mother, her face pallid and sweaty, crumpled to the floor bringing the tablecloth and glasses and cards and money and bleeding-bowl with her.

There was a general confusion of first-aid and departure. I felt sick with terror but found myself seeing out Mr. Leaf, Maidment and Uncle Hector. Mr. Leaf shook my hand when he left, murmuring obscurely, "Lady Macbeth all over again." Maidment said to Uncle Hector, "How about a wet? Bloody silly to keep this up, eh?" Uncle Hector turned to him briefly. "Piss off!" he said. Maidment moved off into the rain. Uncle Hector turned to me—awkwardly, I thought. He drew his hand from his pocket to proffer a half-crown. "You'll be all right, lad," he croaked as I accepted it. "She's got a lump, yer know. Your mother's got a lump. Your auntie will look after her. You'll be all right."

When my head touched the pillow that night it was not to sleep. The doctor had come and gone. Mother must 'take it easy.' Aunt May would stay until Bell came back.

I could not worry about Bell any more. Mother had a lump. What was a lump? Would Mr. Bagnall know what a lump was? Could a lump make her face wet like that and then make it look as if it had been dusted with flour? I felt myself going all hot; from my throat to my stomach I felt weak and hollow. Suppose . . . suppose . . .

Bell must come home soon. I didn't care where she had been. It no longer mattered. I resolved I wouldn't ask her. Nothing should add to the anxieties of the night. I just wouldn't ask her and then I wouldn't have anything to add to the sick fear that kept me awake and staring into the dark.

I heard Bell come in by the back door. For a long time I could hear voices—hers, my father's and Aunt May's. Then the front door went. My father and Bell talked for a long time before I heard her step on the stairs. She came into my room, shading her candle with her hand.

"Are you awake, Arthur, dear?" she whispered.

"Yes, Bell. Bell . . ."

"Yes, dear?"

"Bell," I whispered. "Bell, where were you to-night?"

"At Madge's," she said.

"All the time?"

"Yes, of course, dear. All the time."

V

THE PASSING DAYS drew the sharper teeth from my gnawing anxieties over my mother; but I couldn't put from my mind the ghastly spectacle she made as she lay drained of colour at our feet. She now went upstairs every afternoon for 'her rest'; sometimes she pushed her food away untasted; but when I asked her if anything was the matter she always said no and urged me to run along. I vaguely resolved to 'do something', and eventually saw, as so many have done, that my help might come from the Lord who hath made Heaven and earth. Not exactly from the Lord himself, but from his representative, our vicar, the Reverend Benskin.

Mr. Benskin used to come to Friday-night choir practices. Not that he joined in—he did not even sing the versicles during service —he would sit there with the tenors, thumbing the sheet music with a look of amused tolerance as if he knew a much quicker route to God's ear than the path we were trying to follow. We choirboys found him a rewarding man to listen to. Though not spiritually.

He had a goat's voice. He was known to us as Billy Benskin or sometimes Twobags Benskin. One of our number, Jimmy Pawsey, used to work for Mr. Dighton, the grocer, during the holidays, and he had reported more than one of Mr. Benskin's shopping encounters. Mrs. Benskin refused to go into Mr. Dighton's shop, and it was, I suppose, a wonder that she allowed Mr. Benskin to go either. On Saturday evenings, Mr. Dighton kept open half an hour longer than any other shop, thereby obliging other shopkeepers and their assistants who were hard-pressed to buy provisions for the Sunday. Just before half-past six one Saturday evening Mrs. Benskin had come into Dighton's and set about compiling a big order. She queried the price of everything she bought; but the tins and parcels began to pile up on the counter; the minutes passed; Mr. Dighton told the assistants they could start packing up; he would take over the order. The blinds were drawn, the door locked. Still Mrs. Benskin probed and purchased or rejected. At five to seven she was still there, inspecting butter. Half a pound of slightly salted was at last approved, wrapped and bagged. She asked the price. She was told by the ominously tight-lipped Mr. Dighton.

"Oh, but I can get it a halfpenny cheaper down the street," she said. "The same thing."

Mr. Dighton leaned forward from the waist; his white-sleeved arms encircled the heap of packages. He drew them to his side of the counter. "Well, bugger off and get it," he said.

The Twobags incident was nothing, really. Only that Mr. Benskin had stood at Dighton's counter and bleated, "I want tew pounds of demar-rah-rah sugah in tew begs."

But Mr. Benskin did win some respect from us, and at a time, too, when you would have said he had lost it. He was bleating a powerful sermon based on the proposition that there are none so deaf as those who won't hear. He had taken some twenty minutes in propounding the point and then had concluded conclusively with the exhortation, pitched in the considerable upper register of his bleat, "He that hath yahs to yah, let him yah." Harold Witty, one of the second trebles, had then called out, "Yah, yah." We all laughed, and Mr. Benskin ordered us out.

Anyway, it was to Mr. Benskin that I half decided to turn. It came to me when we were practising an anthem, "The spirit of the Lord is upon me because he hath appointed me to preach the gospel, to teach the acceptable word of the Lord; to give unto them that mourn a garland, for ashes, the oil of joy . . ." and, I thought, 'Why not? Why not ask Mr. Benskin?' Only if Mother got worse, of course. I didn't want to say anything at the time because we believed that he was on to one of our best jokes and best secrets. Whenever we had the hymn "Through all the changing scenes of life, in trouble and in joy . . ." we used, by custom, to sing the first two lines as 'Ha, ha, she cried, the kid's boss-eyed; and she wagged her wooden leg.' No one so far as we knew, had ever detected the interpolation; but the last time we did it in church Mr. Benskin, who usually mouthed the hymns facing the congregation, had pivoted with a look of shocked disbelief.

Although Mr. Benskin as a man had never inspired me he had won me over by his fine stole, his Geneva bands, the way he held his hand up when he gave the blessing and the dignified but humble way he knelt at the altar, elbows out, head buried on hands, soles and heels (always unfrayed) meekly bordered by the heavy folds of his cassock. It was to Mr. Benskin I would turn if I was in trouble, sorrow, need, pain, sickness or any other adversity.

I had at the back of my mind someone else to turn to if something terrible happened. There was a possible refuge in Grandfather.

My mother's father was never spoken of, but he existed just the same. He wasn't spoken of in our home not only because he had never stepped inside it but because my father had forbidden anyone to refer to him.

Grandfather looked like the Boer leader, Kruger. A wiry black beard, a huge forehead, stubby fingers, a frock-coat. But he was not disagreeable. Far from it.

Grandfather lived with my mother's sister, Auntie Lucy, in what used to be called a market town, twenty miles away. Sometimes my mother talked to me about him, and she said he was an agent of some sort. I always thought of him as a mayor, or at least a town councillor, and there was one period, when, influenced by my reading of *The Secret Agent* (how I got through it I don't know), I was quite sure he was either an anarchist himself or one whose job it was to track anarchists down. I got most of my information about him from my cousin, Arnold. When Uncle Hector and Aunt May were out Arnold used to become quite expansive. Not only did he let me go behind the brass-wire pen in the shop but he talked about 'the family'—rather, I thought, as if he were an outsider and not one of us at all. He said that Grandfather 'undertook things', and made it sound very grand.

Arnold told me why Grandfather never came to our house. There had been a family row. Years ago.

Grandfather had objected to my mother marrying my father. Of course he wasn't my father then. What Grandfather had objected to, Arnold said, was the fact that his daughter was marrying beneath her, for mother had been a piano-teacher at a High School, and father, well, apparently father hadn't been anything for very long at a time. When he married he was a traveller for a grocery firm ("peddling cocoa and arrowroot," Grandfather said). He hadn't any money, and Grandfather had refused his consent to the match. Grandfather wouldn't go to the wedding; but when it was done he gave my mother a hundred pounds and said he'd finished with her. And he had, too.

46

I ought to have been the victim of divided loyalties over this, but somehow I wasn't. Bell and I paid a state visit to Grandfather every winter starting off sometimes in Mr. Bagnall's cab and being met always by Grandfather in his trap. Auntie Lucy used to give us sausages for tea; Grandfather used to give Bell a gold sovereign and me a half-sovereign. Going home in the train we used to compare them, and I can still see their rich lustre and feel their eloquent weight in my hand. When Auntie Lucy served the sausages Grandfather used to sing, "When we are Married we'll have Sausages for Tea." When we got home Mother used to ask us how we got on and how Grandfather was, and was he well wrapped up and was the house warm; but she didn't ask us that if Father was in the room.

Grandfather used to ask how Mother was; in fact, he asked us that in different ways many times during the afternoon. He never mentioned Father though he was less reticent on the subject of Uncle Hector whom he referred to in varying degrees from 'that counter-jumper' to 'that jumped-up errand-boy'. My father used to take my half-sovereign from me 'to go in the Post Office.' Since we were not allowed to mention Grandfather's name it wasn't possible to contest this transaction though my conviction that it was going straight into Uncle Hector's pocket made it very hard for me to surrender it meekly.

We were practising *The Spirit of the Lord is upon Me,* not for Christmas but because Mr. Asher, the curate, was leaving to be a missionary in Africa and this was the choir's tribute to him. Once we had satisfied Mr. Dyball that we knew *The Spirit of the Lord* . . . we went straight into carols for the Nine Carol Service. This was a service I always looked forward to, but now any mention of it sent a sharp spasm of fright from my heart to my stomach; for this year, Mr. Dyball had said, I was to read one of the lessons. One Friday night when we had first begun practising the carols Mr. Dyball had called out to Mr. Webster, "D'you think Hook could read a lesson this year, Mr. Webster? I know he can't count, but d'you think he can read?" The men and the boys had laughed, but Mr. Webster had replied gravely, "He won't let you down, Sir." But I did let Mr. Dyball down and Mr. Webster, too, and myself, I suppose, though I'm not sure how one does that.

The service was the night before Christmas Eve. Mr. Dyball

said it ought to be after Christmas and it was silly, really, to sing "Unto us a Child is Born" and "Lullay my liking, my own dear sweeting," and things like that before Christ's birthday; but Mr. Benskin said no-one wanted to hear carols after Christmas Day; it was like having the soup after the Stilton. So we went ahead with glory to the new-born King who was Virgin-born on that morn, Procreated for us, and I don't suppose anyone minded very much. We had *The noble stem of Jesse hath flourished at this time* and *Lo, star-led chiefs Assyrian odours bring* (what were Assyrian odours?), and my real favourite, *While shepherds watched their flocks by night*.

The lesson I had to read was only a short one: Adam and Eve hiding from God because they were naked. I had practised my reading alone. I didn't like to ask Bell to hear me through it because of the bits about being naked. I thought she or I, like Adam and Eve, might be ashamed. I don't think it occurred to me to ask my mother. I used to smuggle our Bible to Mr. Bagnall's stables when he wasn't there and read my piece to Dinah or Prince. I did think of copying it out but I wanted to get used to seeing the printed chapter-heading and text because ever since Mr. Dyball had said I'd got to read I had wretchedly wondered what I would do if on the night I couldn't find the place. So I practised with the Bible propped up on the manger in the stable, and it wasn't until years later that I realised that territorially I could scarcely have done better. Acoustically, however, I could hardly have done worse, or so it seemed to me when Mr. Dyball made me read my lesson in the vestry.

"You must speak up, small fry. They'll never hear you. Hold your head up. Your chin's in your chest. Now then; hold the book away from you and imagine you've got to make them hear up in the belfry. Are your people coming?"

"I expect so."

"Then read to Aunt Freda by the font, not to Aunt Cora in the crypt."

"I haven't got . . ."

"Well, Uncle Charlie in the clerestory, not Uncle Tommy in the tomb. Now, deep breath; stand up straight."

On that particular night, the night when I saw Mr. Benskin as a hope and refuge in trouble, the spirit of the Lord might have been upon us all, or so it seemed to me. The trebles used to start the practice at half-past seven; the men did not arrive until eight,

48

and Mr. Dyball usually contrived a break for us while they took their places. In they came, and behold! they were all dusted with snow. And they were jovial and free and, merry gentlemen, were dismayed at nothing. The carols we practised came out warm and round, full of promise and hope. You felt as if the Star was passing over the very roof; you saw the Magi's three ships a-sailing; you joined the humble animals kneeling outside a stable through whose rough planking poured a radiance like the moon, like the sun, like heaven itself.

We were let out early. Our torches probed. There was the snow, enough to be scooped into handfuls, enough on the flat tomb of Henry Rabjohn and his wife to make a small snowman, enough for me, if I cared to do it, to see what footsteps led to the grave-digger's shed by the red brick wall. The vestry windows threw a yellow light on the flakes, for the men were still at practice; the elms disappeared gauntly upwards in the flurried gloom. No one wanted to play Tombstones. Snowballs scuttered along the ground or with a soft thud starred on the flint walls. The chilblains on the knuckles of my left hand demanded to be stratched to shreds; the toes of both feet felt wet; my ears ached a little.

Ernest Green called us together round the Rabjohn tomb and said that he had bought some braces for Mr. Dyball and that any-one who let on had better look out and that there had been enough money left over to buy four eightpenny cigars in a box and he was going to present them to Mr. Dyball after the morning service on Christmas Day and that anyone who pushed off before the presen-tation was made had better look out and Jackie Dawes and Fred Fish whose job it was to hold candles for the readers at the carol service had better have clean hands or they could look out, too. Greeny didn't say it as fluently as that, but no snowballs were thrown while he spoke.

Willie Waites and I didn't wait long after that. He gave me a paregoric from a limp, sticky paper bag and we agreed to see if any shop windows were still lit up. I complimented him on the size of the amber tablet, remarking how quickly the paper peeled off once you'd got the sweet in your mouth.

"Got them from Mr. Parker's," he said. "Eight a penny. Spies have to eat paper if they're caught with plans for fortresses and things."

"What do they do that for?"

"So's they won't fall into the hands of the enemy."

There were shops which in deference to the season had left their

49

window-lights on. We went first to Askew's because Willie wanted to show me a steam-engine. The glass was a bit blurred on the inside as if the engine had been busy, but we could see it well enough: a beautiful little donkey-engine with a copper boiler and a powerful little cylinder worked by eccentric gear. Willie said you could run a dynamo off it, and he thought his electric motor might work as a dynamo if it was driven backwards. Off the dynamo he could work a little induction coil, he said, and give people shocks or light up geissler tubes. The steam-engine was what he wanted for Christmas. I wanted a carpentry set so we went along to Fletcher's to see if it was still in the window. It was, but the glass was so steamy that we could only just make out the long fibre box with its lid propped open by a chisel.

I didn't need to see it to know it was there. Since it had appeared in Fletcher's window hardly a day had passed without my inspecting it. Its price was nineteen and elevenpence. For that you got a saw—not one of those feeble boy's-carpentry-set saws that stay bent after their first trial, but a real saw, only not very long—a saw, a hammer (I still have it), a chisel, a screw-driver, a gimlet (useless), a bradawl, a conical oil-can (which I never filled), a pair of heavy pliers (awfully stiff at first) with wire-cutters, a wad of sand-paper and a book called *Simple Joinery*.

It was somehow very urgent to me that I should possess that tool-set. I don't know quite why. It wasn't primarily because I wanted to make things or mend things; it was just that I had to have it. I had had that kind of craving before. There had been a pocket-watch in Schusters, the jewellers. It had a small dial which occupied only half the watch-glass; under the dial was the exposed balance-wheel busily pumping away for you to see. The gun-metal case at once housed a chronometer and a little power-house. I never possessed it.

There had been a pocket-knife, too. Not one of those which bristle with miniature picks and probes and levers, but one with two strong blades and a cork-screw. I didn't want the cork-screw, but I did want the knife. I got it. Shutting the larger blade carelessly I cut myself deeply in the webbing between thumb and fore-finger. I had promised my father that if he bought me the knife ("It's too big for a boy. It's a man's knife") I'd be awfully careful. Now I was going to die of lock-jaw; no doubt of that. If you cut yourself there you were sure to get lock-jaw. I didn't die. My jaw did not even lock.

Willie and I slowly did the round of the shops in the High Street. Altogether they were rather bleak, like eyeless faces. Some were forbidding. The fishmonger's was dark and bare but enlivened by an illuminated tank of darting goldfish; the butcher's, whose windows were masked during the day by pendent and (I thought) sad rows of pheasants and other feathered friends and hares strung up by their hind legs, their heads decently buried in tin cups, was now nothing but a cavern of marble and wooden slabs. The cash-desk, framed with holly-twigs and red crepe paper, where during the day Mrs. Plastow presided over the great ledger, looked like a garish glass cenotaph. We pressed our faces closer to the window, wiping away our breath-marks with the palm of our gloved hands. Axe and cleaver, steel and saw could be seen laid out on a great wooden block. The mighty scales and weights gleamed brassily with a subdued lustre. From a grating beneath our feet came the searching smell of raw meat.

Snow was packing under the soles of our boots by the time we reached Bradshaw's Sports Shop. Whatever treasures were there, the Meccano sets, the Diana air-guns, the chess-sets with a black and a white knight standing on their half-opened lids, the miniature billiards and the ash bows which cracked the first time you bent them, were revealed only in dim outline, for there were no lights in Bradshaw's. So we made a slide where the pavement sloped.

Why we did not at first notice the two figures huddled in the recessed doorway I do not know. Our icy track carried us right past them. We saw them only because when Willie chose to try the slide from top to bottom when I was trying it from bottom to top we collided and fell not exactly at their feet but within a few yards of their retreat. Picking ourselves up we saw that we were not alone. That it might be Bell and Marcus Daveney did not at first occur to me at all. We had none of the niceties of discreet be-haviour in these circumstances. We peered into the dark doorway.

"Hop it, you kids. Go and play somewhere else." A domineering voice; yet a whining voice. A voice I knew. Marcus Daveney? Surely he had not roamed so far from the security of Mr. Annesley's boundary wall? And Bell? Whatever niceties we had or had not, I was sure that it was not fitting for my sister to be huddling against a man in some shop doorway. A man? It was hardly a man's voice that petulantly invited us again to hop it.

"Didge oo do this?"

Another voice. We turned from the dark cavern of Bradshaw's

51

doorway. In the flakes, huge and glistening in his great conical tarpaulin cape—a policeman. No stranger to us. This was Alligator Juniper. With his right boot, its great domed toe-cap, superior to the elements, glistening like jet, he was demonstrating that we had been guilty of a misdemeanour in that we had acted in a way likely to cause a mischief to the public by converting a safe footway into a dangerous passage. From his manner you would have thought that we had sowed the entire English Channel with horned mines.

Police Constable Juniper was known as an officer timid but vindictive. It was said that his confidence in himself had been undermined by the many occasions in Court where he had made himself ridiculous. Now, they said, he was out to strike an indisputable blow for law and order and pass into retirement not a buffoon but honoured and respected. This would take some doing. There had been the occasion when the magistrate had asked, "Who makes this allegation?" P.C. Juniper, sure that for once he had nailed his man firmly, replied with barely-concealed pride, "I am the alligator, my lord."

Alligator Juniper's hands moved mysteriously under his cape. At length raising its hem in front as if he were going to commit a nuisance he produced a heavy notebook. Savouring the situation he pointed out the enormity of our offence and had us whining false abject apologies; then he pointed out that he wasn't going to enforce the law this time (the scales of justice being solely his to tip) and had us whining false heartfelt gratitude. By the time he had done with us we found Bradshaw's doorway sheltered nothing but a discarded newspaper.

"Coming to my place?" said Willie.

"No. You come to mine."

"Wonder what the time is."

"Don't know." (What a pity I didn't have the watch with the works showing!)

"Shall we chuck snowballs at Jimmy Leaper's front door?"

"Better not. Not with Alligator on the prowl."

We plodded silently on through the busy flakes. I didn't want to talk. I had really been a bit scared of P.C. Juniper's ponderous charge. I knew my mother and father wouldn't like it if I got into trouble. Then there was the couple in the doorway. I don't know how I expected an earl's son to talk, but I felt disappointed and humiliated. "Hop it, you kids. Go and play somewhere else."

We stamped our feet and shook the snow off our coats at our back door. Our cat, Tinker, glided round my ankles waiting to be let in. My mother had cocoa and bread and dripping for us as if she had known precisely when we should arrive and what we should like most. I had had in mind not to say anything about the slide and its consequences; but Willie spilled it all out and had my mother and father so laughing away over Alligator Juniper that it seemed the most natural thing in the world for two boys to be near arrest and disgrace.

"And d'you know who we saw in Bradshaw's doorway?" prattled Willie, conscious of his attentive audience.

There was no reply.

"Praps Arthur doesn't want me to split."

"What's it got to do with Arthur?" asked my father, rather sharply, I thought.

"Well it was his cousin," said Willie. "It was Arnold. His cousin. And that girl Elsie Catcher."

When I went to bed my mother came up to my room before I had blown my candle out." Grandfather wants you and Bell to go and see him tomorrow. You'll like that, won't you?"

I don't know what I had expected her to say. Something about Arnold. Something about Bell.

"I'll tell Bell when she comes in," my mother said. "I do hope the snow will stop soon. I can't think where she's got to. And she's only got her thin shoes on."

This I knew. I had seen their print in the snow by the shed in the churchyard.

VI

"It was given to me by a dying hermit," said Grandfather gravely. "He said—I can hear him now—he said he would roast in unquenchable flames because he had kept it. When I found him he was suffering from an attack of the galloping jim-jams. I nursed him as best I could on Bath Oliver biscuits and stomach bitters, and this is what he gave me just before he died."

"Let the boy look at it, Father," said Auntie Lucy, "and stop spinning your yarns. It's a different one every year!"

I believe it was, too. But there was something in Grandfather's stories that carried conviction. The latest story always effectively cancelled out the one before it, establishing itself as genuine after a host of spurious histories.

"What happened to him?" I asked.

"The other hermits living with him must have known his secret," declared Grandfather. "They never forgave him. When he died he was buried in a shallow grave. No one came to see it, and no grass would grow on it."

"Come along, Bell, dear," said Auntie Lucy. "You don't want to listen to that stuff. Come upstairs, dear. I'll show you the new curtain material. There may be some pieces for you."

So Grandfather and I were left alone. There had been silverside of beef followed by apple-pie and cream. I had had cider to drink, Bell and Auntie Lucy red wine. (Did I see Bell pull a face at her first sip?) Grandfather drank ale which he poured into a thin silver goblet from a long-necked beer-bottle wearing a smart frilled paper cap over its stopper. When the meal was done there was port wine for Grandfather and me, and for Auntie Lucy and Bell an amber drink which, Grandfather told me in confidence, was pure weasel's water. In a silver dish there were nuts—cobs, brazils, walnuts; and Grandfather showed me how to get them whole from their shells, unchipped and smoothly oily.

"Mustn't eat too many nuts, Arthur, lad. You'll get a stoppage, else."

"A stoppage." What was that? I did not know; but it reminded me of Maidment and the night he came to play 'Newmarket' with us. And that reminded me of Mother's collapse. And I felt such a rush of misery and of love for her that I feared that if Grandfather chose this moment to ask how she was (it couldn't be long now before he did) I would be able to do nothing but cry. As it was, the well-chewed nut went round and round in my mouth but refused to be swallowed. One of Uncle Hector's standing jokes was about the boy at the Christmas dinner who at his third helping confessed, "I could eat it, but I couldn't swallow it."

Mercifully, Grandfather was engaged in detaching the greedy hermit's golden jewel from his watch-chain. The chain itself, which would have held a mastiff, threaded a button-hole of his waistcoat and dipped mysteriously into bulging pockets. From its middle, brought into prominence by the bulge of the stomach, the little gold sphere depended like an expensive pom-pom. Grandfather clucked impatiently at its fastening; then it lay in his outstretched hand. You pressed minute levers. Tiny hinges opened. The gold shell flowered into a cross, its arms and upright encrusted with the little opal pyramids which had fitted together so snugly when the jewel was closed.

Once every year I was allowed to open and close the little cross. Once a year, conducted by Grandfather, I made the tour of his house and garden and sheds and stables. We didn't go far outside this time, for a light snow was adding itself to what already lay. Grandfather seemed gratified that snow was falling; it confirmed his views on a blackthorn winter and the urgent call which snow on the ground made to snow yet unfallen to come and join it. He was anxious that we should do the rounds outside the house before Auntie Lucy came downstairs. I noticed that he crossed his heavy muffler over his chest in exactly the same way as my mother made me cross mine. He grunted his way into a huge black overcoat, drew on black woollen gloves, fitted a black bowler hat, peculiarly flat as to the crown, took up a thick cane with a gold knob and declared himself ready to face the yellow-bellied devils.

"See this stick, boy?"

"Yes, Grandfather." He must have remarked my surprise.

"Given to me by a dying British tea-merchant in the Boxer Rising. They'd burnt his warehouses and broken his heart. Here, hold it, boy. Notice anything?"

"It feels very heavy, Grandfather."

"You grip the stick and pull the Harry Randle. No, not like that. Give it a twist first."

From the shaft of the cane slid the upper part of a greasy but sinister steel blade.

"Did you ever kill anyone with it, Grandfather?" I didn't know he had ever been in China.

"That sword could tell a story, Arthur. Better not tell you, I suppose. Have your aunt after me."

We went to the stables first. Two fine black horses twitched and shuffled in their clean straw; glossy and well covered, they made poor Dinah and Prince seem very lowly creatures. They smelt the same, though. There were black brass-mounted plumes hanging from wooden pegs. Grandfather was a little disconcerted when I asked him what they were for.

"Oh, ah. Well. Well, you see, these two were circus-horses once. Part of the act, you see. Don't use them now."

As usual he hurried me past the closed doors of a big barn-like building of red-brick and timber. I remembered that the year before when I had lingered and asked him what was inside he had told me it was full of empty boxes. I asked him this time.

"In there? Oh, nothing you'd want to see. Old boxes and things. Now, d'you know what this is?"

It was a fine, upstanding pump; six feet high with a graceful curly handle which terminated in an iron whirl like a swiss-roll. From its pouting iron lip hung a long clear icicle.

"Have a go, lad," said Grandfather. And as I laboured at the long handle he sang to himself a ditty of which only a little remains in my mind—"The Village Pump. The Village Pump. The village pump, pump, pump, pump, pump."

No water rose. There were only sucking noises and wet gurgles.

"It's the washers, you see, lad. They don't like the cold. And no more do I."

Flakes of snow were nesting in Grandfather's fringe of whiskers. It was time to go indoors. It was a little while before Auntie Lucy came downstairs with Bell. Grandfather did not actually deny that he had been outside but it was somehow conveyed to my aunt that although he hadn't, I had. So I was felt all over for humidity and pronounced damp as to the feet. My aunt went up again and came down again, this time with a pair of socks mysteriously wound round each other to form a ball. Separating them she deftly folded so that instead of my tugging them on they somehow rolled themselves at a touch over my feet. Did Auntie Lucy, I wondered, keep socks to fit all her visitors? These fitted me. The changeover was made to a musical accompaniment, Grandfather singing catches of a song the meaning of which is no clearer to me now than it was then —"Sailing, sailing, over Niagara rocks; there's many a man will change his mind, but few will change their socks."

Though it was not late Grandfather lit the gas in the drawing-room. The fat glass globes on either side of the tall mantelpiece hissed pinkly so that I could not tell if Bell, holding against herself a bunch of curtains, blushed when Grandfather said, "Those for your bottom drawer, girl?" In a gentle joking way he had made so many references to 'young men' and 'beaux' and even though sharply pulled up by Auntie Lucy, to 'slap and tickle', that I became almost convinced that he knew what I knew.

Bell and Auntie Lucy busied themselves measuring the stuff with a yellow tape-measure; Grandfather made up the fire from a brass-bound scuttle, manipulating the long brass tongs with a dexterity which he declared he owed to his use of chopsticks during his long stay at the palace of an Eastern potentate to whom he was confidential adviser. Auntie Lucy, her mouth bristling pins, said that he'd never set foot outside his native land. He, unabashed, said, "You're forgetting Nebraska, aren't you?" I was left to make my annual exploration of the drawing-room.

There was the mantelpiece clock to look at (but not to touch). It lowered itself on a toothed metal column and was an ugly thing, though still fascinating, when it neared the foot of its ratchet. There was a bowl with holes in its lid which gave out the smell of faded roses of summers long ago. There was a little Taj Mahal (Grand-father said, or, rather, I took him to say, that he had had his shoes stolen while inspecting the real thing) under a cracked glass dome with rivets in it. There was a West African dagger in a fringed leather sheath hanging on one side of the fireplace and a brass toasting fork with a telescopic handle hanging on the other. And there were the history books. Faded and crumbling leather, tiny print and a musty smell. But what a wealth of pictures! In stark steel engravings there must have been every bloody deed known to history. Edmund had his chead chopped off; Normans cut off Saxon hands by the dozen; Becket's brains were spilled on the pavement; the Black Prince massacred Limoges; Clarence drowned in Malmsey; Titus Oates had his tongue ripped out; Byng grovelled in his own blood; Marat bled in his bath. While Grandfather

57

settling in his chair dropped instantly off to sleep and while Auntie Lucy and Bell grew serious over false hems and pleats I sat on a big round leather cushion (Grandfather said it was stuffed with love-letters) under one of the gas-lamps rustling greedily through the thin pages, the discarded volumes piling up round my feet, soft shreds of perished leather littering the carpet.

I have them before me now as I write, those books. I have not looked into them for years.

Auntie Lucy and Bell gathered up their materials whispering to me that they were going to do some sewing and that I might come and work the treadle if I liked. I had done this to my delight on previous visits, both legitimately as Auntie Lucy anxiously guided cloth under the busy, stabbing needle, and in the interests of science as in a make-believe world the machine became for me an aeroplane or a submarine. It somehow did not seem right to desert Grandfather just then, so I whispered back that I would come presently and was soon back in my book.

When he woke up he wanted to know not about Mother but what I had been doing at school. There wasn't much to tell, really. We had only a few days left. Exams were over, and all that remained was the announcement of results, my inevitable disgrace in arithmetic, the second attempt at answers shoddily done and the filling in of a lot of blank time while our masters, each one claiming that by some cruel trick of fate he had been prevented from marking our papers earlier, busied themselves with their piles of foolscap sheets.

He asked me how I had got on at sums. Had he wanted to know about any other subject I could have answered with less awkwardness. There was *Sohrab and Rustum* to tell him about, and *Macbeth* and *Great Expectations* and *Brigadier Gerard*. But he wanted to know about sums. I had had my usual experience: the exam over, there was the inevitable stock-exchange in the corridor outside the class-room. We had been engaged during the term with grocers who found it difficult to mix coffee and chicory in the correct proportions and with sailors who, for unspecified reasons, were unable to get together at the same time to work the pumps of their sinking ship. There had been, too, a brief excursion into the world of paper-hangers and paviours. Their lives were considerably bound up with converting everything they touched into square yards. As answers were compared after the exam it became obvious that my future lay not on the sea nor behind a grocer's counter; neither should I get very far in the interior decorating or landscape-gardening business. Where other candidates' answers were in round figures, I had grotesque fractions; where they estimated that you could paper that particular room for three pounds fifteen shillings, I had pledged my belief that it would cost one hundred and twenty-five pounds, twenty-two shillings and sixpence. As Mr. Webster pointed out later, not even the grocer's errand-boy would have put eight pounds of chicory to three pounds of coffee. But even Mr. Webster might have been wrong there, for everyone knew that Mrs. Benskin had once said that Mr. Dighton's coffee was nothing but chicory and sweepings off the floor.

I couldn't tell all this to Grandfather, so I said that my sums 'weren't bad'.

"You've got to be good at sums, boy. If you aren't it'll be a burden to you all your life. You'll have every smart alec scoring off you, see? I know their tricks—eighteen pence are one-and-eight; that sort of thing."

Before I could verify the accuracy or knavery of this calculation he was on to a baffling conundrum about the weight of brick being a brick and half a brick. Soon out of my depth I could do no more than pretend I knew what he was talking about. I was saved when I said that for Mr. Webster we sometimes did sums not about bricks but about paving-stones, and that Mr. Webster sang in the choir, like me, and that Mr. Webster sang a song at the end of term concert.

Grandfather wanted to know all about that concert. "What did you do in it, boy? Sing; eh?"

"Yes, Grandfather; Harold Witty and me sang a song called 'Heigh, Ho, Come to the Fair' by someone called Easthope. It wasn't very good."

"Did they clap?"

"Yes. They clapped all right."

"Well, then . . ."

"We sang it too fast, Grandfather. We knew we were too fast, but we didn't seem to be able to slow down, somehow. We got faster and faster."

"Oh, well. As long as they clapped. What else?"

The headmaster, I told Grandfather, had started a violin solo called 'Melodie D'Amour', but had stopped to object to the dazzling effect of the lime-light which had been coaxed into life half-way through his piece. He had peered down the beam waving his open hand at the operators until they dropped the brass disc over the lens and stood like disconcerted Wright of Derby figures round their radiant apparatus; then he had found that his concentration on the light had robbed him of sight. Not only could he not see the notes, he could not see the sheet of music on the stand which supported it. In his groping he knocked the stand over the edge of the stage and would no doubt have followed it, had not Mr. Selby, his accompanist, restrained him by leaning back on his stool and catching him by the coat-tails.

Grandfather chuckled away, and I was about to tell him how Mr. Webster sang a wonderful song called 'Nirvana,' all about the dumb gods and the temples being shattered, when all the laughing creases on his face opened and he said, "How is it with your mother, lad?"

"She's all right. She . . . sends her love."

And then my throat went all tight and I couldn't speak. And it was as if the unformed words came up behind my eyes, dissolving into hot tears. Grandfather's arm went round my shoulders; he drew me to him so that my cheek was against the rough stuff of his coat. His fringe of whiskers was in my hair. I felt very ashamed and pathetically grateful all at the same time.

"I know, lad, I know," he said. "She hasn't been very well, has she. And you'll help her all you can, won't you, lad?"

I could still say nothing. He pulled out a big white handkerchief from his coat pocket. "Have a good blow," he said. "Nothing like it."

While I attempted to blow my tears away through my nose Grandfather told me about the village where he was born. "There were three bells in the church tower," he recalled. "One was made of iron; and one was made of wood, and one was made of leather. And do you know what happened when they rang them?" I sniffed that I did not. "They went—Ding—Bong—Flop. What d'you think of that?—Ding—Bong—Flop!"

I managed to tell him that Mother had told me that I wasn't to say she hadn't been well, and so he must pretend not to know.

"Bless you, boy," he said. "It's not a secret. Your aunt doesn't spend all her time in the kitchen, you know." I didn't really see what Auntie Lucy's absence from her kitchen had to do with it. I told him, as best I could, how Mother had fallen down that night. I didn't say anything about the card-game and Maidment, though. That part of it seemed . . . what did it seem? . . . I hadn't words for it. It had seemed a shameful and pathetic thing for Mother to

60

lie there at Maidment's feet with the débris of the evening's entertainment around her on the floor.

"They tell me the doctor's no fool," said Grandfather. "Matson, isn't it? Does she see much of him?"

"I don't know," I said miserably. I didn't know; but Mother had said I was to say she was all right. "Mother said there's nothing to worry about."

"That's because she doesn't want me to come over."

I think he was going to tell me everything then. I didn't say anything, but just waited. The clock ticked noisily on its ratchet; the coals settled themselves audibly on the fire. Grandfather drew a deep breath.

" There was a time . . ." he began. Then Bell and Auntie Lucy came in.

"I thought you were going to do the machine for us," Auntie Lucy accused. "And now it's tea-time. Turn up the gas, Father. Pull the curtains, Bell, dear."

"I think we ought to be going, Aunt," said Bell. "It's getting late and Grandfather oughtn't to be out in the snow. I think we ought to get the early train."

"Grandfather's a step ahead of you, young miss," chuckled the old man. "He's arranged for Hatch to take you to the station."

Did I see a flicker of disappointment and pique on Bell's lips? Perhaps she didn't like Hatch. I didn't see why she should object to an arrangement that gave us the freedom of Auntie Lucy's tea-table. Besides, I liked being with Hatch. Like Grandfather, he gave you the feeling that he was equal to any calamity. You would never miss a train if Hatch was looking after you, nor, I was sure, would you ever be ship-wrecked, or molested by bandits, or struck by lightning or transfixed by lock-jaw.

Besides, Hatch had only one thumb. There was a story about the other. Hatch had been driving one of my Grandfather's closed wagonettes up a steep hill. Half-way up, whatever was in the back had started to slide. Hatch got down, and in order to take the strain off the pulling horse while he put things right, placed the big iron shoe behind one of the back wheels. The horse, knowing the procedure, had mistaken Hatch's grunt of satisfaction for the expected order to ease back. The iron tyre of the wheel ground along the sides of the shoe and Hatch's severed thumb lay in the gutter. Hatch had picked it up, put it in his waistcoat pocket, straightened the load and driven on to town.

They couldn't put his thumb back on again, but they let him keep it. I never saw it, but I saw the stump lots of times. He said it was better than a weather-glass.

So we sat down to tea. Grandfather had wanted to have it round the fire, and I wanted that, too, because there was a table on wheels, and a kettle with a blue flame under it and a cake-stand thing made of brass that had flaps on it that came down to hold plates, but Auntie Lucy said we'd got to have a proper knife-and-fork tea because we'd got a long way to go and it was fit to starve you outside.

We had bread and butter and two sorts of home-made jam and haddock with egg on it (which I didn't like very much) and rock-cakes with big pieces of peel in them and Christmas cake with thick marzipan on it and lots of little silver balls that went crunch when you bit them hard and had a taste you never forget.

I had saved my marzipan until last; and I was just going to put it into my mouth when Auntie Lucy said, "When do you sit for your scholarship, Arthur?" My thoughts, I suppose, were not on scholarship just then; but when she repeated her question a cold thrill ran down my inside as if I was going to be sick.

"What scholarship, Auntie?"

"The one to the Big School."

Bell intervened. "Arthur doesn't know about it yet, Aunt. It was only arranged last week."

"Oh. And what do you think about it, Arthur?" said my aunt, as if this little exchange over the tea-cups had put me in possession of all the facts and marshalled my response to the prospect.

"I don't know," I said. I couldn't eat my cake any more.

"It's nothing to be frightened of, Arthur," said Bell. "It's only that it's a chance for you to go to the Big School."

"Will I have to leave home?"

"Well, you wouldn't be far away," said Auntie Lucy. "It's your education, Arthur. That's the important thing. I expect you'd be able to look in at home whenever you liked. And there would always be the holidays."

Grandfather said, "Suppose you tell us all about it, girl."

"It was Mr. Leaf who told Father . . . told us . . . about it. It's an experiment. They'll take in boys from Arthur's school, or any school in the district, it doesn't matter, and teach them along with the real College boys. It's an experiment, you see."

"I can't do sums," I said—not miserably, for I suddenly saw

my shortcomings in that direction as a way out of the trap which my elders had prepared for me.

"You don't have to do an exam paper, Arthur. I thought you knew that."

Had she forgotten that this was the first I'd heard of the scheme? or had it been discussed so much in the family that it was naturally assumed that I, the sacrificial lamb, knew all about it?

"I don't know anything about it."

"Go on, girl," said Grandfather. "Don't hold back. He doesn't have to prove he can write. What do they do? Make sure he washes behind the ears and doesn't bite his nails, and give him the money?"

"Mr. Leaf," said Bell with a quiet defiance no doubt calculated to silence Grandfather's banter, "Mr. Leaf says they judge on a boy's character, and circumstances, and age, of course, and Arthur's just the right age for next September. He says that what they're looking for . . ."

"Who is this Mr. Leaf?" asked my aunt. "And how is it that he knows so much?"

Bell told her how Mr. Leaf worked in the College library and no doubt saw lots of notices about College business. "He says that what they're looking for is a boy with curiosity and resolution who would benefit by a college education."

"Very nice, too," said my aunt. "And do they put a roof over his head and feed him on the fat of the land, too?"

"He can live at home if the parents want it," said Bell. She didn't say anything about feeding on the fat of the land. Judging by the way the college boys went for my father's ham and sausages they were either very greedy or extremely hungry.

"It's an experiment, you see," said Bell again. "Father . . ." She hesitated and looked confused; but she had gone too far to withdraw. "Father's very keen. Says it will be the making of Arthur."

"Everyone seems very confident," observed Grandfather. "And what do you think about it all, Arthur, lad?"

For the second time that day I burst into tears.

We received our golden sovereign and half-sovereign when we left. Auntie Lucy wouldn't let Grandfather come to the door when Hatch came round. She said his chest wouldn't stand it. So we made our good-byes in the dim hall under the many-coloured lamp. Auntie Lucy insisted on wrapping my scarf round me in the

63

regulation manner—though I was quite capable of doing it myself, and indeed would have known no other way. She promised to send my wet socks on when she had washed them. We promised to take care of ourselves and come again soon. We promised to give Grandfather's love to Mother. Father received no mention.

Hatch, holding the right rein coiled in a funny way round his gloved hands, unerringly delivered us through the snow to the station where he got the assurance of the porter, the booking-clerk and eventually of the Station Master himself that our train would arrive at his station on time and deliver us to ours on time and that we would be safely on it. He even gave me a penny to insert in the red multiple slot-machine and helped me to pull out the stiff tray which delivered a tiny box of minute red throat-pastilles.

In the train, which was five minutes late, we didn't compare our coins this time. I expected Bell to be cross with me because of what I did at tea-time. But she wasn't cross. She held my hand and told me to cheer up, and said that lots of boys would be only too glad to go to the College and that education was something they couldn't take away from you, and that it didn't mean I'd have to leave home yet, and that there would only be an interview with the College Headmaster, no papers to write, and perhaps there would be one or two others who would want to talk to me, and wouldn't it be fun.

It never occurred to me to wax indignant. No one had consulted me. It had all been arranged. I was, I suppose, in a strong enough position to upset the whole underhand business. At the time, though, I did not see myself as a rebel. I wondered why they all seemed so sure that I should be so acceptable to the College; from the way they talked you would suppose that there would be no other candidates at all, that I had only to present myself to be snapped up.

At our station we were met by Mr. Bagnall and Dinah, both under glistening tarpaulin. Inside the cab was a warm rug and a leathery, rubbery, sweaty smell quite at odds with the unfriendly snow hissing on the two big carriage lamps either side of Mr. Bagnall's unsheltered seat. I was ordered to 'get in quickly' while Bell stood outside talking urgently to Mr. Bagnall. The cab stopped when we came to the foot of the hill leading up to the church. Mr. Bagnall clambered down to turn the stiff brass handle of the door.

"This do, dear?" said Mr. Bagnall.

"Thank you, Mr. Bagnall. Arthur, tell Mother and Father I shan't be long. I have to collect some typing."

The door plugged shut with a thump. Mr. Bagnall heaved himself aloft. Bell disappeared into the snow. We moved off.

VII

AT THE END of the last day of term, always a Friday, we weren't allowed to go home until the headmaster had given out reports. We had to line up outside his study, form by form, and go in, boy by boy, to stand in front of his desk while he slid our report from the great stack in front of him, while he read it, muttered over it, signed it and handed it to Mrs. Ednay to fold and seal in a long envelope.

From this ceremony Mrs. Ednay had earned her name, Spittle Ednay. She was thin and balding. It was said she lived solely on gum arabic licked from the flaps of envelopes. This had somehow gummed up inside and denied her scalp the power to let hair through. If the headmaster frowned, she frowned. If he smiled, which he did sometimes, Mrs. Ednay smirked in a toothy, quick twitching way, quite mirthless, but especially striking if it was done whilst her long wet tongue was fully extended in the act of licking.

We were always apprehensive as we waited outside. Jokes about Mrs. Ednay somehow fell flat there: experience had taught us that to laugh aloud, shuffle or even to blow your nose in an extravagant way could mean instant relegation to the end of the line in the lowest form. I felt empty and scared as I took my place in front of the desk; school had suddenly meant much more to me since the frightening scholarship had been rolled like a boulder in my path. I didn't want the scholarship, yet I didn't want to be held unworthy of trying for it.

The headmaster drew my report in front of him. "You'll have to do something about your arithmetic, Hook," he said. "If your uncle had you to do his sums for him you'd have the Post Office Inspectors round in no time." He permitted himself a smile. Mrs. Ednay twitched indecisively, caught between frowning at my sums and smirking at the notion of my being in Post Office employ. "However, it's not so bad. Not so bad." Mrs. Ednay smirked. "You know you'll be representing the school when you go up for the scholarship? Think you can do it?" I did not really know what he meant by doing it. Had I, after all, to put pen to paper? Here was my chance to get the whole thing settled once and for all: ask him what I had to do and why I had been chosen to do it; put it to him that I was happy where I was and didn't want to go to the College at all; that was it: ask him what I had to do and when I had to do it; get him to tell me what would happen to me if I succeeded—and if I failed.

These things passed through my mind when he asked me if I thought I could do it. What passed through my lips in reply was an inane, "I hope so, Sir."

He nodded, dipping his pen. He made some flourishes in the air over the place where his signature was going and brought the nib down carefully on the paper as if he were lowering the needle on to a gramophone record. A pause, a deft scratchy whirl of the nib—and I had lost my chance. The report was in its long envelope; Mrs. Ednay's long tongue spittled the flap, and I was outside in the corridor again.

When I got home my father took the envelope with his usual question, "Are they giving you a budge up?" I replied, as usual, that no one moved up at the end of this term; but he was sufficiently impressed by my report when with my mother he read it over the tea-table to give me two half-crowns. This was half-way to making up for the loss of Grandfather's half-sovereign which had gone into the Post Office. I badly needed funds if my hopes for my mother's Christmas present were to come to anything.

After tea I was taking books out of my satchel—for I had promised Mr. Webster and at least two other masters to 'do some work in the holidays'—when Willie Waites burst in. He had come straight through the shop, under the counter and in by the door behind it. This meant a crisis of some sort. "There's a fire. Coming?"

Just as people in seaside towns turn out to see the life-boat launched, so we would never fail to attend the fire-engine on its way and, with luck, at the conflagration. So Willie and I followed until we were out of breath. It was our custom to call out to drivers of crawling vehicles, "Hey mister, your back wheel's going round!" or even to try to hang on to the tail-board of a creeping cart—until the driver was advised by well-wishers to 'whip behind'—but we had no voice left as our Merryweather fire-engine glimmered away into the gloom, and no run left in our legs. Willie was for going on, but it was choir-practice later on and I did not want to.

When I got home, my father, summoned to the shop-door by a late apologetic customer, came back with the news that the fire was at Major Birkitt's house, Great Lodge, and that the library was a ruin. What the flames had spared, the Fire Brigade had saturated. Maidment had heroically tried to extract a case of whisky from a cupboard and had been singed and driven back. The housekeeper, Mrs. Chelvey, had . . .

But the knowledge of what the housekeeper, Mrs. Chelvey, had or had not done was denied me, for my mother rather sharply observed that that was quite enough gossip and that that was how stories got about and that she would be surprised if the fire had been big enough to boil a kettle on.

I had been in the library at Great Lodge, though I would hardly have called it a library. On the walls hung a set of pictures called the Bluemarket Races, and some prints of cricketers, rather static cricketers, but all looking very knowing. They were drawn by strangely-named artists called Spy and Ape. I knew this because Major Birkitt had pointed them out to me, saying that he didn't know whether Ape had aped Spy or Spy had spied on Ape. As for the books, there was a set of the Badminton Library in shiny, brown cloth, lots of red Surtees, a shelf length of Trollope, Youatt on The Horse, Fuller Pilch on Cricket, two rows of *Blackwood's Magazine* bound in a royal if knobbly blue cloth, and on a shelf over the door a foreign legion of books with French names, all with shaggy leaves and paper covers. I knew they had shaggy leaves because when Major Birkitt had gone out to find his big magnifying glass I had climbed on to a chair to look at them. The chair had a leather seat which gave me away by retaining my footprints when I got down. But I covered them with *The Morning Post*—one of the dozens of newspapers with which the room was strewn.

I was thinking what a blaze the papers must have made and could see Major Birkitt trying to gather them up and stuff them in the fire-grate—which, I learned later, he did, having first put on his wicket-keeping gloves—when my father lowered his *Daily Mirror* and said, "How about your choir-practice?"

For our final practice before the carol-service we always went into our places in the choir-stalls. So when we had briefly looked at difficult verses in the psalms for the coming Sunday and prac-tised the entries in the anthem we formed up in the vestry to process into the church. Out of the west door of the vestry through the little passage lined with square wooden organ pipes and into the dimness of the Lady Chapel. Mr. Dyball had once told us that the Lady Chapel was always to the North of the altar because Christ's head had fallen to the right when he was on the cross; but I have never heard anyone else say that. A right wheel and we could file into our stalls. The nave was unlit; pews glimmering faintly disappeared into the darkness. We should, said Mr. Dyball, be flattered by what an empty church did for our singing; "And you small fry," he added, "stop staring down there. There aren't any ghosts." I was having some difficulty at that time in accepting and visualising the Holy Ghost, and it struck me that if He was to have a habitation on earth the dark West end of the church was just the place for Him to be located. However, Mr. Dyball was always very strict about our looking down the church ("They don't want to see your ugly faces; they want to hear your lovely voices") so I didn't add to my knowledge that night.

Not all the lessons were read at this practice, but there was no escape for me. The first lesson was read by a chorister, the second by one of the men, Mr. Empson, who every time we did Stainer's *Crucifixion* sang the part of Pilate and, by the twisting and jerking of his body as he sang, had earned himself the name of 'Jumping Jesus'. After that the readings fell progressively to more senior members, culminating in Mr. Benskin himself. I had to go first, but not until we had sung *Hark the herald angels sing*.

So we practised that and then I had to leave my place, march to the brink of the chancel steps, bow to Freddie Horton, the probationer who held the Bible ready and who stood between two other probationers, Jackie Dawes and Fred Fish, who held candles in big brass holders, take the Book (would he present it to me upside down?) and read my piece.

I muffed the bit "who told thee that thou wast naked?" stumbling over "thee that thou," and Mr. Dyball made me do it again. But when it was over I could have laughed and shouted for joy it went so easily. Jumping Jesus told me afterwards that I would have to hold my head up more on the night or the people at the back would never hear me, but considering the knots he had tied himself in over "as soon as the voice of thy salutation sounded in my ears" he was a fine one to talk.

After that it was splendid. From *The noble stem of Jesse* to *Oh come, all ye faithful* I sang with more pleasure than I had ever known in singing. I almost looked forward to the real service three nights away. For once in a way Bell was in when I got home (it never occurred to me that the College had broken up) so I was able to tell her of my success at the reading. "I shouldn't look at it any more," she said. "You've got it off pat; you'll only muddle yourself." She sounded really concerned and I determined to take her advice. I said, "You'll come and hear it on the night, won't you?" She said she wasn't sure. I said, "You must come and hear it. You always come to the service." She said, "I'll see." I wonder she didn't say she couldn't because she'd got a bone in her leg, for she spoke in that putting-off way that grown-ups have; and I felt baffled. She said she hoped Mother would be well enough to go.

That was it, then. She thought she might have to miss the service to look after Mother. The glories of the evening crumbled away. Was Mother really not well enough just to walk up to the church and sit in a pew?—no kneeling, and very little standing. Was she really as bad as that? I thought I should never go to sleep that night; but, somehow, instead of turning over in my mind what Bell had said, I saw myself again and heard myself again reading my piece, loud and clear. I must have fallen asleep very quickly.

Saturday mornings were always good mornings, but Saturday mornings in the holidays were very special. Not that we did anything different, but there was a stronger sense of freedom; we were slower and later, and it didn't seem to matter. On that Saturday morning no shadow of what Bell had said the night before clouded my mind, and my satisfaction over my part in the choir practice glowed comfortably inside me. Willie Waites called for me; we went to Empson's and Mr. Caxton's, planning our day. There was a new serial beginning at The Cinema. There was also a message from Major Birkitt. While we were out Maidment had called with a note.

Although it was addressed to my father the message was really meant for me. Major Birkitt would be most grateful if I could call at Great Lodge that afternoon taking with me my British Colonials and my Cameroons.

I didn't like putting Willie off. We had decided on the cinema unless it snowed again. But his disappointment would have hurt me more had I been less excited about my summons to Great Lodge.

Most of the snow had gone. What remained (waiting for another fall, if Grandfather was right) was stiffish slush by the side of the road so no one objected when I said I would go to Great Lodge on my bike. There were considerable objections, though, to the style of dress I proposed to adopt for the expedition, and in the end you would have supposed, had you looked at my top half, that I was setting off for a funeral, though my bottom half recalled rough-going on the Klondike. My mother said I was to be sure to wipe my boots when I got there and I was not to stay too long because Major Birkitt wouldn't want me there all the afternoon and it got dark very quickly these days. Father said I was to be sure to look Major Birkitt in the eye and grasp his hand firmly if he shook hands on my arrival. Bell said I was only a boy and Major Birkitt wouldn't shake hands and I was to call him Sir because that was safe whoever you were speaking to, even the Archbishop of Canterbury, and that I was to be sure I had a clean handkerchief and that if I wanted to go to the lavatory I was to say so instead of getting white-faced and miserable. I didn't know I did that so I told her not to be silly.

I was Nanook of the North driving my huskies as I pedalled towards Great Lodge. The satchel on my back held not two stamp-albums but pemmican and a small keg of brandy. The laurels of the drive were towering pines. Some of the time I was a King's Messenger bearing stolen enemy plans now safe in the leather pouch to which I was attached by a steel chain, my revolver loose and handy in its holster. When I came to the front door with its polished brass bell-pull big as a pear I was a bit scared; my boots felt big and my satchel clumsy.

Maidment let me in. No reference to his visit to our house; no mention of Mother's health. "Wipe your boots, son," he said; "these polished floors are buggers to keep clean." He left me in the porch—all ferns and walking sticks—until I began to wonder if I'd got the wrong day, or had been forgotten, or for some reason wasn't wanted at all. "The quality and gentry won't be a minute," he said when he came back. "Give us yer coat and step in." The hall was polished and cold, but there were big pictures to look at even if they were mostly of horses. A little uncomfortable by Maidment's attendance, I stared hard at a horse with a thick neck that tapered into a tiny head. "You like pictures?" I didn't know what to say to that. "It's a gee called Mambrino by a feller called Stubbs," said Maidment—information I had already gained from the gilt tablet on the frame (unless the horse was named Stubbs and the artist Mambrino). "Shall I give you a tip?"

I wanted to explain to Maidment that although I was quite

familiar with racing parlance I was not much interested in placing bets. He clearly did not expect an answer, though, for he went on without a pause. "When you come to look at a pitcher, never mind how pretty it is or how grand it is, never mind that, just look for the faults. See how many things you can find wrong with it. They'll expect you to say something about it." (Who would?—not Major Birkitt, surely?) "And they'll think far more of you if you pint out that a feller in it 'as two left feet, or got 'is medals on the wrong side of 'is chest, or the shadows are going the wrong way—something like that. Now look at that gee, there. Ever see one like it? Course you never did. Nor me, neither. If that gee went two furlongs at Newmarket, you could . . ."

Major Birkitt's appearance closed Maidment's mouth. The Major didn't shake hands with me, nor did he look me in the eyes. He put an arm round my shoulders and guided me out of the hall saying, "How about some buttered tea-cakes, eh? Got those Colonials with you? Not much of a day for a bicycle, eh?"

He took me into the library. It smelt of scorching and smoke, but apart from a tulip-shaped brown patch on the wall and some charring on the skirting and floor-boards near the fire-place it didn't seem much damaged. Mother's assessment of the fire was probably right. It was awfully cold, though, and I saw that a big pane in one of the windows had been shattered. The carpets were up; there were rows of little nails, some flying shreds of Wilton, to show where they had been. If the fire-brigade had really given the room the dowsing that was credited to them they must have been very adroit at taking away what they had so freely given.

We went into a room which seemed to be almost completely furnished with brass. I wondered who cleaned it. Not Mrs. Chelvey, of course. What I had heard of Mrs. Chelvey did not lead me to suppose that she spent much time with rags and a tin of Bluebell. It was beautiful to see. The bright fire in the tiled hearth was reflected everywhere you looked; even the brass shell-cases on the mantelpiece seemed to carry the flames higher. The fire-irons, the fender, the coal-bucket, the embossed discs on the walls, the gasbrackets, the canterbury, the Indian tray on ebony legs, bearing an assortment of lesser brass-trays and racks for letters and pens, all contributed to the general exchange of light from the brass-coloured flames. There was a kolza-oil lamp. There was a beautiful little model of a Borodino cannon. Solid brass.

Major Birkitt said that it was jolly nice of me to come. In that dam' fire he had lost a box of cigars, dam' expensive ones, and two stamp albums. The stamps in them hadn't been catalogued; he knew that half of them were duplicates of mine and it would be jolly nice of me to let him see my Colonials again so that he could make a note or two.

So I opened my albums on the brass tray, and Major Birkitt, from time to time giving the tip of his thumb and forefinger a quick lick, creased up the corner of each page the easier to turn it as he examined my collection. I wondered if wicket-keeping had knocked the life out of his fingers, they seemed so fat and slow. Once or twice, he said, "Very nice. Very nice," but he didn't take any notes and he didn't ask me any questions. I was surprised at this until I remembered he had only to tell his dealers that he wanted this or that to have it, though at the time I liked to believe that my steam-yacht overprinted Cameroons were unique. I was just beginning to think that nothing more than a final "Very nice" was coming from him when he said, "I wish they were mine, Arthur. You've got a nice little collection there. Very nice. Let me know if you find any more. You know the ones I mean. And put it round, will you, that I'm re-building my sets. Never know who your friends are, eh?"

I was not sure what he meant by this—his friends, or my friends; but I said I'd be on the look-out and that I would tell my little circle he was a keen collector and that he could borrow my albums if he liked. He would have nothing of this, though; he said it would do if I just kept my eyes open and told other collectors and that he thought tea and toast would be just the thing. He twitched a little brass lever by the mantelpiece. A wire scraped. Somewhere a bell, a brass bell, I supposed, tinkled weakly. There followed a rather awkward silence. He asked me if I wanted to pump ship. I didn't know what he meant, so I declined and was relieved when the door opened. Tea is always an easy meal to talk through; the business of cups and saucers and rattling spoons encourages conversation. It isn't like dinner when you have to manage tough meat and parch-ment-like cabbage. But it wasn't tea that came in. It was an elderly gentleman in narrow dove-grey trousers which lapped over shiny, pointed boots and gave way upwards to a rose-coloured velvet jacket, a high collar and a severe face fringed with grey whiskers.

"Come in, Harry," said the Major. "Just in time for tea. This is young Arthur Hook I told you about. Come to teach me a thing or two about stamps. Arthur—Lord Rutherstone."

I remembered to call him Sir, though I think I didn't remember to look him in the eye. The grip of his hand would not have damaged a butterfly. Whatever did one say to a Lord?

There was no need for me to pursue the panic-stricken ideas that tried to scurry out of my mind. Between them the Major and Lord Rutherstone set flowing a conversation so easy and natural that I felt no impediment at all. To them it seemed as easy to listen as to talk, but everything they said fell so easily into place and seemed so much worth saying that I wondered if this was what Mr. Selby meant by the art of conversation. But he had been telling us about Dr. Johnson then, and there was nothing massy in what passed that afternoon at Great Lodge—unless it was what Lord Rutherstone said to me just as I was putting on my satchel to go home—though at the time, of course, I didn't see anything of weight in his good-bye. When I told Bell afterwards how easy everything had been she said I had probably talked too much, bored them to distraction and made a fool of myself into the bargain. I daresay she was quite right, but 'cycling home that afternoon I felt a kind of elation. I had no words for it of my own, but found myself declaiming again and again to a gaunt and stiffening countryside—"now felt I like some watcher of the skies when some new planet swims into his ken." I was shouted at by a farm-labourer crunching his way home with sacks tied round his legs, but in a way I was quite glad to share my feelings with anyone at all.

Mrs. Chelvey—I supposed it was Mrs. Chelvey—brought tea in on a silver tray as a brass clock on the mantelpiece busily struck four. I don't know what I expected her to be like—certainly not the soft, gentle, firm, melting, strong, business-like, retiring person who put the tray down, declined an invitation to stay and was gone.

I didn't feel at all awkward at tea; perhaps a little put out to find that Lord Rutherstone, by closely describing the steamer on French Suez Canal 20 centimes 1868, unwittingly showed that he knew far more about stamps than I did. Nothing went wrong. I took only one spoonful of sugar in my tea though I really liked lots more than that; I put up with the very strong bloater paste from a flat white pot though it tasted bad; I accepted only one piece of Christmas cake though it was of a size which Uncle Hector would have ridiculed, and I didn't mess my linen napkin with the butter that dripped from the toast.

Lord Rutherstone and the Major both saw me off. Even Maidment was there. And I was sorry that he was; Major Birkitt gave me a folded ten-shilling note when I had got my coat on, and for some reason Maidment's presence made me clumsy in my thanks. The Major had said, "It was jolly nice of you to come. Here's something for a few stamp-mounts." I wanted to say something fitting in return. I suppose now I could have done worse than to say Thank you very much; but I am not sure that I even said that. It was having to speak up in front of Maidment that spoilt it. Lord Rutherstone gravely said if ever I came Oxford way he would be glad to see me. I took him to add that his place was tame but the Major would give me details. I think he meant it, about going to see him; I don't think he was just being polite, though Willie Waites, when I told him about it next day, said that people, posh people, had to speak like that. It didn't really mean anything. It was like beginning a letter with Dear and ending it faithfully.

Mother said I shouldn't have accepted the ten shillings. Father said it was all right. Bell said it was sometimes easier to give than to receive. I asked her what she meant by that, but she didn't tell me, though Mother said, "Quite right, dear." I wanted to keep it, not put it in Uncle Hector's Post Office. Although I had a little money saved, the ten shillings would more than double it. Christmas was only four days away, and I hadn't bought my presents. Sunday wasn't any good. The carols were on Monday. Tuesday was Christmas. There wasn't much time to add to my savings by casual labour, so unless I bought even more modest gifts than I usually, and I was afraid he had come to take the ten shillings for stamp-mounts would have to be diverted.

My father came up to talk to me when I was in bed. He didn't usually, and I was afraid he had come to take the ten-shillings for the Post Office. He didn't say much about that, though, only advising me not to let fly at the bung-hole with it and that people didn't want expensive presents. I think what he really wanted to talk about was my afternoon with the quality and gentry. He didn't so much want to know what we had done or said, but was anxious to discover how I had been received. Did they make me feel at home? What room were we in? Was it a proper tea or only a cup? And all the time I felt that as gratified as he was that I had apparently been accepted at Great Lodge so he was fearful lest I had imposed myself on the Major, poking my nose in, as he unguardedly put it. In the end he had me wondering if I hadn't been too full of myself. Perhaps Bell had been right.

As for Lord Rutherstone's presence, my father clearly regarded this as a kind of social windfall, something quite unexpected. And yet he made it clear that such a brush with the aristocracy, though it might come once, was not to be regarded as a permanent invitation to join the exalted circle. By the time he had asked his questions and said his say I was left wondering whether I had missed something of tremendous significance about my visit to Great Lodge. When is a cup of tea not a cup of tea? That is the way with grown-ups towards the young; they always seem to be saying that things are never as simple as they seem.

Strangely enough, what he did say finally was something of the utmost simplicity to him, gratifying, no doubt, but unclouded and uncomplicated, while to me it was a statement that set my thoughts racing—scurrying, rather—for they had no direction.

He had wished me Good-night. He was standing, candle in hand, outside my door about to close it.

"You know who he is?"

"Who?"

"Rutherstone. That Lord Rutherstone."

"What do you mean—who he is?"

"He's young Daveney's father. You know him. Daveney. Always in and out of the shop. You must have seen him."

VIII

I THINK I had forgotten all about Lord Rutherstone when I woke up next morning. I had finally gone to sleep with Father's revelation heavily weighing on my thoughts: had Bell met him? did she even know he was so near? had he slyly been getting me to talk about her? (I didn't remember anything about our family coming into our talk); had the Major got me there for something more than a look at Colonials? had Father known all the time about Marcus Daveney and Bell? (I was sure he hadn't.)

And in the morning all those questions no longer needed answering for they had lost themselves in the mists of the night.

Sundays had long ago fallen into a pattern. There was morning service, an afternoon expedition with Willie Waites, and evening service followed by a family gathering in the best room with both gas-mantles glowing, a bright fire and the grandfather clock treading on time with its measured metallic click.

Sunday afternoon expeditions with Willie were usually of a kind which could get us into trouble. There had been mild trespassing and a few memorable afternoons when we had let ourselves loose on the strawberries in the allotments beyond the churchyard. Since to get at them we had to climb railings near the seats on the churchyard terrace, we had to go through an elaborate duologue to fool anyone who was sitting there enjoying the view. It had taken the form of references to an uncle who was supposed to be waiting for us to join him on his vegetable patch. "I hope uncle's there," we said, very loud. "I expect uncle will be surprised to see us," we broadcast. We would certainly have been very surprised to see uncle, for on a Sunday afternoon you could never find anyone at all on the allotments.

There were many major enterprises inspired mostly by Grandfather's reminiscences. We intended, one night, to fit half walnut shells on a cat's feet and set it on the corrugated iron roof of Mr.

Seely's house. We had once resolved to put a sack over Jimmy Leaper's chimney, and we had once planned a hoax which, according to Grandfather who in another age had successfully brought it about, was the masterpiece of all jokes: you discovered a farmer who drank heavily at market in the morning (Grandfather claimed that when he was a boy farmers who drank heavily at markets in the morning were two a penny); you followed the pony and trap which without his guidance took him home (Grandfather apparently had no difficulty here); you waited until he was snoring in his kitchen (Grandfather's farmers, it seems, always lived alone), and when he was safely off you silently unharnessed the horse, took the wheels off the trap (no difficulty for Grandfather), tipped the trap on its side and carried it into the kitchen, brought in the wheels, righted the trap and fitted them, led in the horse, put it between the shafts, harnessed it and waited. According to Grandfather, the perplexity of the farmer who woke up to find he had the company of his horse and trap was worth all the trouble— though the way he told it made it sound as though it had been the easiest job in the world.

We never did this. We were too frightened of Jimmy Leaper to go near his house let alone climb on to his roof with a sack. We thought the cat and walnut-shell business rather cruel even though we did once use up the whole of a Sunday afternoon in pulling the wings off daddy-long-legs—an exploit I had quite forgotten, no doubt by choice, until in an English lesson Mr. Selby had asked for 'the plural of daddy-long-legs'. And now that I cannot forget the little heap of severed gossamer wings I cannot remember what that plural was.

On this particular Sunday, Willie and I resolved to try our hand at another of Grandfather's prime jokes. I never told Willie the source of my ideas. I believe he thought me a most original wag.

When he wasn't working, Mr. Ewart, the road-sweeper, kept his wheel-barrow, shovel and brush under a big iron sheet bearing the word BOVRIL behind a hoarding on the road to the railway station. Sometimes it was full of dust and rubbish; at weekends it was empty.

What you did, according to Grandfather, was to take the barrow and wheel it into the next parish. How it got there would baffle everybody. It would be talked about for months, and when you heard people talking about it you would keep quiet, knowing all the time how it was done. Therein was the cream of the jest.

78

Light snow had fallen when we took over Mr. Ewart's barrow—not enough to obliterate BOVRIL, but enough for snow-balling. After some dogged cross-country pushing we finally burst through a hedge on to a straight stretch of road so inviting with its untrodden snow that we had the barrow bumping and banging as we raced it along. When we came to a barn, we knew, though we did not consult each other, that that was enough. As if we had planned all along to do it, we ran the barrow behind a rusting seed-drill, abandoned it and at once started on our way home.

We had not gone far when Willie pointed at the tracks we had made on our outward journey. He said that anyone could see where we had taken the barrow and anyone could trace it back. He somehow made it sound as though the trackers would be taken right up to our very door-steps, and when I told him I thought he was being over-cautious if not scared he said that Indians would run us to earth in no time and that we had better do something. So we did something.

It was Willie's idea that we should return to base, as it were, and go back with Mr. Ewart's broom to brush away the tracks we had so carelessly laid along that straight piece of road. I had been for taking the barrow all the way back, but wiser counsels prevailed and so we went through the whole journey again. The broom, like the barrow, was really too big for us to manage, but with its help we obliterated the marks of the wheel on the road substituting a swept passage far more likely, we realised later, to arouse suspicion and lead Indians to us than the everyday track we had made first.

We got the broom back under the BOVRIL sign as dusk was falling. No one had seen us. Provided that our tracks did not reveal us we could now enjoy the cream of the jest—"Who moved old Ewart's barrow?" "I hear they haven't found that barrow yet." "What went with the sweeper's barrow?" "Some joker's pinched the lengthman's barrow!"—and all the time we should be sitting there not letting on! As Willie said, "Won't it be lads, knowing all the time!"

We somehow expected it to be the talk of the vestry when we arrived for evening service, and for a little while our adventure took priority in my mind, so that it was not until Mr. Benskin read out a notice about the carol service "tomorrow night at eight" and I saw the congregation brighten at the reminder that my courage fell down a lift-shaft from my throat to the well of my stomach, and the backs of my hands grew hot and prickly.

When I got home Mother and Father and even Bell were in the sitting-room. So was Tinker. There seemed to be something wrong, for the talking stopped when I came in. I wondered if the misplacement of Mr. Ewart's barrow had been discovered and if the tracks had led to me. But nobody said anything about it. There was just that feeling of tension and uncertainty as if there was something to be said or a move to be made and everyone was waiting for everyone else. Sometimes in the middle of the night you hear a door creaking and banging. You are sure everyone else can hear it, too. You wonder who will go down and shut it.

We (except Bell) played a game of dominoes; threes-and-fives; we (except Bell) played 'I Spy with my Little Eye'. We all had cocoa and bread and dripping with salt and pepper on it. As soon as I closed the sitting-room door after saying goodnight their busy talking began again. Not arguing; just anxious voices, pleading voices.

I woke next morning aware that the day had in it something to be feared, but not sufficiently alert to recall what it was. I had to parade its contents before me to find out. The carol service was not long in presenting itself. But, I thought, the carol service isn't until tonight; no need to worry about that yet. All the same, I felt a little sick.

There were jobs to be done; but who resents doing jobs on the day before Christmas? Willie called for me at nine o'clock, burdened, as usual, with his list of jobs and a shopping basket. He was not, however, burdened by the prospect of having to read a lesson at the carol service; but when he spoke about my part he lightened my load by letting it be known without exactly saying so that anyone who read one of the lessons at the carol service, except Mr. Benskins, of course, was something of a hero. Heroes are sometimes martyrs, and he may have been confusing the two.

But there was a more serious topic for conversation—not that we were able to develop it.

"What about old Ewart's barrow?"

"No-one's said anything."

"Same here."

"Think they've found it?"

"Don't know. It was lads, wasn't it?"

"I bet old Ewart's furious."

"Same here."

As a matter of fact, old Ewart wasn't furious at all. We heard

80

later that uncomplaining though denied the use of the apparatus of his trade he spent the day in, or not far away from The Axe and Cleaver.

The shops were crowded. If you listened to the conversation of waiting customers you would have supposed that Christmas-time was a season wholly reserved for triumph or disaster. Frank heard to-day: he's passed his exam. all right. Now the little boy's got mumps too; so they won't have much of a Christmas. Fancy, they ordered it weeks ago, and the butcher said he didn't know anything about it. So John will be home for Christmas after all—isn't that wonderful. They say he won't last the day, poor old chap. All the way from Australia and it came this morning. It's her hip—she's broke her hip—and you know what that means. They might have written: only a card; it's not asking much. They say he won twenty pounds; couldn't have come at a better time. She's been sick half the night—can't keep anything down. Never gave them a penny piece—miserable old sod.

But we liked doing the shopping on that day. No-one was grumpy; some shopkeepers even gave us something 'for ourselves'. Mr. Dighton gave me a thick syrupy piece of candied peel cradling solid opaque sugar; Mrs. Brill gave me a little ginger-bread man with a beady currant eye when I collected the loaves. Mr. Plastow picked a handful of sawdusted gobbets of fat from the floor, screwed them into newspaper and said they would do for the birds. Since Mr. Plastow was notorious for being very 'tight' and since he was to be seen every early-closing day and on most evenings with his gigantic twelve-bore bringing down pretty well everything that flew, this generosity could only be ascribed to the triumph of the Christmas spirit.

Shopping done, we had of course to see whether our hoped-for presents were still being offered for sale. No carpentry-set was in Fletcher's. Askew's revealed no steam-engine. This, we decided, was entirely in our favour—or distinctly against us.

I had to make other calls. Every year on this day my mother gave me a little load of neatly packed and gaily tied parcels to leave at certain houses (which were neither neat nor gay). I had to knock at the door and say, "Mrs. Hook wishes you a merry Christmas." Then I was supposed to say, "She begs you to accept this little gift for the children," but I felt so silly trying to get that out that I usually said, ". . . and here's something for . . ." and hoped that that would do. Usually it did. Mrs. Abrams always said, "God bless her! You're her eldest, aren't you?" Mrs. Cook said, "You wish your mother the same, dear. How you've grown. Hardly knew you." Mrs. Vosper said, "She shouldn't have. I've got a little bag of cakes for you, dear. I expect you've got plenty, though." There were two surprises this year. Mrs. Hedges burst into tears. Mrs. James said, quite sharply, I thought, "Thank your mother nicely. You're reading at Church tonight. You speak up loud. Never heard a word last year. Not a single word."

In the afternoon Willie and I did some shopping on our own account. I bought an ounce of Player's White Label, a cake of Pears' soap and a packet of pipe-cleaners for Father (Mr. Empson taking my word for it that I personally did not smoke a pipe) and a box of Wax Vestas for Uncle Herbert (though these never reached him and had to be replaced by Father's pipe-cleaners). Auntie May was always difficult. This year I bought her a fancy box of hair-pins, remembering too late that I had bought her exactly the same thing the year before. Bell was easy. She liked silly little handkerchiefs, or lace mats, or embroidered pin-cushions; and a small velvet pin-cushion 'stuffed with best kapok' (whatever that was) was well within my compass. I added a sheet of pins to it—but might have saved myself the trouble as she later complained that they had all rusted to the paper.

I had my eye on a bottle of eau-de-cologne for Mother. A card in the window said it was 'an aid to the toilette and indispensable in the sick-room'. Not until I got it home did I find that it wasn't eau-de-cologne at all, but 'toilet-water eau-de-cologne.' I think they might have pointed it out at the shop.

Uncle Hector's Vestas were sacrificed to pyrotechnics. Willie said he knew a trick with Wax Vestas and Uncle Hector would never miss two from the box. So I gave him two. He shredded one into its waxy threads compounding the whole into a tight ball with the head in the middle. The second Vesta he struck by drawing it smartly across the seat of his trousers. He lit the little ball and it burned sullenly. I was about to ask him what was so remarkable about that when it exploded smartly and brightly.

He let me do it—though I had no success with the seat-of-the-trousers part, and then he said he knew an even better trick with the head of a match, a key and a nail. So we had to find a nail and a key, and by the time we had got our little detonator exploding faultlessly whenever we swung it against a wall there wasn't a great deal left in the box for Uncle Hector.

The carol service was to begin at eight o'clock. By five o'clock I could think of nothing else; and though there was the promise of a special supper I had no appetite. Father closed the shop soon after five declaring that he wasn't going to keep open a minute longer for man nor beast. He drew down the blue blinds as a preliminary to the ritual of making fast for his two day holiday. I was allowed to return errant biscuit boxes to their rightful places and to flip shut the lids of the cardboard chocolate boxes on the counter. Then there were the piles of milk chocolate bars to be dismantled, the pyramids of whipped cream walnuts to be razed and the mosaics cunningly fashioned from blocks of Turkish delight to be transferred to their powdery wooden casket. Father said it had been a good Christmas, so I did not feel guilty of treason in rejoicing that among the left-overs were two oval boxes of crystallised fruits, each oozing stickily, and two mottled drums of what I later learned to call Elvas plums. In syrupy crinkled paper cups on a tray there were a few syrupy crinkled brown confections like tiny brains. "Better take these to your mother," said Father, pressing one with his thumb. "I should never of stocked 'em. Cost a mint of money. Only conkers, too, when you come to think of it." On a sticky board there was the last slice of crystallised melon. The whole thing had also cost a mint of money, and over the past two weeks Father had reported at every supper-time how much he had sold during the day. I had respected its rarity enough to refrain from helping myself to a sliver. Now I expected virtue to be rewarded.

On his way to fetch the bucket and mop preparatory to the swabbing of the oilcloth, Father crammed the last slice of the crystallised melon into his mouth, asserting, I think, that he wouldn't give twopence for muck like that.

I liked the ceremony of swabbing the floor. The oval mop-bucket, smelling of soapy steam, was fitted with an inverted perforated cone into which Father squeezed the sopping and soiled mop-head after it had swabbed and dabbed the muddy floor. Just at the point where he was going to open the shop door to cascade the contents of the bucket into the gutter there came a shy tap at the glass. Father said something I didn't catch, then *stong* went the bell and there was Miss Partridge who twice a year generously laundered the surplices for the choir.

She was very sorry. She knew it was after closing time. She had tried other shops. She didn't quite mean that. She meant she hadn't wanted to disturb Father. She was giving a little party on Boxing Day. She wanted some little prizes. She wondered if there were any of those lemon-pigs left. She thought they were so clever. She was sorry to be such a nuisance.

Every year Mother made a few little pigs by sticking almonds into lemons—four legs, ears and a tail, with two cloves for the eyes. Father placed them cunningly here and there in the window. He said they brought more people into the shop than a cart-load of holly; and though they caught everyone's fancy and could be easily copied he wouldn't sell them.

When Miss Partridge came in, bringing her muddy footprints with her, the lemon-pigs stood in an expectant kind of way where I had placed them on the counter. So Father could hardly say he hadn't got any. She wanted them all, of course. All six. Father said they weren't for sale. Miss Partridge, putting her basket down on the damp floor, as good as said she didn't see why not. Somehow I couldn't steel myself for what must follow, so with an air of purpose I took up the steaming mop-bucket, and with bent back I managed to slop it out of the shop door to the gutter where I made a great business of emptying it.

I stayed outside long enough for the transactions inside to be completed, for Miss Partridge, all smiles, was coming out as I clanked the empty bucket in. There were not six pigs on the counter. There was one pig. A one-eyed pig. The two sticky oval boxes of crystallised fruits had gone. The two drums of Elvas plums had vanished. Like Miss Partridge, my father was all warm smiles. But smiles notwithstanding she froze me with her parting shot. "I'm sure you'll read very nicely tonight, Arthur."

There was an air of restraint when we sat down for supper. I had no speech (and no appetite) because of the carols. It looked as if we were to eat the meal in silence when Father asked the question I wanted to ask.

"Where's Bell?"

"Packing," said Mother.

"Oh, ah," said Father, flatly, not surprised, as if he were resigned to anything Bell might choose to do on Christmas Eve.

"PACKING? BELL?" That was me.

"She's going away for Christmas, dear."

"GOING AWAY!" Me again.

"Some friend," said Father. "Stephanie Haywood. Something like that." His voice was grey.

"She'll only be away for a few days, dear." Mother.

"But it's CHRISTMAS." Me.

"Not that you'd notice it." Father.

"She's going to stay with a friend, dear, in a big house at a place called Thaime. And she'll soon be home again. You'll see."

Bell came down, then, in her going-away clothes. She set herself—even I could see it—to cheer us all up. She wouldn't eat anything as she 'had to go in a minute.' She wouldn't be hungry because 'there'd sure to be something waiting' when she got there. She would soon be back; it was 'only for three days, after all.' But Father wouldn't be comforted, and it was a relief when a knock came at the outside door. "That's the car," said Bell. And I didn't think to ask her what car. Nor did anyone tell me.

She gave me a big kiss at the door. "You'll read ever so well tonight," she said. "I wish I could wait to hear it." I was going to ask her why she couldn't wait, when she said, "There's a present for you on top of the wardrobe in the spare room," and I made her stay until I had been upstairs for her pins and pin-cushion. "Will you write, Bell?" I managed. "Will you write from Thaime?"

" It's not Thaime," she said; "it's called Tame." And she spelled it out, T—H—A—M—E.

"Where is it, Bell?" I said.

"It's near Oxford. This side of Oxford. Now I must fly."

When she had gone I somehow couldn't bring myself to ask Mother and Father if they were coming to the carol service. Neither did I want to look on top of the wardrobe in the spare room. In fact I didn't want to do anything. The time seemed to drag if you watched it, but darted ahead as soon as your back was turned. I did not have to be told that they weren't coming to the service. They didn't say they weren't, but somehow established the fact by the way they went about things. Willie called for me soon after half-past seven.

In the vestry a merry Christmas was being observed, but of course I couldn't join in. As well as having the reading shrew-like in my mind, nagging more tauntingly as the sober joviality grew around me (did anyone hear tell of gloomy carol-singers?), there was the bald fact that Bell had gone. There was something else, too.

What it was did not strike me until we were processing to "Oh come, all ye faithful." Lord Rutherstone. That was it. Lord Rutherstone had gravely said that if ever I came Oxford way he would be glad to see me. He had said his place was tame. No. He had not said that at all. He had said his place was at Thame. Thame. Not Mother's Thaime. Bell's Thame. Bell was going to Thame. To stay with Lord Rutherstone and the Honourable Marcus Daveney?

No. It couldn't be that. She was going to stay with a friend, dear. Stephanie somebody. Near Oxford. This side of Oxford. Thame. The Major would give me details.

We had done *Oh come, all ye faithful,* and I suppose we did *Ding-dong merrily on high* (and I ought not to have failed to notice that one, for 'ding-dong' was our private word for belly-button) before I remembered that in a minute I had to go out there and read 'And the angel of the Lord called unto Abraham a second time . . .' No. That wasn't my piece. My piece began, 'And they heard the voice of the Lord God walking in the garden in the cool of the day.' The bit about Abraham was Greeny's bit. Mine was the voice of the Lord God walking in the garden, because we had joked about a voice walking. I knew Greeny's bit by heart as well as my own.

We were more than half-way through *Hark the herald* when I began to find it possible to believe that mine was the piece about Abraham, after all. It was just as well that Freddie Horton would be there with the book of Lessons.

I walked to my place at the final rallentando of Glory-ee tooo the newborn King. Fred Fish and Jackie Dawes swung round with their big candles flickering. Freddie Horton moved round between them, holding the Book open. Freddie Horton and I bowed to each other. I took the Book. I looked down at the piece I was to read.

It was not the right one. It was nothing like my piece. I did not know what it was; but it was not mine. I knew I mustn't read it. It would put everyone else out if I read that piece. I stared at it—and it blurred. I stood there, the back of my neck beginning to fill with a heavy heat. And I said nothing. I just stood there.

I heard a rustling beside me. A fat forefinger was laid flabbily on the ornate initial letter of the page.

"Well go ON, boy. READ IT!"

Mr. Benskin had come to my rescue. I did what he said. I read the page. It was my piece. I don't know why I thought it wasn't.

I went up quickly when I got home. Mother brought me a cup of cocoa when I was in bed. She put it on the little table by my candle, pulled back a corner of the eiderdown and sat down by my pillow. Then she leaned over me, steadying herself by putting one hand on the table, and she kissed me, and when she had done that she smiled at me.

I began to tell her about the reading, but she said I was to drink my cocoa first, then I'd feel better.

I told her everything—except what I believed about Bell. I told her everything, and it all came alive again as horrible as it had been in church. "It didn't look like my piece," I said. "I don't know why, but it didn't. I stood there for hours, and didn't say anything. It was awful, Ma. People must have thought I . . ."

"It wasn't so long, dear; and the people round us thought you read beautifully."

I began to cry. "You weren't there, Ma, were you!"

"Of course, son," she said. "You don't think we'd let our little boy do that all alone, do you. I wonder you didn't see us—you looked straight at us once. We were very proud of you, Arthur, dear. Now go to sleep, dear. It's Christmas day tomorrow."

She kissed me again, took up the cocoa mug and blew out the candle.

The whiff of the candle and the glimmer of light under the door were nearly the last things I remembered. There was something else—old Ewart's barrow. I remember feeling indignant that no one had wondered where old Ewart's barrow had gone.

IX

By the time I was awake what had been on top of the wardrobe in the spare room had somehow reached the foot of my bed.

There was also one of Father's stockings—he wore breeches and a Norfolk jacket when holiday-time came—and I knew what filled it. There would be nuts in the toe and a half-a-crown wrapped in silver paper. And there would be a tangerine and a Cox's Orange. And there would be a little pair of tin scales and half a dozen miniature sweet bottles holding cachous and hundreds-and-thousands, and a generous set of cardboard money. There might be a pen-knife and a little bright-red magnet; there was almost certain to be a little tin cyclist (who would whizz round a plate if you set his one-wheeled bicycle in motion by spinning the heavy lead wheel).

I unhooked the stocking from the bed-post, scooped up the parcels and was in beside Mother before the lino made my feet cold. Father was downstairs making a cup of tea. His place, impressed deeply in the feathers, was still warm, but I snuggled up to Mother who was warm in a way that nothing else was ever warm. No fire had such warmth. No sun-drenched hay. The warmth of deep water was not like her warmth. "Cosy-coo," she said. "Cosy-coo."

But there was that heavy oblong parcel that must be the tool-set from Fletcher's. I shook it. Dull thuds—but distinctly metallic. I turned it up on its end. A slithering clatter. The conical oil-can or the little tin of Croid glue travelled from top to bottom. There were knots and stiff brown paper before I raised the lid.

We didn't have much breakfast on Christmas day. Our feet were soon awash in wrapping paper, with Mother saying, "That's a pretty piece; we mustn't throw that away," or "Save that string, Arthur. It will come in for something." Father was always for 'throwing the lot away,' but he was overruled by Mother who collected all the whole pieces and pressed them into one of the empty boxes—which she somehow never managed to find when wrapping-up time came round next year.

The biggest surprise came when Father went upstairs to the shop and came back with a little package clumsily done up, for me. "Present from Miss Partridge," he said. It was one of the sticky oval boxes of crystallised fruits. You often read about people chuckling; but you don't often come across real chuckling. Father began to chuckle as he told us about Miss Partridge. She had so badly wanted to buy the lemon-pigs. But he wouldn't sell them. Not likely. He never had, and he wasn't going to now. Did we know what he did? We didn't know. He gave them to her! Said take them. Gave them to her, that's what he did! And then she'd bought half the blessed shop. You couldn't stop her. Half the blessed shop. And she had wondered if I'd like a little box of crystallised fruits.

There were lots of jobs to be done after breakfast because Uncle Hector and Auntie May and Arnold and Mr. Leaf were coming to dinner. I had to take down all the Christmas cards in the best room upstairs and dust where they'd been. Then there was holly to go up behind the pictures and nuts and raisins to be taken up, and then there were logs for the upstairs fire.

There were so many extra things to be done because Aunt May mustn't find anything out of place or dusty or obtrusive or elusive that I was still struggling with my Eton collar when Willie called for me. I was secretly proud of my Eton collar—once I had subdued it. Mother wouldn't let me wear a celluloid collar. This one, heavily starched, had a saw-like upper edge which chafed my clipped neck if I turned my head (Mr. Dyball would not disapprove of that) and an unexpected latent springiness capable of flipping the ready-tied bow from its socket if I put a finger between the garotting rim and my lacerated flesh.

There was still a dusting of snow; half-hearted flakes blew in our faces. Willie said that his dad predicted a real fall before the day was out, and wouldn't it be lads if we got snowed up. We tried to make snow-balls but found ourselves scraping up only grit and mud, so we contented ourselves with clawing out a huge MERRY XMAS on the grass bank beside the lychgate as we exchanged news of our presents. Willie had got his steam-engine; he had even had it working. What had impressed him most was that they had remembered to give him a bottle of meths. with it— which accounted for the pervading smell which he gave off. I told

89

him about my tool-set. He told me about his John Bull Printing Set, exhibiting purple finger-tips and a torn piece of brown paper smudgily but undeniably stamped WILLIAM WAITES in purple. I told him about my Boys' Chemistry Set (Bell's top-of-the-wardrobe parting gift) and how you could turn water into wine and back again. He told me about six linen handkerchiefs, and I told him about a pair of galoshes.

The vestry was all scarves and overcoats and little pools of muddy water and chatter and compliments of the season and a happy Christmas. No one said anything about my disgrace of the night before—except Mr. Dyball who cornered me when I was buttoning my cassock. You didn't mind Mr. Dyball telling you off. He just said straight out what he wanted to say; and somehow, although he was the one who was saying it, you didn't feel that he himself was personally surprised or hurt or affronted or let down or shamed. You felt as if some adjudicator who wanted you to do better next time was telling you exactly how things stood so that you'd know. On this occasion Mr. Dyball said, "You were in a blue funk last night, young Hook. No need, you know. No need at all. You were only the middle-man delivering the goods. You weren't on trial. You'll be all right."

I thought that Jumping Jesus was going to point out my shortcomings when he sidled over, but it wasn't that at all. He put his hand on my shoulder saying, "Give your mum and dad the compliments of the season, will you." Greeny came round to each one of us to whisper, "Sssstay afterwards. Ber-ber-braces." And that, innocent as it was, made me feel more ashamed of myself than any reproaches anyone could have made. That Greeny had been able to deliver his "And the angel of the Lord called unto Abraham a second time" with perfect precision and clarity when I had stood there tongue-tied and spell-bound made me feel wretchedly foolish.

We had Stanford's *Te Deum* and the wonderful bit that begins, "And there were in the same country shepherds abiding in the field, keeping watch over their flock by night," and for a little while it didn't seem to matter that Bell had gone away and that I had failed at the carol service and that Mother had a lump. I did not at that time know the *Messiah,* and the simple story seemed to me (though at that time I did not know the word) sublime. Bell would come back; I hadn't been as bad as I thought; Mother would get better.

Mr. Dyball was pleased with the 'Mikado' braces. He said he

was more sure than ever of our support—and all the men laughed, though I didn't see why. And he said he'd smoke one of the cigars after his Christmas dinner and we were not to stuff too much and he wished us a happy Christmas, and we all said, "Same to you, Sir!" And then we were free.

When I got home the house was full of a roasty-toasty smell. Mother was wearing an apron; Father was in his best blue serge. She was bustling round the dinner-table with a bunch of spoons in her left hand; he was on his knees in front of the fireplace holding a sheet of newspaper over the grate. From time to time it was drawn inwards with a smart smacking noise, but for the most part it flapped inconclusively below Father's thumbs.

"Help your father, Arthur," said Mother. "They'll be here in a minute."

"Bloody thing's out," said Father, and you could see him preparing himself for Mother's rebuke at the word. But before it fell on him the newspaper bellied deep into the grate again; there was a scurry of sparks darting upwards and a sudden brown patch of scorching that thumped into a blaze before Father could draw the paper away.

It was at that moment that the door-bell rang. Father said, "Blast and damn", as with the poker he tried to quell the flaring paper. Mother said, "They're here," and her apron was off and under a cushion before the tinkling had died away. Father said, "Ought to have had dinner in the kitchen, like we always do. No room for everybody in here. And it's cold as bloody charity."

When Uncle Hector and Auntie May came upstairs the room was smoke-filled and chilly. Uncle Hector's Christmas greeting was that it was a good thing King Alfred wasn't there: he wouldn't have burned the cakes in a month of Sundays. I asked where Arnold was—merely to be polite, I think. I was delighted that they had not brought Arnold with them.

"Pigtail-pulling, I shouldn't wonder," said Uncle Hector.

"Now, Hector!" said Auntie May. "He'll be along soon, dear. He's got a little friend you know."

I said, "It's Elsie Catcher, isn't it?"

"Ah-ha; that would be telling, wouldn't it?"

"Have some sherry-wine," said Father.

So they had some sherry-wine, and the fire took heart with a spirt of flame and Mother said though she really oughtn't she'd have just a thimbleful, and she and Aunt May began to enumerate the niceties of sage and onion stuffing. Uncle Hector even remembered to thank me for the pipe-cleaners and promised that after dinner he'd show me a trick or two with a pipe-cleaner. Meanwhile I'd have to content myself with 'that.'

'That' he drew from an upper pocket in his waistcoat: a green baize bag about six inches long and two wide with a neat flap and press-stud at one end, all reeking of linseed-oil. Inside was a beautiful little cricket bat. "Real willow, that is," said Uncle Hector fondly stroking it with his thumb as it lay in the palm of his hand. "Here you are, lad." I took it gingerly. Even though it was so small you felt that it was full of sweet shots and stout defiance; it was a live little bat; no mere carving. Its handle was bound with real sticky wax thread; the splice flowed smoothly into the blade; in minute precise Indian-ink printing it was dubbed "The Arthur Hook Special," and under my name three tiny stars.

My pleasure at possessing that little bat was clouded by a feeling of guilt. It must have taken Uncle Hector hours of patient work to make this little gem for me. I had always felt that for Uncle Hector my presence and my absence were as one; that to him I was some kind of domestic animal for which he had no great affection but whose right of existence had to be tolerated. And now he had done this for me. I had misjudged him. He did nothing like this when he made his own bats: though he enjoyed local respect and even renown for his handiwork, the bats he made were crude clubs by comparison with my tiny blade. There had, in fact, been a good deal of murmuring against some of the maces he had fashioned for his own use; on one occasion, when he had come out to bat with something that looked like a clumsily lopped trunk with brass straps round its splice, a visiting captain had had the temerity to question whether the spirit if not the laws of cricket were not being broken. The brass, he said, was dangerous. Uncle Hector had successfully challenged him to say why, and finally floored him with a bit of expertise. "Ever see E. H. Budd's bloody bat?" demanded Uncle Hector. "No, 'course you never bloody did. Brass halfway down the bloody blade. Used it at Lord's he bloody did. No smart alec or clever dick got on his hind legs with a bloody bleat then. I'm telling yer."

Glowing from the admiration his gift had excited, Uncle Hector grew expansive demanding to see all my presents. He seemed especially interested in the tool-set, but had me almost crying aloud at the way he proved to us all that the saw was of excellent temper—

taking the handle in one massy fist and with thumb and forefinger bringing the tip of the blade almost full circle. I expected him to hand me back a saw like a pruning hook, but the steel sung musically back as Uncle Hector said it would. He didn't dwell long on Bell's Chemistry Set, which wasn't remarkable.

What was remarkable was that no one said anything about Bell —why wasn't she there? where was she? why was she where she was? And once more I had the helpless feeling that all the grown-ups knew something I didn't and wasn't intended to know.

It was Aunt May who got nearest to forbidden things. Perhaps it was the sherry-wine. "And what did your grandfather give you?" she demanded.

To tell the truth I had forgotten about Grandfather. His presents never failed to appear and never failed to make all other presents seem rather ordinary—though this year the tool-set would take some beating.

Mother, very flustered, said, "Oh, yes; I've got Grandfather's parcel in the spare room." There was an awkward pause while she fetched it. It was a heavy parcel, expertly done up. I wanted to open it myself, but Uncle Hector, with a brusque "Give it here, lad" produced a pruning-knife from his trouser pocket and snipped the taut string. I believe he would have unwrapped it himself had I not said, "Thank you, Uncle," and taken it from him. They all stood round while I pulled back the stiff brown paper. A mahogany box with a brass catch; a perfect cube. They all leaned over while I lifted the lid. Inside, heavy lacquered brass, a gyroscope. And had Grandfather wanted to give everyone there a present for Christmas he could not have done better, for that gyroscope hardly ceased humming its grave, exciting note in someone's fascinated hands throughout all that day. No one, including myself, thought of asking how the parcel had reached our house. No one, except Mother, showed much interest in the next parcel I opened. Auntie Lucy's present, a heavy woollen scarf and a pair of socks.

The humming gyroscope all but spoilt the entrance of Mr. Leaf and Mr. Bagnall, who arrived together for 'a little drink before dinner', but neither was slighted. Mr. Leaf soon became so engrossed with it that he forgot to go and wash his hands. Mr. Bagnall was, I think, impervious to any lack of social niceties, for with ponderous joviality he insisted on shaking everyone by the hand, some twice, bellowing as he did so, "Put it there, for it weighs a ton."

93

Then there was a spell when nothing but the weather was discussed and Mother went quietly down to the kitchen. There were stories of deep and deeper snow and long and longer icicles, of frozen milk and burst pipes, of trains in snow-drifts and bodies preserved in ice. It seemed quite fitting that when Mr. Leaf and Mr. Bagnall said 'goodbye' at half-past-twelve, Mr. Bagnall insisting again that everyone should put it there for it weighed a ton, it should be snowing.

I think my mother was a little put out when Aunt May assumed command of the kitchen, and at the dinner-table took it upon herself to help everyone to the vegetables and gravy and bread-sauce as if she had prepared them herself, but she didn't say anything, and though I think she never harboured any resentment about anything at all in her life I expect it helped when Uncle Hector congratulated her on a fine turkey and trimmings done to a turn. She was allowed by Aunt May to carry in the pudding glowing a fitful blue and with holly scorching in the brandy flame. There were threepenny joeys to be had: until we remembered it was his annual pantomime Uncle Hector alarmed us all by pretending he had swallowed one. When, after a great show of bringing it up, he slapped it with a muffled clink down on my plate I could hardly bring myself to touch it; but when the mince-pies came round and he slipped two shillings (the others had brandy in theirs) under the lid of mine, I once more found myself wondering how badly I had misjudged him in the past. Perhaps Christmas did something to Uncle Hector. Perhaps it did something to me.

It was unanimously decided to 'leave the washing-up', and there followed a drowsy intermission in front of the fire enlivened by riddles and conundrums until one by one the grown-ups dozed as a prelude to the heavy but uneasy sleep, marked by little snorts and sighs and gasps, of people obliged to be half-upright when they would have preferred to be completely horizontal.

Before they dropped off, Uncle Hector asserted that you never saw a dead donkey. Father said that for that matter you never saw a fat postman. Mother said something about the merits of old candles and new soap—or was it new candles and old soap? Aunt May (of all people!) said that if you wanted to kill a tree you should drive a copper nail into it, and Uncle Hector (of all people!) said that if you wanted to keep cut tulips fresh you should put a penny in the water. This exhausted riddle and conundrum time except for Uncle Hector's demanding to know why New Year's

Day was like a dead chicken. No one knew the answer (though Uncle Hector later told me it was because 'its neck's weak') and when he had observed that it was a good thing he wasn't travelling by train because he'd have to pay excess fare, and had asked me if I knew that there were enough bones in a pig's foot to lay on every doorstep in London, he fell instantly to sleep.

I was not dismayed at finding myself thus cut off from my elders. I should have been surprised if they handn't settled for a nap. I was put out, though, to see the gyroscope firmly wedged between Mother and Aunt May on the couch; I felt I had not had my fair share of Grandfather's gift. I could take it downstairs on to the kitchen table and have it humming for myself alone until the house stirred again. But though I could see the corner of its box I dare not try to lever it out.

I couldn't very well use my carpenter's set because Father had said he didn't want any banging about while Aunt May was in the house. There were my lead soldiers, of course, but I really needed a ridged hearth-rug for their deployment, and the hearth-rug just now had four pairs of sleeping feet guarding it. Besides, I didn't want to expose my soldiers to Uncle Hector again. Whenever I thought about it I hated Uncle Hector; Father didn't come out of it very well, either.

Father had bought a Diana air-pistol to kill the rats that had appeared at the bottom of the yard. It was a heavy thing, with a plunger too obstinate for me to manage and it sent its lead slugs with a smart slap against the fence thirty yards away. I was forbidden to touch it. No rat was known to have succumbed to it. Mother was terrified of it. One night, in the summer of that year, I had heard the pistol coughing its slugs out, and, unable to sleep, I had slipped downstairs to see the sport. Uncle Hector and Father. In the kitchen. Not shooting at rats. Shooting at my soldiers lined up in front of a rolled door-mat on the kitchen table. They were of my favourite regiment, baggy-trousered bearded Frenchmen in pale blue, moulded for ever in a state of charge. Now their heads were about them; their hollow bodies, still running, lay on their dented sides.

It was said afterwards that my behaviour was disgraceful and that I ought to be ashamed of myself. When my tears were dry Uncle Hector mended my gallant Frenchmen by giving them a match-stick for a neck, pointing out that they could now see where they were going as well as where they had come from. This only made me cry again. Nothing they could say could make up for what they had done.

So though it was just the afternoon for having all my troops on parade I was not going to allow Uncle Hector to wake up with a massacre ready to hand.

Taking a handful of almonds and raisins as I passed the sideboard I opened the door to leave the sleepers. I doubt if I left them sleeping, for the catch on the door was made on the same principle as the latches on church doors: impossible properly to open or shut the door without its giving out a sharp, metallic report. Perhaps latches on church doors have to be like that so that you're always found out if you arrive late or want to leave early. Glad to get away, I crept downstairs.

There was a scuffling in the kitchen. Before I had the door properly open I knew that someone was there. It was Arnold and his 'little friend'—not so little, for she made Arnold look pretty weedy—Elsie Catcher. I think that they felt as awkward about my arrival as I did. Elsie gave a kind of simpering giggle; Arnold said, "Hallo, kid." He had never called me kid before, even in his rôle as dashing journalist and deputy Postmaster General, so I supposed he did it to impress Elsie. Then he said, "Have a fag," and neatly flipped open a slim curved case. "Do you know which end to light?" tittered Elsie. "They're all asleep upstairs," I said, and, shutting the door, withdrew. It struck me afterwards that they must have thought I had come down especially to tell them that it was quite safe for them to—to do whatever they were doing.

My advance and retreat cut off, I was left only the shop to manoeuvre in. It was gloomy in there for the big blue blind was down muffling the glare from the snow outside. I did the rounds of the bottles taking a sticky piece of almond hard-bake, and a paregoric cushion; I played with the scales weighing against each other half-pound packets from rival firms or trying to find the difference between nett and gross. I made incursions into the Huntley and Palmer biscuit tins dwelling longest at the Garibaldi and Petit Beurre. But I was bored, not hungry; with so much upstairs on the sideboard there was little piquancy in helping myself down in the shop. I took all the paper bags out of the big drawer under the counter and arranged them in a pyramid before putting them back; I climbed the little ladder to re-arrange the Heinz bottles on the top shelves of the fixtures; I took down a large card which said OXO and replaced it with a picture of the Matterhorn which said VELMA; I tested the toffee pincers on Everton toffee; I scooped French gums from their ranks with the brass scoop, and put them back in their box. I unscrewed the top of the cylindrical string-box. I opened the till and examined the small collection of foreign coins which had illicitly infiltrated.

That reminded me of the superior collection at the Post Office, and that reminded me of Elsie Catcher and Arnold downstairs. Obeying an over-mastering curiosity I was on my way down to see what they were doing when I was overtaken by Mother who said that everyone was awake now and that she was going to make a nice cup of tea. I carried the tray upstairs for her and was surprised to find Arnold and Elsie Catcher already up there. I had not heard them when I was in the shop, and I felt a twinge at the thought of the hold it gave them over me had they watched me opening the sweet-bottles. They didn't say anything, though; indeed, Elsie was on her simpering best behaviour. She refused Arnold's airy man-of-the-world offer of a cigarette, saying she never smoked the nasty things; she refused cake, saying she would love to but daren't, and causing Uncle Hector to pat her knee and observe that thoroughbreds never put on weight. She drank her tea (four lumps from the basin which I held before her) holding the cup as if but for the crook of the handle it was covered with wet paint, and said, no, ta, she wouldn't have a second.

Another conundrum session looked like developing until Arnold, speaking like a man who knows that what he is going to say will floor everybody, floored everybody by asking what happened when an irresistible force met an immovable body. Aunt May was clearly delighted at Arnold's tour de force. I could have gone one better by giving the right answer if only I could have remembered what Mr. Webster had said about this particular situation. For he had said something about it. It had come up in class when he was telling us about Achilles and the Tortoise; and that had somehow come up when he was telling us about dropping weights from the leaning Tower of Pisa. But of course I couldn't remember what it was Mr. Webster had said. I couldn't even remember what he said went on at Pisa though in my mind's eye I had a clear enough picture of a clever-looking man in a white robe carrying up brass weights like the ones in the shop.

Uncle Hector, as jubilant as Aunt May at their son's success, declared, "We've got to give you best, Arnold"; and he patted Elsie's knee again as he added, "Clever lad. Clever lad."

"Mr. Webster knows the answer," I burst out with a rush of memory. "There isn't an answer—or something like that."

They all laughed at me. "And who might this genius, Mr. Webster, be when he's at home?" said Arnold—though he knew very well.

"He teaches me sums."

"I thought Mr. Gentleman taught you arithmetic," said Elsie, "or was going to teach you."

"Mr. Webster."

"But Mr. Gentleman's going to," she persisted, though what authority she had to speak on matters like this I didn't know.

"Mr. Webster," I said. Rudely, I suppose.

My mother intervened. "Mr. Gentleman's going to give you some special lessons next term, dear, to get you ready for the scholarship."

That knocked me out of the discussion on irresistible forces, though obviously such a force was at work against me. Mr. Gentleman! Godfrey Gentleman! Known to us as Goddy or Gent. Mr. Gentleman! He was a laughing-stock at school. He was, I believed, very junior to Mr. Webster. None of us liked him. He tried to mix with us. Got his glasses knocked off and smashed when he joined in a football game in the play-ground. Serve him right, too. Ought to have minded his own business. And his was such a soppy name, too! Fancy anyone being called Mr. Gentleman! Of course, you get used to names. We had a Shufflebottom at school, and when he first came no one could leave him alone. When Ivor Brokenbrow arrived Harry Shufflebottom was forgotten. But—Mr. Gentleman!

Arnold became the irresistible force as the evening wore on. Mention of Mr. Gentleman (taken so calmly by all but me) led to the propounding of a series of mathematical problems whose answers only Arnold knew. I thought of introducing the Achilles and Tortoise problem to see what he'd make of that, but somehow I couldn't fit it in. He scored neatly off me by asking if I knew that the hairs of my head were all numbered. I replied, neatly enough, I thought, that the Bible said so, whereat he smartly jerked a hair from my head saying, "And what number is this one?" And they all laughed.

My school report was handed round for perusal as it always was. Arnold observed that Mr. Gentleman would have a hard furrow to plough when he took me on. Aunt May looked it over for a long time, and when asked what she thought of it said she'd left her glasses at home and couldn't read it.

Meanwhile whites outside were turning to purples, and you could sense the brittle iron grip of coldness on the evening air. The gas was lit; I was commanded to lower the heavy venetian blinds—a job I liked doing, though I liked hoisting them up better.

There was 'a little drink before supper', then in came cold turkey and ham, and cold Christmas pudding, and mince-pies and blancmange and jelly, and celery in a glass jug, and potatoes in their jackets. And they all said they'd never seen such a supper and congratulated Mother and wanted to know when she'd got it ready. (When *had* she?—I didn't see her.) Even Elsie did justice to it, rewarded by a pat on the knee from Uncle Hector when she accepted a second huge potato. My father and Uncle Hector had beer, Uncle Hector asserting that you couldn't get up an argument on tea. Arnold had beer, but I found his glass half-full behind the plant on the piano when clearing-up time came. Elsie wrinkled her nose and said it was nasty stuff; she drank tea, experiencing the same difficulty with her cup as she had earlier. Uncle Hector all but spoilt my supper by somehow giving the conversation a medical turn. Celery was good for rheumatism, he said. You could always tell if someone was going to be rheumatic—their nails would get crinkly first. And he went at his celery as a fire consumes dry twigs. From that point, by way of the scream lobsters gave when you dropped them into boiling water, and the fact that if someone broke a bone he always went white behind the ears, and if your neck gets fat you've got heart-disease, things gots worse—until, when Uncle Hector was explaining the origin and course of a hairy naevus, Aunt May said we'd had quite enough of that.

There was singing afterwards. Father sang a sad song called 'Watchman, what of the night?' and a hopeful song called 'The Lost Chord'. Mother played a strummy piece called 'The Harmonious Blacksmith' and Uncle Hector sang 'Good King Wenceslas', but it wasn't really 'Good King Wenceslas' because the words were, "Good King Wenceslas looked out, we sang with splendid pow-er; several neighbours looked out, too, to see what all the row were."

I was invited to sing a carol but refused on the grounds (false) that Mr. Dyball had forbidden the choir boys to go carol-singing (true). I had to recite, so I did *The Inchcape Rock*. Arnold and Elsie whispered to each other all through it.

Then Uncle Hector told stories of his cricket and how the Major was counting on him for the big match in the summer, and I had a brief moment of glory when I had to tell of the Major's hobby of stamp-collecting and of his utter dependence on my advice in that pursuit. Then Uncle Hector told stories of his cricket and how the Major was depending on him for the big match in the summer, and I fell asleep.

Mother brought me up a cup of cocoa and a piece of Christmas cake when I was in bed. But I didn't really want either. She said wasn't it nice of Mr. Gentleman to help me with my sums, and wasn't it kind of Mr. Bagnall to say he'd take me to the circus.

I fell asleep with a merry-go-round of thoughts twirling in my head. Mr. Gentleman's good intentions—known to everyone but me before that day; Mr. Bagnall's invitation to the circus—known to everyone but me, I supposed, before that minute. And Bell's whereabouts—unguessed at by everyone. Except me. No one had mentioned Bell.

X

BELL CAME HOME the day after Boxing Day and she brought me the whole of the bottom layer of a wooden cabinet of chocolates. Without exactly asking her what she'd been doing I asked her if she'd had a nice time. Yes, she had had a lovely time. How had I got on?

There wasn't much to tell, really. I told her that Mr. Gentleman was going to take me for sums, which, of course, she knew, and that Mr. Bagnall was going to take me to the circus, which she didn't know. I didn't tell her about my failure at the carol service, but I expect she knew about it already. But however little there was to tell, there was much for me to do. There was my tool-set; there was Willie Waites' steam-engine; there was deep snow.

Willie and I met daily in the store-room at the back of the shop. Our day was carefully parcelled. If we weren't out with our home-made toboggan we were burning our fingers on the bright little boiler of his steam-engine as with spluttering churnings in the intoxicating smell of methylated spirit it brought itself to readiness. Willie would hold back the fly-wheel until I was sure that the boiler could contain itself no longer, and then give it a twirl which set the engine humming and vibrating so that of its own volition it threatened to jump off the upturned crate on which it was set. Or if we weren't engrossed in steam we were busy with wood.

It hadn't taken us long to see the commercial possibilities of carpentry. Willie's John Bull Printing Set provided us with hand-bills, purple in every sense, announcing that Hook and Waites, Carpenters and Joiners, were ready to undertake all kinds of construction work in timber and solicited your esteemed enquiries. We were not quite sure how joinery differed from carpentry, but Willie said that since we joined things we must be joiners. Nor were we altogether certain what the soliciting part meant; but we got that off the placard outside Mr. Davis' rag and bone yard, so we were fairly confident that it was meant to attract trade. To call wood timber was Willie's idea, too. He said it sounded better. Our handbill announced that we specialised in the construction of dog-kennels. Had we not had a supply of grape-barrels—often offering flabby grapes and half-filled with promising but useless chips of cork—from Mr. Dighton we should probably have specialised in something else.

We made four dog-kennels. We sold two: one to Miss Partridge and one to Mrs. Vosper. We found out much later—we should have known—that neither Miss Partridge nor Mrs. Vosper kept a dog.

I became awfully conscious of the fact that I ought to be starting my holiday-work. I didn't mind not doing my arithmetic because I felt that since I had been sold to Mr. Gentleman that Mr. Gentleman took sole responsibility. But I was supposed to be reading for Mr. Selby. I never thought of it as reading for myself; it was for Mr. Selby. It is true that he had said, "This is for your own good, mind," as he handed a little pile of books to me on the last day of term; but books you don't discover for yourself are always strangers. Reading Mr. Selby's books—they were his very own, each with a cyclostyled book plate "Ex Libris Ricardus Selby. Ut quocunque paratus"—was like looking through Mr. Selby's private photograph-album. I didn't get on very well with *Lorna Doone* except the bit about the shooting in the church and Jan Ridd tearing Carver's muscle out of his arm. Mr. Selby had said that I 'ought' to read *Tom Brown's Schooldays* as it would 'help me in the future'. It frightened me. *Under the Greenwood Tree* I read in a day and thought it just the book for me—until I got to the last sentence, which made me think of the secrets that my sister would never tell.

I was supposed to be studying History and Geography, too. But what can you do with Geography? The books say Liverpool is a port, that at Nottingham they make lace, that at Luton they make hats. All right, then: at Luton they make hats, at Nottingham they make lace, and Liverpool is a port. Our history book was not like the ones Grandfather had. It certainly had a few pictures in it, but they depicted nothing like the drama of Grandfather's. There was a foppish-looking Charles I, not helped in majesty by the recent addition of a pair of spectacles; there was a static Boston Tea-party; there was a very dull representation of the Signing of Magna Carta—all those participating in the event wearing beards and moustaches and, of course, spectacles. The editors had devoted a whole page to a diagram showing the disposition of the two sides of Naseby; to this a contemporary military historian had added not only cannon but three battle-cruisers.

Perhaps it is understandable that the crisp air outside and the snow were not seriously challenged by school-books. Willie discovered that by some freak of nature the large pond near the spinney where we had left Mr. Ewart's barrow was frozen over but had no snow on it. We tried unsuccessfully to knock a hole in the ice; we skidded broken twigs across; we spent a whole morning sliding on it. Then it lost its magic; it wasn't getting the best out of us; we were not getting the best out of the ice. Hook and Waites, Joiners and Carpenters, had a little cash in hand thanks to the dog-kennel business. The One-and-All Stores sold skates. We would become skaters.

The skates we bought were probably of another age. The blade was somehow mounted in a kind of wooden patten which bore a screw and a strap. You screwed the screw tight into the heel of your boot and then pulled the strap tight over the toe-cap, and there you were. Or, at least, there you were until you took to the ice, when the strap which you thought rigid as a clamp somehow became lax allowing the blade to move on a line at variance with the one your boot was taking. The screws which engaged your heels, having over the years lost most of their thread, were more like nails than screws.

After two days on the pond we considered that we had mastered the art of skating. Luckily for us the snow which by rights should have been covering the ice had somehow piled itself up round the edge so when our turns were too ambitious or were influenced by the wayward blades we came to rest suddenly but safely. We knew nothing of inside-edges and outside-edges nor of figures of eight or Dutch runners: it was enough for us to make a circuit without the slithering clatter of a lost skate or the wild thrashing of the arms which usually led to a thudding fall. After two days, then, I announced with pride at tea-time that I could skate.

I could not have expected the kind of reception that this announcement would have. Mother was horrified. Father was angry. Whose pond was it? Where did we get the skates? How thick was the ice? Supposing we'd been drowned? Had we got permission to be on the pond? How would they have known where to look? Did we know the One-and-All Stores sold rubbish? Did we know we were asking for trouble? Why hadn't we told someone where we were?

In vain I said we'd only been skating. I didn't think we had done anything wrong. Then we ought to have had more sense. There might have been a terrible accident.

The upshot was that Father had to come with us next morning to test the ice and to ask someone's permission for its use. While we stood on a mound of snow on the bank Father gingerly put one foot in front of the other until he had completed a St. Andrew's cross inside an oval. He then stood in the middle, and with a little jump brought both feet down hard. A painful cracking, like a tooth coming out, then Father, in the best of moods, strode over to us. "Crack she hold; bend she break," he said. "She's all right." Round the edge of the pond muddy water slopped up from underneath the ice.

He didn't find out who the pond belonged to, either then or later. As for Willie and me, I think it had never occurred to us that the pond was owned by anybody at all, or the field it was in, or, for that matter, any other field—or copse—or path. We did not see ourselves as interlopers or marauders or trespassers. We meant no harm, and I don't think we did any—if you don't count tying acorns to the lower branches of a conker-tree or putting an old blackbird nest with three cold eggs into the font. That was Willie's idea, and it was going to set tongues wagging for weeks. In fact, like the illicit removal of Mr. Ewart's barrow, it moved no one to wonder or surmise. But perhaps we moved in the wrong circles.

We were in those days very trusting and undemanding, I suppose. Just as I had never for a moment seen any necessity to ask about the ownership of the pond, so I saw no reason to enquire about my engagement with Mr. Gentleman. The pond was there. We skated on it. I had to do sums with Mr. Gentleman. When, where, for how long? These were not questions for me to ask or answer. The grown-ups would know. I would avail myself of what was presented, just as we availed ourselves of the ice—well, not quite in the same frame of mind, but certainly without thinking deeply on the matter. With the promised visit to the circus it was rather different. I didn't ask Mr. Bagnall where it was going to be because that would have been rude, but I asked Bell and Mother and Father. Father said, "I don't suppose he meant it. He didn't know whether he was on his arse or his elbows that morning." Mother said, "We must wait and see, dear. I'm sure Mr. Bagnall won't forget. I shouldn't ask him, if I were you, dear. He mightn't like it." Bell said, "Why not ask him? He wouldn't mind. He'll only forget if you don't say something."

Since Bell had come back from staying with her friend over Christmas I had been wondering whether she was forgetting something herself. At first I thought she was, as it were, entirely inside the family circle; then I noticed that every day she had a letter to post, or was writing a letter, or wanted a stamp, or didn't want to be disturbed. I never saw any letter come for her. Whether she got up early or had an arrangement with Mr. Alston, the postman (though I don't see how she could have done that without Uncle Hector's finding out), I don't know.

I needn't have worried about Mr. Bagnall and the visit to the circus. Word soon reached me—though I had to interpret it for myself since it was conveyed in casual breakfast-time conversation —that Mr. Bagnall and I were to go on the last Saturday of the holidays. Why I couldn't have been told directly, I don't know. It seemed to be assumed that it was sufficient for the grown-ups to know; that I might have an interest in plans which concerned me was something that did not arise. It was worse when it came to my first arithmetic lesson with Mr. Gentleman. I didn't know about that until half-an-hour before it began.

We were having a late tea, the sort of tea we had when I was to go to choir-practice on Friday nights. Willie and I had been out all the afternoon getting the last out of the snow and melting ice, and I thought I had missed out tea-time altogether. So when I turned up at dusk with numbed hands and my feet miserable in sopping boots, and Mother announced, "Sausages for tea,"—but not before she had ordered, "Get those wet things off and put on your best suit"—I was doubly pleased. Ever since I had heard Grandfather, in similar circumstances, sing "When we are married we'll have sausages for tea," there had been something very special about sausages for tea. So we were having sausages for tea, all of us, and because Bell had asked me what Willie and I had been up to all the afternoon (what had she been up to?) I was telling them (though Father, reading the evening paper, wasn't listening) how Willie and I had managed to roll a huge log on to the middle of the ice on our pond and how we had waited (in vain) to see it break through and submerge and how . . . when Mother said, "Hurry up with your sausage, dear; you've got to see Mr. Gentleman at half-past six."

I didn't let it spoil my tea altogether, though I did feel a little done at the way I had been got into my best suit and had my attention taken from sausages for tea. Father stirred from his paper to say he wished he'd had someone to teach him sums when he was a boy. Bell said that I'd better see that my hands were clean. I said, "How long will I be there?" They didn't know that. Mother said, "Not too late, dear. I expect Mr. Gentleman won't have had supper." "How will I know when to go?" I wanted to know. They didn't know that, either. "Mr. Gentleman will tell you, dear," Mother said. "Don't sit there half the night," Bell said (as if I would!). "When the time comes, just stand up and say, 'Thank you very much, I think I ought to go now'."

I never found out if Mr. Gentleman was being paid for his services. And I didn't find out because, of course, I never thought to ask.

At half-past six I pressed the button by Mr. Gentleman's front door. Above the bell-push was a curled card secured by a rusty drawing-pin. 'Mr. Godfrey Gentleman,' in copperplate. Nothing happened. I tried again.

Mr. Gentleman lived above the coal-office in the High Street. It was an establishment which never looked cared-for or even attended. It was shut half the week. It was certainly shut now. The glass-panelled door leading up to Mr. Gentleman's lighted but curtained rooms above, turned a blind eye on to the street as did the main door and windows of the coal-office. I tried the bell again, feeling rather silly standing there on the pavement, but just as I was about to turn away there was a thumping clatter on the stairs. Mr. Gentleman's street door opened. Madge Ingles came out and Mr. Gentleman stood behind her with a hand on each door-post. Madge said, "Hallo, Arthur." Mr. Gentleman said, "Goodbye, dear. Is that young Hook? Forgot all about you. Come in, young Hook. Don't be shy. Up you go. Mind how you do it; the bulb's gone. Left at the top."

I fumbled my way upstairs, and presently Mr. Gentleman thumped up to join me. "Let's have your things, young Hook, shall we. Andrew, isn't it?" I said it was Arthur. "Come in, Arthur. Welcome to Parnassus. Know what Parnassus is?" I said I did know, and I think he was a bit disappointed. He put his hands on my shoulders and propelled me to Parnassus. It was a big room, somehow larger than the coal office below. There was a bright fire in a small grate, two Minty cane chairs, a long table with a cloth and tea things at one end and a tall typewriter like a loom at the other; and everywhere there were books and papers—packets of papers tied by string, wads of papers held by huge paper-clips at the corner, stacks of papers fastened by nothing at all and curling at the edges like the card over the bell-push outside.

"Now, young Arthur. Take a pew, lad, take a pew. Now, it's French, isn't it? Do you know Henri Bué?"

I had no idea what he meant, so I sat on the edge of the long cane chair and waited. He put into my hands a shabby little book bound in red cloth. "Where shall we begin, eh? Subjunctives all right? Tricky little devils, eh? Just like those Frogs. What do you say to a cup of tea, eh?" And he laid aside his own shabby little red book, struggled out of his long cane chair, and from the middle of the tea things removed an old trilby hat. A metal tea-pot shaped like a bomb was underneath; putting the back of his hand to it he said, "Wet and warm, eh, young Andrew? That's the stuff. Always room for a cup of tea. Picked up the habit in my acting days."

He gave me a cup of lukewarm tea with a digestive biscuit in the saucer. The tea had slopped over; the biscuit was soggy, but I didn't like to leave it. Mr. Gentleman had nothing himself, but went through an elaborate process of filling and lighting a heavy curved pipe on which as the evening passed he had to use a heap of matches. And as I sipped at my lifeless tea he told me how he had given up an acting career for teaching, how he had been kept out of good parts by jealous professionals who should have given up long before and how he was 'doing a little bit with the locals' just to keep his hand in and how we must be sure to see their next production which was called *Outward Bound* and was very mystical and suitable for Easter.

"Do a bit of writing myself," he said with satisfaction. "See these?"—and he waved a hand, unnecessarily, to indicate the biggest pile of papers. "Novels. Just waiting to be finished. Well, they're finished, really. You know—just dotting the i-s and crossing the t-s, so to speak. Publishers are funny, young Andrew; send 'em something and they say it's just what they want, but will you re-write the first dozen chapters and alter the plot and all the names, and will you say if it's for the juvenile market, because if it is you'll have to simplify it a bit. That kind of thing. Of course, I dash 'em off when the inspiration comes. I'm not one of your paragraph-a-day-men like Augustus Flaubert—heard of him, young Arthur?—no, that's not me at all. Take my latest—well, it's not my latest, really—did it three years ago; just wants the finishing touches, you know . . ."

And he told me about his latest, which was the story of a young man wrongly imprisoned for treason and how he escaped from the castle by pretending to be dead and how he revenged himself on his enemies. And while he unfolded the story, or attempted to—for he had to keep going back to uncover bits he'd left out—I began to wonder what on earth Madge Ingles had been doing there (Doing sums?) and what right Mr. Gentleman had to call her 'dear', and whether she called him 'dear'. For though I considered Mr. Gentleman was OLD I didn't think that he had that degree of age which lets you call people 'dear' when you don't really mean it. I studied him. Sandy hair plastered down, a ragged moustache, gingery-brown like the tips of two of the fingers of his right hand and covering most of his upper lip, a snuff-coloured, hairy suit, bulging pockets, black socks with scarlet clocks, and heavy, un-polished brown shoes. His glasses spent their time on his nose or being waved in his right hand to gloss over some intricate turn in the plot. And enthusiasm glowed from him like heat from a furnace.

The story he was telling might, I think, have gone on deep into the night had he not crossed it with the plot of an earlier novel and found himself with two heroines and a mad woman shut up in a turret. He promised to get it right next time I came and thought I'd better be going as it was getting late and 'they' might wonder where I was. He said I'd better come next Friday, and I said I couldn't because it was choir-practice. He said, oh yes, Mr. Webster had told him Fridays were no good and I'd better come Saturday. I told him I thought I was going to the circus on Satur-day, and he said, how silly of him, he couldn't manage Saturday anyway because of course he'd be rehearsing *Outward Bound*. He was the steward who wasn't really going to Heaven or Hell because he had to stay on the steamer to help the others who were, you know, and I'd better bring my arithmetic book next time I came.

I was out on the pavement as the church clock struck eight, and I spent some time standing there wondering if I ought to knock on his door again and ask him when in fact he did expect me next. It seemed the right thing to do. But I didn't like to.

When I got home not much notice was taken of me because Uncle Hector was there. He had, I found by listening, come round because he'd had a 'bit of bother' with the Post Office money. It was a pound short. And, come to think of it, it had been short once or twice lately; not so much as a pound, but a bit here and there, just enough to make him count all the Post Office cash again and look on the floor.

"Of course," said Uncle Hector, "I'll have to put my hand in my pocket. I can't afford it, but I can't afford to have it on my mind. If there's one thing I hate it's not having the books square."

We supported him with nods and grunts, knowing what was coming next (though it was years before I discovered where it came from).

"He who steals my purse steals trash," declaimed Uncle Hector. "But he who takes my good name takes all that I have." Then in more business-like tones he added, "Your good friend the Major was in today. Now, he was on a funny thing—writing letters to himself! What do you make of that?"

I began to say that I supposed Major Birkitt wanted to get a particular postmark on a particular stamp, but Uncle Hector wanted to tell us himself, so he interrupted.

"It appears," he said ponderously, "it appears that these stamp collectors like their stamps cancelled. Can't see why, myself, but that's how it is. So happens there was a new stamp out today. We've got sheets and sheets of 'em. Nothing rare about 'em. But the Major comes in all excited, buys half a dozen, sticks 'em on envelopes and hands 'em in to be franked. 'Do it carefully, Hector,' he says. 'Don't blot 'em right out; and see that you get the date clear.' So I do it for 'im. Careful. 'But they're all addressed to you,' I say. 'That's a funny thing. And there's nothing in the envelopes.' 'That's all right,' he says. 'Alston will see that I get 'em.' Good thing he said that. I was just going to hand 'em right back to 'im. Have to go through the proper channels, y'know. Did you know that, Arthur?"

As a matter of fact, I did. What the Major was doing I had done many times. But clearly Uncle Hector did not want to be interrupted. "That's what they do, you know, these stamp collectors. Can't see much in it myself, but that's what they do."

He paused to reply to Mother's enquiry. He didn't mind if he did have a bite. A bit of that cheddar would slip down very nicely, especially if there were some of those onions, same as he had last time. I was not sorry that a second supper was coming up; it would make up for my first one from which some of the taste had been taken by my impending visit to Mr. Gentleman. I didn't mind if I had a bite myself, but having to listen to Uncle Hector scraunching his pickled onions and glutching his beer was a high price to pay for my enjoyment. Anyhow, a second supper was laid in accordance with Uncle Hector's wishes, and though it was late I was allowed to have a little cheese. No beer for me. Milk. Uncle Hector then contrived to do five things at once, managing all at the same time to hold his breath, to hiss, to grind his pickled onions to pulp with the sound of packing-cases being smashed in, to turn the diminishing wedge of cheese on his plate into a head-quarters with earthworks of crust and a redoubt of pickled onions—and talk.

"Had that new curate, that Gedge fellow, in today," he said. (I noted that Mr. Gedge whoever he was had not lost much time in losing status in the eyes of Uncle Hector.) "They tell me" (Uncle Hector always made it sound as though he was a kind of confessor for the community), "they tell me he's a bit of a trouble-maker." And, munching, he looked round at our faces.

"He seemed a very nice young man to me," said Mother.

"Can't think what old Benskin wants with a curate," said Father. "Laziest person I ever knew. Not enough for one man, let alone two."

"Now, Father," said Mother.

I didn't say anything because I didn't know we had a new curate. When Mr. Asher went into the missionary field it was said that Mr. Benskin would run the parish on his own.

"They tell me he's had a row with Dyball," said Uncle Hector. "Wants to change the service, or something."

"Now, Hector, it isn't that at all," my Mother said, rather severely for her, I thought. "Mr. Gedge only wants Mr. Dyball, and I happen to know, to do something different this Easter. That's all."

"Well, there you are then," said Uncle Hector, triumphantly. "Muck about with Easter and you, ah, strike at the, ah, heart of things, don't you!" And he let out a long hiss as if the whole Christian religion had been suddenly deflated.

"It isn't that at all," said Mother again. "Mr. Gedge asked Mr. Dyball, and he was very nice about it, I'm told, if the choir couldn't do something new at Easter . . ."

"Well there you are!"

". . . He said it would be nice if we didn't have *The Crucifixion* but had one of the other pieces instead. That's all."

Though Mr. Gedge and his hopes were new to me, the great *Crucifixion* controversy wasn't. The choir had always sung Stainer's *Crucifixion* at Easter, and as long as Mr. Dyball had anything to do with the choir, always would. Mr. Dyball had said so himself. He had said more, too. One Friday night, when the men were all there, he told us that he was well aware that Stainer's *Crucifixion* had its critics. He had a letter in his hand, and kept glancing at it, so I suppose someone had written about it. "I am not going to pretend to compare it with the St. Matthew or the St. John," he had said (meaninglessly to me); "but I believe it has a place in the hearts of many. I do not for a minute accept that it is sentimental slush" (he looked at the letter) "or musical drivel" (he looked at the letter again). " 'Gentle Jesus, meek and mild' is no less effective because it is simple in words and homely in music. I am prepared to discuss the matter."

The matter seemed to be closed, and whenever we sang the great chorus, 'From the throne of his cross, the King of Grief cries out to a world of unbelief', I wondered that it had ever been opened.

Here it was again.

"What other pieces are there?" demanded Uncle Hector, music critic, village Hampden, Defender of the Faith. I had never known Uncle Hector to go to church so I was surprised at his zeal.

Mother said in a funny voice, "Well, there's *Olivet to Calvary*, for instance. That's very nice . . ." and then she went very white and sat down quickly and asked for a glass of water. Bell flew to her, taking her head into her arms and hugging her gently; Father pushed his chair back and strode into the kitchen; Uncle Hector said he'd be going; Mr. Bagnall, like an actor on cue, appeared at the door. "Wot's up, Missus?" he said kindly. " 'Ere, you lie down a bit, eh? Bit hot in 'ere, in't it." He went to raise her up, but Mother, miraculously, was well again. She sipped the water Father had brought, but said she didn't really need it. It was silly of her, she said, but just for a moment she'd come over a bit faint. We weren't to fuss.

So we didn't fuss, and Mr. Bagnall said he and I had better go outside and look at the stars because Saturday was the great day and we wouldn't want to go if the stars were wrong, would we?

According to Mr. Bagnall everything you did had to fit in with stars, or, put another way, he said, the stars made you do everything that you did. And there was one star up there, we'd find it in a minute, that kept its eye on circus-riders and cabbies and jockeys and them sort. "And if that star—ah, there it is plain as plain—if that star in't bright or if it in't on top of its form, then, lad, our old circus on Saturday will be arse in the grass and we might as well stay at home. D'you believe it, lad?"

I said I wasn't sure.

"No more am I," he said. Shall I show you where it is?"

Eventually he guided me in, apparently satisfied that the stars were in their courses and propitious. No one was in the kitchen, but voices came from upstairs.

"I expect yer mother's having a little rest, lad," Mr. Bagnall said. "I wouldn't disturb her if I was you. You tell 'er I'll be along for you on Satdy at three o'clock. Three o'clock, most decidillum. We'll have a nice time, Arthur, lad. You'll see. I'll let myself out. Don't disturb yer mum and dad." He winked and smiled. "A nice time," he added.

Bell came downstairs soon after Mr. Bagnall had gone. "Mother's gone to bed," she said. "And how did you get on with Mr. Gentleman?"

"What's the matter with Mother?"

"Nothing's the matter. She's gone to bed, that's all."

"Why has she gone to bed?"

"Because she's got a little headache. You know what a headache is, I suppose."

"Yes, but . . ."

"You have headaches sometimes. Mother has a headache now; that's all. Do you want some cocoa?"

"No. I've just had milk. Is the doctor coming?"

"Why ever should he?"

"I just wondered."

"Well stop wondering, and tell me about Mr. Gentleman."

"His feet smell."

"Don't be disgusting, Arthur. You know very well what I mean. Did he teach you anything?"

"Not really. I don't think he likes arithmetic any more than I do. He likes books and things. He's an author. He was a famous actor once. He gave me a cup of tea and a biscuit."

"I hope you said thank you."

"Don't be silly. Of course I did." (Did I? I couldn't remember actually saying it. But I couldn't just have sat there and taken it without saying anything at all.) "Bell . . . what was Madge Ingles doing at Mr. Gentleman's?"

"What do you mean, what was she doing?"

"Well, she was there."

"Why shouldn't she be?"

"I don't know. I only wondered. It seemed funny."

"Since they're engaged to marry each other I don't see anything funny about it."

XI

FRIDAY NIGHT choir-practice and (as it turned out) another
lesson with Mr. Gentleman lay between me and Mr. Bagnall's nice
time. I didn't mind the practice, even though it was holidays, but
the visit to Mr. Gentleman filled me with near panic. I got home
early for Saturday dinner so as to be ready for Mr. Bagnall's most
decidillum call at three o'clock. I was at once ordered to wash and
change so as to be down for dinner by one and ready to go out at
two. I said I hadn't to go out till three. They knew that. I said it
was silly to dress up an hour too soon. They knew that, too. They
said I was to go to Mr. Gentleman's at two, and when I said I
couldn't and reminded them that Mr. Bagnall was calling for me
at three they said they also knew that. I was not to be silly. I
could manage both engagements quite easily.

Choir-practice the night before had been marked by the first
appearance of Mr. Gedge. For the sake of Stainer's *Crucifixion* I
was predisposed to dislike Mr. Gedge, and so my guns were spiked
when I somehow took a liking to a young clergyman wearing a
Fair-isle pullover sitting in the second row of the tenors, who
turned out (I asked Harold Witty while the men were practising
'Come Holy Ghost') to be the renegade himself. He didn't look
like a rebel. He seemed to be getting on very well with his neighbours. He seemed to be enjoying the practice.

I waited for Mr. Dyball to make a profound statement about
The Crucifixion. He didn't. At least, he didn't actually say anything. But when the routine things had been practised, he nodded
to Greeny, and Greeny scooped up a tall pile of stiff-covered music
scores. Steadying it with his chin he went the length of the vestry,
right down to the basses. Copies were passed along. Basses first;
then tenors; then altos; then us to share one between two. If Mr.
Gedge felt that war had been carried right into his own camp he
made no sign. Having taken the copy of *The Crucifixion* into his

hands he could scarcely hand it back. I suppose he had, in every sense of the word, to accept it. All Mr. Dyball did say was "We're looking at this a little early, gentlemen. Not prematurely I hope." Thinking it over, I suppose that that might have been one in the eye for Mr. Gedge, though had you seen Mr. Gedge a little later—flinging his head back ("Don't overdo it, tenors; it isn't Jericho," from Mr. Dyball) to bawl 'Fling wide the gates' you would have supposed that Mr. Gedge was Stainer's most vociferous supporter. I had another look at him ("Look at ME, trebles. Don't keep your noses stuck in your copies," from Mr. Dyball) during "Cross of Jesus, cross of passion." He was singing with all his heart.

At a quarter to two I was nearly ready, physically, to pay my second visit to Mr. Gentleman's Parnassus. I was in my room trying to get my tie right when Bell came in. "Arthur," she said, "just drop this in at Mr. Annesley's House as you go by." And she laid a typed envelope on the bed.

"I can't," I said. "I'm in a hurry."

"It's on your way."

"No, it isn't."

"Arthur, you know very well it's on your way to Mr. Gentleman's."

"Oh, all right, then."

"And Arthur . . ."

"Yes?"

"Here's a little something towards your train-fare."

She did what they do in story-books—'pressed half-a-crown into my hand.' This would have been more welcome had Bell not been present when Father had financed me for my outing with Mr. Bagnall. She had even protested that Father was giving me too much; but he had had his way 'in case Mr. Bagnall lets you pay his train-fare', and Bell had had to bow too in the face of his superior knowledge of the world. "You always want to have some money in your pocket," he said. "And if you're going to enjoy yourself—enjoy yourself. Don't stint yourself."

So it was that Bell's half-crown seemed to me more like a bribe. I didn't need to look at the name on the envelope.

It had not fully struck me that the College boys were back from the holidays. I suppose I knew, really, for I had seen many arriving that morning with their trunks and square iron-cornered boxes. Some came in splendid motor-cars; some came packed in Mr. Bagnall's cab, their luggage piled on top.

I felt awfully out of place as I crossed the yard of Mr. Annesley's House to the big green door. There were piles of luggage round it, and, in spite of the cold, groups of fine gentlemen in splendid overcoats round the luggage. I was wearing my best coat. No one took any notice of me. I might have been an errand boy. I was an errand boy.

The stone corridors were cold and running with water but the air was rich with smells of cooking as if the first care of every boy returning from the holiday had been to fry sausages and bacon. I wasn't sure where I was going with my note. Bell had said I was to put it in the letter-rack; but I hadn't seen a letter-rack. Neither did I see Mr. Cater until he appeared from behind the trunk he was carrying hugged to his green baize apron.

Mr. Cater remembered me. "Got something for Mr. Annesley, lad?"

"Er . . . No . . . I don't think so."

"What, then?"

With an unreasonable sense of being caught out I pulled Bell's envelope from my pocket.

"Oh, ah," he said. "Praps you'd like to give it to Mr. Annesley himself. He'll look after it."

I could see no logic in this, but clearly Mr. Cater thought it was the thing to do so I meekly followed his green baize apron through the green baize door.

We had to wait in Mr. Annesley's hall while Mr. Annesley said good-bye to a gentleman and a glorious lady like a princess. He assured them that he would 'keep a special eye on young Arthur,' at which they seemed gratified and I felt a shooting in my stomach. When he turned from the door it was as if he had changed one face for another. The brilliant smile of the beautiful lady was not reflected in the face he wore now. "What is it, Cater?" he wanted to know.

"It's the boy, Sir. With the note."

The note? The boy? Why not a boy? With a note?

"Oh, yes. Well, perhaps you'd like me to take care of it? I think that would be better, don't you?"

Flustered as I was I none the less felt the unfairness of his question. Why should I like him to take care of it? Why should I think it would be better if he did?

I handed it to him. He thanked me. No sixpence.

I was late when I got to Mr. Gentleman's, but he didn't mind.

He was eating tinned pears. I told him I had to go early, and he said he remembered. Would I like a cup of tea? And would I like to look at THIS while he brewed it?

The table which on my previous visit bore the remains of a meal and drifts of papers now bore the remains of a meal and the paraphernalia of an artist. There were screwed-up tubes, a jam-jar full of brushes, a flat tobacco-tin full of clear bat-oil and a fish-paste jar of murky turpentine. Pinned to the table-top by four tin-tacks was a square of thick grained paper half-concealed by a shapely new palette blooming with patches of glorious colour. I supposed I was to view what was underneath the palette so I boldly removed it—not without fitting it over my left thumb—and looked.

I made nothing of what I saw. The glistening paint rose thick in ridges, rough like dried skin. There were whirls and explosions, comets with flying hair, a sunset, a sunrise, a breaking wave and, in the bottom left-hand corner, what I took to be a bare foot. Perhaps I was looking at it from the wrong side of the table.

"No training," said Mr. Gentleman, coming back with two cups of tea. "It's what you call impressionism. You simply paint the ideas that come into your head." He put the cups down unthinkingly on a corner of what had just come into his head (where they stuck and refused to come away without lifting rings of paint from the sunset) and with a tea-spoon pointed out his impressions.

"These are Man's Lofty Aspirations. This is Life like a many-coloured dome. This is a man's Ambition. This is Hope. This is Genius on the wing."

He dug the spoon into the sugar-bowl but then remembered the bare foot. This—to my surprise, for I thought he had done it on purpose—received a fine coating of sugar. He was merely explaining it. "This," said Mr. Gentleman, "shows that Man, for all the sublimity of his Thoughts, must keep his Feet on the Ground. And now, young Andrew, I think that is what you and I should do. Got your Maths book?"

I showed him my Pendlebury's Arithmetic. He seemed, I thought, taken aback by my demonstration of the maxim he had just propounded.

"I wonder," he said, briskly stirring sugar into the tea, "I wonder if you'd like to hear me do my part? Won't take a minute, and we've got that big rehearsal tonight."

From his roomy jacket pocket he brought out what I first

thought was a scroll. He put it in my hand. "You sit there," he said. "Page twenty-six, I think it is. Near the top."

I unrolled the papers to form *Outward Bound* and found page twenty-six.

"Scrubby," he said.

Scrubby's part was heavily underlined in green ink. On the margin someone had written in actions to suit the words—Pause; look up; scratch head; adjust port-hole curtain; pull lobe of l. ear with r. hand; look at feet—each action arrowed to a word in the text, so that Scrubby's lines looked something like Man's Lofty Aspiration in the painting.

I began at the top of twenty-six. Mr. Gentleman, in a stiff unnatural voice, put his own lines in at more-or-less the right place, more-or-less as they were written. What he could not remember he made up.

"Right," he said, at last. "Now the real thing. Top of twenty-six again."

He went to the far end of the room and drawing a deep breath stood tensed as if he feared someone was going to jump on him from behind. I began again at the top of twenty-six.

It was then I realised that Mr. Gentleman was not taking the stage directions lightly. He must have written them in himself. I realised too, though it should have struck me before, that almost every word of every sentence uttered by Scrubby was fully annotated. The effect was alarming. It was as if Mr. Gentleman was a mechanical man, motivated by clockwork and levers. As soon as he began to say his lines he became animated in every joint; beginning with a kind of twitching all over he progressed to an unbroken series of mechanical actions, some, as far as I could see, bearing no resemblance to natural movement, others a kind of jerky travesty of looking up, scratching head, adjusting port-hole curtain, pulling lobe of l. ear with r. hand and so on. He might have been a puppet. I thought he couldn't keep on vibrating like that as he spoke. But he did. He all but rattled.

When he subsided while I looked for his next entrance he confided to me that the trouble with most amateur actors was that they didn't know what to do with their hands. Watch any amateur, he said, and you would see what he meant. He believed you should act naturally. Then he drank off his luke-warm tea and spooned out the sugar from the bottom of the cup.

We got round to Pendlebury's Arithmetic at just about the time when I knew I should be getting home. I didn't like to say so, for Mr. Gentleman seemed suddenly as keen on arithmetic now as he had been on painting before. We were just seated at the table, Mr. Gentleman having shifted the plates and cutlery, canvas and pots to the sideboard, when the door-bell rang.

"Just look through Fractions," he said. "You'll find the page." And he thumped off down the stairs.

I heard a voice I knew down at the front door. They came up. Madge Ingles and Mr. Gentleman.

Madge said, "Hallo, Arthur," which made his "Well, young Andrew, that had better do for today" sound silly. "Jolly good luck at the, er . . ." he added. Then to Madge, "Young Andrew's going to the er . . ."

"Look after Mr. Bagnall," said Madge. "I hope you have a lovely time."

I realised that I had been dismissed; but without knowing quite why, I was conscious of not wanting to go, and that in spite of being fearful that I should be late for Mr. Bagnall. It wasn't because of Mr. Gentleman, or his paintings, or his dramatics, or his sums that I wanted to stay.

Mr. Bagnall was waiting for me when I got home, having a cup of tea. I had never seen him like this before: shining boots, a thick blue overcoat and a new black hat which missed being a top-hat but was something better than a bowler. He wore a blue suit and fawn-coloured waistcoat with transparent orange buttons that looked good enough to eat and might well have gone into one of Mr. Caxton's jars next to the Colonial gums. Across his waistcoat hung a heavy gold chain, a miniature of those you see hanging on dungeon walls, and from the chain hung half-a-dozen little gold horses' heads. He had a tight stiff collar and a loose grey tie stuck with a horse-head pin. I was glad I was in my best clothes.

No one seemed in a hurry to get us away, and I began to wonder if it would be in order for me to draw attention to the passage of time. When Mr. Bagnall finally buttoned his heavy coat and declared that we were under starter's orders there was a further delay while I was ignominiously sent to the lavatory 'just to make sure'.

We had hardly left the house when Major Birkitt's big Napier drew up just ahead of us and Maidment from within called out, "'Op in, Billy-boy. You, too, young shaver."

We hopped in—Mr. Bagnall as if he had ordered driver and cab specially, I timidly, terribly anxious lest Major Birkitt should appear and want to know what we were doing in his Napier. I relaxed a little when Maidment told Mr. Bagnall that 'is nibs was away—on the job, he shouldn't wonder.

At the station I was saved the embarrassment of offering to pay my own fare when Mr. Bagnall, drawing two tickets from the right upper pocket of his waistcoat, propelled me past the ticket-collector ("'Allo, Freddy-boy!" "'Allo, Bill. Enjoy yourself!") on to the platform. He gave me a penny for the slot-machine when he went to see a man about a dog. He returned as the train, its engine throwing out a steamy warmth, pounded to a halt. He marched me at once to a First Class compartment labelled No Smoking. We were on our way. I do not remember much about the journey except that Mr. Bagnall smoked a pipe with an amber stem that matched his waistcoat buttons.

My sadness at leaving the train vanished when we boarded a taxi-cab—an experience new to me, but obviously holding no wonder or terror for Mr. Bagnall who had summoned the vehicle by the merest twitch of a finger and who spent the journey expertly calculating how many miles we had covered.

I don't know what I expected of the circus, but I never expected the glittering, noisy, bustling world on which the cab dropped us. There were roundabouts and shooting-galleries, stalls where they made pink toffee, ladies with all sorts of fascinating and lucrative deformities and men who could bend pokers and rip packs of cards. There was a boxing booth with the professionals all lined up outside, each with his arms folded to show his muscles and wearing black tights and a red sash, with gladiators' boots nearly up to the knee. There was, at least a placard and a man wearing a fisherman's jersey and sea-boots said there was, a mermaid in a tank swimming for all to see, and a man with the Great Wall of China and the Taj Mahal tattooed on his chest and back. There was an Indian on a bed of spikes ready to charm snakes or climb up a rope which hung from nothing, and there was a Chinese Opium Den.

I very much wanted to go into the Den because I had seen a book called *Confessions of an English Opium Eater* in Major Birkitt's library, but Mr. Bagnall said we'd got to hurry or we would miss the jamboree, and putting his hand on my shoulder again he hurried me past the opium den into a tunnel decorated with flags. Two tickets came out of the left upper pocket of his waistcoat and we were at the arena.

I had been to a circus before, but that was in a tent in a meadow and the ring was no bigger than our skating-pond. This one was huge. There was real sawdust and there were circles of seats starting at a little padded wall and going up and up. There were rope-ladders and trapezes, a brass band in a gallery, hundreds of little flags and opposite the band a great wooden cannon. I thought it was made of bronze, but Mr. Bagnall said it was good old English oak. And he then told me that they were going to fire a man out of it into that net over there. A human cannon-ball! Somehow it took my fancy and I felt that I would gladly sacrifice all the other wonders of the circus if only I could see a man shot from a gun.

We had seats at the ring-side: I might have expected it after the first class railway carriage, and from the moment when the Ringmaster first flourished his top-hat and swish-cracked his long whip it seemed as if all the performers were doing their turns for us alone. The clown with the big boots and diamond eye was the first. He made as if to throw a chair at Mr. Bagnall but caught it just in time; then to make up he jumped on to the little wall, arm outstretched as if to shake hands. Mr. Bagnall stood up and put his hand out whereupon the clown turned his back. Everyone laughed, and I felt hurt and angry because Mr. Bagnall had been made to look silly. But it was all right in a minute because another clown, this one sad-faced with huge trousers, and braces much more elastic than 'Mikado' brand, came and sat on the wall in front of us. When big-boots came along he was accosted by big-trousers who pretended he could see acrobats on the highest trapeze. As soon as big-boots gazed up, out came a bucket of water from the capacious trousers, skip over the wall came big-trousers, up jumped Mr. Bagnall as if he'd known all the time what was going to happen, the bucket changes hands and—swoosh!—big-boots was drenched. Mr. Bagnall was cheered by everyone.

The performing dogs ran round the little wall under our noses and the naughty one of the troupe who wouldn't do their tricks hid himself in Mr. Bagnall's overcoat and wouldn't come out until the trainer offered him a biscuit.

A glittering lady on one of the shuffling, gentle elephants slid down his trunk into Mr. Bagnall's lap and stayed there until her elephant knelt down in the sawdust in front of us as if asking her to come back.

And all this time I was longing to see the man shot from the cannon. Even when the acrobats with their hups and their heys made frightening pyramids or tottering towers I found myself glancing up at that ominous mouth whence a real man would shoot before my eyes. I thought of Major Birkitt's little brass cannon, which I coveted; I thought of the terrible cannon of Borodino; I thought of Mons Meg; none of them seemed to me to count half as much as that great tapering tube up above our heads.

I didn't like the lions much though I didn't tell Mr. Bagnall. They seemed shabby and weary, with big bare patches on their coats. Perhaps we were sitting too close. The only thing I did like was the big revolver sticking in the lion-tamer's belt though I desperately hoped he wouldn't have to use it.

There came high-stepping white horses with gay huntsmen and lovely ladies on their backs. Mr. Bagnall who I thought had dozed a little sat forward in his seat. "The Tupplers", he said to me. "The Tumbling Tupplers. Now you'll see something, Arthur boy." And see something we did. But for all the wonderful tumbling and leaping and bounding they did they did nothing that excited my wonder more than the regard they paid to Mr. Bagnall and me. The flying girls smiled and winked at us; the scarlet huntsmen shouted a-hey every time they pounded by. And Mr. Bagnall sat there like a king reviewing his troops.

When the Tumbling Tupplers trotted triumphantly out Mr. Bagnall spoke again. "Like to go and see 'em, Arthur lad?" he said. I didn't really know what he meant, for we had surely seen all their tumblings and it must be nearly time for the human cannon-ball to make his flight; but Mr. Bagnall seemed to want me to like the Tupplers so I said I would like to see them again.

He crouched low as he left his seat so as not to spoil anyone's view of the ring. I, quite mystified, did the same and followed him. So, like two fugitives from Justice, we hurried down the beflagged tunnel turning our back on a troupe of performing seals black as wet top-hats and happily honking. Mr. Bagnall, quite at home in the bustling world we found outside the arena, picked his way, one hand on my right shoulder, to a splendidly painted caravan, all curlicues and scrolls and cornucopias, with a serpentine fascia-board —The Tumbling Tupplers. All round the door, which had shiny brass handles, there were painted rich amber pineapples. Mr. Bagnall said they were a way of saying come in. So in we went.

I think all the Tumbling Tupplers were inside, and there were also inside some whose tumbling days were either over or yet to come—an old woman in a black silk shawl, a wiry young man with his arm in a sling and two naked babies on a rug in front of an empty brass-bound stove. I was awfully embarrassed because two of the lady Tupplers were almost naked, too, and the men had stripped to their tights. When Mr. Bagnall and I went in there were shrieks and giggles from the women who without much hurry pulled on white dressing-gowns (embroidered 'Tumbling Tupplers' in black) and shouts from the men who practically engulfed Mr. Bagnall in their welcome.

He introduced me as Young Arthur, whereupon the ladies, who looked much older close-to than they had in the ring, pulled me to them and gave me great kisses heavy with perfume, sweat and beer. There was a babble of voices; there was laughter and shining eyes; there was slapping on the back and shaking of hands. There was excited chatter in a language I did not understand and which, I suspect, was lost on Mr. Bagnall, but which none-the-less conveyed the fact that we must stay to tea.

The old lady busied herself in cupboards and recesses, and in no time at all up came a table-flap and out came a big metal tea-pot already jetting steam and along came plates of sticky cakes, thick with nuts and chocolate and up from a tin box came a painted bowl full of stiff green ice-cream. Bottles of beer were already there.

Short of pushing food down my throat they could not have looked after me more attentively. While Mr. Bagnall, declining cakes and ice-cream on account of having a bone in his leg, drank bottled beer I (I'm afraid) ate all that was put in front of me. I didn't like the thick brown tea much and wondered if Mr. Bagnall knew what he was missing. It never occurred to me to wonder how it came about that they knew Mr. Bagnall or he knew them. Even the two who had no English and the old lady who didn't speak at all behaved as though they had known him for years. The men looked foreign, but in an athletic kind of way were like Mr. Bagnall in build; in fact, all the men in the caravan were of the same height. They might all have been guardsmen once—save that they lacked twelve inches. What they really did have in common was—horses.

When the flurry of greetings and the echoes of reminiscence had stilled they all got down to horses, and they listened to Mr. Bagnall as if he were Youatt himself. Some people can tell you the where-abouts of every railway-engine in Great Britain; Mr. Bagnall had the same knowledge of horses. You would have thought he was the Inspector General of horses. So detailed did the talk become that one of the lady Tupplers, the one I rather liked, said she'd take me outside and show me—the Tuppler horses. I very much wanted to see the man shot from the cannon, but I didn't like to say so and I followed her round the canvas stalls where the graceful creatures, with a twitch here and a twitch there, stood patiently waiting to comply with the Tuppler demands. It was while she was explaining to me that the Tuppler horses were trained to ignore distractions, even the firing of a pistol, that I heard a dull report followed by a storm of applause from within the arena. It was quite true; the horses made no move. I made no move. Inside I felt sick with disappointment.

It was late when we left the Tupplers. There had been more to eat and there had been mysterious paper transactions between the Head Tuppler and Mr. Bagnall. When we left I was given a bag of popcorn by the old lady, a ten-shilling note (folded in a funny way) by Mr. Bagnall's business associate, and a kiss by each of the Tuppler ladies. Mr. Bagnall received a wad of pound notes and two bottles of beer. They said we must come and see them again and at the time there was nothing I wanted more; I felt I was saying good-bye to the most exciting people I had ever known. I never saw them again.

Mr. Bagnall elected to take a taxi-cab back to the station. He said he had noted the fare for the outward journey—so there wouldn't be any hanky-panky from the driver on the return. Taxi drivers had been known, he told me, to take you from here to Timbuctoo if they thought you didn't know the right way. As we threshed along I noticed that he was watching the taxi-meter keenly, but I was too much taken up with the bright lights and the bustling crowds outside to watch with him. He got very excited as we neared our station, pointing out how the fare for this journey was going to work out exactly the same as the other one, right to a penny-piece. And so in the end it did, or would have done had Mr. Bagnall not begun to dig deep in an inner pocket for the money instead of stepping out on to the pavement. Just as he found what coins he wanted and was leaving the cab the meter ticked up another three-pence. The taxi-man saw it. I think Mr. Bagnall saw it, but, whether he did or not, it was the old fare that he put into the taxi-man's hand. The taxi-man took it, counted it, pointed at the meter, announced the discrepancy. Mr. Bagnall put on a simple idiotic look, cupped his right hand behind his ear, and, mouth open, craned his head forward. The louder the taxi-man shouted the more helpless Mr. Bagnall looked, and the more he strained to catch what the man was saying. Passers-by stopped and stared. The taxi-man began to use swear-words; but Mr. Bagnall's deafness was not to be overcome. When the taxi-man threatened to get out of his cab Mr. Bagnall put on a puzzled but pitying look, and shrugging and shaking his head sadly he took me by the hand and led me down the steps to the station. He left me, terrified of pursuit, at the far end of the platform while he went to see a man about another dog and did not come back until I was sure he had been arrested and our train came lumbering in.

In the train Mr. Bagnall was in high spirits chuckling away at the taxi-man's efforts to diddle him and going through again and again the antics of the clowns. He mused a little of circus-life. "Everyone ought to see a circus," he said. "It does yer good." He looked hard into the bowl of his pipe. "They do say . . ." (he drew on the amber stem and stretched his legs) ". . . they do say every man ought to see three things before he snuffs it. Know what they are?—A Derby winner, a ship in full sail and a naked woman." He seemed a little uncomfortable at saying this and began to grope deep in the big pockets of his overcoat as if to show that the subject was changed.

To my surprise he at length drew out a packet of Banbury Cakes. He got me to undo the neat red cord that fastened it and unfold the stiff grease-proof paper. The three Banburies inside were flaked and bent, but we devoured them, meticulously sharing the odd one, as if we had not eaten all day. Where he got them from I don't know. We had Banburies in the shop, but not in the holidays. They were special favourites of mine, but how he knew that I don't know, either.

No one got in our compartment. Mr. Bagnall said he'd have a little shut-eye and advised me to put my feet up on the cushions and do the same. I was afraid that we might both be asleep when the junction came and tried to see where we were; but the windows were steamy and only reflected the inside of our cosy box so I could see none of the Hall's Distemper men carrying their planks which had marked our outward journey. We pounded so fast through the lighted stations that I could not read their names.

Mr. Bagnall woke me at the junction. I was inside Maidment's Napier before I was properly alert. Mr. Bagnall and Maidment left me there for some minutes while they went off together to see if the roads were safe, for it was bitterly cold then and, as they pointed out, it would be silly to set off if there was ice about. I must have dozed off again for I do not remember their coming back, only turning out into the cold at the top of our street where Mr. Bagnall presented Maidment with two bottles of beer, which, he said, he had bought in London specially for him. I said good-night to Maidment and remembered to thank him for the ride. He said that that was all right, that any friend of His Nibs was a friend of his. The tracks of his wheels made thick lines in the frost as he drove away. Mr. Bagnall unbuttoned his heavy coat and contrived to get me under it. Thus we walked home.

It wasn't really as late as I fancied it ought to be. There was cocoa and biscuits for us and lots and lots of questions; but I was really too sleepy to bother much with my answers, and I remember wondering if Mr. Bagnall would think me ungrateful: I heard him telling Father that we'd had a champion day; top rate. So that was all right. I thanked him very much when I went up to bed, but in front of everybody I didn't like to offer to pay something towards the train-fare.

Before I went to sleep I heard them saying good-night at our back door as he went off down the yard. And I heard him singing "Goodnight Maria, then he snored.—She didn't like it, 'cos her name was Maud." I remember wondering who had looked after Dinah and Prince while he had been away; then I fell to thinking about Bell, then the pretty Tuppler lady who had kissed me twice and squeezed my hand. But most of all I wanted to know (and somehow I couldn't picture it) what it was like to see a man shot from a cannon.

XII

I SUPPOSE THAT it was quite by chance that the College boys began their Easter term on the very day that we began ours. This meant that so great was the preparation in the shop that no one had much time for me or my departure on the first morning. I would have liked to have stayed and helped Father; there were so many exciting things to be done. A York ham which had simmered on the gas-stove all Sunday, filling the house with a smell that gave me a craving for food, had to be shorn of superfluous fat, dressed in breadcrumbs and mounted on its china pedestal; boxes of loose chocolates had to be opened and displayed with at least one row of their contents broken to show that they were not sacrosanct; fat had to be heated for the creation of scotch eggs; the tall jars of boiled sweets had to be shaken to make sure that the freshly-polished brass scoop could have free play inside them; stacks of chocolate bars, like log-cabins, had to be built; pyramids of marshmallows, all pink and white and powdery, had to be thrown up.

The floor had to be swabbed, the brass weights polished, the chef's knives sharpened on the big steel that hung on a nail behind the counter, the paper fastening the lids of the new biscuit-tins had to be slit.

Someone (Bell) would have to go to the bank to get bags of coppers for the till; Mrs. Brill, leaning to one side like a Russian peasant woman, would bring a great basketful of hot sandwich-loaves; Mr. Plastow's errand boy, riding his carrier bicycle without ever sitting on the saddle and with only one of his raw, chapped hands on the bare handle-bars would bring strings of sausages in a shallow basket and fill our kitchen with his smell as he sucked at hot, sweet tea.

Father was not the only one to be up early on that day. The whole household stirred once he was about. Bell came into my room before I was properly awake. She was getting the breakfast that morning, she said, and she didn't want to be kept waiting by me. I asked her what was the matter. "Nothing," she said. "Mother's staying in bed for a little while; that's all. You can take her breakfast up to her, if you like." As it happened Mother didn't want any breakfast, only a cup of tea. She seemed more concerned that I should wrap my scarf round me the right way when I went to school than that I should wait on her. Bell went up and argued with her about not eating, but it wasn't any good. Nor would Mother stay in bed. So we had an uneasy meal made the less comfortable by my thoughts of school and by the arrival of Mr. Alston with two letters, one for Mother and one for Bell.

Father was clearing the mist from the shop window when Mr. Alston came with the letters, so they were delivered straight into his hand. We were at the breakfast table when Father brought them through and laid them down. Bell took hers and immediately opened it; Mother left hers where it was until Father said, "Aren't you going to open it?—It's yer father." Then we had Mother and Bell reading their letters, with Father and me unreasonably and involuntarily waiting for them to read an extract aloud or say something or pass them over, or somehow let us share them. The letters were folded and put back in the envelopes.

This was too much for Father. "Well, what's he on about?" he demanded. "He's not on about anything," said Mother patiently. "He thanks the children for their Christmas present and says . . . and says he wonders how . . . how I am keeping."

"Nice of him to take an interest. As long as he sticks to enquiries by post. Because he's not coming here. That I'll swear . . ."

"Father!"

I think Father knew he had gone too far. He said no more than the single word 'sorry', and drank his tea as though he didn't like it any more. I believe that he had at first had a mind to challenge Bell about her letter too; but whether he forgot or whether he felt he'd said enough I don't know. Bell got up, saying "I'm going to change my dress", and went out taking the letter with her. She did not try to conceal it. The envelope was large; the paper was blue and stiff and, somehow, very regal. She was a long time changing her dress.

School wasn't as bad as I thought it was going to be. Everyone had some story about the holidays; most had spoils to show—pen-knives, purses, pocket-watches, packets of foreign stamps; one or two even had a bright sovereign to display. In spite of the cold we spent break outside in the play-ground; and it would have been thought soppy to wear an overcoat.

School became more like school when break was over. We sat in our places waiting for Mr. Webster. It wasn't Mr. Webster who came, it was Mr. Gentleman. Before he taught us any arithmetic that morning he told us a great deal; but it wasn't about sums, it was about everything he'd done in the holidays. He didn't tell us why he had taken Mr. Webster's place.

I was terrified that he would put me on display and recount my visits to him, but he took no notice of me at all, and I doubt if he realised that I was there. He was listened to with some attention at first, but his reminiscences tended so much to show him as the intrepid traveller, gifted raconteur or generous host that incredulity dwindled into ridicule and his flaccid grip on the class lost what hold it had. Mr. Gentleman was not in the least dismayed at this as far as I could see. If there were interruptions, whether groans or counterfeit applause, he marked them only by talking faster and louder or by pausing a moment to say "Why this thusness?" His other favourite observation was "Time is of the essence", and he made it to indicate how urgent his message was and to avoid awkward questions. If he taught us anything on that first morning I cannot recall what it was, but I remember that I didn't want anyone to know that I owed a kind of allegiance to Mr. Gentleman: I suppose I felt that I couldn't very well drink his tea (however insipid) one evening and run him down the next morning.

When I got home for dinner I found that everything was all right again. Bell even asked me how I'd got on and seemed interested in the emergence of Mr. Gentleman. She asked me if I had seen Mr. Webster, and when I said no she said she wondered if he would be at choir-practice in the evening. I reminded her that it was Monday and that the men came only to Friday practices. Then she wanted to know if I would be going as usual, and when I said yes she said she'd probably want me to take a note to Mr. Annesley's. And suddenly I felt it wasn't Mr. Gentleman she was interested in, or Mr. Webster, or the school, or the choir. It was only the note.

As it fell out, I nearly didn't go to choir-practice at all that evening, and there was no note. Maidment had called during the afternoon; Major Birkitt would appreciate it if Father and I could call on him at about eight o'clock. He would like to see me about some of his stamps and he had a guest staying a short while who would like to meet Father.

It was, I suppose, a straightforward message; one that delivered to friends of the same standing would have caused no more stir than the arrival of a post-card from holiday-makers. It both paralysed us and threw us into a state of ant-like activity. Father, completely mystified as to the identity of the guest who wanted to meet him, said we couldn't refuse. Mother said we couldn't go. Bell said we'd have to go because it was too late to let Major Birkitt know that we weren't coming. Father said it would give offence if we just didn't turn up. Mother said they had no right to expect people at such short notice. Bell said we could telephone. Father said that would be rude. Mother said we couldn't get there; it was too far. Father said we could get Mr. Bagnall to take us. Mother told him not to be silly. Bell said we'd have to make up our minds.

I was sent upstairs to change 'just in case'. But I didn't change. I messed about in my room wondering why I hadn't pointed out that I had to go to choir-practice. I hadn't pointed it out because I wanted to go to Major Birkitt's. Once again I was elated that I was invited into his house, almost into his household. I found myself, and tried to stop myself, half resenting that Father was going, too.

When I went downstairs soon after six no one noticed that I was not dressed for visiting. There was a diversion. Uncle Hector and Aunt May had arrived.

"I know it's that girl," Uncle Hector was saying. "Now, Hector, you mustn't say things like that. We've no proof."

"I don't want proof. I know she's taking the money. I don't need to prove it."

"Now you're just being silly."

"Being silly, am I! I suppose I was being silly when I looked in her handbag!"

"If that's what you did you were asking for trouble."

"She's the one that's asking for trouble, my girl. It was all there, I tell you. Every penny."

"How do you know it was money from the till?"

"Well, I do know, because it wasn't in the till any more."

"But," broke in Father, "how do you know it was the same money? Had you marked it?"

Uncle Hector let out a long-suffering sigh. "Look," he said, "I keep the stamp-money separate, see. And I keep the postal-order money separate; and the registered envelopes' money separate; and the float separate. So I can run my eye over 'em easy, see? Tell at a glance what's what. I cashed up before she'd gone tonight. Seven an' six short. I got her back in the shop, and while she was there I went and looked in her bag in the lobby. Three half-crowns."

"But how do you know, Hector, that they came out of the till?" persisted Father.

"Because all the half-crowns in that till were Queen Victoria ones. I'd taken care of that, see. All Queen Victoria ones. And that's what was in her bag."

There was a long pause. Then Mother said quietly, "And what about Arnold? Arnold and Elsie Catcher seemed so friendly when they were here. Does Arnold know anything about it?"

"Haven't asked him," said Uncle Hector. "Don't intend to. She'll have to go; that's all there is to it."

"Well, she can't go unless you've got proof," said Father. "Be a hell of a row. You'd have Arnold wanting to know what was up, for one thing. For all I know the girl could sue you, or something. You'll have to mark some coins, or put some of that powder on 'em; the stuff Juniper told us about."

"I don't want the Alligator sticking his oar in," said Uncle Hector. "Silly old fool. That would put the cat among the pigeons. He'd have the Attorney-General in before we knew where we were. No, thank you."

At this point Bell interrupted. What about our visit to Major Birkitt's? And Uncle Hector and Aunt May had to have that explained to them in detail.

It was somehow thereupon decided that Father and I couldn't possibly go to the Major's that evening. No one actually said we couldn't or shouldn't, in fact no firm proposals were made in any direction; but when Mother said, "Well, someone will have to tell him," out came the irrevocable conclusion that we were not going. It seemed to be generally assumed that, whoever told the Major, the message was that we were not coming, for Father said that he wasn't going to phone, he'd only 'get landed' with some proposal for 'something else'; it was considered far too cold for Mother to go out; obviously no one thought me capable of communicating with Great Lodge. Bell would have to do it.

I think Bell was only too anxious to do it. She was upstairs and down again—wearing her new fur-trimmed green Cossack coat—

before the consortium had begun to work out exactly what she should say and how she would say it. She seemed a little taken aback when I pointed out that since I was about to leave for choir-practice, and since the nearest phone-box lay on my route to the church she'd better come with me.

We left them deep in mixed cogitations; who was Major Birkitt's friend who was so anxious to meet Father? What would Elsie Catcher say if squarely confronted? Had the Major expected us to walk, or had he intended to send Maidment? Should Arnold be told?

When Bell, grumbling that she ought to be 'getting on', and I went outside to wait for Willie Waites it was bitterly cold and I was glad of my scarf. Though it was not late everything was very still; the bright moon and diamond stars, cushioned in blue, looked down on a frosted, brittle street. Bell said it was too cold to stand about, but I pointed out that Willie was sure to bring his winter-warmer, and she could use that. "And smell of smoke all night!" she said. "No, thank you." When Willie did come, running, and windmilling his right arm to keep his winter-warmer going, we all linked arms and set off with a fine clatter. Suddenly Bell pulled us up short. "Oh, I am silly," she said, "I've forgotten to bring any money for phoning. I'll have to go back." She turned and was off before Willie and I had time to see if by chance we had any pennies in our pockets. Willie gave the winter-warmer an extra twirl as we stood watching her go. "Didn't Bell look topping!" he said. "What was she so excited about?"

When I got back from choir-practice there were two slices of bread and dripping, already salted, waiting for me, and a mug of cocoa on the stove. Mother had gone to bed early; Bell was out with friends, and Father was at the kitchen table with orderly heaps of silver and copper round him and a great roll of squirming paper and the new cash-register in front. There was a discrepancy in the figures.

There had been long arguments between Father and Mother before the cash-register had been bought. Father said that every shop had one and therefore we ought to; Mother said that she didn't see that entering every purchase on the roll brought you in any more money and wanted to know what the contrivance did for you if the total on the paper didn't tally with the money in the till. Father said it helped you 'to keep an eye on things'. Obviously the register had not helped Father keep an eye on things this day: he had fifteen shillings more than the paper roll said he ought to

132

have; and now he was trying to recall every transaction, or, as he put it, every piddling ha'penny.

I was still doing my homework when Bell came in. I had, in truth, little to do, for the masters had not entirely shaken off the effect of the holidays; but Bell found me identifying the causes and estimating the effects of the Civil War. She said Father and I were to go to Major Birkitt's on Thursday evening. She had phoned and the Major had quite understood. The mysterious guest who wanted to meet Father would still be there.

I pointed out to Bell that I was supposed to be going to Mr. Gentleman's on Thursday. She, unfeelingly, I thought, said I would have to make other arrangements, wouldn't I. Then she relented a little. She had already fixed up, she said, that I should go for my lesson the very next night.

All the same, I did feel aggrieved that I had been cast in my usual rôle of pawn. I didn't think to ask her how she had managed to make the new arrangement so quickly, though from something she said later I think Madge Ingles must have had something to do with it. Madge, I gathered, had been round (but if Bell had been where I think she had been—how had she seen Madge?). Madge's father was in trouble again; and this time it was boils. Madge had been round to borrow some boracic powder.

Madge Ingles wasn't at Mr. Gentleman's when I went for my lesson next night. I could not decide whether I was glad or sorry. He didn't say anything about the change of evening, but there was fresh tea, the pot kept warm under his old trilby hat, and two cups waiting when I climbed the steep stairs.

Mr. Gentleman had obviously transferred his interests to chess, for two boards were set up on the table and *Staunton's Chessplayer's Handbook* lay open. Over our tea he told me how he was engaged in a postal match with a man in Rugby. There had been a muddle over whose move it was and a cessation of hostilities for over three months while each player waited for a post-card from the other. Now the struggle had been joined again. It was Mr. Gentleman's move. Another post-card was addressed and stamped. Unfortunately Mr. Gentleman couldn't decide what move to make.

I thought at first he was going to take me through the game move by move, but instead he explained a scheme he was working on to make reading easier. As far as I could make out it entailed a complete revision of the way letters were printed and words set out on the page. Using the post-card addressed to the chess-player in Rugby Mr. Gentleman demonstrated that if you covered the lower half of a letter you could still make out what it was, that, in fact, your eye reads only the top half. The second part of his plan, to have words printed vertically in columns, was based on the proposition that the eye, moving from the end of one line to the beginning of the next, takes no longer than it does to move from word to word, therefore the reader's perception is jolted backwards and forwards like a goods-waggon in a siding.

The bit about a goods-waggon in a siding eventually set Mr. Gentleman going on sums concerning the vagaries of railway trains, and we spent some thirty minutes on trains approaching each other at different speeds, trains on gradients and trains on the level—none of them straightforward, punctual trains, but all encumbered by some deficiency which turned them into problem-trains. The best part of it was that for each sum Mr. Gentleman drew beautiful little pictures of the wayward locomotives. As it happened, he drew them on the back of the post-card destined for the chess-player at Rugby, so I suppose that that particular contest, like some of the trains in the problems, was destined to be held up.

When it was time to go Mr. Gentleman said that he'd like me to call him Godfrey. I didn't know what to reply to that. I think I remember saying I should like to, and then saying, "Good night Sir" as he shut the street door on me with "Good night, young Andrew". I do remember resolving that whatever he called me I could never bring myself to call him Godfrey.

News had reached home that Maidment would call for Father and me in the car on the great night. Father was anxiously discussing with Mother what he should wear. Mother, who knew about these things, had no doubt that we must appear in our Sunday clothes, and it was no good Father talking about Smoking Jackets—in the first place no gentleman would wear one while visiting, and in the second Father hadn't got one. We would find that Major Birkitt would wear what he wore for church (right) and that his guest would have to do the same (wrong).

More urgent than the doubts about what to wear was the consideration given to the propriety of availing ourselves of Maidment's services. Nothing had been said about him since that Saturday evening when he came to play cards, but it seemed to go without saying that we required no favours from him. At the same time we couldn't very well wait for him to drive up to the door and then tell him that we had made other arrangements. We hadn't made other arrangements, neither did it seem likely that we should —or could. I said that Maidment had been jolly decent when he met Mr. Bagnall and me on the Saturday before; Mother said that Major Birkitt was trying to do us a kindness and that it would be rude to refuse.

So when Maidment turned up we didn't refuse. He had to be asked inside to wait because Father wasn't ready. He didn't take much notice of me, but he was once more most attentive to Mother. He trusted that she had quite recovered from her indisposition. He understood that he would not have the pleasure of driving her to the Major's that evening. He hoped that she didn't find the frosts too severe: they played him up something awful. I am not sure whether I did or did not want the neighbours to see us riding off in the Napier. Father sat in front with Maidment who had made an appraisal of my Sunday best before telling me to sit at the back. "Since you're got up like a fourpenny ham-bone you'd better go in the three-and-sixpennies."

So I sat in the three-and-sixpennies feeling over-dressed and clutching my loose-leaf album of swaps which I thought I'd better take along in case I could find nothing to talk about—the exhilaration I had felt after my last easy meeting with the Major having worn off a little.

Major Birkitt was waiting for us in the hall. How long he had been there I don't know, but it was nice of him to be there at all for it was bitterly cold. He shook hands heartily with Father and put his hand on my shoulder. "Nice of you to come," he said. "Busy man like you. And young Arthur. Have you finished your homework, young Arthur?" Father said he was honoured, he was sure. I said I had not had much to do. "Come along into the library," said the Major, "and we'll see if we can warm you up."

So we trooped into the library which was in shadow save for a mellow patch of light round the hearth. A bright fire was reflected fitfully in the glimmering leather of the deep button-back couch and arm-chairs, and from the chair nearest the fire rose Lord Rutherstone.

Major Birkitt said who we were. Lord Rutherstone said he remembered me, and proved it by asking me about the Suez Canal stamp. Then he said he had met Father years before when he had reviewed the Special Constables after the war; and although he didn't specify in which rank Father had stood, he said enough about the time and the place to have Father delightedly filling in all the details for him. Major Birkitt groped in the shadows to produce a brass tray bearing a shabby bottle and four rattling glasses. "You'll like this, Mr. Hook," he said. "Daresay you won't object if young Arthur has a thimbleful." Father didn't object, so I was given a careful half glass. I watched fascinated at the way Lord Rutherstone put his cigar through its paces before he approved it and lit it. Even then he held it up from time to time and looked at it suspiciously. I noticed that he had removed the paper band, and hoped that Father would do the same with his.

We had settled in our yawning chairs with our glasses, and the Major had just laid a bulging album in my lap when there came a discreet tap at the door. Mrs. Chelvey's head and shoulders, beautiful in the firelight, appeared. "Excuse me, Major." "What is it, my dear?" "The hot tap in the kitchen. Only steam will come. I think the tank may be empty. I wonder if . . ." "Blasted pipe's frozen," said the Major. "Of course, my dear. Will you excuse me for a moment, gentlemen." And taking his glass with him the Major closed the door firmly on us.

"You may have met my son," said Lord Rutherstone to Father.

"I, ah, don't think I've had, the, ah . . ." said Father.

"Marcus Daveney."

"Oh, ah. Yes. Ah. Yes."

"You have a daughter, I believe. Arabella."

"Oh, ah. Yes. Yes."

I didn't know what Father was making of this, but I felt my stomach turn over. I expected Lord Rutherstone to add, "Well, you'll know what I'm talking about, then, won't you!" But he said no more for a moment and contented himself with drawing thoughtfully on his cigar and then holding it up to look critically at the glowing tip. Then he held his glass at almost arm's-length and stared through it before putting it to his lips.

I think that in any other circumstances I would have laughed to hear Bell called Arabella. It was a name once used for teasing, but almost forgotten. Coming from Lord Rutherstone it sounded rather like an accusation, almost as if it was the accused's prison-number.

"This port," said Lord Rutherstone. "Very good. At least sixty years old, I'd say. Do you care for it, Mr. Hook?"

"Very nice. Very nice," said Father. He was, in fact, having difficulty in keeping his cigar alight and had hardly tasted his wine.

"It's not only the age, though that has a great deal to do with it," Lord Rutherstone went on. "It's the rejection of grapes and even whole vines that are not worthy of the stock. When you have grapes of quality, wines that have been cherished and tried and tested so that not as much as a single suspect leaf goes unextirpated, then in the end you have something great, and anyone who has an eye for these things knows as great."

Father said he supposed so. I miserably turned the pages of the Major's stamp album.

"Everyone knows about old wines and new bottles," went on Lord Rutherstone. "If you are going to mix something new with something old, you must be sure that the new has the same potential stature as the old."

Father said he supposed that was so, too.

Lord Rutherstone was not done yet. "You know your Chaucer, Arthur, I expect."

I wondered what was coming.

"Chaucer knew wines. You'll remember what he says about the wines of Lepe. And what he says—though I won't malign Lepe, because I don't know the place—in principle, what he says is as true today as it was then. Don't you agree?"

Father agreed.

"And you can't assume that port has vintage—for that's what we're talking about—vintage—just because it smells good, or looks pretty in the glass. Fine bouquet and elegant style are all very well. But there are more important qualities than those; character, that's what counts. Character built on solid foundations of character. A thing can look pretty and turn everybody's head, but it won't last; it won't last. Style. We hear a lot about style. But mere style is not good enough. It's careful preparation over years and years, that counts."

"You get these cheap-jack fellas stamping their corks. Just because the bottom of the cork bears a lodge's stamp it doesn't mean to say the wine is fit for a discerning man. Outward show's no good, Mr. Hook, no good at all. It's pedigree that counts. You won't disagree with that."

Father did not disagree.

"Time is the thing," said Lord Rutherstone ("Time is the essence," said Mr. Gentleman). "Time."

"You get these butler fellas cleaning the silver. You'll see them putting their thumb over the hall-marks so they won't be rubbed away. What's the good of that?—hall-marks. Names on corks.

Just advertisement, really. Looks nice. Catches the eye. Catches the eye like a pretty girl. It's a pity . . ." He sipped his wine. ". . . It's a pity that people can't see these things."

Father was still trying to get his cigar to go when Maidment took us home. "Interesting, what the old boy was on about," he said. "I think we've still got some port-wine in the sideboard. I'll take a look when we get back."

He did take a look, but he didn't find any reference to vintages or lodges or pipes. Neither did the cork have any secrets to reveal. He didn't pour any out, but no doubt, mongrel as it was, it would have looked pretty and caught the eye—just as, no doubt, Bell had caught the eye of Marcus Daveney.

XII

ONE OF THE bitterest kinds of wretchedness is being left out of
things. I hadn't wanted to go back to school, but a few weeks after
the beginning of term when I caught a cold and Mother said I
must stay at home I pleaded and argued and pretended. It wasn't
any use. She got, for her, quite stern and said strictly, "Well, you're
not going, so you'd better make up your mind to it."

I was desolate at the order. At a distance school seemed a jolly
social club, a university, an outing, a brotherhood. I think I knew
all the time, though, that it wouldn't be any good. I just couldn't
stop coughing. I went on and on. Father said I could stop if I
tried, but I did try, and I couldn't stop.

As I lay in bed with the stone bottle that was either so hot that
it burnt your feet or so cold that it seemed to freeze the sheets
Mother used to rub my chest with warm camphorated oil. It was
worth being put to bed just for that, but it didn't really do any
good. I went on coughing. The great decision was made: the
doctor must be sent for.

The whole house, I think, had to be cleaned out before the doctor
came. My room of course received special attention though I
didn't like lying there watching Mother, sometimes standing on a
chair, dusting and polishing as if the whole room as well as my
cough was about to be examined.

Dr. Matson talked to me about cricket while he tapped and
prodded and listened. His hands were warm and somehow comforting on my chest as if they were sending out their healing
properties, but the mouth of his stethoscope was icy-cold and
made me start. Saying he'd soon have me batting for England he
drew Mother outside for a conference from which I picked up
nothing at all.

After that Father and Bell somehow treated me with more
respect, as if I supported some rare complaint. The word 'bron-
chitis' became common currency; a dumpy kettle over a spirit

burner breathed out an aromatic herbal steam; a nightlight marooned in a saucer of water glimmered hopefully after dark.

Then there followed a confused jumble of time when I couldn't really tell whether I was awake or sleeping. I only know for certain that whenever I opened my eyes I would find Mother sitting at my bedside. If it was in the night she would give me a drink of lemonade, pouring from a glass jug where slices of lemon floated and whose beaded net made a cheerful sound when she whisked it off. Sometimes at night she would bring me mysterious comfort by placing in my hands a gold trinket from her jewel-box, an anchor, a cross and a heart, each on a short gold chain leading to a gold ring. Where it came from, what became of it I have never found out.

Father said you'd never get a fire to burn in the grate in my room: it wouldn't hold two penn'orth of coal. But he brought up newspaper and sticks and coal in a biscuit box all the same. Mother pared a candle to help the little fire-place to make up its mind.

It is a special kind of luxury having a coal fire in your bedroom, like having meals in a dining-car. When I was alone I used to lie gazing at that lively little fire behind the three heavy black-leaded bars; but the best thing about it was that when Mother and Bell brought up my tea on a tray they would stay and have their tea, too. At night, long after the glow had faded out, you could hear the embers settling down. The only thing I didn't like was waking in the morning to see the grey, dead ashes flat in the bottom of the grate.

My first visitor from the outside world was Mr. Leaf who bore the *Boy's Own Annual* for 1910 and laid it on my bed saying that it would keep me out of mischief.

I am ashamed to recall that I lay there fingering the heavy book and longing for Mr. Leaf to go so that I could get on with it, but there was Mr. Leaf talking about the impregnability of those with an Education and asking me how my studies were going and whether I was able to do any work now that I was getting better. He had heard, he said, that there were a good dozen, a baker's dozen, who were going to sit for the scholarship along with me. "Don't let them get the better of you, Arthur. For your Mum and Dad's sake."

At length, when he said he must go and wash his hands, I no longer felt fully accredited to the *Boy's Own*. I would devote myself to the few school-books I had; but first I would run through a few pages of the *Annual* just to remind myself of what lay in store. Sitting up I drew it on to my lap. I was still reading it when Mother came up with beef tea and thin slices of bread and butter.

For once she seemed ill at ease. She sat on the side of the bed holding my tray safely on top of the book. She told me I must drink all the beef-tea; she had made it herself and it was very good for me. I mustn't spill any on Mr. Leaf's book. Wasn't it kind of him to bring it? He was a friend if ever there was one.

When I had finished she put my tray on the floor and took my hand in hers. "Bell is going away for a little holiday," she said.

"Bell going away! What for?"

"She wants a little rest, dear, that's all. It won't be for very long."

"A week?"

"No, dear, longer than that."

"Two weeks, then?"

"Well, perhaps a little longer. We'll have to see."

"She's not going to get married, is she?"

"No, dear, she's not going to get married."

"Where's she going?"

"To Grandfather's, perhaps. We'll see."

"What's she going for?"

"I told you, dear. She needs a little rest and a change."

"You're not going with her, are you?"

"No, dear. I'm not going away."

Mother wouldn't say any more than that. I asked her more questions, but she said I must rest. She asked me if I'd like Willie to come round. I said I would, but not when Bell was at home.

"When's Bell going?" I asked.

"Not yet, dear. Not for a day or two." She stopped and took up the tray. "Now I'm going to have my little rest," she said. "You go to sleep."

When Mr. Gentleman called he came like a whirlwind, blowing away some of my anxiety over Bell, presenting me with a large orange and giving me the choice of 'doing a bit of arithmetic' or 'hearing his jolly old part'.

He got through his jolly old part at high speed, including his actions and everybody else's jolly old part, too. He was proposing to do it all over again 'just for luck' when Mother brought him a cup of tea and a piece of Christmas cake on a tray. That reminded

141

him that he had something for her. He absolutely insisting on presenting her with four front-row tickets for the jolly old show—which wouldn't be long now.

As he ate his cake, starting at the bottom and leaving the marzipan until last, he added a little to my mathematical stature by warning me about trick questions. "At the interview" (my stomach clenched at the word), "at the interview, young Andrew, they'll try to catch you out. There'll be some kind of trick question—you mark my words." Then he suddenly said, "The yolk of the egg is white. The yolk of the egg are white," and looked at me searchingly.

Bell came to see me later on, but I didn't like to ask her directly about going away, and to any kind of question remotely connected with her movements, she replied that I was not to be silly, or that I must wait and see. I thought she looked troubled and tired. Her eyes were all puffy and heavy. She left a crumb of comfort: I was going to be allowed downstairs before long; the doctor said so. And if the sun shone I might even go for a short walk—provided, of course, that I wrapped up well and didn't do anything silly.

There followed a run of placid days when I sat downstairs in my dressing-gown by the fire, or, wrapped like an Eskimo, went in uncertain sunshine on slow anxious walks with Mother. It was a time of beef-tea and crayons, Virol and plasticine.

No one seemed especially glad or sorry to see me back at school, though those masters who had noticed my absence did not fail to urge me 'to try and catch up', none pointing out where my effort should lie.

I was allowed to start going to choir-practice again provided I didn't do anything silly. Then there was a duty call to be made on Uncle Hector and Aunt May on the very first fine day after my release from house-arrest. Aunt May, I now learned, had been 'very good' while I was ill, sending round milk-puddings and beef stock and a wing of chicken.

For once I was not well received at Uncle Hector's. When I got there the blue linen blind was drawn over the glass of the shop-door, and Uncle Hector, breathing deeply, made a great clangour in unbolting, unlocking and unchaining to let me in. He had company. With him was a short, bald man with a huge dome of a head, neat white cuffs and a blue serge suit (later to be described by my uncle, to the outrage of my aunt, as 'that perky little sod').

"You see, Mr. Eustace," said Uncle Hector as he fastened the door, "we don't do things by halves when it comes to looking after Government Property."

As Uncle Hector raised the mahogany flap of the counter and with his eyes directed me through the coloured glass door into the parlour Mr. Eustace said something about locking the stable door after the horse had bolted, and laughed in an official kind of way.

"Oh dear. We've had more trouble. And a Man has come," was Aunt May's greeting.

I said my piece about her kindness, but I think she rather wanted to hear what was going on inside the shop, for she stood by the door listening to the muffled voices and peering through the more transparent parts of the glass.

"It's that girl," said Aunt May. "That Elsie Catcher. Anyone with sly looks like hers and a name like hers can't be any better than they should be. There's proof positive that she . . ." But Aunt May was interrupted by the appearance of the two combatants. Their business was done. "Until you have proof, real proof, not just suspicions, however strong those suspicions may be," said the man from the Government, "you mustn't do anything drastic. Might bite off more than you can chew, if you see what I mean. You've made good the money, so as far as I'm concerned, that's that. It could have been a mistake in booking. It could have been what you think it was. We haven't got proof positive. Nor won't have. That's the long and short of it. Nor won't have." And having in a brusque kind of way refused Aunt May's repeated offer of a cup of tea, obliged Uncle Hector to unbolt and unchain so that he wouldn't miss his connection. It was while the shop-bell was tinkling cynically that my uncle referred so impolitely to Mr. Eustace and added that it was all right for some, but that he himself was three pound bloody ten the poorer.

I tried unsuccessfully to bring the conversation round to beef tea and chicken legs; I even asked how Arnold was. I asked if they were going to Mr. Gentleman's show. Hadn't heard of it. Nobody told them anything. All they knew was that there was something funny going on with the Post Office money and they'd be lucky if Mr. Eustace didn't make an Official Report when he got back to the Department.

At last the time came for taking the tickets for Mr. Gentleman's play from behind the white china mouse on the mantelpiece. Even Bell was coming. And it was Bell who, on the night, so goaded us

143

that we were all ready to set out a good hour before we needed.

Arriving much too early we had to wait in the vestibule until a little ticket-window went up with a bang and by magic there appeared at the doors gentlemen stewards in evening-dress and satined ladies with sheaves of programmes and Mr. Webster with gold studs sticking out of his shirt to welcome us 'in the name of the Society'. I got a wink as well as a strong hand-shake.

There were few witnesses to our shuffling but triumphant advance right down the centre aisle to the front row: the stewards were still fiddling with chairs, and the orchestra was engaged in a kind of general post in which they bustled from stand to stand as if they could not decide what parts to play. Father was rather grudgingly groping in his trouser pocket for threepence for a programme when a beautiful lady came up and gave us four "with Mr. Gentleman's compliments". This was considered to be so generous and thoughtful that it put even Father in a good humour. He didn't really like being in the front row, with the nobs, as he put it: he couldn't see who was in the cheaper seats. He unashamedly put one elbow on the back of his chair and with his mouth half-open ranged his eye over the filling auditorium. Mother looked straight ahead. I was told to stop fidgeting. Bell, with the help of a minute mirror, making sure that no wayward tendril of hair should disgrace her, must have seen something else out of place for she suddenly blushed deeply and like Mother gazed straight in front of her. A well-controlled commotion, and a small band of College boys with easy self-assurance clattered into two rows at the back. Then the orchestra played *Fingal's Cave* before a hand parted the curtains for Mr. Benskin, holding a rolled-up programme, to sidle through to the edge of the stage.

Mr. Benskin said twice over that with Easter approaching he could think of a no more appropriate play than *Outward Bound* and that he had been asked to say that coffee was available in the interval. He was sure that he would be voicing the sentiments of us all in thanking the good ladies of the Society for this agreeable service and the Society as a whole for putting on a play which, with Easter approaching, could not be more appropriate. Then the orchestra played a piece in which *Abide with Me* was cunningly mingled with *Ye Mariners of England* and the curtains were drawn up.

We must have passed the top of twenty-six by a good many pages before I realised that Mr. Gentleman was on the scene. It was only through recognising a long rehearsed piece of stage-business that I associated our Mr. Gentleman with that totally alien figure up there whose gestures and accent and bearing and appearance were so unlike anything I had known before. Only once did he need the help of the prompt-lady in the wings, and this he obtained by suddenly becoming the Mr. Gentleman we all knew, putting on an agonised expression of bewilderment and snapping his finger and thumb sharply in the air. It was the only time when I came, as it were, ashore.

At the end everyone clapped for a long time, but I don't remember if I clapped or not: I sat there done and empty and sad that the curtains had robbed me of a glimpse into another kind of world. I had believed everything I had seen. I had been enthralled.

It wasn't until we all stood up to go that I realised that Bell was no longer with us. She had gone for coffee in the interval, I remembered, and had not come back.

We found her waiting for us on the pavement. They had taken, she said, so long to serve the coffee that the curtain had gone up before she'd finished. And she couldn't very well walk the length of the hall once the play had begun, could she?

It was choir-practice next night. When the men arrived Mr. Webster, still with gold studs, but a white flower this time, came over to me. "You enjoyed that, Arthur, didn't you? I was watching your face through the curtain." I said I wished I could see it all again. "There's a good house tonight," he said. "The word's got round. Why don't you try the matinée tomorrow? I expect you'd get in all right if you went along." He stopped Mr. Benskin as he passed. "Keen student of the drama here, Vicar," he said. "Wants to see it again."

Mr. Benskin seemed pleased. "Hook, isn't it?" he said. "Saying goodbye to one of the family soon, eh? Could you hear me at the back, er, Hook? No actor meself, but I know about reaching the back rows, eh?" And he laughed in a fruity kind of way.

We did a lot of *The Crucifixion* that night, but my heart wasn't in it. I wanted to get home—to see if Mother and Bell and Father were still there, I suppose. Mr. Dyball became impatient with the trebles. "I'm sorry, gentlemen. The small fry are wasting your time tonight. Once again, please, Letter H, top of twenty-two." And I wondered if Mr. Gentleman had reached the top of twenty-six, and if Bell had contrived to return for more coffee at the back of the hall.

At dinner-time next day it seemed to be generally agreed that Mr. Gentleman would be expecting me for a lesson at two o'clock. I said he couldn't be because he was in the play in the afternoon. Bell said that if he wasn't expecting me he'd have said so, wouldn't he. I said it was silly to go to his place when I knew he wouldn't be there, but they all came up with the conviction that in every play there was always a substitute for the big parts—what would happen, Father wanted to know, if one of the important actors broke a leg? —and the substitute was always allowed to do the part in afternoon performances, which was only right, wasn't it—learning all those words for nothing!

So at two o'clock I rang Mr. Gentleman's bell and knocked on his door. But you can tell if a house is empty by the hollow sound the bell makes—not that Mr. Gentleman's bell made any sound at all—and the hopeless rattle the door makes in its frame as you try it. Mr. Gentleman was not in. The coal-office was empty. There was no one to ask.

With my satchel on my back I went along to the matinée. Because the first act was nearly over they let me in without paying. There were not more than thirty in the audience and they were all huddled together up at the front. And they were all silent. For me the mystery of the place had gone. I longed for a return of the magic spell that had made me oblivious of my surroundings. But all the time I knew where I was; the actors postured in vain, and even Mr. Gentleman, as if disillusioned too, reverted to being Mr. Gentleman. I didn't stay to the end but slipped away as quietly as I could, my satchel catching on a chair and nearly turning it over as I went.

When I got home Bell had gone.

XIV

THEY SAID THAT Bell had wanted to slip away quietly (that made two of us) without everyone coming to say goodbye. I felt many unhappy things and I felt especially done at being classed with 'everyone'. She wouldn't be away 'all that long'. She would be writing to me 'by and by; as soon as she's settled'. She had thought of going the next day, but Mr. Bagnall happened to be going to the station empty that afternoon and it had seemed silly not to accept his offer of a lift.

I have tried very hard to remember how it was that Mother and Father didn't tell me where Bell was going or why she was going there. I cannot be quite sure that I really pressed them. It was difficult asking them straight out if she was at Grandfather's because Father wouldn't let us talk about him; but I felt so desperate, and somehow I couldn't get Mother on her own, that I had to do it. The result was disastrous. Father flew into a terrible rage which quickly had me, in spite of my resolution to get an answer, in angry, futile and helpless tears.

"Your sister's gone away for a rest," he shouted. "There's nothing peculiar about that, is there. Now let's hear no more about it. D'you understand that? No more about it!" And he brought his hand flat down on the table with a terrifying crash.

I think Mother was near tears, too. "Come along, dear," she said. "Your Uncle and Auntie May are coming in for cards tonight. Help your Mother do some nice things for them."

There was no Maidment when they came, but Mr. Leaf turned up as usual. He made me feel very guilty when he asked me about my studies, and his "Well it's only a month or two now, Arthur," paraded before me the weeks when I might have had my nose in my books. "Pretty stiff opposition, they tell me," he added; "but what you've got in your head is yours, and they can't take it away from you."

What I had in my head just then I would have gladly parted with.

147

I was allowed to play 'Newmarket' until ten o'clock. I won, or was allowed to win, eightpence. Uncle Hector gave me five shillings when I went up to bed. Mr. Leaf slipped me a half-crown when he went to wash his hands before supper. They talked about the weather, simnel-cakes, soft-corns, home-made beer, the date of Good Friday, onions, Major Birkitt's cricket, the way Miss Partridge washed the surplices, Mr. Dighton's new errand-boy, Mr. Gedge's old clothes, cricket, Elsie Catcher, indigestion, Seville oranges, celery, horse-manure, sprouts, Queen Mary, Patsy Hendren and Elliman's embrocation. But nobody mentioned Bell.

When I went to bed I resolved to think out what I should do. They say that thinking is a process of comparing notions and rejecting the misfits until at last you are left with what is wholly acceptable and credible. With my head on the pillow I rejected and rejected until at last I was left in no doubt how I should act. Mr. Benskin had said I should soon be saying goodbye to one of the family. Bell had gone the day after he said it. That proved it had all been planned. Father had refused to say anything when I asked him if Bell was at Grandfather's. That proved she was, because Father would never bring himself to admit to being obliged to Grandfather. If Bell wasn't there he would have scorned the idea that any daughter of his would accept hospitality from that man.

I saw that everyone except me knew about Bell. I would have to find out for myself. I would go to Grandfather's. That was the thing to do. Sleep came easily when I had made up my mind.

I put it about at breakfast, without actually telling a lie, that I shouldn't be coming straight back after church. I even managed to eat a big breakfast—not that I tasted anything—hard as it was to swallow. I was 'wrapped up warm' by Mother when Willie called, and nearly blurted the whole thing out to her when she gave me sixpence to put in the collecting-bag because she didn't feel quite well enough to come to church herself. Willie inadvertently saved the day for me by bringing Mother a little bunch of snow-drops. It was a cold, damp, miserable day, and how any flower had managed to put in an appearance was the topic they discussed while I swallowed and fought back tears and looked the other way.

The service could hardly have been less conducive to the aspirations of a renegade had Mr. Benskin known of my intentions. It is true that it began with the sentence, 'Remember not our offences nor the offences of our forefathers', but I felt that the plea would have been better addressed to my earthly father. The psalm for that morning wanted to know Wherewithal shall a young man cleanse his way; one of the hymns (usually a favourite of mine) contained the accusing line, 'Perverse and foolish, oft I strayed'. I felt far more perverse than foolish in what I was going to do. Mr. Benskin's sermon was (it would be!) about Duty, especially to those in Authority; how we must submit to Authority; and for many of us, especially the younger ones, the prime Authority was to be found under God, within the Home.

It was during the sermon that I managed to convey to Willie, who sat next to me, that after the service I was pushing off to see Grandfather. I didn't tell him why, but I did tell him not to spread it round. I somehow did not want to sever all connections with home: I think I looked upon myself as an explorer departing for the unknown. If I did, as it turned out, there was some justification for it.

Mr. Benskin wound up with his second-favourite topic—purging in the refiner's fire, dross, lees, being burnt away, smashed like a potter's shard (we always enjoyed the bit about the potter's shard even if we did not know what he meant by it), refined seven times seven, cast out like useless potsherds, burnt like tares in the oven.

After that we sang 'The King of Love my Shepherd is', and I went on my way.

I walked and walked. There was a thin drizzle in the air and a coat of wet mud on the road. I began to feel I was getting nowhere. I was not going to turn back, but going forward began to seem pointless.

Salvation came in the form of a smart pony and trap, all yellow and black, driven by a short, stern-looking man with yellow leathery gloves and a flat bowler hat like Grandfather's. He pulled up the splendid bay with a swift splashy clatter.

"Where are you going, son?"

"To the station, Sir."

"So am I. Want a lift?"

"I don't mind."

"Nor do I," he said cheerfully. "Gee-up, Drummer!"

Wondering what I had done wrong, I watched the glistening chariot as it spanked ahead and out of sight. It seemed more lonely than ever after that, but I whistled (as best I could, for no part of whistling comes easily to me) and walked in the middle of the road, as did all determined foot-travellers of fiction. It was this

149

that nearly ended my expedition. I had rounded a sharp bend when a slithering screech from behind spun me round. An open touring car had come to a stop a foot from me. Rising from the driving seat to address me was a young man in a leather coat. He wore his cap back-to-front; goggles concealed his eyes; a knotted Belcher guarded his neck. "Where the Hell d'you think you're going? That's a bloody silly place to walk! Might have rooted you right up the arse!" Then he asked me where I reckoned I was off to.

He told me to hop in. Above the noise of the engine and the swish of the wet air I learned that his name was Basil Dicken, that the car was an Angus-Sanderson, that he was an apprentice motor-mechanic, that he didn't like the disc wheels because in a high wind you didn't know where the hell you were, that he was on his way to have dinner with his girl's family, that he always bought his oil by the drum, at Gamages, that his girl's name was Ivy ('same as sticks to the wall', as he put it), that he'd got the car cheap because the chassis was bent, that once you drove an open car ("the hood's a bloody nuisance to put up, anyway") you'd never want to drive anything else, that he'd put me down on Grandfather's doorstep in a brace of shakes.

Watched as I was I could not help admiring the calm way in which Auntie Lucy took the handing-over ceremony. But once the Angus-Sanderson, having refused a nice hot cup of tea, was on its way back down the drive she was all questions and scolding and pity and warmth. Grandfather was upstairs in bed 'with a little cold on his chest'; I could not go up until I had been dried out and given a nice hot drink. The nice hot drink was milk—a drink I loathed because of the smell and the skin. (Grandfather called it 'tepid puke'.)

I had known that Bell was not there as soon as I entered the house.

Grandfather in bed looked much smaller than Grandfather downstairs. He didn't scold me, but just said, "You'll have to be put in the Bloody Tower if you do things like this"; whereupon Auntie Lucy said, "Now Father!" and left us alone.

It was much easier telling him all about Bell than I thought it would be. He seemed to know what had happened though I didn't see how he could. When I had told him everything he said, "Your mother and father know what's best, Arthur, old chap. Doesn't do for a young feller to go against his mum and dad."

"But where's Bell? Why's she gone?"

But he didn't really tell me. "We all need a rest sometime," he said. "Look at me, poor old codger."

"Is she ill, then?"

"No, not ill, Arthur, old feller. Just wants a bit of a holiday."

Then he said I was a good brother to want to find her, but there were awful penalties for what I'd done, and if I'd gone anywhere else but there it might well have been twenty strokes with a bull's pizzle. He'd known families split right down the middle by sons who didn't trust their mums and dads, and he wouldn't be surprised if the peasants didn't rise, take to the hills and start rick-burning because of what I'd done.

Auntie Lucy came up with supper on a tray for both of us. There was a poached egg for me, a piece of toast with the crusts cut off; Grandfather had to be content with a boiled egg. He confided in me that he had been hoping for haddock. Auntie Lucy confided in me that Grandfather had been hoping for haddock, but fish in bed wasn't nice, and in any case it would make the house reek, and she wasn't going to have that on a Sunday. Grandfather's tray was wheeled under his nose on an ungainly trolley that he called a literary machine; mine was placed on a low square lidded cabinet beside his bed. He made the most of his egg, drawing an Indian's face on it with a heavy oval pencil before scalping it with round, spiked scissors. After my egg there came, for me, but not for Grandfather, a heavy wedge of home-made simnel cake. Grandfather said it was 'a bit previous' and that Auntie Lucy had 'jumped the gun', but he accepted a piece of mine after extracting from me a promise that I wouldn't let on.

It was quite dark outside by the time supper was finished and there came over me the feeling of half-scared melancholy that Sunday evenings usually brought. It wasn't that I was a long way from home, though that was beginning to weigh heavily on me; it was the affinity which Sunday evening in my mind had with Death. And still has. I always felt it at evening service when the gloom of the church was only emphasised by the feeble yellow of the pendent lamps. And hymns like 'Abide with Me' and 'The Day Thou Gavest' did nothing to push back the dark shadows of apprehension which were the fringe of despair and terror.

I wanted to go home; but I didn't like to say so. I had got myself to Grandfather's and, daunted as I was and quite without knowing how to do it, I considered it up to me to take myself away.

I felt a kind of panic creeping up from my stomach to my throat.

"I expect you'd like to be getting home, Arthur, old chap," said Grandfather. Then he coughed and coughed and coughed until his face was purple and his eyes full of tears. He reached for a covered cup on his bedside table and shot a string of spittle into it. He seemed to feel better after that, though he suddenly looked drained of blood and had a kind of haunted, scared look.

"Are you all right, Grandfather?" I said. I knew it was a silly thing to say, but I couldn't sit there in silence. He spat again severing with his little finger the thread of spit that dangled from his lower lip. "Right as rain," he said. "Right as rain." Reaching for his gold watch and chain on the bedside table he dragged them on to the turned-down sheet. At one end of the chain (the hermit's jewel was in the middle) was a neat open-work cylinder in gold; he fiddled at this with his big brown, horny thumb-nails; there was a pinging whizz and a sovereign lay on the eiderdown.

"Your aunt will see to you, Arthur, lad," he said. "Buy yourself an Easter-egg, eh? I'd like to come down, but when you're suffering from galloping dandruff and the chronic oopazootic you don't feel very ignifocious. P'raps you'd like to take the trays, down, boy: nothing more lowering than dirty plates." With his hand palm-down he pushed the sovereign towards me with his finger-tips.

When I got downstairs Hatch was waiting to drive me to the station. Auntie Lucy dressed me, regulation-fashion, for the Arctic and gave me a packed basket to take to Mother. I was to keep it the right way up because there was some nice beef-tea in it, and there was a packet of sandwiches and cake, the one in grease-proof tied with string, for me. Hatch would see to my ticket. I didn't mind going in a train by myself, did I?

I forgot to say thank-you for having me.

Hatch was most affable. It was bitterly cold in the open trap, so he wrapped me round in the big plaid rug and showed me how to blow on my hands and beat my arms round my body. He said that on really cold days when he had a 'long waiting job' to do he poured a spoonful of whisky into his boots. I offered to undo my packet to share my cake, but he, most un-Barkis-like, refused, saying that Mrs. Hatch would have a nice piece of cold brisket waiting for him when he got back.

Like Mr. Bagnall at our end, he was on intimate terms with the entire station-staff at his. They were all glad to see him; all assured him that the young shaver wouldn't come to no harm.

The young shaver was glad to remember the assurance as he jolted slowly towards home in a cold, empty carriage.

Mr. Bagnall was there to meet me. Though it had been worrying me terribly how on earth I should get home from the station I never thought to ask him how it came about that he was there. Nor did I ever hear. It seemed to me quite natural that he should be, and he did nothing to make it seem otherwise. I see now that I should have thanked him for being there, should have said what a shame it was that he and Prince should have had to wait for me; but, of course, I didn't think of it.

Mr. Bagnall asked me if I'd like to ride outside with him. There was just room for us both up there even if the only barrier between me and a six-foot fall over the side was the tall whip swaying in its socket. When I had climbed up he drew the big rug off Prince's back to wrap me like a mummy. It smelt of hay and manure and boot-polish, but had in it all the deep warmth of Prince's big body. "Better not tell your ma you was up 'ere with me," said Mr. Bagnall. " 'Ave a fit! And I'll tell you another thing, young Arthur, while we're on it" (I wondered what we were on), "something to last yer all yer life: never say 'I'm sorry if I offended you,' like, or 'I apologise if I let yer down,' like, because that isn't no apology. Say 'I'm sorry I hoffended you', or 'I apologise for poking me finger in yer eye'—that's a real apology, that is. Get the idea, Arthur, lad? No hifs about it. No givin' with one 'and and takin' back with the other. See?" I said I saw, and he said he'd tell me something else while we were on it. "Yer mum an' dad," he said, "know what's what. And when a young feller's mum an' dad 'ave got the reins in their hands it doesn't do for a young feller to say 'e thinks their going arsey-versey. Yer see, in a manner of speakin', you're only an apprentice-boy—know what I mean?—you're learnin' the trade. And do you know who yer masters are? They're yer mum and yer dad—and yer sister, too, I dare say. And when you're only an apprentice, Arthur, lad, you don't go tellin' the bosses 'ow to run the business. Do you get me? You've got to shrug yer shoulders, Arthur, lad, and say to yerself, (and I know you'll take it right), 'when the grown-ups are on to something important you've got to let 'em get on with it.' In other words, Arthur, lad, as the poet says, 'never nudge yer Granny when she's sitting on the po'." Thereupon Mr. Bagnall called upon Prince, who had taken his monologue as an excuse for dawdling, to come on and smarten things up.

The stars were shining brightly, and Mr. Bagnall showed me Orion's belt and the Little Bear. He said he'd like me to clap eyes on Mercury, but reckoned that it would be a night or two before Mercury poked his nose in and reported for duty. "Bit shy, Master Mercury, this time of the year," he said. He then added, "Yer Uncle Hector's had a bit of a do today."

I did not know why he associated shy Mercury with Uncle Hector.

"Come over all peculiar," said Mr. Bagnall. "Locked hisself in the store-room. Wouldn't come out. Said he'd had enough. Shouldn't say nothing about it when you get in."

"Why did he do that, Mr. Bagnall?" I said.

"Don't know," Mr. Bagnall replied after a long pause. "Something the Major said about the cricket next summer. Upset yer uncle. Went all peculiar. Don't you say nothing. Yer Mum and Dad 'ave got worries enough—what with your little capers an' all."

"Are they very cross, Mr. Bagnall?"

"They're yere Mum and Dad."

"What does that mean, Mr. Bagnall?"

He seemed at a loss for some time, and we thumped and rumbled along to the smart iron slap of Prince's shoes as if my question had muted us both.

"It means," he said at length, "that . . . well, it's like this, I reckon: it means that being yer Mum and Dad they've got every right to cut up a bit rough; it's their perogative, as you might say. At the same time it doesn't mean there's any ill-feelin'. They're only a bit ratty, as you might say, because they've got 'igh 'opes in you and want you to do well for yerself. So in a way, if you see what I mean, the crosser they are the more you can tell 'ow much they care for you. When you want to start worryin', Arthur, lad, is when they don't give a brass farthin' where the 'ell you are or what the 'ell you're up to. That's when. See?"

There was supper waiting for me when I got in. There was no questioning. They seemed to know everything I had done, and why I had done it. I do not remember whether Mr. Bagnall came indoors or whether having lifted me down he left me on the door-step. I know I did not at the time thank him for bringing me home.

Mother got it all over and done with when I had got into bed. She had put the big stone hot-water-bottle in already, and presently she came up with the camphorated-oil bottle. "Skin a rabbit," she said, as she unbuttoned my flannel jacket. Then she made me hoist the hot-water-bottle from the bottom of the bed so that she could warm her right hand on it. Soon she was smoothing and rubbing, smoothing and rubbing, with the heavy camphor smell gliding into my nostrils.

"You mustn't worry yourself about Bell, dear. I expect she'll be writing to you soon. I got Willie to take a note to Mr. Dyball about the evening service. Your father's a bit worried about Uncle Hector. He hasn't been very well today. You go to sleep now, dear, and we'll talk about it all some other time."

Soon she buttoned my jacket and drew the bed-clothes up over my shoulders. I felt very sleepy, but I remember she kissed me before she blew out the candle. I thought she had gone, but it was a long time before I heard her treading softly downstairs. She left the door ajar.

I remember parading in my mind all the events of the day, but whether I was trying to, or trying not to, I do not recall. I got up to the time when Mr. Bagnall was telling me about the stars (though I must have skipped some parts of the day). It came over me then that I hadn't achieved very much, but all I could think of then—it kept going over and over in my mind—was a piece we had learned for Mr. Selby the week before.

> Our bugles sang truce—for the night cloud had lowered,
>   And the sentinel stars set their watch in the sky;
> And thousands had sunk on the ground overpowered,
>   The weary to sleep, and the wounded to die.

I felt numbered among the weary, if not the wounded, but it was a long time before sleep came to me. When it did, I was riding behind Prince with Mr. Bagnall. With his whip he was pointing at the sentinel stars.

XV

THE BEGINNING OF the Easter holiday brought *The Crucifixion*
nearer. It was said that Mr. Benskin was against having it on Good
Friday—until he was asked to name a better day. People wouldn't
come to the three-hour service, he said, with that in the evening;
but he was finally persuaded that the Easter Offering might come
to no harm through the added attraction on Good Friday. At least,
that is what Father said had happened. He claimed, and made it
sound a powerful merit, that as regards Church he was himself a
Christmas and Easter man, so I don't know how he became privy
to the forces at work on Mr. Benskin. Not through personal con-
tact, I am sure, for Mr. Benskin was somewhat scornful of those
who came to the Lord's Feast 'only when there was something
special on the menu'. 'Mahogany guests' he called such people,
though I didn't see why.

This holiday, too, there was Work. School work. Mr. Gentleman
was going away to Ostend for ten days, so I'd have to 'Keep my
end up' until he got back. Mysterious powers had been busy: Miss
Ednay informed me that the Headmaster hoped I would work hard
during the holidays; Mr. Selby sent for me on the last day of term
and packed my satchel with books—Lamb's Tales, *The Last of
the Mohicans, The Moonstone, The Mill on the Floss* and a fat,
heavy (though 'Abridged for Students') *Decline and Fall of the
Roman Empire*; Mother told me that Mr. Leaf had arranged for
me to work in the College library. He would be giving it a good
spring-clean so I shouldn't be in anybody's way up in a corner. I
was not dismayed that no one had said precisely what I was to
work at; in fact it never occurred to me that anyone should.

Nothing more had been said about Uncle Hector since the
Sunday when he had come over all peculiar. I had forgotten his
peculiarity until on the second day of the holiday Mother told me
I was to go and have dinner with him and Aunt May. Then, fearful

of how I might find him, I asked Mother if he was still funny. She would have none of it. I wasn't to say anything about it; not a word; not a single word. Did I understand?

Aunt May was busy in the kitchen when I got there. She started me chopping parsley on a board, but at length said she could do it herself in half the time and I should find Uncle in the store-room at the back.

Everything about the store-room was exciting. It might have been the sight of so many household things grouped together in plenty—a scrubbing-brush on its own is not remarkable; half a gross of them on a shelf is a wonder—it may have been the smell.

The store-room door was open. Maidment smoking a cigar was sitting on a crate of Lifebuoy soap; Uncle Hector was dabbing expertly at a cricket ball in a sock suspended by a length of sash-cord from a bacon-hook in the roof. His tongue was between his teeth. He did not appear to be breathing.

"I don't reckon it's the Major," Maidment was saying. "He's got to do what the committee tells him to do."

Uncle Hector lowered his bat and left the ball swinging. His breath came out in a long hissing escape. "Committee!" he said. "Bloody committee! He can do what he likes, and you know it. He doesn't need a committee to tell him what to do and what not to do. Committees are very useful sometimes—to hide behind." And he brought his bat smartly across to the swinging ball to send it up among the bundled candles on a top shelf. "For some reason, though God knows what, he doesn't want me to play. That's the long and short of it. He daren't tell me to me face, so he says it's the committee's decision."

"No one said it was a bloody decision," said Maidment. " 'Recommendation' was the word. You said so yourself. That doesn't mean bloody decision."

"It's the"—and he thumped the ball again—"thin edge of the bloody wedge. And you know it."

Uncle Hector drew in a long breath. There was a silence, and I thought I had better show myself.

"Hallo, young Arthur," said my uncle. "Here, take a dab at that. Get your eye in."

He put his heavy home-made bat into my hands. Maidment pitched his cigar-end out into the yard. "I expect I shall hear something," he said. "Let you know."

"It's his own ground, isn't it?" said Uncle Hector. "He doesn't have to have a committee to tell him who plays on it and who doesn't."

"Let you know," called Maidment. "With this bloody weather, who wants to talk about bloody cricket!"

We had an uneasy dinner. To say we ate it in silence would not be quite true. Uncle Hector champed and clicked and hissed away; Aunt May kept pointing out on my plate the pieces I had missed or (how did she guess?) looked like missing. When we had reached the stage when I was desperately preparing myself to take into my mouth the remnants of veined cabbage and wax-like fat, and when Uncle Hector had cornered all the fugitive pieces on his plate for a final onslaught, Arnold came in. He didn't want dinner. A bit of rhubarb tart would do for him. He had just seen Dr. Matson leaving our place. Did I know he was there?

No, I didn't know. But now I knew why I had been sent out to dinner.

I couldn't eat any more. I wanted to go home. If Dr. Matson had left, it wouldn't matter if I went back.

When I got home Mother was upstairs resting. I didn't wait to see if Father was going to tell me that the doctor had called, but asked him straight out. "Your Mother has got to take it easy," he said. "The doctor says she's got to rest up all she can, then later on they may be able to do something for her."

I wanted to know what that meant, but all Father would say was that the doctors were wonderful-and-clever these days and it wasn't like the old days when he was a boy, and he and I would have to look after Mother, wouldn't we.

This was the moment to ask why Bell couldn't come home and look after Mother, but somehow I couldn't bring myself to ask just then. Looking back on it I can't see how my activities or those of Father changed in any way at all in the process of our 'looking after' Mother. She went up to rest on the bed every afternoon, but she made the bed first. She had regular if skimpy meals, but she it was who cooked them. The housework was never allowed to get on top of her, but she it was who scrubbed and dusted. I shook mats or dried plates or carried the cinders out into the yard, but I had always done that. Father carried in the coal-bucket or lifted the household-steps, but that was nothing new. Mother was always up before I was. When I came down the fire was bright in the kitchen range (and who black-leaded that?—I never saw it lustreless; I never saw anyone polish it), the breakfast table was laid, the porridge was gently erupting in the saucepan.

Mother, indeed, gave me little opportunity to help her. Except on Saturdays and Sundays I was sent off, best suit, at nine o'clock to the College library. Mr. Leaf was waiting for me on my first visit. It was rather like being in church: he spoke in a hushed voice. I trod reverently on the plum-coloured drugget.

I was led to a huge leather-topped table in a niche behind a book-stack. It bore two pewter ink-pots with wide circular aprons, and a yellow duster. The chair I sat on was heavily upholstered in buttoned plum-coloured leather; my feet scarcely touched the ground.

"If anyone comes—anyone who is anyone," said Mr. Leaf, "just pick up the duster and start dusting the books. They won't say anything. If you want to wash your hands it's through that green door over there." And he shuffled away to the neat piles of books he had on a table near the entrance and himself set to work carefully fanning through their leaves and dusting them meticulously. I couldn't start work at once, even if I had known on what I was to begin. I looked around me.

I was in a huge book-lined box. There was an inviting spiral stair-case up to a gallery; neatly labelled in old-fashioned lettering touched with gold-leaf, were mahogany book-stacks on whose top glimmered trophies in silver, goblets and mugs and urns. There were flat glass cases enclosing faded parchments or old books held open by taut green ribbons. There was a tremendous brass chandelier whose shining orb mirrored in fascinating curves Mr. Leaf's stock-in-trade (for I somehow thought of all the books as his). I wondered if Mr. Leaf had to polish that brass, and, if he did, how he got up there to do it.

I opened Mr. Selby's *Decline and Fall*. I found that abridgement was the only concession made to students: to me any one page seemed like any other, though here and there I found myself unable to skim or skip. The sentiments of the Primitive Christians concerning marriage and chastity. Sedition and massacre of Thessalonica, A.D. 390; the Revolt of the British army A.D. 407;—such cases caused me to pause, but I could not guess Mr. Selby's intentions. Did he mean me just to read the whole thing through? Would some great principle of history emerge? Was this one of Mr. Selby's famous 'things you ought to know about'? You ought to know about certain things, said Mr. Selby—and he said it more than once—whether you like them or not.

I did my best with *Decline and Fall*, becoming quick to find the bits about sudden death, both public and private, but I certainly didn't read it all. I moved on to *The Last of the Mohicans*, but quickly shied off that for *The Moonstone*. I would have managed that all right had not Mr. Leaf found me reading it. He shuffled off to return with *No Name*. "Worth two of that one," he said. So I began *No Name*; but I found myself enjoying it so much that I began to feel guilty.

Mr. Leaf wouldn't let me take the book home, but he considered I could 'look round the shelves' without 'making things awkward' for him 'if any questions were asked'; so on some mornings, yellow duster in hand, I looked round the shelves. I even climbed the spiral staircase. I even mounted the mahogany ladder and stood on its little carpet-covered platform to pull from the upper shelves undusted, uncut, unopened, undiscovered fugitives.

I was up my ladder one morning when the High Master of the College came in. With him—I had never seen one in black close to—was a Bishop. Mr. Leaf, ill-at-ease, but somehow unperturbed at the same time, contrived to give the High Master a kind of bow ("Good morning, Mr. Leaf") and to give me a kind of 'start dusting' glance. I dusted away with my yellow duster. The High Master gave me a close look. The Bishop wished me good-morning. And if I needed a spur to my studies, somehow that encounter gave it.

Though I had read some history (especially the chapter on the Causes and Results of the Civil War) and tried to do some Geography, I had done nothing in Mathematics since Mr. Gentleman went to Ostend. I tried, as I tried the Geography, but it seemed pointless. I was left disheartened if I couldn't do the sums; if I did them I couldn't tell if I had the right answers. So I was more than half glad when Mr. Gentleman came back. He called on the Thursday evening before Good Friday. His visit to foreign parts had made its mark on him. He wore a blue beret at a jaunty angle and he smoked cigarettes which, Father said later on, must have been made from French sailors' socks. But he did bring a pretty little bottle of scent for Mother and an enormous cigar in a long cedar box for Father. I got a pencil-sharpener shaped like the Eiffel Tower and the promise that in future all my lessons would be conducted in French.

Mother made a pot of tea, and though Mr. Gentleman said he couldn't stay, the grown-ups settled down comfortably. Willie called for me for choir-practice just as Mr. Gentleman, having drawn deeply from his cup and smiling all round, said, "And how's Bell, these days?" Mother said I'd better be getting along; it wouldn't do to keep Willie waiting, would it?

When I got home she asked me how the practice had gone. Had I been in time? Had Mr. Dyball been pleased? I didn't tell her that for once Mr. Dyball hadn't been pleased, because I desperately wanted her and Father not to miss Friday Night. The year before, Father had said that he didn't care a lot about it, that he had a bone in his leg, that he would think about it. He hadn't come. So I said the practice hadn't been bad, and hoped that Father would be in a good mood in the morning.

The chances were that he would be; for though we were not an Easter Egg family we were a hot cross bun family, so Good Friday, generally, of course, a gloomy day, always started well, thanks to the spicy, doughy, humid pile on the breakfast table. After that came a sombre wait, best suit, no larking about, no getting smothered up to the eye-brows, until it was time for Willie to call.

This time the day passed more slowly than ever. Mother spent the afternoon resting on the bed. Father inscrutably went out to see a man about a dog. I didn't dare ask if they were coming to church in the evening. It was easier to suppose that they were than to bear the disappointment if I knew they weren't. Willie called for me early and I left home without knowing.

Stainer's *Crucifixion* has been described somewhere as a second-rate but sincere little work. Perhaps Mr. Gedge secretly thought it was, but for us it had no equal and in stature it lacked nothing. Perhaps we should have said the same about *From Olivet to Calvary* if that had been the only oratorio we knew. As for sincerity—if Stainer was short of it, we, in our way, made it up, if you could call the uneasy, hushed, wanting-to-do-well air in the vestry a measure of sincerity. There was another unexpressed feeling, too—an urge to get the whole thing over and done with; not to have it out of the way for another year, but to see it safely through, to let it speak for itself again. Perhaps that was because we were nervous. I think we were nervous. Greeny said he was, and if he was—we were.

I daren't look too hard down the church to find Mother and Father, but somehow I knew they weren't there. I had told them where to sit—by the pillar where the tattered ensign, safely home from Zebrugge, hung on its sagging pole, where, according to Mr.

Dyball, we made a goodly noise unto the God of Jacob—but not all the lights were on in the nave and I had to wait for 'Cross of Jesus, Cross of Passion' before I could make sure. The congregation were supposed to join in then ("Be careful, gentlemen," Mr. Dyball had said, "or they'll carry you before them like a river in spate") so all the lights had to be turned on.

Mother and Father weren't there. But Mr. Bagnall was. Mr. Bagnall, in his blue suit and the fawn waistcoat with the amber buttons, the grey tie and the big gold watch chain. Dear Mr. Bagnall. My throat stiffened. No sound would come. I remember hoping (or was it praying?) that the Stainer was impressing him. I dearly needed the second-rate little work to warm Mr. Bagnall and make him doubly glad that he had come.

He was waiting for me outside the vestry. "Yer Mum couldn't manage it, Arthur, lad," he said. "Not feeling too sharp, y'know. Nothing to worry about, or anything like that, but best indoors on a night like this."

He didn't say what had brought him to the church. I had never known him to go before.

"Yer Dad went to see yer uncle. 'E's 'ad another bit of hoo-hah with the money—yer uncle, I mean."

Mother was downstairs in her dressing-gown when we got in. She wanted to know all about it: were there many there, was it cold in church, was Mr. Dyball pleased, what did Mr. Bagnall think of it?

I knew Mr. Dyball was pleased this time. When we did *The Crucifixion* he would stand by Mr. Benskin's desk and conduct. A friend of his from Hereford cathedral played the organ. You could tell by the look on Mr. Dyball's face what he thought of us, and there had been at the end that look of pride and humility, of confidence and thanks; the glow in his eyes, the quiet smile on his lips and the little nod.

Mr. Bagnall said it had been cold in the church and that Mother would have been chilled to the marrow had she been there. He had felt a bit of a caikaftina at first sitting there on his Jack Jones, but lots of people had spoken to him and Cyril Dighton and his wife came and sat next to him and he was glad he went. He had liked the piece, especially that bit—how did it go, Arthur, lad?—ah, that's it, "Is it nothing to you, all you that whatever it was." Very touchin'.

I wanted to go on talking about the evening, but Father came in and wanted to talk about Uncle Hector. So we sat round the kitchen fire, me with my cocoa and dripping, Mother with her Benger's and Father and Mr. Bagnall with whisky and hot water ("You couldn't get up an argument on cocoa," said Mr. Bagnall), and Father told us that Uncle Hector had more money missing and that Maidment had been in to get him to frank more stamps on blank envelopes and that Uncle Hector had told Maidment it was against Post Office Regulations but had done it all the same and that Maidment had said it had all been a mistake about not having Uncle Hector in the cricket team and that the Major was counting on him.

Father said he thought Uncle Hector was getting a bit tetchy again and Mother said I'd better go to bed because there was a lot to do tomorrow. Mr. Bagnall said I'd better come and see him in the morning; I might be handy in giving Dinah and Prince a rub down.

I didn't go to Mr. Bagnall's in the morning because Willie Waites called with the cards for the Cricket Club Subscriptions. I did remember to go down the yard to tell Mr. Bagnall I couldn't come, but he wasn't there. Nor was Dinah; nor was the cab. Prince stood shining in a dust-filled ray of sun that came in over the stable door.

Mother said that if I'd got to go round worrying people for money the least I could do was to look respectable, so I was subjected to a Sunday morning clean-up although it was only Saturday. She said we weren't to pester people nor were we to tell anyone what other people had given. Since they had to enter the sum on our card I didn't see how we could stop their knowing. We usually called first where we knew we might get the biggest subscription (Dr. Matson's)—"pour encourager les autres", as Willie put it. Mr. Benskin's half-crown was not likely to encourage anybody. There was Mrs. Clutterbuck, of course. Mrs. Clutterbuck who in the span of the year gave her guineas to Dr. Barnado's, The Shipwrecked Mariners, The Distressed Gentlewomen, The Royal National Lifeboat Institution, The Red Cross, The Diocesan Fund, The Organ Fund, the S.P.C.K., The S.P.G., The Mission to Seamen and to Miss Partridge who collected every Christmas for a Home for Donkeys.

But Mrs. Clutterbuck was very deaf. She had to use an ear-trumpet. Calling on Mrs. Clutterbuck was an ordeal. She didn't part easily with her guineas: she wanted to know where they were going, and she wanted to know who you were and how it came about that you were the one chosen to collect. She wanted to know how her last subscription had been used. And the trouble was you couldn't tell how much of your reply was lost and how much she caught.

The mistake was not to go to Miss Clutterbuck's alone. We had found that her speaking trumpet could accommodate only one speaker. This meant that if two of you went one had to stand by, a mere witness to the awful contest, and this, somehow, made the interview irresistibly comic—for us, if not for Miss Clutterbuck.

Katharine, Miss Clutterbuck's maid, let us in. In a way it was a pity she did, for whether it was in anticipation of what was to come, or whether it was that Katharine was not wearing her top teeth (which for size and direction bore favourable comparison with those of Miss Ednay)—we got the giggles.

Nothing could stop us. There were moments of explosive silence while we held our breath and tried not to laugh, then out it would come, inane giggling that nothing could keep back. What Katharine thought of it, I don't know. I was ashamed of it then; I am ashamed of it now. Willie and I tried looking at each other. We tried not looking at each other. It didn't make any difference. Even the unnerving business of waiting outside the shining mahogany door of Miss Clutterbuck's drawing-room could not quell us. There was nothing that didn't seem comic. There were brass bell-handles either side of the marble fire-place. I said to Willie, "I expect she was a tram-driver once." A stupid-enough remark, I suppose; but at the time it seemed rich with wit and set us going again.

It was my turn to ask for the subscription. Miss Clutterbuck, sitting gracefully in a velvet chair, made things easy to start with: she said she remembered us from last year. Then she wanted to know what we had come for. Then she seemed to muddle 'cricket' with 'ticket' and told us that when she travelled by train nowadays she always went first-class and she thought everybody else should, too, because it was so much nicer. Then she told us about her nephew, Hugh, who had built a railway in India. Then, when she said 'Hugh', I thought she was saying 'you', and when she said with tears in her eyes, 'I wish Hugh were here', I got completely lost and couldn't find any reply at all.

She must have thought I was saying something though, for she brought the bell of the big, black trumpet round and up towards my mouth. At that moment I caught Willie's eye.

"Spit down it," he said.

XVI

BELL'S LETTER CAME the day after Easter Monday. It's funny
how some things impress themselves on you: it was a warm
morning; I was out by our long, narrow flower-bed wondering if I
ought to tie the daffodil-leaves into knots. I remember having in
my head, just as you do a tune, the lines (Who wrote them?
However did I know them?):

> And throw sweet garland wreaths into her stream,
> Of pansies, pinks and gaudy daffodils.

You wouldn't have called our daffodils gaudy then or at any
time. They may have danced for Wordsworth. For us, at their
best they were haughty flowers. Now I thought their tired, stragg-
ling greenery wanted tying up, but I was no gardener; in fact I
was forbidden to do any weeding because I did not know the
weeds from the accredited flowers.

Mother came down the path to me. I remember she was wearing
a blue check apron with a pocket in it. "Look, dear, there's a
stranger. Just there. It's a celandine; the small celandine." To me
the flower looked like a buttercup. "There's a letter for you," she
said. "From Bell." And she took a folded envelope from her apron
pocket, yellowy-green like the leaves of the celandine.

It wasn't really a letter. It was a note which had been enclosed
in Bell's letter to mother, but it was sealed and addressed to me as
if she had been going to post it.

Dear Arthur, Are you being a good boy and looking after
Mother. I am having a nice time and people are very kind. I
have two type-writing pupils and I do a lot of sewing and things
so you see I am kept busy. How is Mother? Aunt Lucy said in
a letter that she thought she needed a good rest. Would you
like to write and tell me, Arthur. How is Tinker? Can you go
into my room and see if my little Birthday Book is in the top
drawer of the dressing-table. Mother will send it, or you can

send it yourself when you write and tell me how she is. Don't
worry Father with it. I had a nice letter from Grandfather. He
said you'd been to see him. I wonder if you had apple-pie!!!
Look after yourself, Arthur, and see that you wrap up when you
go out. How is Mr. Dyball? Don't forget to say about Mother.
And be a good boy. I'll buy you a nice prezzy when I come
home. Love. Bell.

It was a long time before I noticed there wasn't any address, and
longer before I realised that she hadn't really told me anything
about herself. I am ashamed to admit that I didn't at first see that
her letter was really about Mother.

It was two days later on the morning of the Choir Treat that I
saw for certain. And the moment I realised—'the moment of truth'
they would call it these days—I knew again the sickening, hot bile
of terror welling and curling from my bowels to my throat.

The Choir Treat was going to be a visit to the Waxworks in
Baker Street ("and if you want to go to the Chamber of Horrors
you'll have to pay for yourself") and then, for those who wanted
it, a concert at a place called the Queen's Hall. For those who
didn't fancy that ("it's not really for you small fry, but if you go
in you're not leaving until the end") there was the London Palla-
dium which was a music hall, though the music was not like the
music in the Queen's Hall.

I had never been to a proper concert so I had put my name
down for the Queen's Hall. Willie, who once went with his uncle,
said the best part was seeing all the violin bows going up and down
together and watching how the audience behaved. He said that
everybody sat quite still, looked suspicious and alert and yet all
dreamy as if they were thinking lots of sad thoughts. He said what
you must never do was clap in the wrong place. Everyone turned
round and stared at you if you did that.

We were to start outside Uncle Hector's Post Office at 12 o'clock
sharp. When Willie turned up, the first thing he noticed was that
my jacket pockets didn't bulge as his did. "Got your grub?" were
his first words.

Mother had made me liver-sausage sandwiches and packed them
in greaseproof and tied them with string. There was an apple, a
piece of lardy cake and a bar of Nestlé's milk chocolate in silver
paper. I had left them on the dresser in the kitchen. My only
words to Willie were, "Bag us a place".

When I got home, out of breath and with that feeling of near-panic that being late always gave me, I saw two gentlemen going into our house. One was Dr Matson and the other was a grave-looking man in a grey suit.

Dr. Matson's motor car was down the yard. I thought of standing beside it until they came out, but I wasn't brave enough to wait. I wasn't brave enough to go into the house, either, but hung about round the stables, terrified. I do not know what I expected. I felt weak and sick. I think I pledged myself to a life of religious devotion if only things could be all right again. I was bitterly conscious of the fact that I had not been much help to Mother. I would make up for it. I ached with love for her.

Dr. Matson and the gentleman were nearly in the car before I saw them.

"Hallo, Arthur," said Dr. Matson. "Shouldn't you be on the choir outing?"

The Choir Outing! And I had forgotten all about it. They would have gone by now. I didn't so much mind missing it, but they would have waited for me; Willie would have been mystified; they would feel I had let them down (which I had)—I didn't like that.

"Your mother needs a little rest and a tonic, Arthur. Happened to be passing with my friend Mr. Rice and thought we'd look in and see your dad. Glad we did, eh, Charles?"

Charles said he was glad.

"Don't let your mother work too hard, eh, Arthur. I told her we'd have her in hospital if you two men made her do too much."

Dr. Matson made it sound as if this was a promise, not a threat. The two of them chatted cheerfully as they backed the car out. They waved like old friends when it moved forward. It must be all right, then. Mr. Rice was Mr. Rice, not Dr. Rice. And it stayed all right for just forty-five minutes.

When I went in Mother was in bed. Father was boiling a kettle. I thought they looked strange, as if they'd been caught out at something; then I remembered that they must be surprised to see me there, and without telling them about Dr. Matson and the man, I told them about the packet I'd left behind and how I had come back to fetch it and missed the Treat.

They said that Dr. Matson and a friend of his had just dropped in for a chat. A very pleasant gentleman. We'd better have my sandwiches in Mother's room. She wouldn't be wanting any dinner, but she might have a glass of hot water and milk.

Just before one o'clock, a little table set up by Mother's bed with all the food on it, Father gave me the usual ten-pence-ha'penny and said he'd get me to pop along to Mr. Empson's for an ounce of Player's White Label. Mr. Empson was just locking up for dinner when I ran up to his door. He gave me a long-suffering look through the glass before ponderously unbolting, unlocking and letting me in with a ping.

"They tell me you've had Mr. Rice to see yer mum," said Mr. Empson. "Very clever doctor, so they tell me. He'll get her right if anybody can. Specialist, you know. They call 'em mister. Now that's a funny thing, isn't it?"

Not funny. Horrible. Terrible. Deadly.

It was on my way home with the tobacco that I resolved to call on Mr. Benskin in the evening. I could go to Mr. Gentleman for a lesson at six. I would go on to the Vicarage after that. I cannot remember wondering if it might be inconvenient to Mr. Benskin; I suppose I never thought of Mr. Benskin's having meals as we had meals. I should have done. Mr. Benskin always looked very well fed. His face was ruddy in a flecked kind of way. His cheeks bulged a little by his nose.

Nothing seemed to have changed when I got home and after dinner I found myself with an empty afternoon stretching in front of me. Mother was having a rest; Father was painting the fixtures in the shop. I offered to help but he said I'd only get smothered to the eyebrows and in any case he'd only got one brush. Mr. Bagnall was out, so was Dinah. I forced myself to go to my school-books.

It wasn't much use. I have often wondered why it is so hard to study. To study!—not even to study. That was too grand a word for it. To sit down and read and try to understand. That was all I was setting myself to do. And I couldn't do it. Mr. Gentleman must have done it, for he was a Schoolmaster and had letters after his name. But even Mr. Gentleman had sometimes found it hard. Often in class (so often that we no longer laughed) he had said, "It isn't work we don't like; it's work we don't like that we don't like," and set us something to do while he himself had allowed the day to drift away, gazing out of the dusty window with unseeing eyes.

There was Bell's letter, of course. I had to answer that. But somehow I couldn't bring myself to do it. The truth was, I couldn't bring myself to think of Mother's two visitors, let alone write about them.

I took Kennedy's Latin Primer (cunningly re-entitled "Eating Prime Beef" by a wit, with a pen and pen-knife) and settling by the fire in the kitchen set myself to master the third declension neuters. Kennedy was keen on neuters, but he was keen on all sorts of out-of-the-way things as well. The Romans, it seemed, had to be careful when it came to remarking on aromatic roots or tumours or spleens. But for Kennedy, the words were unknown to me in any language. Though I did not know it at the time, I was better off not knowing anything about tumours or spleens.

I had wasted two hours playing at work when Father, smelling of turpentine, came down from the shop to see if I'd like to make Mother a nice cup of tea.

Tea round Mother's bed was usually a great treat, but somehow this tea was an uncomfortable and almost silent meeting. Mother pecked at her Hovis and butter; Father drew steadily on his tea-cup; I didn't know what to say, and I didn't feel like eating any-thing. I was glad to collect up the things on the tray and take them down to the scullery.

When I got to Mr. Gentleman's at six there was a light upstairs. I was just going to knock on the street door (having long ago lost faith in the bell) when a blur filled its glass panel and it was almost wrenched open. Madge Ingles and I stood face to face. No sign of Mr. Gentleman. She did not look behind her, nor did she look up or down the street. What she did was to fling her arms round me and kiss my face all over. Between her sobs she got out a kind of moan, "Arthur. Oh, Arthur," she whispered. My satchel strap slipped from my shoulder so that the weight of the books was on her forearm. When she stood back to look in my face wet from her tears the satchel fell to the pavement. "Dear Arthur; I'll tell you one day," she said. And she hurried away from me: a purposeful walk breaking into a run. Not the way girls run with their heels flying out sideways, but a sharp, determined, compact run.

I didn't really count Madge Ingles as a grown-up or I would have put it all down to the unaccountable ways of grown-ups—suddenly baffling—that one simply had to accept. I didn't know whether I ought to go up to Mr. Gentleman's room or not. What I most wanted to do was to run after Madge, but even I could see she didn't want me. Probably didn't want anyone. I felt that Mr. Gentleman didn't want me either.

I made as much noise as I could going up the stairs.

Mr. Gentleman was in the act of writing. A sheet of writing-paper twice as large as anything we had at home was already one-third covered. "Hallo, young Andrew!" he said, closing the blotting-paper down on what he had written.

I was right. For once he did not seem altogether pleased to have me there.

I asked him if he wanted me to have my lesson some other time, but he wouldn't hear of it. He said that time was of the essence and that there was nothing like work. So when he had made two cups of tea ("Nothing like tea," he said) we set to on the theorem of Pythagoras. A lot of time was taken up by Mr. Gentleman's narration of his successful employment of the theorem to mark out a football pitch where none had been before and of someone's grand plan to mark out the Pythagoras diagram in white linen on the Sahara Desert so that observers on Mars would spot it through their telescopes and know that we were a thinking people, but in the end I really did know about squares on the hypotenuse of right-angled triangles, and agreed with him that not only would it be a jolly good thing if Pythagoras came up in my exam., but that working it all out and seeing the truth of it was jolly satisfying. When he saw me to the door he rather spoilt it all by saying, "You can see that the converse is true, can't you." I didn't, of course.

The closer I came to the Vicarage the less stomach I had for calling on Mr. Benskin. I rang his bell at length only because I thought I would despise myself if I funked it.

What I didn't want to happen happened. Mrs. Benskin came to the door. I thought at first I would have to explain everything to her. "I want to see your husband," I said like a simpleton (or like a policeman). She knew who I was. The Vicar was out. Would I like to wait? She expected it was about the choir. How was my dear mother? The Vicar wouldn't be long. I'd better wait in the study. She lit the gas-fire holding the match at arm's length and turning her face away.

When Mr. Benskin did come he let in a strong smell of boiling fish and a flood of yellowy-white gas-light from the hall. The first thing he did was to light the gas-lamp in the study; the second was to turn the gas-fire out.

"How's your father?" Mr. Benskin asked. Nothing about Mother. Nothing about the Choir Treat. But he might have made a worse start.

"It's about my mother," I said, nearly choking over it because the real reason for my coming flooded up into my throat.

"Ah, yes. Well, I hope?"

I was near tears and couldn't answer. My silence must have jogged his memory.

"Ah, no. Not up to much, I believe. Well, we're none of us getting any younger. No, indeed. Well, we're both busy people—what can I do for you?"

He tipped his head to one side, pouted out his lips and listened.

"Mother's not well," I said.

"Yes, yes. I know," said Mr. Benskin.

"I wondered . . . I wondered if you could help."

"My dear boy, I'm not a medical man. It wouldn't do for me to, to . . . There's a code of ethics, you know. Is your father not satisfied?"

I was out of my depth by this time. I wanted to say 'Jesus healed people', but Mr. Benskin's pout and his twitchy anxiety to be done with me seemed a long way from his warm assurances from the pulpit. So I didn't say anything. And the marble clock ticked away.

"Would you like a glass of ginger-beer?" he said, just as I had plucked up enough courage to remind him about Jesus. "Mrs. Benskin makes it herself. Much better than your bought stuff. Here, you have a look at this and I'll go and see what the kitchen department can do."

In my lap he placed a heavy red book—The Army and Navy Stores catalogue.

"Something in there for everyone," he said. Then he went out and after two attempts shut the door.

For a long time I sat quite still. Then I began to wonder if Mr. Benskin had forgotten me, and I couldn't just sit there waiting. Holding the catalogue to me I had a look round. On the upright piano was a copy of *The Entry of the Gladiators*; over the mantelpiece was a large print showing Christians (mostly undressed) being Thrown to the Lions. There wasn't really anything else to catch your attention. I tried the Army and Navy Stores catalogue, and of course Mr. Benskin was right. But somehow I couldn't do it justice. Even the pages showing pistols and rifles (could one really go into the Army and Navy Stores and say 'I'll have this Webley and that Remington'?), even these pages couldn't excite me then. I began to grow scared. I couldn't hear anything outside. I would have to open the door (Supposing it had jammed?) and call out.

The door opened with a sticky thud.

"Mr. Benskin had to go out," said Mrs. Benskin. "He left his tobacco pouch in the vestry." She set down a metal tray. "Mr. Benskin said you might like a cup of tea before you went."

For many reasons I didn't want a cup of tea. I thanked her. I drank it. I thanked her again, and in a minute I was on the front steps and the front door was shut. I had another look at the only memorable feature of the whole vicarage—the bell pull: a brass hand holding a short brass bar.

Mother was by the fire in her dressing-gown. Father had the table littered with invoices and fell across them dramatically when my entry caused them to stir like autumn leaves.

"There's cocoa for you in the kitchen, dear," Mother said. "I think I'll go to bed now. Perhaps you'll come and say good-night."

She was nearly asleep when I went up. There were three little bottles and a small glass on her bed-side-table. There used to be a prayer-book with ivory covers and a blue ribbon and a picture, of her mother, I think, in a velvet frame. These were now on the chest of drawers. She said it was a pity I had missed the Choir Treat, but she'd make it up to me. Had I seen Willie Waites? she asked—so I knew she was dozing a little and would soon be off.

But I didn't go to sleep easily that night. I thought of Mother and Mr. Benskin for a long time, wondering if Mr. Benskin would go on preaching about the Goodness of the Lord. If he did, and Mother didn't get better, I would know that as the Christian soldiers marched Onward I was going to be left behind. It was all very well for us to sing "Oh, taste and see how gracious the Lord is", and "Come unto me all ye that labour and I will give you rest" if it applied to everyone but me. And yet, and yet perhaps Mr. Benskin was not imagining a vain thing. All the bitterness I felt could not stand against the promise contained in one thing I had heard. It hadn't come from Mr. Benskin. It had come from Mr. Empson.

When I had gone to buy Father his ounce of White Label Mr. Empson had terrified me by what he said about Mr. Rice. "Very clever doctor, so they tell me. Specialist, you know. They call 'em Mister. Now that's a funny thing, isn't it."

But Mr. Empson had said something else. When he was about to shut the shop-door on me he had paused. "They tell me," he said, "your sister might be coming back to look after your mother."

And yet when at last I went to sleep it wasn't about Bell I dreamt, or of Mother, or of Mr. Benskin.

Madge Ingles was kissing me outside Mr. Gentleman's door.

She was wearing a little jacket with mauve flowers on it and tights like the Tupplers at the circus. Suddenly she said, "I must go now." There was a puddle in the road. She ran to it, turned a neat somersault in it, gave me a thin parcel wrapped in orange-coloured paper and ran off into the night.

XVII

MY SISTER DIDN'T come back to look after my Mother. No one at home so much as hinted that she might, so I supposed that Mr. Empson had told me what ought to happen rather than what was really going to happen.

What was going to happen was that Aunt May or Auntie Lucy would come 'to help out if anything happened'. Anyway, Father and I had to get Bell's room ready, not for Bell, but for Auntie Lucy or Aunt May. I didn't see how Auntie Lucy could possibly come. What would happen to Grandfather? I somehow never considered Uncle Hector's welfare.

I'm afraid we didn't prepare for Aunt May with very good grace. Mother from her bed told us what to do. The only thing we did thoroughly was the airing of the sheets. These we scorched so badly that we had to soak them in the bath when Mother was asleep in the afternoon. We had thought of dusting the top of the wardrobe, but when Father stood on a chair to inspect he said we'd better leave it or we'd only smother ourselves up. I don't think anyone wanted Aunt May to come.

The holiday, as all holidays do, rushed to an end. There seemed an age of leisure when a whole week remained; even three days seemed long enough. But with only two days to go there crept in a kind of panic tinged with regret for all the opportunities missed. When on the first morning of the new term we sang the plaintive 'Lord, behold us with thy blessing', I felt depressed and guilty. I had half-heartedly suggested at home that I shouldn't go back to school until Mother was better; but of course no one would hear of it. Mother surprised us by shaking off whatever it was that had put her to bed, and running the house as she had done before Mr. Rice called. On the last day of my holiday she had assured us that she was perfectly all right and that there was no need for anyone to fuss. Doctors didn't know everything. She even said I could ask Willie to tea.

In the great wave of relief that soaked warmly into me when Mother declared she was all right I told Willie about my visit to Mr. Benskin. What Willie said surprised me; amazed me. I think frightened me. This was a Willie I didn't know and at the time I wasn't sure that it was a Willie I ought to know.

"So you didn't get anything out of him?" said Willie.

"No."

"How did he take it?"

"As if . . . as if we were miserable sinners, I suppose. Didn't say much."

"Did he laugh?"

"No."

"Did he smile?"

"No. I don't think so."

"Christ never laughed and Christ never smiled," said Willie.

"How d'you work that out?"

"Well, did he?"

"I don't know. I never heard of it."

"There you are then," said Willie. "What did he look like?"

"Who?"

"Old Benskin."

I thought about this before answering. "Like a fish," I said.

"That's because he's got a weak face," said Willie. "Jesus had a weak face."

"How do you make that out?"

"Well, he had, hadn't he? Look at all the pictures."

"They're only pictures."

"Well, they're all alike," said Willie.

"Come off it, Willie," I said. But Willie wouldn't come off it. He said he'd thought about it a lot. If he became a clergyman, and he thought he might, he was going to be a leader. How many clergymen did you see who looked as if they could open an innings for England? Did Jesus?

Cricket did not come easily to me at the start of the term—in spite of the one-sided practice with Uncle Hector. The bowlers were always faster and the ball harder than I was ready for.

We took our cricket very seriously. Every break time we were out in the playground with a narrow bat, chalked stumps, and a ball which began its career as relentless leather orb and finished a floppy bundle of rags in a gaping case. We played in any weather. But on Wednesday and Saturday afternoons it was cricket with

Mr. Venables. And that meant boots dazzling with Blanco, an oiled bat, snake-buckle belt in the correct colours. For Mr. Venables was a Tartar.

We never questioned his methods or his decisions. We were reconciled to being given out L.B.W. or run out on a judgement made at an impossible angle or an absurd distance. After each game he gave a penny to the best batsman, the best bowler and the best fielder. No prize was more eagerly tried for nor more warmly treasured. I won only a single penny. I have it still.

At this time of the year, just about when the cuckoo began to call, Rogation Sunday, Uncle Hector entered into serious practice with the local club on the ground down the hill behind the church. It was many years before I learned that Uncle Hector was not a popular member of the local club. They fawned on him in success, but they found him a sight too high and mighty. What they didn't like was his lording it over them at net-practice. He didn't turn up until there were plenty of bowlers taking a turn; then he would take off his jacket, tie and collar, buckle a pad on his left leg, pull a spiked glove on to his right hand, and, completely out of turn, with his bat over his shoulder, march down to the wicket for 'a few quick ones'. No one had known Uncle Hector to help with roping off the pitch or marking out the crease or getting the numbers out for the score-board. As for standing umpire, Uncle Hector said he had a doctor's certificate expressly forbidding him to stand umpire. He would name half a dozen jobs that he would be perfectly happy to do instead (though somehow he never did them) but to stand umpire would in five minutes, less than five, three, clog up every bloody vein in his bloody legs. So, No, thank you; he wasn't going to stand bloody umpire.

I was particularly anxious to keep my uncle and Mr. Venables apart. Failure to do so would put too great a strain on my allegiance to each, for in my eyes each was a god. A god of cricket. And, everyone knew, they loathed each other.

I didn't want Uncle Hector to know that I admired Mr. Venables, nor did I want Mr. Venables to know that I had an affiliation with Uncle Hector.

Of course, Mr. Venables must have known all the time who I was, and what Uncle Hector was to me. But perhaps he didn't become involved, as it were, until that term began. I appeared, much to my embarrassment, that for one term I was a rather special case: I was going to Represent the School. I had a grave if one-sided interview with the Headmaster, who said I was carrying the school banner, that I mustn't waste time, must I, and that I must prepare myself for the ordeal ahead. He said 'ordeal ahead' with a kind of laugh as though he meant the opposite, and Mrs. Edney echoed it with a toothy bleat, but it struck my stomach cold. The Head said that to bring me up to scratch and polish me up I was to drop Scripture and do General Knowledge with Mr. Venables instead. The General Knowledge class, everyone knew, was for good boys who were good for nothing.

So I started with Mr. Venables in a little book-lined room at the very top of the school. It was not a library; it was the bookstore, and we sat, six of us, at a long table presided over by Mr. Venables and surrounded by faded and tired sets of Shakespeare, Collier's History, Kennedy, Hall and Stevens, and the pale blue Macmillan Elementary Classics. Behind Mr. Venables' chair was an open iron water-tank lagged in newspapers tied with string. The tank gurgled most of the time; sometimes it hissed a jet down into its rumbling depths; and when it did that Mr. Venables would cover his face with his hands and say, "By the waters of Babylon we sat down and wept."

I liked him because he always remembered why I was there, and though many of the pieces of advice that he gave were prefaced with frightening words like, 'when you go in front of the examination board', or, 'when you're under the microscope, as you're going to be . . .', he made me feel that there must be a point in everything we did. But I believe I didn't understand half the things he propounded. It was a long time before I found out what an examination board was: my mind had presented it to me as some kind of chess-board with numbered squares on it.

As for General Knowledge, we ranged about the continents and centuries as if time and distance had no meaning. One day we were with Galileo dropping weights at Pisa, another we were with Morris designing wall-paper. One week was devoted to gunpowder; the next was given over to church architecture. So it went on and on. I wonder now if Mr. Venables had a master-plan in his mind and taught to a pattern. If he did, I never discovered it.

It was Mr. Venables who told me when the Exam. would be: 'The fifth day of flaming June'. There would be questions to answer—Mathematics and English. There would be an interview with the High Master and a board of examiners. I felt as much indignant as frightened. Had I not been told, 'Nothing to write'?

I found out later that everyone had known the date long before Mr. Venables told me, and I felt more strongly than ever that 'They' knew lots more things, too, pertinent to my situation, but in Their grown-up way weren't going to tell me.

Mr. Venables took it upon himself (I don't know what Mr. Selby thought) to give me some of his maxims on Essay-writing, on a piece of rough paper. I had to write the last paragraph first so that the reader was left with my most striking thought ringing in his mind. The final words must be the very words of the title so that the examiner could not but recognise that I had stuck to the subject. "The scheme is," said Mr. Venables, "that your essay, like all Gaul, is divided into three parts. Very simple, my dear boy: you say what you're going to say; you say it; you then say you've said it." There also had to be somewhere in the essay as a kind of *bonne bouche* a quotation and a foreign expression. He asked me how many foreign expressions I knew, but I could think only of 'post mortem', and he said that that didn't really count.

In a moment of confidence I told him of Maidment's precept for judging works of art. Mr. Venables thought it 'rather negative'. He would, if I liked, give me something a little more constructive. "The yardstick for any work of art," he declared, "whether it's a picture or a book or Tit Willow, is to answer three questions for yourself: look at the thing, or read it, or listen to it, then say to yourself, 'What's he saying? How does he say it? Is it worth saying?' "

I tried very hard to do what Mr. Venables said, but I daresay I did not really know what he meant.

Whatever progress I made with Mr. Venables I did not think I was getting far with Mr. Gentleman. I found it hard to work with him. The evenings with their promise of summer called me to games with Willie Waites and the others. I felt that if I did not make use of them they would somehow never come round again. Perhaps Mr. Gentleman felt the same. His lessons, dropping all semblance of continuity, became patchwork. He began to speak of question-spotting and inspired guess-work. And the evenings became longer and warmer, and there was cricket to be played and rambles in the woods and fishing in the pond and building a hut and making a raft and catching newts and training for the School Sports and putting ha'pennies on the railway-line to change them into pennies.

We kept quiet about putting ha'pennies on the railway-line,

assuming, correctly, that parents would not approve and that the Railway Company might object. It was a simple sport: a long bike-ride to the cutting near the junction, a furtive Red Indian approach through the furze-bushes, a fearful reconnaissance against any nosey plate-layers, a short dash to the burnished rails and a long vigil from behind the squat tarred hut.

On a certain calm evening towards the end of May, this particular summer sport came to an abrupt end. We had reckoned we could lay our ha'pennies before the goods-train went through at six o'clock. Our reckoning was wrong; we were scarcely bending over the rail when we heard a trembling rumble. Without a word we pelted for cover. Too late. As we scrambled over the ballast the engine, with spats of steam, came grandly and terrifyingly round the bend.

We ran for the hut, but the fireman had spotted us. He yelled something from his footplate. He and the driver threw lumps of coal at us. We were sure they would stop the train to search the line. We cowered paralysed. The swaying guards-van whipped past us with its bull's-eye glowing a baleful red.

Willie recovered first. We mustn't come to the cutting again. We must separate. The railway police (I didn't know there were railway police) would be after us and they would be looking for two trespassers. We must go home by different routes. Ducking and weaving we made for our bikes. We separated at the first fork in the road. "That was lads, wasn't it!" was Willie's summing-up as he rode away. I felt slightly sick.

I made as wide a circle as I could, but in the end I had to enter P.C. Juniper's territory. I especially didn't want to encounter P.C. Juniper.

I did encounter P.C. Juniper; but when I did he was too busy to take me up. I encountered him at the bottom of Church Hill where the road divides.

By the big notice that told drivers to ease the reins and give the horse its head, Mr. Bagnall's cab lay on its side, a black, shapeless mass with white splintered spars sticking from it like spikes. A Foden steam-wagon, bull-nosed and ugly, rested steaming half over it, its sacks of flour spilling on to the road. Dinah lay on her side shrieking. Feebly kicking one hind leg and frantically dragging sparks from the road with her fore hooves, she was trying to pull herself from the touch of the still red fire-box of the wagon. Two men were trying to free her from the smashed shafts; P.C.

Juniper, with a heavy hammer, was trying to smash the iron away from her side. A group of helpless men and women stood mutely looking on. The clang of the hammer and Dinah's screams drilled into my head. The hiss of steam burnt into me.

I did not see Mr. Bagnall at first. There was a row of bent backs, coats off, braces stretching, over the fore part of the wreckage. Men were lifting, lifting. And failing, failing. They groaned in their efforts. They were in an agony of effort. One had his boot in a pool of heavy blood.

A man came down the hill on a bicycle with something under a coat across the handle-bars. He jumped off by P.C. Juniper, and someone near me, I don't know who it was, called out, "You go home, son," and then, "You, young Hook; you go home to yer dad, son. Somebody send that kid home, for God's sake." And then a woman behind me put her hands on my shoulders and turned me round facing her. And then she put her hands behind my head and drew my head into her breast and covered it with her fore-arms.

I heard a dull bang. Dinah's screaming stopped. The woman released me. "You go home, dear," she said. "Time enough for you."

But I couldn't move. Then men still bent over their terrible task, heaving and groaning. I watched stunned. Then P.C. Juniper came dragging the heavy iron-bound tail board from the wagon. He shouted to the men to stand clear. Reluctantly straightening they drew back while he tried to ram his lever under the wreckage. It was then that I saw Mr. Bagnall.

He was looking directly at me. Only his head and his shoulders were showing. He was all sideways, his head hard against the hub of the smashed wheel.

He was looking directly at me, and as he looked a change came over his face. At first his cheeks seemed to be forced up under his eyes, half shutting them. His mouth was a long straight line. Then came a wonderful smile, as soft and gentle and loving as I had ever known, but sad, somehow, as if he were smiling in defeat. I am sure he wanted me to go to him. I think I moved towards him. But then, staining his teeth and breaking from the corner of his mouth, came a burst of dark blood.

I turned and ran for my bike. Driving the pedals down with a strength I didn't know I possessed, I rode for home.

Aunt May was there when I got in. They didn't take any notice of me at first. There had been more trouble over the Post Office money, and Uncle Hector had had a turn, emptying all the drawers and cupboards and locking himself in the shop for almost an hour. As soon as he had come out, apparently quite calm, he had gone off to his store-shed and his captive cricket-ball and Aunt May had come to us. My entry did not dam her flow of words. It was that girl Elsie Catcher who was taking the money, and they'd have to give her marching orders before any more harm was done. Aunt May was just about to go through everything that to her certain knowledge Elsie had bought in the last six months when Uncle Hector opened the door and announced, "There's been an accident."

"It's Mr. Bagnall," I burst out. I couldn't stop the tears coming. Mother said, "Come to me, dear," and pulled me tightly to her.

They had known all the time. I don't know how they knew, but they did. Aunt May went into the kitchen to make a nice cup of tea while the others went through the events of the evening minute by minute.

Uncle Hector said they had got Mr. Bagnall out. He was on his way to the hospital. He didn't look up to much if Uncle Hector was any judge. Drinking their tea they talked about anything but Mr. Bagnall until they seemed to resign themselves to the fact that I wasn't going to bed early and I wasn't going to find Willie and I wasn't going to do anything that took me from Mother's side, and then, quietly and, as it seemed to me, hopelessly, they began to talk about the accident again.

All sorts of people called that evening; some just to look in to see how Mr. Bagnall was, some to stay for a cup of tea and a slice of bacon-and-egg pie to see how Mr. Bagnall was getting on, some to see if they could do anything, some to gossip, and some, subdued and fearful, who could scarcely trust their voices, to ask if we knew any more. No one said anything about Dinah, though I did hear some whisperings, and Father, going down to the stables to see how Prince was, said it wouldn't seem right not to have Dinah there. I didn't dare to ask.

By ten o'clock an uneasy silence had settled on everyone. There seemed nothing left to say about Mr. Bagnall. I had agreed to go to bed, had had my cocoa and a piece of pie, and was about to kiss Aunt May's turned cheek when Maidment arrived.

Although he brought no news (he had telephoned the hospital but they wouldn't tell him a ruddy thing) he somehow brought a whiff of relief and hope. He reckoned Mr. Bagnall was as tough as an oak barrel; lots of life in the old dog yet; it was wonderful what doctors could do these days.

As if to complete the card-party Mr. Leaf came in at half-past ten. He had seen a light and wondered if there was any news of Mr. Bagnall. He accepted a cup of tea and a slice of pie; he went out to wash his hands; he came back to his chair. No one seemed to have anything more to say.

P.C. Juniper walked in at eleven. Mr. Bagnall was going to be all right.

"The Sarge", said P.C. Juniper, standing stiffly in the doorway, "telephoned the porter at the hospital—an old mate of his, you know—and asked him for the real griffen."

The real griffen was that a nurse had told the porter that Mr. Bagnall would be all right.

Everyone relaxed. Father brought out bottles of beer and Mother knelt in front of the side-board to bring out the cherry brandy left over from Christmas. P.C. Juniper took off his helmet and undoing the stiff hooks of his collar sat in the best chair and stretched his cycle-clipped legs.

They began to tell stories of terrible accidents of old, Maidment and P.C. Juniper being restrained only because I was there. I was by then very sleepy, but I could not have enough of the buoyant air of relief and begged Mother to let me stay up a little while longer. Mr. Leaf reminded me of my studies; Aunt May said that when Arnold was studying he never went to bed late; Uncle Hector thought it wouldn't do me any harm.

I think I must have fallen asleep in the middle of one of P.C. Juniper's longer stories. I remember the beginning, how he was called in to deal with a sudden death, and I remember the end, ". . . and the jury brought in a verdict of death by tubercollosis after being hit on the bloody head with a crow-bar," but the middle was lost. Father gathered me up and Mother put me to bed.

Mr. Bagnall was going to be all right. P.C. Juniper had said so. Mr. Bagnall was going to be all right. I could sleep easily. Mr. Bagnall was going to be all right.

XVIII

MR. BAGNALL DIED next morning. The last words anyone heard him say were, "Tell the bees"; and no one knew what they meant.

It was thought better that I should not go to his funeral but go to school as usual. I played truant for the first and last time. I hid in the shrubbery by the lych-gate and then I stood outside under the big window near the pulpit until the service was nearly over. I saw the coffin carried into the church by four men in black, led, to my dull amazement, by Grandfather's Hatch who seemed to be in charge. I remember wondering if Arnold's paper would describe the little procession as 'Hatch. Eight Hands. W. Bagnall up.' I remember wondering who had chosen the hymn whose stirring hopeful sound reached me under the window—Winchester New. 'Ride on, ride on in majesty'.

Hatch, very black and subdued, came back to our house to tea, and so did lots of others who had been at the funeral. For the second time in the day he surprised me—this time by telling me, what no one else had told me, that he was taking me back to Grandfather's for a couple of days. I protested to Mother and then to Father, but was told it was 'all arranged' and that Grandfather, who had been a little bit poorly, was looking forward to having me and that Auntie Lucy had aired the bed all ready and that it wouldn't be a surprise if she hadn't baked a special cake, too. Mr. Gentleman had been told. Mr. Dyball had been told. Willie had been told. And now I was told. I would be at Grandfather's from that very night, Friday, until Sunday night, and then I could come back and work ever so hard for the exam.

So Hatch and I went back to Grandfather's that evening after a tea of ham and jam-tart, and in the train he told me that Grandfather had been in bed for a week and that there were lots of jobs I could do and that the way to stop a horse eating was to rub tallow on its teeth and that you could mesmerise a lobster by rubbing its back and that coffins were lined with pitch and that he had once seen his grandmother's ghost. But he didn't tell me about his thumb.

Auntie Lucy received us as if we were explorers back from Greenland's icy mountains. She gave us cocoa and ham and jam-tart. But she didn't ask about Mr. Bagnall.

I was allowed to go up and see Grandfather in bed. Auntie Lucy said he wasn't to be worried. He spoke in a funny, strained sort of voice. He had caught a chill, he said, by sitting too long under the ooperupus tree and then drinking out of a damp glass. Auntie Lucy had given me his evening tray—beef-tea and little squares of brittle toast, but he hardly touched it while I was there, saying it would fly straight to his stomach. "Now I wouldn't say no to a nice little bit of cheddar," he said, "and a nice little onion or two to go with it; and a nice little corner of crusty bread to keep them company." I think he wanted me to try my hand at persuading Auntie Lucy, but I suppose we both knew it was a waste of time to try. Grandfather consoled himself. "You can always think about it," he said. "Hoco, poco, stylo, smoko, cropickerumpus—bread and cheese, oh father." And he tried a piece of toast dipped in his beef-tea.

"I expect you think about your friends when you're over here with us?"

I said I liked being with him and Auntie Lucy.

"Ah, but you've got your own special pals, I reckon. I reckon you miss 'em. Who's your best friend?"

I told him about Willie Waites.

"Wish he was here, Arthur, lad?"

I said it would be nice to have Willie, but I didn't want to offend him and didn't keep on about it.

"He's not as far away as you might suppose," said Grandfather. "Now, that's funny, ain't it. You think that because you can't clap eyes on him or have a yarn with him tonight that he might as well be at the bottom of the sea, eh, lad?"

I suppose I did think that, though not quite as strongly as Grandfather put it.

"You've only got to think of people, wherever they are, and they come alive," he said. "They may be hundreds o' miles away; you might suppose they're gorners; but they ain't, y'know. If you think about 'em, they're alive in your head, just as if was a room and they'd stepped right into it. Now, you're probably thinking your poor old gran'dad has gone and got a screw loose. But you take your mum, now. Haven't seen her for three years or more, but, I'll tell you, Arthur, lad, she's as if I saw her yesterday. And why? Because so long as I think about her—and I do think about yer mum—whatever lies between me and her doesn't mean a thing. So don't you go and get thinking your pals are gorners just because you can't pass the time o' day with 'em. It's only that they're waitin' for you, all nice and comfortable, waiting for you to join 'em."

For a long time he stared straight ahead. I didn't like to say anything; indeed, I could think of nothing to say. Auntie Lucy came up and scolded him for pecking at his supper and me for hindering him, and made him eat it all up, but for two little squares of toast. She whisked the tray away and said she'd put a fresh hot bottle in my bed and I'd better join it before ten minutes were out.

When she had gone Grandfather said that the only way to treat women was to give way to them. He reckoned there was room even for the bossy ones. The country would go to the dogs he said if it wasn't for strong-minded women. The Bards would flee to the mountains and there'd be skeletons in the hedges. But he wished Auntie Lucy wouldn't treat him as if he were a disabled imbecile of six.

"Now, don't forget what I told you," he said. "When you think of all your pals tonight . . ." He paused for a long time. Tears sparkled in his eyes. When he spoke again it was as if he was choking. ". . . You can raise 'em up as if you had blown a trumpet. As if you had blown a trumpet, lad."

I was glad of the hot water bottle. The sheets were icy. You slid down between them as if they had been starched and you had been starched, too. I wondered if it would be all right if I put my vest on under my sleeping-suit, but decided that Auntie Lucy wouldn't like it. Before I went to sleep I tried to think of Mr. Bagnall, but I don't think I sounded a trumpet for anyone that night. I believe I did not stay awake long once I was warm. I dreamt about Madge Ingles. I told her I loved her. She said, very gravely, "I know." She didn't laugh.

On the Saturday afternoon Hatch let me help him with the horses and even let me harness the little cob, 'Dandy', to the trap for a spin before supper. In the evening Auntie Lucy and I played 'L'Attaque' after I had taken up Grandfather's tray of Benger's and brown bread and butter cut very thin, and placed it handy for him on the literary machine. He said he had had Benger's Fluid when he was six years old and he had loathed it then and he had loathed it ever since.

Auntie Lucy and I went to church on Sunday morning, but there was no choir so we said the psalms and fended for ourselves in the hymns. We had a box pew to ourselves, so unless we were standing up it was like having a private service, though I expect Auntie Lucy could see more than I could. Grandfather wanted to know all about it when we got home. All I could remember about the sermon was the text, "Let me build three tabernacles". I always thought of a tabernacle as a kind of side-board with long handles on it for carrying. I remember wondering why anyone should want three, but I couldn't very well tell Grandfather that. Anyway, he was nodding and dozing before I reached that part of the service. Auntie Lucy came up just as I was tip-toeing away. She roused him gently saying he had better say good-bye to me because I would be going soon after dinner. I don't think he woke up properly. He asked me how I was going to get home, and when Auntie Lucy said that Hatch would put me on the train, he said, "Aldgate East; Aldgate West; all get out." Without turning his head he groped with his right hand at the bedside table where his watch and chain and hermit's jewel and his gold sovereign-case lay. I think he intended to give me—give me what? A sovereign for Bell? My usual half-sovereign? But his hand slid feebly over the edge of the quilt and Auntie Lucy gently lifted it and tucked it inside. Then she took my hand. And so we went very quietly out of Grandfather's room.

Hatch put me on the train with a packet of ham sandwiches and a jar of beef-tea and six fat, brown eggs for Mother.

All the way back to our station I thought about Bell. I tried to think about Mr. Bagnall and about Grandfather and about the Exams.—for the truth was that I felt guilty about Bell and wanted to put her out of my mind. And every time my thoughts turned to her I felt a sick spasm shoot from my heart to my stomach, because I knew I had done nothing about her. It was true that no one had uttered her name, but then nor had I. I knew, in the train, that I had been a coward. Just as I had run away from Mr. Bagnall when he seemed to want me, so, as it seemed to me, I was running away from Bell when no one wanted her. Why hadn't I said to Auntie Lucy, "Where's Bell?" It would have been so easy. I comforted myself that I couldn't very well have asked Grandfather because he wasn't to be worried; but I knew deep down that I could have asked him. And I knew he would not have put me off. I suppose I was so used to the putting-off power of the grown-ups, or took it so much for granted that their plans were not to be questioned, that I held my peace. The only thing was, it wasn't my peace that I held. It was a feeble writhing at my lack of courage. Only when we got near our station did I begin to wonder how on earth I would get home.

The growns-ups had, of course, thought of that, too. Mr. Gentleman in Burberry and huge leather gauntlets was there to meet me. He obviously had a surprise for me for he said only, "Come along and see what I've got," as he propelled me through the booking-hall with a heavy gauntlet at the back of my neck.

Outside was an open Arrol-Johnston. We did not get away at once because at first Mr. Gentleman did something which made the car jump upwards instead of forwards. When, with screaming engine and slithering wheels, we did advance he spoke of overhead valves and circulating pumps and metal-to-metal clutches that were 'a shade fierce'. Nothing at all about Mr. Bagnall; and nothing about work until he put me down. "After Whitsun, young Andrew, we'll really have to buckle to."

Before I went to bed that night I took my flat torch and slipped out. Mr. Bagnall's stables were silent and unlocked. Prince wasn't there. Up in the loft the walls were bare. The clock had stopped, its weights hanging lop-sided on the floor. From their half cotton-reels hung his two whips. On their nails hung his three hats, the greenish bowler, the tarred bowler and the big top-hat in which he was wont to 'see them home'. It was the most melancholy sight I ever saw. I wasn't really afraid; but whether that was because Mr. Bagnall was a long way away or because he was very close I do not know.

It was Mr. Gedge's turn to preach when the next Sunday came. He talked about Mr. Bagnall, at least I think he did, though he never mentioned him by name. I think he wanted to speak of Mr. Bagnall but didn't want to offend Mr. Benskin by making it sound as if Mr. Bagnall had been a pillar of the church. I could think of nothing he had ever said to me to suggest that he was. He had once told me that the first man mentioned in the Bible was Chap I, and that the wettest chapter was the thirsty-first of Guinnesses, and that the most slippery happening was when Baalam went through on his ass, but I don't suppose that Mr. Benskin would have considered that these observations justified a mention, let alone a sermon.

Anyhow, Mr. Gedge went as far as he could. His text was a long one. Perhaps he need not have enlarged on it. I expect everyone knew what he meant. "And an highway shall be there," he quoted, "and a way. And it shall be called the way of holiness; the unclean shall not pass over it; but it shall be for those, the wayfaring men, though fools shall not err therein."

I saw Marcus Daveney on Whit Monday. We had a holiday. The College boys did not. They had a grand cricket match with the Free Foresters—or was it with I Zingari?—with the regimental band glittering through waltzes and 'Light Cavalry' and 'William Tell' under the lime trees, and lovely ladies drifting with flannelled escorts round the gay pennanted marquee. Willie and I, chewing grass stalks, watched from a safe distance.

We braced ourselves as a languid group floated our way. It was clear that they were not going to ask us to produce proof that we were allowed to be where we were; if they were intent on anything, they were intent on walking round the ground, from one neapolitan ice-cream back to another. Still, we sat very quiet and looked our most respectful.

A girl was speaking as they came up. She held the brim of her huge hat prettily with both hands. Her voice was clear and musical. "I've heard Marcus writes poetry," she said. "Not a bit surprised, m'dear," replied her father (uncle? brother? husband?); "he can do anything, that fellow. Pots of money, too. Favourite of the Gods, if you ask me. Byron without the game leg."

And while Marcus Daveney, on two sound, long legs, shuttled effortlessly between wicket and wicket, touching his bat down like a wand, I wondered yet again about Bell. I had left too much in the hands of the grown-ups, that's what it was. I hadn't questioned enough, insisted enough, acted enough. And now Time had stretched a skin over it all, a film like the film on top of paint in a tin, a film that would give a little if you touched it, but was best to leave if you didn't want messy fingers. Perhaps I had imagined too much. It seemed hardly possible that that dashing white figure out there had anything to do with Bell. Bell sending notes to the poet? Bell in the arms of the Favourite of the Gods? Bell, my sister, a shop-keeper's girl, kissing that Hyperion? I had imagined it. Bell had been ill. She had gone away to ease

Mother of the burden of extra house-keeping. That must be it.

Meanwhile, Marcus Daveney, no doubt fancy-free, moved serenely past his fifty (and applause rippled round the ground like the popping of a million ripe ears of wheat) into the uneasy bridle-way of the nineties. I did not hear Major Birkitt come up behind us. "Well, young Arthur," he said, "an innings your Uncle would be proud of, eh?"

Willie and I scrambled to our feet. I managed a kind of introduction for Willie, feeling an awful fool, until the Major shook Willie's hand. Up to that point I had been looking on the ground, noting, I remember, how the Major's pointed shoes glowed a rich tawny in the buff of the wiry grass, and how the crease of his check trousers made a sharp, precise vee at his ankles. At the success of my halting presentation I felt encouraged to take a little more in. The Major shone in the sun, his cigar-smoke was azure, his loosely knotted silk tie blazoned some élite band of cricketers. He turned to the game, his thumbs sticking out over his jacket pockets, his cigar waggling as he spoke. "Got something you'd like to see," he said. "Prince Edward Island, '64." I was out of my depth here, so I just waited. "But I'm coming right up to date," he went on. "Historic days, these" (I couldn't think why), "and I'm not letting many of 'em pass without a stamp properly franked on an envelope to show for it. I expect yer uncle thinks I'm a bit mad. You'd better tell him, young Arthur: the Mad Major's keeping tabs on History, eh? Make a fortune one day these stamps will. Mark my words. Good shot, Sir! Good shot!"

He clapped his hands slowly and heavily. Willie and I after a glance at each other, clapped our hands, too. I felt foolish applauding a stroke I hadn't seen, and suddenly I felt guilty, too, because I had meant to spend the whole afternoon studying, not assisting at someone else's triumph.

As the day of the examination drew near I began to get scared. I hadn't done enough work and I didn't know where to begin to make it up. Each subject I had to take seemed to expose great tracts unexplored by me. If I wasn't careful all the Georges, all four of them, merged into one. Pitt the Elder and Pitt the Younger united likewise. The trade routes passed through the Suez and emerged at the far end of the Panama. Nothing I could do would prove that triangles on the same base and between the same parallels were equal in area.

I was the recipient of much advice. I see now that the advice I needed was on what to study and what to leave out. The kind I got was more on strategy than tactics. Mr. Venables said I must 'read anything and everything'. Mr. Webster said I must study right up to the last minute, the last second. "Do what I used to do," he said. "Half an hour before the exam. take your book, whatever it is, and go and sit in the lavatory reading it until you hear the bell go. Then you go straight into the examination hall and write it all out." He did not know what terror struck into me by his use of the words 'examination hall'.

I even had advice from the Headmaster. Encouragement, rather. I was called to his study by Mrs. Ednay to be reminded that I was representing the School. Then he conducted me round the room stopping before each black-framed diploma and pointing out what it was for, how and why it had been awarded to him. Mrs. Ednay simpered in the background making 'Go, thou, and do likewise' sounds. We finally got round to the door, which the Headmaster opened for me. "There's a half-holiday for the School, Hook, if you don't let us down. Think of that. Good luck, my boy! See that your boots are clean."

A week before the exam. Mr. Gentleman showed his hand. "What you don't know now, you never will," he pronounced. "So what you've got to do is to give your brain a rest. Wash it right out. Don't do another tap between now and next Monday. I've fixed it with your Ma and Pa—next Sunday you're going on a refresher-walk with me. You're going to walk so far that you'll want to go to sleep standing up. And when you go into that exam. on the Monday you'll be as fresh as a daisy."

I did think of telling him what Mr. Venables and Mr. Webster had said, but he seemed so enthusiastic and so sure of his scheme that I didn't like to say anything.

Various exhortations came in as the week slipped away. Mr. Dyball sent a message to say I could skip choir until after the exam. if I wanted to. Uncle Hector said I was to get into the way of eating bigger meals or I'd never stay the bloody course. Aunt May brought round six Scotch eggs. Grandfather sent a sovereign via Hatch who came to take Prince away. My form-mates encouraged me as if I were an aristocrat about to leave them for the guillotine. Mr. Leaf gave me a copy of Tennyson's *Princess* bound in calf.

I simply could not accept Mr. Gentleman's advice. The knowledge that he was going to take up all my Sunday was enough to drive me to my books. Mr. Venables had added a rider to his dictum. "You must," he said, "read yourself full, and, when the time comes, write yourself empty." So I tried to read myself full; but while I was reading I was worrying about arithmetic; and while I was doing sums I was fretting about History.

Mother wasn't very well on the Saturday, but she got up in the evening to beat me a raw egg in milk and inspect the suit I would wear on Monday and to polish my shoes. She didn't get up for breakfast on the Sunday and I meanly hoped I could put Mr. Gentleman off on that account, but Mother said it would do me good to get away, and Father said he could manage, and Mr. Gentleman who appeared at nine o'clock dressed like a mountaineer said he'd got "grub enough for two".

His idea was that we were to visit seven parish churches. He had selected what he called the batting order and would explain as we went along. Before we went along, however, there was the walker's ritual to perform. I had to wash my feet, he insisted. Then I had to smear tacky soap all over them. Then I had to turn my best woollen stockings inside-out and soap them, too. Then I had to cut my toe-nails and test my laces. Then I had to tighten my belt and loosen my collar. Then I had to select a walking-stick from the drain-pipe by the front door. We got off at about ten o'clock. I don't think that even Mr. Gentleman thought we shouldn't be back until ten at night.

I remember the first part of our Seven Parishes walk better than the last. That was a confused rhythm of chafed flesh and aching muscle, of broken blisters and cold sweat. We were doing seven parishes, Mr. Gentleman explained, breathing rather heavily, because of the Seven Churches of Asia and the Seven Hills of Rome. There was something mystic in the figure seven, and Mr. Gentleman was going to write a book about it, when he had time. He knew the way to the first two churches like the back of his hand; after that we should have to use his survey map and compass.

When we left the road for the first short cut you could see the distant tower of our first church, and when we got there another tower seemed to pop up obligingly from a far wood. By lunch we had done three churches, one from the outside because there was a service on, two closely from within. Mr. Gentleman didn't seem to miss much, but his observations were irritating because though he used no guide-book for reference he used guide-book abbreviations and jargon. "The N. fenestration is Perp." he would say; or, "just look at the ogee-headed crocketed recess!"

We had our lunch sitting on a Rabjohn-like table-tombstone under the elms of our third church. I was afraid some indignant verger would order us off, but we saw no one. A robin joined us for crumbs, and a weasel looped busily over a bank, a bull bellowed remotely. Mr. Gentleman recited Gray's Elegy and I ate corned-beef sandwiches with my jacket off. When we had finished the luke-warm lemonade he spared my embarrassment by suggesting that I should "go and find a place" while he studied the map. "Sure to be somewhere behind the grave-digger's hut," he said. "Always is." You would have said that no grave had been dug for years in that church-yard. Tall grasses waved lazily over gentle mounds. Crosses leaned in a romantic, hopeless way that Tennyson would have appreciated. But there was a hut; and there was 'a place'. When I got back, the map was spread out over the tomb and Mr. Gentleman, somewhat baffled because he could not make the church lie E. and W., was sliding his compass about trying to free it from the pull of undetected iron.

We found our fourth church by three o'clock and were in-advertently back at our third by four. Mr. Gentleman couldn't explain this. Nor could I.

From that time it became clear that we were running late. I didn't like to suggest that we should ask someone the way: Mr. Gentleman obviously made it a point of honour that we should do our own navigation, and it was clear from the breezy way he spoke of our setback that we were jolly well going to do our seven churches, come what may.

I was becoming dreadfully weary by the time we reached the porch of the fifth. There had been diversions on the way: we crossed two fields to try to find the nest of a Sedge Warbler; we were twenty minutes outside a cottage while Mr. Gentleman sketched the pargetting; we walked the length of a lane solely because it was rich in speedwell and red campion. We had his cold tea and lardy cake with our legs stretched out in front of us. Mr. Gentleman said we mustn't take our boots off because if we did we'd never get them on again. He added that when mountaineers fell down mountains their boots always came off.

At first I could scarcely get going after tea. We had a false start when Mr. Gentleman had to hobble back to the porch clutch-ing the calf of his left leg. "Cramp! CRAMP!" he groaned.

"Push my toes back. Harder! Harder!" His teeth were clenched and he was sweating. When we set out again he hardly dared put his foot to the ground, but he soon started swinging out. We must get on, he said; there were pew-ends waiting for us at the next stop—pew-ends showing the Seven Deadly Sins. Sloth was one, and we mustn't be slothful.

We were denied the carved sins because the evening service was on. I think Mr. Gentleman wanted to wait until it was over, but he said we must keep walking because it wouldn't do to go off the boil. The sun was there all right, but it was beginning to make its big slide to the West and the stirring breeze was chilly.

The walk from church number six to church number seven seemed to me to be all in the shadow of trees and all uphill. I was reduced to pledging myself to do a hundred paces at a time—making a fresh resolve for another hundred at the end of each. Mr. Gentleman felt, I think, that we were reaching our testing time. He fumbled in a hairy pocket to produce a thick packet labelled simply MARCHING CHOCOLATE. It was soft and warm and wonderful stuff. I divided my piece, but he put almost half a slab into his mouth declaiming in a muffled kind of way, over and over again, "I bit my arm and sucked the blood." Then, when he had finished the chocolate and the Coleridge he said, "Now we shall have to suck buttons," and began to take notice of the trees. In a vague way I took it all in because, tired as I was, I was still dreadfully conscious of my coming exam. and felt that Mr. Venables would want me to cram myself with any kind of knowledge.

A path by a stream led us to our seventh church while Mr. Gentleman sang 'Tit Willow'—a sad song in its right place, but like a chorus of triumph as it brought us to the last lych-gate.

I hardly knew what to do with myself, I was so weary. Mr. Gentleman was like an exuberant Stout Cortez. He shook my hand heartily and stared at our last church as if he had never believed in its existence.

In the orange sun-light he spread his map.

It was then he realised we had reached our furthest point from home.

We had to walk another four miles before we could hire a car, and we had to wait three-quarters of an hour before the driver was ready to start.

I fell asleep on the way back and I do not remember saying Goodnight to Mr. Gentleman. I am certain I did not thank him.

Father said I'd better have a glass of milk and go straight to bed, and I mustn't make a noise because Mother was trying to get some sleep. The Doctor had been, and she wasn't very well.

I do remember the utter relief with which I stretched myself in the sheets. As Mr. Gentleman had predicted, my brain was washed out. I could have slept standing up. The 'fresh as a daisy' part did not seem the least bit important. All I wanted to do was to sleep.

Bell, holding a flickering candle, woke me up. She said I must put on a dressing-gown and come. Mother wasn't very well, I must come down and see her before it was too late. She put my slippers on my feet for me. With her arm round my shoulders she guided me to Mother's room. The light was shaded and I couldn't see properly. There were people round the bed. Uncle Hector and Aunt May were there. Grandfather and Auntie Lucy stood at the foot. Father sat on a chair holding Mother's hand.

She lay very still on her back, her head tilted forward a little by the pillow. Her eyes were closed.

Grandfather took me from Bell. He brought me gently round to Mother's side. "Give your mother a kiss, Arthur, lad," he said in a funny voice. I bent over and kissed her. She opened her eyes. "Dear Arthur," she whispered. And her free hand stroked the back of my head. "My little boy."

Grandfather led me away. Hatch was outside the door. He picked me up, and Bell led us back towards my room. I think I was asleep even then.

XIX

FATHER WOKE ME in the morning with a cup of tea. I must look
slippy, he said, because we were on our own. I took the tea,
slopping it in the saucer and splashing my chest with it. My dream
was so vivid in my mind that I expected him to talk about the
night, but he added only that I was to have a special good wash
and put my Sunday suit on and that Mr. Leaf was going to call
for me at ten to nine.

I was awfully sore and stiff, but I hurried as much as I could,
for although it was only eight o'clock I was already fearful that I
should be late and turned away from the Examination Board. And
the more I thought of that the more I began to feel sick with
apprehension.

Uncle Hector's advice about eating a good meal didn't help me.
I managed a cup of tea. My slice of fried bread went round and
round in my mouth like a ball of putty. By twenty to nine I was
as ready as I could be and asked Father if I could go up and say
goodbye to Mother.

"Your mother's in hospital, Arthur. They took her away before
you were awake."

Up to that moment I had thought that I could not feel more
wretched, but when Father told me that, my inside turned to water
and I felt myself going hot all over. It was as if I had been drained
by the pulling of a plug.

"Is she very bad?"

He didn't seem to know what to say. "She'll be all right," he
got out at last. Then Mr. Leaf came.

Mr. Leaf made sure that I had my pen and pencils before we
could set out. He said Mother would be well looked after. He said
wasn't it nice to see my grandfather. He said he expected I was
surprised to see Bell. He said I must write slowly and speak up
when spoken to.

I hated the other candidates as soon as I saw them outside the hall. They looked big and looked clever. They were all talking together, and some of them were even laughing. They didn't take any notice of me; even so I was glad when Mr. Leaf went. He said, "You'll be all right now, Arthur," and somehow melted away before I remembered to say thank-you for coming.

The laughter and chatter stopped when a master in his gown appeared at the door. He called out something and everyone began crowding into the door. I was last. "Last but not least," he said, kindly enough. "Hook, isn't it?" I said it was, and he ticked a name on his list. "Desk number eleven, on the left," he said.

Chairs scraped; feet shuffled. "You have two hours," said the master. "You may turn your question-papers over and begin now." The gusty sound of leaves turning, and then the scratch of nibs.

At first I was mentally paralysed by the mere number of questions: I could not switch my brain about in the way they seemed to demand. Closer and cooler inspection revealed that I was required to answer only one question from each of the first three groups, and one question from any one of the remaining groups. I was to write on one side of the paper only and was to pay special attention to handwriting, spelling (how do you pay special attention to spelling?), punctuation and presentation. I was not to draw diagrams except in answering questions on History, Geography and Mathematics when I could if I wanted to.

The first group was sums. I warmed towards none. There was a man who invested money in gold mines and put the interest in the Post Office Savings Bank for his son. There was a builder faced with the awful problem of having to build a wall of a certain dimension with bricks of a certain size. There were two gardeners who (unaccountably, as far as I could see) had to make gardens on the sides of a triangular lawn with a square corner and were fearful lest one should have more ground that the other. There was a huge layered fraction to be resolved.

I chose the fraction. I got an answer running into five figures, abandoned it, saw too late that the gardeners needed the help of Pythagoras, drew a diagram, botched that and moved unsteadily into Group II.

Here the examiners wanted a description of any important battle in British history. I looked no further. Naseby! I described it. I drew a diagram (without battle-cruisers). I was tempted to draw a diagram of Charles I.

Group III required, among other things, a description of a

196

journey from Paris to Bangkok or from New York to Vancouver. If I didn't like that I could describe the foodstuffs on my breakfast table and reveal from what part of the world each item came.

I found myself thinking that neither the question-paper nor my answers bore much relation to anything I had studied at school, but the third group was altogether less turgid. 'My Favourite Hobby' finally ousted 'How I spent Five Pounds' and 'Why I am sitting for this Examination' (which I regarded as an intrusion), and I gave a concise account of British Colonials and How to Collect them, adding a dash of Major Birkitt and Lord Rutherstone, but reluctantly deciding not to mention them by name. I became so engrossed in my answer that when the master called, "Ten minutes more" I had yet to select my fourth Question.

As it happened, no great loss to the world of learning was involved. I was unable to say what happened when a candle was lit. I did not know how a gramophone worked; the circuit of an electric-bell was a secret I did not share; I could say nothing worthwhile about Amundsen, Madame Curie, Pasteur, Edison or Ross. Nor did I know why grass grew, rain fell or volcanoes erupted. I did know why Macbeth was alarmed to see Birnam Wood coming to Dunsinane, and said so in four quick lines.

There was an uneasy break after we had handed our answers in. The boy next to me burst out crying because he found he had written on both sides of the paper. Someone was sick in the lavatories. The longer we waited for The Board the worse I felt.

When my name was called I remembered to turn and close the door quietly and to stand until I was invited to sit down. There were only three on The Board. I recognised the High Master from his visit to the library. The others I did not know. There was a grey, severe man with a long, thin face and shoulders flecked with dandruff, and a fat jolly man in a hairy tweed suit which revealed most of his black socks. He had a bristly moustache, gold pince-nez, a celluloid collar and a heavy silver watch-chain looping between his waistcoat pockets without going through a buttonhole.

The grey man asked me to confirm that I was Arthur Hook and invited me to sit down. Then he said that I needn't be nervous. The High Master said he should think not. "You're our good Mr. Leaf's protégé, are you not?" he said. "We met in the library, I think."

I couldn't say 'met' was hardly the word. I thought it wonderful of him to remember me at all. Then he was even more wonderful. "I hope your mother will soon be well again," he said. I was so taken aback and, I believe, so near to tears that I could only just thank him.

The grey man redressed the balance by asking in slow patient French how old I was. I fear that I told him I was nearly forty. He then wanted to know, or I think he wanted to know, if I had ever been to France; and after that (for I hadn't, and managed to say so in more words than one) how I passed the time in *les vacances*. Even in the kind of stupor I was in I was amazed at my inability not only to find a single French word to fit any activity at all, but to discover anything worth mentioning that I did in *les vacances*. I could think only of stamp collecting, but I didn't know the word for 'stamp'. I knew 'postcard', though. I tried to believe afterwards that the grey man was convinced that I collected postcards and had several thousands of them carefully arranged in accordance with their country of origin.

When he had done with me, the jolly man rubbed his hands together and began to chuckle. As if it was the biggest and best joke in the world he put his first question to me. "If one man goes to the top of a castle wall and sees three miles, how far will four men see?"

If in the written part of the exam. I had felt that nothing was related to my special studies I was now being reimbursed. For this was undoubtedly the kind of trick question that Mr. Gentleman said I was to look out for. So I didn't answer at once. I tried to think it out. My thinking in fact didn't amount to much more than visualising four men peering from battlements. At length I answered firmly, "Twelve miles".

The jolly man was delighted. He slapped his knee and chuckled away, his jolly face creased with pleasure before he propounded his second joke. "There's a frog, Hook," he said, "at the bottom of a slippery thirty-foot well. He wants to get out, Hook—and who should blame him?—but although he can jump up three feet at a time, for every three feet he jumps up he slips down two. Now what we all want to know is . . . how many jumps before he jumps out?" Somehow he made me feel as if they and the frog all depended on me for salvation. But was it another of Mr. Gentleman's trick questions? It couldn't be. If he jumped three and fell back two he moved up a foot at a time. Thirty feet; thirty jumps. "Thirty," I said.

This made the jolly man's day. "Thirty!" he spluttered. "Thirty! Splendid! Thirty! Well I never!" And he guffawed away and rumbled away to himself. At last he managed to get out, "If you were in an aeroplane, Hook, over Glasgow, and flew dead South (know what I mean, eh?), what's the first English county you'd fly over?"

This was quite beyond me. I was so flustered at trying to switch my mind to geography that I feared for a moment that I was not going to be able to name any county at all. The grey man was looking at columns of figures; the High Master was writing something; the jolly man was beaming at me. I was desperate. "Devonshire", I said at last. The three of them suddenly looked at me as if I were an imbecile.

The High Master put down his papers. "Talk to me about books," he said quietly. Had anyone else said it I think I should have been quite done. "Books?" I should have said. "What books? What do you mean—'books'?" But in my mind's eye I saw him in the library, his library, and somehow it didn't seem a silly request. He made it sound as if he really wanted to hear what I had to say about books, as though there might be something I knew that he didn't. And I thought of the Major's books in his smoke-smelling library, and of Grandfather's history books, and of the few we had at home in the frail bamboo set of shelves by the fire-place in the best room, and their spines presented themselves to my inward eye as if they were a parade especially for a review by the High Master. *With Edged Tools, Silas Marner, We Three—a Novel, Longfellow*, covered in faded velvet, *Enquire Within Upon Everything* (with that horrible section on Poisons and their Symptoms), *David Copperfield, No Name, Multitude and Solitude.* They and their fellows stood to attention waiting for us.

But between them they broke the spell I was under. I began to think less of them and more of their whereabouts. I began to think of Mother and of Bell and how terribly I missed them and how terribly I wanted to know where they were and what they were doing. Mother in a hospital, and I here with those three men! I became aware of the room we were in, its brown paint, its marble clock with the busy claws and cog-wheel on its face, the heavy green curtains on tarnished brass rings, books behind glass. I could even see the title of one of them—Browning's Poetical Works. Mother and Bell and Browning. Could Browning bring me back to the task in hand? "What's become of all the gold used to hang and brush their bosoms? I feel chilly and grown old." That's what Mr. Venables used to say up in the tank room when someone opened the iron-framed window. And after a pause he would say, "Browning". Mr. Venables. Mr. Selby and his reading-list. I was back with the High Master and books.

So I talked to him about books. And before long he talked to me about books. Then, after a long time, he said, "Well. Thank you. That will do. I hope you won't be frightened of us again." I believe I said what needed to be said as I backed to the door, but they were engrossed in their lists. I let myself out. "What was it like?" a big, blazered boy wanted to know. "All right," I said. "The headmaster's quite decent." "High Master, you mean," said he with a kind of suppressed derision for my simple ways.

Mr. Leaf was waiting for me in the courtyard place. I was to have dinner with him because Father had gone to the hospital and wouldn't be back.

Mr. Leaf lodged with Mr. and Mrs. Dance near the One and All Stores. We had pressed beef and peas and new potatoes and a kind of rhubarb-custard which Mrs. Dance said was good for the blood. Mr. Leaf couldn't hear enough about my exam. He had spoken to some of the boys while he was waiting for me. They had all seemed very nice, but one of them, a big fellow in a blue blazer, was as sharp as a plum. If they'd all been like that one I shouldn't have anything to worry about.

I had forgotten to ask—and no one had told me—if I was expected to be back at school for the afternoon. Mr. Leaf was sure it would be quite all right if I didn't go. In any case there wouldn't be much afternoon left. I said I would like to go and see if Father was home from the hospital, but I agreed to wait until we had had a nice cup of tea. When Mrs. Dance went to the kitchen to boil the kettle Mr. Leaf said she was a wonderful woman, and cleaned his pipe with a sticky brown skewer. He said that hospitals did wonderful things these days, but that Rome wasn't built in a day and it was no use trying to run before you could walk.

Father wasn't there when I got home. The shop was shut; the side door was locked; the back door, with Tinker sitting outside it, was locked, too.

Uncle Hector's wasn't shut, though. When I clanged my way in Aunt May came indignantly out of the parlour and shut the coloured-glass door firmly behind her. "Oh, it's you," she said, crossly. Then she softened a little. "Do you think you could look after the shop, Arthur? Not the Post Office. Just the shop." She didn't say anything about my exam. or about Mother or about my not being in school. "The man's here," she said. "Your uncle's got trouble again." She lifted the flap of the counter. "There's won't be hardly anybody in. All the prices are plain-marked. That Elsie Catcher's in there. Don't you touch anything in the Post Office, whatever you do. And don't give no change without asking me first. And don't go eating anything. Just tap on the glass if you want me; and I'll come."

I didn't have to tap on the glass. Through the parlour door came the sounds not quite of argument, but of accusation and denial, of patient, dogged explanation and of heated assertion. I think Aunt May had forgotten all about me. She came and went once, her lips tight shut, and took away the date-stamp from the Post Office counter.

Elsie Catcher came out next. She was crying and twisting a little handkerchief round and round one of her fingers. When she saw me she sniffed, "Oh, it's you." She got her hat and coat out of the lobby and flung the counter-flap over with a crash. She wrenched the shop-door open so violently that the bell still hummed when she was out of sight.

When I was becoming quite certain that I was destined to look after the shop until it was time to put the shutters up and with the big hooked pole roll up the heavy sun-blind, the parlour door opened to let out Mr. Eustace. He and his soiled brief-case looked even more forbidding than they had when I had seen them before. Aunt May had an infinitely pathetic smile; Uncle Hector was pale but bustling. "I name no names," he was saying to Mr. Eustace, "but you can see for yourself the size of it."

Mr. Eustace took no notice of me at all, in fact he didn't seem to be taking much notice of Uncle Hector, either. He put his G.R. case on the counter while he buttoned his blue serge jacket and, narrowing his eyes and looking hard at one of the upper shelves where Epps's cocoa was, said rather grandly, "You are not accused of anything, Mr. Hook. My department is gravely concerned. Gravely concerned. Nothing can be proved. Nothing. But facts are facts. The girl must stay on. And you must be viligant, Mr. Hook. *Very* viligant, I should say."

"Are you sure you won't have a cup of tea?" pleaded Aunt May. "It won't take a minute."

But Mr. Eustace wouldn't have a cup of tea, however quick it was. He smoothed back his hair with his left hand and thumped his bowler-hat on with his right, and let me open the flap and the shop-door. "It could be quite nasty," he said. "Quite nasty."

Aunt May said I must bring Father round for supper. There would be lots to talk about.

There was lots to talk about. Mother was 'as well as could be expected', but we had not been invited to supper to talk about Mother. Neither did my exam. appear on the agenda.

A book-maker in London (by dint of listening I reasoned out what a book-maker was), a book-maker in London had been receiving postal-bets from Major Birkitt. Major Birkitt had shown uncanny skill in picking winners, but he had, they noticed, always delayed his selection until almost the very last moment. There was nothing very remarkable in that; some of their regulars often found it necessary. What had put the fat in the fire was that one of the clerks had by chance twice seen 'a man' slipping a letter into their letter-box just after the postman had delivered the early-morning mail. They had kept watch after that, and, sure enough, it had been done again, and they were certain, or practically certain, that the late letter smuggled in was the one containing a winning bet from Major Birkitt. The 'man' had not been identified. The letter bore a postmark timed before the starting-time of the race. Could it be, wondered the book-maker, who under a proud claim of 'never owing' had always paid up, could it be that Major Birkitt had somehow contrived to get his stamped envelopes franked at Uncle Hector's Post Office without surrendering them at the same time?

If Major Birkitt had an envelope timed say, 11 a.m. on the 25th, he could wait until by telephone he found out the name of the winner of the three-thirty, make out a letter placing a fat bet on that winner, seal the envelope, address it and pop it (himself?) or have it popped (Maidment?) in the book-maker's letter-box with the next-morning's delivery.

Question was, would Major Birkitt stoop to such a trick, and if he would—and the consensus was that he would—how could he get hold of envelopes bearing Uncle Hector's official stamp?

It was that girl Elsie Catcher, of course. She'd do anything for anyone who gave her the glad eye. That's who it was.

All this was propounded by Aunt May as she laid the supper-table, dealt hot plates and spooned out bubble and squeak.

Elsie Catcher had been rigorously questioned by Mr. Eustace but had proved obstinate as a mule—which, said Aunt May, was no more than you'd expect.

"Why doesn't someone tackle the Major about it—or Maidment?" said Father.

Uncle Hector had hardly spoken up to then. Keeping his eyes on his plate he had busied himself in building ramparts of greens and potatoes and creating a great lake of tomato ketchup. He raised his head. "I'd look a right bloody fool, wouldn't I, going down there and asking the Major if he'd been diddling the Post Office. A right bloody fool. Wouldn't I? And if he said he had . . . Suppose he said he had . . . How d'you think I'm going to look when it comes out he'd got the doings across the counter here? Where's that put me? I'd like to know."

The meal continued in a silence broken only by the swishing scrape of Uncle Hector's knife as he dexterously rounded up some stragglers on his plate and interred them firmly in a burial mound he had created near his mustard.

"Did Hector tell you we'd had more money gone as well?" Aunt May spoke to Father in a whisper we could all hear.

"Five bloody quid," said Uncle Hector. "End of last week sometime."

"Did you tell your, what's-his-name, Mr. Eustace?" asked Father.

"Not bloody likely. Trouble enough without that coming out. Absolutely beats me. I've watched that girl ever since we had that last lot of trouble. Watched her like a bloody hawk. Haven't seen a damn thing. But she's getting it somehow. Seen the clothes she wears? She's got . . ."

Aunt May, no doubt feeling that Elsie Catcher's wardrobe was more her province than Uncle Hector's, took over. "She's got a silk umbrella now. She's got enough shoes . . ."

"For a bloody centipede," said my uncle.

"Why not speak to Arnold?" Father asked, mildly enough.

"You try it. You just try it. Says it's no business of ours how she spends her money. Says he won't have her insulted. Says she'll leave and he'll leave, too. Says . . ." Uncle Hector paused to clean up his plate with a piece of bread. "Mind you," he said at last, "the lad's got spirit. You've got to give him that."

"You once said you wouldn't let on to Arnold," said Aunt May reproachfully. "It's not fair on the boy."

"Well, we've got to find out, haven't we! Any road up, I'm not going to have that bumptious little whippersnapper, Eustace, going back and putting it about that I'm dipping my hand in his bloody till. Suppose it gets to the Major, eh? Suppose it gets to him— D'you see him having me in his cricket? See me getting my feet under the table on his stuck-up bloody dung-hill? Eh?"

"From what Mr. Eustace says the Major's as much in it as anybody is."

"In it? In it? Nobody's in nothing. There's someone taking his pickings, that's all; and I don't want the world and his wife hearing from Mr. Bloody Eustace that I'm doing very nicely thank you. So let's get that straight."

"Of course not, Hector," said Aunt May firmly; "but the way you're going on won't get us anywhere. There's two things. There's the money, and there's that horse-betting business . . ."

"I know. I know. I only said I didn't want the Major to be put into the way of thinking that I was mixed up in anything here. In the first place it would make it easier for him to wriggle out of the envelope thing—and I'm not saying he's in it, mind. And in the second . . . in the second I'd get as much chance of playing cricket round here, big cricket, I mean, not that bat-and-ball stuff in the middle of a cow-pasture, as a . . . as a . . ."

"I don't really see what cricket's to do with it," said Aunt May. "It's the money that's important."

"Oh, is it! How about my good name, eh?"

"Well, it comes to the same thing, doesn't it?"

"No, it doesn't. I'll tell you straight: if it came to it, I'd . . ."

"You'd pay out of your own pocket, wouldn't you? Anything to get into the Major's lot. You've lost enough as it is without buying favours off the Major."

"Who's buying favours? I don't need to buy favours from that lot. I'm good enough to play cricket alongside anybody round here without going cap in hand."

He glared at Aunt May and then at Father and then at me as if we were going to say he wasn't. Then a kind of far-away look came into his eyes. "They tell me Jimmy Daintry's coming down to play," he said.

James Daintry. My hero. Every cricketer's hero. James Daintry. "Dainty Daintry". Never dropped at catch. Bowled like a machine. Six centuries for England. Still applauded to the wicket when he modestly left the pros' gate at Lord's. Left-hand batsman, right-arm bowler; but known to play the other way round in charity matches. Never refused an autograph. Never rolled his sleeves up.

By what right Uncle Hector called him Jimmy I don't know; but when I heard him say that Jimmy Daintry was coming I had the notion that perhaps Uncle Hector knew him, and perhaps I could get his autograph and perhaps I could speak to him.

When it was time to go I was sent into the shop because the grown-ups 'wanted a few words'. They had more than a few, and in the end they became angry words. Father came stamping out of the glass door, took me by the hand and didn't say anything until we got home.

"Don't you ever tell anyone what your uncle said tonight. Not even your mother."

"When's Mother coming?" I said. "When's she coming?"

He didn't answer for a long time. "I don't know, son. They won't tell you anything, hospitals. I saw your Mother for ten minutes. Couldn't have been more. She says she hopes your exam. up at the College went all right."

This was more than Father had said when I found him at home, back from the hospital. He didn't seem to want to talk about Mother then. Some people can't bear to talk about ears, and some can't talk about snakes. I believe Father was the same about hospitals. He said before supper that he reeked of Jeyes' Fluid and that he hoped he'd be allowed to die in his own bed. Now, after supper, he was saying that they were 'very good' at the hospital. "Do anything for your mother," he said. "There's one nurse there, slip of a girl, couldn't do more if she was her own daughter." He was silent for a long time. "Your sister might be coming home soon," he said. "Depends how your mother gets on."

He couldn't or wouldn't say any more about it. I could go to the hospital 'one day'. Bell might come home 'any day now'. It all 'depended'. You mustn't expect to walk before you can run. I told him about going to Mr. Leaf's. He knew already. He had had a word with Mr. Leaf about that scholarship (Father usually spoke of the scholarship as though it was something very remote from us). Mr. Leaf reckoned he'd hear about the result just as soon as anybody, if not sooner. Anything to do with the College, he heard. Had to put the notices up in the library. Mr. Leaf would tip us the wink just as soon as anything was through.

"It would do your mother good if you got a budge up," Father said. I had never heard him say anything one way or

205

the other about my going to the College. I suddenly found myself wanting very much to be accepted. Father seemed keen, and if it was going to do Mother good then it was something I must be keen about, too. I was keen. I wanted to go. And then I saw more clearly how I had wasted opportunities of making sure. I thought of everyone who had tried to teach me or to encourage me. I even thought of Miss Ednay; but most of all I thought of Mother polishing my shoes and beating an egg in milk. Mr. Gentleman once told me that the saddest words in the world were 'If only' and 'Too late'.

There was a thunder-storm that night. I didn't hear it. Father told me about it at breakfast. He said that things always got worse before they got better and the storm had cleared the air.

XX

ANYONE WILL TELL you that the summers of his childhood were always rainless and sometimes endless. As the day of
Uncle Hector's cricket match came nearer the talk was of
scorched turf and cracked wickets. Hardly a cloud sailed across
the blue skies; the pond outside the Axe and Cleaver dried up;
Harold Witty's grandmother went to sleep in the sun, and woke
up all peculiar in the head; we were allowed to go to school in
shirt-sleeves.

No word had come from Mr. Eustace or the London book-
maker; only one pound disappeared from the Post Office till;
Major Birkitt could have heard nothing of the dark suspicions
he had roused, for almost every day he was in Uncle Hector's
to talk cricket.

Everyone seemed to be talking cricket. I expect it was the
warmth and the blue skies. No one spoke of my scholarship
exam.: it was as though it were a frosty subject thawed out and
quite evaporated by the summer sunshine.

I tell a lie (one of Maidment's expressions). I tell a lie. Mother
could not hear enough about the exam. She wanted to know
about each question and about each answer. Did I think I impressed the examiners? Did I feel deep down inside me that I
had done well enough? Had the Headmaster given a hint or let
anything slip about what I'd done? Father had taken me to the
hospital to see Mother after she had been there for ten days. He
said I might think she looked a bit ill and she probably wouldn't
have her teeth in and I wasn't to mind. I had to borrow a chair
from another bed, but I didn't like doing it: in the bed was an
old woman with skin stretched so tightly over her cheeks that it
looked as though it might split like scorched paper. I think she
tried to say something when I took the chair, but no sound came
and I couldn't tell if she was pleased or angry.

Mother said she was much better now. Her hands were ever so
thin. Her hair was sort of damp, but her eyes shone bright and

she was so eager to know what was going on that you couldn't believe they'd keep her there much longer. Father left us together saying he'd go and have a chat with the porter, and after that I went to the hospital without him. Visiting hours were really three to four in the afternoons, but they used to let me go up even when I was nearly an hour late.

I never went into the hospital without feeling dreadfully frightened. I tried to think of it as a place specially made for getting sick people well, but I really thought of it as a place you went when everything was as good as over and done with, where you didn't have any say in what happened to you, where, if they said you must drink hot milk you had to drink it, and if they said they were going to cut your leg off you had to let them do it. I expected bad news every time the disinfected air and the smell of floor polish wrapped itself round me; kind as the nurses were, and bright as Mother was, I never rid myself of the cold, sick emptiness of fear that drained my hopes and flushed out what little courage I had. It was all right when I reached Mother's bed. She always spoke of coming home, and one day said it couldn't be long, because Mr. Rice had been to see her and he'd said that if someone could help her in the house she could come when she liked. It was then that she told me that Bell was coming back.

The Saturday of Uncle Herbert's match was made for cricket. There was a stillness in the air—not, as it seemed to me, because there was not enough breeze to stir a leaf, but because there was the holding of breath that heralds a great conflict.

Willie and I reached Major Birkitt's cricket-ground ten minutes late, but it didn't seem to matter. The College team was there, lazily bowling or swinging a bat on the springy turf at the edge of the circular arena. They were not in the least impatient. The Major's team numbered six at the time of our arrival. Not one appeared to care whether he took part in a cricket-match or not. Pairs chatted; one splendid gentleman dressed in knicker-bockers leaned against his bicycle smoking a meerschaum pipe; Major Birkitt himself leaned against the big horse-roller, his cricket-bag at his feet, laughing delightedly with a wiry, mous-tached gentleman who negligently practised his shots holding his bat in his right hand. There were some pretty girls round about, chatting happily enough, but with the slightly-lost air that women have at cricket-matches.

Willie said that the man the Major was talking to was James Daintry. I could not claim to recognise him. Willie and I instinctively drew near to hear what the great man was saying. He was clearly in the middle of some well-worn cricketing yarn. ". . . Then the bloody fool changed his bloody mind and ran the other way. I wasn't going to move. I stayed in my bloody crease. 'Make your mind up, Mister', I shouted. That set him off again, and, d'you know what he did?—the silly bugger turned round and came charging back! Laugh! I could have died! Amateurs!" And Jimmy Daintry laughed hugely, and the Major laughed with him and slapped his hand down on his thigh. Willie and I were enchanted.

It was then that the Major spotted me and beckoned me over. I knew he was going to introduce me to the great man, but my first instinct was to pretend I hadn't seen his gesture, for I suddenly felt at a loss, having nothing to say to a man who had even played against Australia. Yet here was the chance for the meeting I had hoped for ever since Uncle Hector said that Jimmy Daintry was coming. So I walked slowly over, busily searching for some remark worthy of the occasion.

"Like to take on the scoring, young Arthur?" was the Major's greeting. "We're a bit thin on the ground today. Had to scrape the barrel, eh." He turned to Jimmy Daintry and they both laughed.

I ought to have taken Willie over with me when I was beckoned. It was his chance to meet our hero. But I didn't. I ought to have told the Major that I couldn't do the scoring. I was going to see Mother in the hospital at three in the afternoon. I should have said so. But I didn't.

"You'll find the book in the pav. Give you the batting order when we've got a full complement. Think you can manage, eh? Just pop over and see if it's where it ought to be, eh?"

Feeling angry and ashamed I asked Willie to tell Father I'd got to score and wouldn't be back. Presently the Major brought me a list of names on the back of an envelope. "The lads'll be batting first," he said. "I'll be back in a jiffy. Just going to spin the jolly old coin."

Spinning the jolly old coin did not disprove the Major's first-to-bat forecast. The College prepared. I was joined at my seat before the rough pavilion table by an immaculate College boy with glasses who set down the College team carefully in an immense leather-bound scorebook as players from both sides nervously relishing the preliminaries, leaned over our shoulders to read the batting order. No one spoke to me. Uncle Hector was busy hurling a ball into the Major's gloved and, no doubt, beef-steaked, hands. Jimmy Daintry did not come near.

Just as the Major, to a sprinkling of artificial clapping led his team on to the field, a light hand touched my shoulder. "Poor Arthur," said Frances Birkitt, "cooped up here all day when you'd much sooner be playing! Never mind! You must come to the supper tonight. Be sure you do. I shall look out for you."

I had already written down James Daintry's name in the batting order. I was copying out the College team and had just reached their third batsman when Frances spoke. Marcus Daveney. Meeting James Daintry would not come easy to me. (Was I really going to meet him?—I hadn't got very far.) But what would it be like if I had to talk to Marcus Daveney?

When Uncle Hector and I arrived at The Lodge for the Supper there was hardly anybody there. Maidment opened the door to us with the whispered information that not many of the toffs had turned up yet and that the iced cup was to be avoided as it was nothing but unadulterated gnat's piss. His nibs was in the library.

I had spent most of the match with mixed feelings about coming, but the nearer the time came for presenting myself the more I dreaded it. I asked Father if he thought I need go. He said it wouldn't do if I stayed away, having been invited. He had told Mother, he said, about the invite, and she was ever so proud that I was going. I was to put on a clean white shirt and my best suit. He himself had given my best shoes a rub up. I wasn't to drink anything the gents drank and Uncle Hector was to see I got home at ten o'clock. Or half-past ten at the latest.

I had hoped that we might arrive in the middle of things, and so not be noticed. The trouble was, Uncle Hector didn't want to miss a minute. He insisted that we should arrive at half-past seven like the invite said; after his exploits of the afternoon, he saw himself, I believe, as a more than welcome and honoured guest. On the way he had scarcely stopped talking about his score. He had shown them, hadn't he! Just like he said he would.

The horrible scene that had ruined the day for me seemed to have passed completely out of his mind as Maidment led us to the library to greet his nibs. We didn't go straight to the library as Maidment wanted to show us the buffet supper laid out in the dining-room. "While you," said Maidment, "were hob-nobbing with the toffs I was seeing to this little lot." This little lot was on two long tables running the length of the room. What impressed me first was the big linen table-cloth. It seemed to be starched. It looked as stiff as my Sunday collar. There were stacks of plates with blue rims, and stacks of bowls with gold rims. There were two hams on china stands like empty cotton-reels; boiled eggs cut in half filled a flat silver dish; onions and radishes made a pattern on a round plate. There were long, twisty loaves and bread rolls, arranged to look like wickets; scotch eggs were heaped like cannon-balls in pyramids; a veal, ham and egg pie revealed its secrets in a field of parsley; little open silver jugs brimmed with salad-dressing (I thought it was custard) and fat pottery jars with flat corks held two sorts of mustard. There was a huge crystal bowl of fruit salad. There was an egg-cup bristling with tooth-picks.

On a separate table were tall glass jugs of straw-coloured wine on which floated borage and slices of cucumber. On the floor was a wooden tub wound with smilax. In it in an arctic of ice and water, champagne bottles sprouted.

Maidment winked at me and suggested that I should 'start now', but I pretended not to hear him. Popping a pickled onion into his mouth he adjusted a fork here and a knife there before telling Uncle Hector that he supposed he'd better get on with the bloody pantomime.

Major Birkitt stood twinkling amid the twinkling candles in the library. He was talking to Mrs. Chelvey when we went in, his hand on her upper arm which was bare. It was a warm night, but she wore a dress of black velvet like a queen. I thought the Major's face fell a little as he greeted us. Greeted us? "I'm glad you were able to come. You did very well, young Arthur. Do yourself proud, eh?" Then there was shouting and laughter outside and a sudden avalanche of young men in evening dress, and pretty, smiling girls in gay colours surging into the room sweeping us aside and bursting out with congratulations to the Major on the match, the supper-table, the weather, the wine and the great day it had been. I stood dumb almost behind the door when a second wave of guests rolled in. This was the College team. Not one of them was dumb. Marcus Daveney carried on, as it were, where the Major had left off. Not that he put his hand on Mrs. Chelvey's arm, but he smiled and twinkled at her just like the Major, and she smiled and twinkled back at him in a gay, grave kind of way until I longed to know what they were talking about. I caught sight of James Daintry on the other side of the room. For a moment no one was with him, and if I could have got through I would have gone over to him, for in the moment I found myself with the courage to talk to him. Of course, in another moment he was the centre of eager, attentive cricketers and I had lost my chance. I felt so much out of it that I squeezed my way past and wandered miserably into the Brass Room. There was no one there and I was just beginning to feel like a trespasser when Maidment, carrying a tray of brimming glasses, halted on the threshold. Before he turned to go he discarded his faithful-retainer face to tell me that he was just going to ring the gong and that if I wanted to miss the bloody stampede I'd better nip in smartly and get among the eats.

It was advice I couldn't follow because I didn't really know what he meant, and I had no idea at all what the rules of etiquette demanded on an occasion like that. Not very much, as it turned out. From the hall came the clanging peal of the gong, and, almost at once, it seemed, I was no longer alone but surrounded by laughing, chattering, happy diners holding aloft loaded plates or slopping glasses as they sought a place to settle. James Daintry in a most matter-of-fact way set up the card table that had stood behind the door; Uncle Hector, in a kind of cheating musical-chairs manoeuvre bored his way to join him at it. He had somehow contrived to bring two glasses of beer with him, besides a stacked plate. He snatched two chairs from almost beneath a surprised couple to join the great man, and the two of them, mouths full, were soon hob-nobbing as if they had played cricket together for years, though Uncle Hector seemed content to do most of the listening.

I groped my way to their table, sure this time that Uncle Hector would tell Jimmy who I was. I stood quietly by while Uncle Hector finished off an anecdote about a cross-eyed umpire and at the same time finished off his ham and pie. He turned to me. "Fetch us another bit of pie, Arthur, there's a good lad," he said, handing me his empty plate. James Daintry addressed me, too. "Do the same for me, son," he said; "there's a good lad."

When I brought their plates back I could hardly get near the table. Jimmy Daintry was telling a chuckling audience about a charity match in which he had scored fifty, and was trying in vain to throw his wicket away. Even when he played cack-handed they couldn't get him out. "Had to turn round and knock my own bloody castle down (excuse my French) or I'd ha' been there half the bloody night."

In view of what had happened that very afternoon I didn't think it very sporting of him to talk about being out 'hit wicket'; but Uncle Hector joined in the general laughter. Some of the Major's team gave each other wise looks. Two exchanged whispers, and two others winked. James Daintry had in fact given himself up by offering a series of towering catches to the over-anxious College fielders. When he was eventually caught, knowing spectators said he was trying to get out once he had got his fifty, so perhaps the winks and whispers and nudges were not directed against Uncle Hector after all, for the great Daintry had never let it be seen that he was hitting up catches on purpose; indeed, he seemed very angry with himself for making such a cow-shot. Even so, I felt suddenly hot and uncomfortable over his 'hit wicket' story. When Uncle Hector had been given out and had come stumping back to the pavilion, at every step banging his bat down on the turf in fury, I had wanted to run from the field and hide. Now I felt the same. But here was Uncle Hector laughing with the others as if the horrible hiatus in the easy flow of the day's cricket had been something he may have observed, but could not possibly have brought about.

I did not eat very much at the supper. Frances Birkitt saw to it that I had a plate and stood in line at the buffet-table; Maidment put on my plate the crusty cone off the end of a loaf remarking that he didn't think that it would break the bank if I had it and that since everybody else were feeding their faces I might as well join in the fun.

Apart from the drinking, which never stopped, there was a kind of lull after supper. The girls disappeared upstairs after insisting on carrying the empty plates to the kitchen and allowing Major Birkitt to dissuade them from doing the washing-up; the men lit their cigars and pipes before a stroll through the french windows to see if the flowers wanted watering. James Daintry told innumerable cricket stories, and with Uncle Hector in close attendance drank glass after glass of beer, bottles of which seemed to come readily to Uncle Hector without his having to ask for them.

A game of indoor-cricket began, with a bread roll for ball and the brass coal-shovel as bat. Far from being put out by this liberty the Major organised sides and insisted on batting first. There was shouting and laughter. I didn't know what to do: I wandered from room to room. Uncle Hector, jacket off, tried to assume control of one of the teams, and somehow the game suddenly petered out. A half silence fell. The girls said it was time they were going. The Major, sensing, I suppose, that his evening was sagging, dramatically called on Maidment to open the champagne.

Each cork that popped brought a cheer. Laughter came up again, and though most of the girls did soon put on their shawls and prettily say good-bye, and though nearly all of the College boys eventually left together, there remained plenty of players for another game of cricket, and almost enough to do justice to the sparkling glasses that Maidment brought round on the big brass tray.

Longing to go home I began desperately to try to catch Uncle Hector's eye. As it turned out he needed me more than I needed him. He steered himself up to me, bent and spoke in my ear. "Lavatory!" he whispered hoarsely. "Lavatory! I want to piss like a bus-horse." I showed him the way, timidly suggesting that it might be time to go home. He would have none of it. In the cloak-room two young men were talking about a girl. They began to speak in French when we came in. "Odeur de corsage!" said one. "Quel odeur de corsage!" I saw them a little while later pouring champagne and calling out, "Electric soup! Anyone else for electric soup?"

Major Birkitt seemed more affable to Uncle Hector now, offering him a glass of champagne from his own little brass tray of drinks. Uncle Hector said he was honoured, took it and drank it in almost one go. "Thank you, Major. A little of what you fancy . . . Mind you," he added very seriously, "I wouldn't give twopence a glass for the stuff. Just gas and water. Not twopence. I stick to beer."

I did manage to ask Uncle Hector again if it wasn't time for us to go, but he said we couldn't go until Maidment had finished, because Maidment was going to give us a lift in you-know-who's motor. So we might as well enjoy ourselves. He picked up a sausage-roll, but dropped it untasted into a brass jug, saying that he felt like a poisoned pup.

How the fight began I don't really know. Maidment could have told because he was in the room all the time, but all he would say afterwards was, "I name no names." It was over another game, I think. There was a crash in the next room, laughter and shouts of "Hit wicket!" A young man near me who was pouring himself a glass of champagne and declaring that he was just going to have one more glass of the pure to warm his gob turned to his companion saying, "Sounds as though the Major's grocer has done it again!"

When I went to the door I saw Uncle Hector, coal-shovel in hand, a broken vase on the floor behind him, facing a large, sandy man with a pink face. "You're out!" roared the sandy man. "Hit bloody wicket! Or are you going to argue the toss again?"

Someone pushed me aside, and when I could look again the large man was holding his face in his hands and two others were wrestling with Uncle Hector trying to get the shovel away from him. They let go when the Major came in. Everyone went quiet. Uncle Hector, breathing heavily, stood holding the shovel; the large, sandy man slowly let his hands fall from his face. From a two-inch gash in the middle of his forehead blood ran down his nose to drip heavily on to the carpet.

Going home in the car Uncle Hector didn't speak. Neither did I. I wanted to say something, but could find no way of beginning. Maidment turned once. He said, "I'm glad you popped him in the gob. Some of those stuck-up bastards want taking down a peg or two".

Someone who hadn't been stuck-up was Marcus Daveney. The dreadful, sharp chill that had fallen when Major Birkitt had said, "I expect you'd like to go home now, Mr. Hook," had been blunted a little when Marcus Daveney stepped forward and, gently taking the shovel from Uncle Hector's hand and laying it quietly in the fireplace, had led Uncle from the room with the words, "Let's find a little fresh air shall we, Sir. We've all got a little over-heated." The unexpectedness of the 'Sir' had been like the unexpectedness of the 'Mr. Hook' from the Major. It was like hearing Bell being called Arabella: you looked round to see if there was someone there you hadn't noticed before.

I had seen little of Marcus Daveney during the evening. He did nod to me once: so he knew who I was; but for most of the time we hadn't been in the same room. I had seen him talking to Mrs. Chelvey at the bottom of the stairs; he had waited on Frances Birkitt at supper. At other times when I had seen him he had been at the centre of some eager circle or deeply engaged with James Daintry. He did better than I did. It seemed to me afterwards that I must have been pretty cowardly not to have spoken to James Daintry when he was the one I most dearly wanted to have a word from; yet at the time, taking the evening minute by minute, there seemed no opportunity except for that once when I lacked the courage to go up to him. I had ridiculously hung about near him, giving him a chance to notice me. Of course, he hadn't noticed me. He had been in the hall when Uncle Hector and I, followed by Maidment, had passed quickly out of the house. Uncle Hector hadn't looked at him, but he had cast an eye on Uncle Hector, giving him a look such as an experienced bowler might give to a young sprig of a batsman who comes and goes, his wicket shattered, without once getting his bat near the ball.

Father was waiting for me when I got home, with a hot drink that I didn't want. He was terribly eager to know how I had got on—wanted every detail from the time I arrived to the time I left. I think I must have disappointed him bitterly. He had, I know, wanted it to be a day I would never forget, and, for reasons I didn't feel like giving him, I expect it was. He was very patient with my 'all rights' and my 'don't knows', especially as he had something to tell me worth far more than anything I could tell him. He didn't ask me anything about the match. I expect he had heard enough already.

For me, of course, it had not really been a matter of Major Birkitt's team playing the College: it had been a day of sickening anxiety. I didn't really mind who won. I couldn't decide whether I wanted Marcus Daveney to do well or badly. But I did desperately want Uncle Hector to come through the game with . . . with what? . . . with honour, I suppose; I somehow wanted James Daintry to show his worth (I need not have worried), and I had to carry out my job as scorer without making a single mistake.

The College batsmen began nervously, so that hardly any runs came in the first six overs. Then, when they found that the bowling was not as deadly as they had thought it must be, they began to glide into a smooth flow of scoring. The Major tried to dislodge them by allowing nearly all of his young men to bowl; but though there was a great pounding up to the wicket from a long, long run, and though there was a flurried windmilling of arms—for all the Major's young men were fast bowlers—the College openers, no doubt coached to invulnerability, seemed to score at will. They reached sixty before a towering hit was held very securely by the big, sandy man with the pink face who stood waiting firmly on the boundary until the ball smacked smartly into his hands cupped in front of his chest.

Marcus Daveney came in next, and soon he began to fill his scoring line in my book with twos and threes and fours.

James Daintry came on to bowl at last. And at last the easy, flowing strokes changed to cautious dabs and hurried parrying. The optimistic chatter in the pavilion ran to silence. It was agreed that Jimmy Daintry knew what he was up to. You wouldn't have thought so to watch him; he took only a few paces up to the wicket; he didn't seem to be trying very hard; but the first of his victims to return—proud, it seemed, to be bowled by so great a cricketer—spread consternation by his report: "Mostly leg-breaks; then off-breaks. And you can't tell one damn ball from the other. He's a wizard."

When Marcus Daveney surrendered to the wizard for forty-four the Major obviously considered that he had the whip-hand. Daintry was taken off. Runs came once more, but the damage was done. Caution had set in. The fast young men whirled their deliveries down again with fresh hope. Even Uncle Hector was given a go when the last batsman came in, and though he four times swished the ball into the long grass of the boundary behind the Major, he did finally hit the wicket, knocking out two stumps and sending one of the bails so far that he stayed behind to pace out the distance, and returned to the pavilion long after the fielding side, holding the bail for all to see. The College boys had scored one hundred and ninety-two runs.

By tea-time the Major's side had scored forty-one for four, of which Uncle Hector had made twenty. It was generally decided that it was "anybody's game".

In spite of cress sandwiches with pickle in them and dough-buns and jam tarts, there was lively interest in the score-book; great speculation on the merits of the Major's remaining batsmen; close calculations on runs per hour and over-rates.

The calculations were soon upset. Wickets fell quickly after tea. Uncle Hector remained, but in ten minutes three young men came cheerfully sad back to the pavilion with tales of not being so young or of having eaten too many buns. Uncle Hector had batted very stubbornly up until then, but when he was joined by James Daintry he proceeded to show what he could do, cracking the ball to the boundary with tremendous power and not bothering to move from his crease when he had made the stroke. Sometimes when he had been forced to defend his wicket he would call down to the bowler, "That was a good one, son," or, "Nearly had me then," and he would laugh as if laughing at himself. Jimmy Daintry, meanwhile, was guiding ones and twos without any apparent effort, and ambling easily between wicket and wicket at half the pace he was obliged to observe for Uncle Hector's runs. He unobtrusively ambled up to his fifty before giving mid-off a towering catch to hold.

When the Major joined Uncle Hector twenty-six runs were needed for victory; Uncle Hector was twenty short of a century. Eight wickets had fallen. Spectators and players who had been wandering round the boundary or chatting in groups now stood still and were silent. The Major's players left in the pavilion now craned forward in their canvas chairs; the one batsman waiting to go in leaned against the corner of the pavilion in a patch of sun heaving prodigious yawns and stretching and restretching the elastic of his batting-gloves.

When only seven more runs were required to win and when Uncle Hector's score was at ninety-four the faster of the two bowlers gave way to one who, taking an intricate grasp on the ball and carefully inspecting his grip before bowling, sent up a delivery which appeared to be of child-like innocence.

The Major made nothing of the first ball, nor did the wicket-keeper. The batsmen ran a bye, and Uncle Hector prepared to take strike. This he did by standing up straight, forcing his shoulders back, looking imperiously all round the field, holding his bat aloft, blade upwards, and spinning it smartly in his hands before slowly bringing it down to the block-hole.

With tremendous power he hit the next ball not only out of the field of play but out of the ground.

His bat must have clipped the wicket in his mighty swing. One bail fell to the ground. There was a yell. The umpire at Uncle Hector's end raised a finger. Uncle Hector had hit his wicket. Uncle Hector had been given out.

He refused to go.

He stood there, first pointing to the boundary then at his broken wicket. Then he turned and shouted at the umpire who had given him out and then pointed towards the umpire at the other end. Major Birkitt called down the pitch—we could hear him from where we were—"You've been given out, man. For God's sake, go!"

For a long time nothing happened. Then Uncle Hector, his bat over his shoulder, marched the length of the pitch to the Major.

He said afterwards that he was pointing out that the ball had crossed the boundary before the wicket was broken and that in any case the wrong bloody umpire had given him out, so he wasn't bloody well out, was he. From where we were it looked as though he had said a good deal more than that before the Major pointed to the pavilion and slapped him across the buttocks with the flat of his bat.

It wasn't until I was thinking about it in bed that night that I realised I hadn't entered anything at all in my score-book after Uncle Hector had been given out. It seems strange to me now that the cricket entered my mind then, for Mother was coming home and Bell was coming back to look after her. That's what Father had told me after he had listened to my halting account of my evening at the Major's.

The Major's team had won the match by a single wicket; Uncle Hector had disgraced himself; Jimmy Daintry had acquitted himself as I had hoped he would.

Mother was coming home and Bell was coming back to look after her.

XXI

ON THE DAY that Mother came home I had to have dinner at
Mrs. Dance's with Mr. Leaf. Father said he had fixed it all up and
it would be better if I was out of the way for a bit. "You understand, don't you," he said. I can't remember much about it except
that Mr. Dance wasn't there and we had tapioca pudding with a
blob of strawberry jam on it and that Mrs. Dance said a funny
thing about Uncle Hector. She said she was sorry to hear that he
had been taken poorly at the Major's and that she expected it was
the rich food that had done it. She hoped he was better now.

Since the match I had steeled myself for any remarks about
Uncle Hector that might come my way. Half a week had passed,
and Mrs. Dance had been the only one to penetrate, as it were,
into the Major's supper-party.

Uncle Hector himself didn't mind talking about his performance
with the bat—and with the coal-shovel. He somehow contrived to
associate James Daintry with both events, making it sound as
though he and Jimmy had had a bit of a lark at the expense of the
toffs. And he would get strangely excited about it all, and laugh in
a wild sort of way. I don't recall, though, that he had ever put it
about that he had been taken ill and so wasn't himself at the
Major's party. Perhaps Mrs. Dance had made it up or I hadn't
caught what she really said. I didn't give it much thought, anyway, because I could think of nothing but Mother's coming back.

When I did get home—and I ran all the way from school—
Mother and Bell were there. So was Auntie Lucy. So was Aunt
May. Mother was resting. Bell was with her.

Auntie Lucy was just leaving. She had been there all day 'giving
the house a going-over'. Now she had to fly to the station. Hatch
would meet her at the other end, and it wouldn't do to have the
horse out after dark. Aunt May had been there all day, too. Her
self-appointed task had been to clean up the kitchen and cook a
good meal.

I am ashamed to have to admit that in a vague sort of way I

resented their coming. It did not occur to me that it might have been difficult for them to get away to spend a day with us. Before the hired car came to pick her up Auntie Lucy told me that Grandfather sent his love and a little something for me (a half-sovereign in a match-box, it was) and that he had been taking things easy and sitting in the garden on sunny days. I was to be a good boy and look after Mother who wasn't very strong yet. Aunt May said I wasn't to be a nuisance and expect Mother to do everything for me. Nor was I to worry Uncle Hector.

I wasn't aware that I ever did worry Uncle Hector, but, from the whispered talk Aunt May had with Father just before she left, I gathered that Uncle Hector had been 'doing funny things' again. I think she said she was glad to get away for half-an-hour; he was like a bear with a sore head and wouldn't listen to reason.

We had supper sitting round Mother's bed in the spare room. She had boiled fish. We had meat roll. Bell was very quiet, slipping away lots of times to change plates or fetch something from the kitchen. Always on the move. You wouldn't have thought that she'd been away at all, and Father didn't treat her as though she had. I expect he was thinking more of Mother.

And as the days went by we fell into a routine. Bell got the breakfast; Mother stayed in bed until twelve; we all had dinner together and then Mother went upstairs for her rest, or, if it was nice enough, sat in a deck-chair outside the kitchen door. I am not sure what Bell did in the afternoons, though once she did go to watch the College boys play cricket. She got quite cross when I said it was rather a funny thing for her to do.

Uncle Hector hadn't played cricket since the Major's match. He offered various explanations—he'd had a bellyful of cricket; there weren't any decent pitches to play on; he was too tired; he was too busy. We didn't see much of him. Aunt May came round almost every other day but if they both came it was only to say they were just passing and wouldn't stay.

Then, one evening, they both came and they both stayed. Something had happened. Bell told me what it was. But not then. Not until Uncle Hector did what he did. Then I understood why I had been sent upstairs. Aunt May, sending a pair of Arnold's white tennis trousers to the laundry, had found in one of the pockets a pound note which Uncle Hector had marked and planted in the Post Office till.

There had been a terrible scene, Bell told me, with Arnold

refusing to say how the damning note came to be there, then saying it probably wasn't the marked note at all and he distinctly remembered being given it over the tea-counter at the Tennis Club, then saying that he thought Elsie Catcher had lent it to him, then going all silent and then saying all right then, he had taken it out of the till. He had taken it, along with a few others, for Elsie's sake: Uncle Hector paid her so little that it served him right if someone made up her wages. He said he couldn't remember when he started taking money or how much he had taken. He was willing to pay it all back. He declared hotly that he didn't know anything about Major Birkitt's envelopes, and Elsie had better be kept out of it because Elsie wouldn't put up with the way Uncle Hector had treated her and she had, moreover, a friend at the Tennis Club who was a solicitor's clerk and knew all about libel.

When Uncle Hector came round that evening he said that two things stuck in his crop—Arnold's attitude and the fact that there was nothing whatever that could be done about the money. One thing he was going to do, and that was to get Elsie Catcher and Arnold and the Major and settle that business of the envelopes, once and for all. He couldn't stand unfinished business; it weighed down on him.

I knew there was something wrong, of course, long before Bell gave me the whole story. Father told me, as Aunt May had told me, that I wasn't to worry Uncle Hector. Bell told me that there was some trouble at the Post Office and that I wasn't to go worrying Mother with a lot of questions because it would only upset her. Mother told me that Uncle Hector wasn't very well: he had had a lot of troubles lately, and now there was money missing at the Post Office and he was very upset.

In the thick of it Mother was the only one who remembered my scholarship. Everyone else seemed to have too much to think about. She used to say, "I expect we shall be hearing in a little while. Mr. Leaf's sure to tell us as soon as he knows. You won't be too disappointed, will you, dear, if nothing comes of it. You've done your best, and that's all that matters." And sometimes she would say, "It won't be long now, dear. I'm sure we're going to have wonderful news! Just think, Arthur. Going to the College! And won't Grandfather be proud!" And she would ask me all over again about my answers to the questions and what I said to the High Master and what Mr. Gentleman thought and if I would like to wear a College suit and if I would be too proud to come home to my old mother when I was a College-boy.

Ancient Mariner-like, I began to want desperately to talk about the scholarship to anyone who would listen. It didn't seem fair to mention it to Willie since I had taken the exam. and he had not; no one at school seemed to remember, except Mr. Venables who said, every time he saw me, "Won't be long now, eh? Gradus ad Parnassum!" I used to try to get the Fates to declare their hand by telling off prune-stones or cherry-pits or orange-pips or iron railings. There had to be at least six to cover the whole range from success to abject failure. You started on a high note, "Pass", and then went down the scale as you spat out your stones or pips or clanked your ruler along the railings—"Pass; bim; bam; bom; arse-in-the-grass; bottom." If you got a bim or a bam there was some hope for you, but from bom downwards you were doomed.

The first indication that the earthly Fates were indeed soon to pronounce came from Mr. Leaf, and the circumstances in which he told me showed again, if ever I had doubted it, how devoted he was to my cause. On the Saturday morning after Uncle Hector's affray with Arnold, Willie and I on our shopping round had to call at the Post Office for postal-orders. We had decided to send for "The Explorer's Friend"—a device incorporating in a flat metal case, a tiny sundial and a magnetic compass. With this you could not only tell where you were heading, but could, by a cunning setting of the dial, tell the time. The advertisement in the *Boys' Own Paper* said that no adventurous boy should be without one, that it was not a toy but a Scientific Instrument and that your money would be refunded in full if you were not absolutely delighted. Willie and I felt that we could not go wrong.

No one could have been completely delighted with what was going on outside the Post Office; Uncle Hector was out on the pavement in his shirt-sleeves and apron, his fists on his hips shouting, bawling, bellowing at an ice-cream salesman whose tricycle-barrow stood at the kerb.

"I pay rates for these premises," Uncle Hector shouted." I pay good money to be where I am. And what is more I pay rates for the upkeep of this bloody road. You come here . . . You come here—nobody asked you to—you come here taking the bread out of the mouths of shopkeepers who have spent bloody years working up a nice little business and getting established. Ever heard of 'good will'? That's what I'm talking about. Good will." Then he shouted, "You're taking my good will!"

"I don't want your bloody good will," cried the ice-cream salesman. "You know what you can do with your good will. As for taking the bread out of people's mouths!—You ought to have more sense. I'm putting stuff into people's mouths—otherwise I wouldn't be much bloody use, would I!" And he rang his bell sharply, calling out, "Who wants a lovely ice-cream! Stop me and buy one."

"I'll stop you, all right," said my uncle.

He advanced on the tricycle, and grasping one of the side-wheels turned the whole thing over with a crash.

It was Mr. Leaf who restored order. He must have been behind Willie and me, watching. "Come along, my lads," he said. "There's work here for good citizens."

The first thing he did was to give the salesman a pound note; then he got us to turn the tricycle on to its wheels, and while Willie and I put the spilled packets of ice-cream back in the containers he spoke earnestly and quietly to the two contenders. We couldn't hear what he said, but when he finished no one else spoke until Uncle Hector had turned about and marched back into his shop. Then the salesman said, "You know he's mad, don't you"; and when he had given Willie and me an ice-cream each, in a gritty paper wrapper, he cycled off through the small crowd that had collected, too late, to see the fun.

Mr. Leaf then gave us half-a-crown each. "I shouldn't tell anyone about this. Wouldn't do any good, you know. You're men of the world. You'll understand." Then he said, "Oh, Arthur, you come along and see me next Saturday morning, not before eleven, mind. There ought to be something then, so I'm told. High Master's secretary, you know. Get all the notices."

Mr. Leaf, having dreadfully alarmed me thus, went into Uncle Hector's shop. Willie and I, though desperately keen to possess The Explorer's Friend, turned away. We needed no conference to reach the unanimous conclusion that it was not the right time to ask Uncle Hector for a postal-order. We never bought The Scientific Instrument, for when we made a second attempt we encountered something terrifyingly beyond the scope of The Explorer's Friend.

We lingered a little while before drifting off to Mr. Caxton's sweetshop. Stocks had to be laid in for the afternoon's expedition to the junction. Willie had heard that there was to pass through a G. J. Churchward Swindon. When he first told me about it I had no idea what a Churchward Swindon was, and pointed this out to him. "It's an engine, a railway-engine, you ass! Everyone knows about Churchward."

As it happened, I was not destined to add to my knowledge of Churchwards that afternoon. We took, or, rather, intended to take a short cut to the junction. Somehow, we never found the junction; we did not even find the railway line. We found a disused brick-kiln, a gravel-pit, a dead sheep and a dried-up canal. At this point we gave up. Turning for home we got briefly lost in a plantation of young fir-trees and there and then resolved that we would never again set off on such an expedition without The Explorer's Friend. Mr. Caxton's Colonial gums sustained us in our forced march to get to Uncle Hector's Post Office before he closed for the week-end. Somehow it had become imperative to us to get our postal-orders before the day was out.

And meanwhile, at the Post Office, there was being enacted a scene which came fully to light only when Elsie Catcher, who heard some of it, and Aunt May, who saw part of it, were suffi-ciently recovered to fill in details of the afternoon's business that Major Birkitt couldn't or, as some said, wouldn't remember.

Just about the time that Willie and I gave up our search for the signal-box, Major Birkitt had burst into Uncle Hector's shop, demanding a cowed Elsie Catcher to fetch her Employer. When Uncle Hector appeared—he had been having a little sleep—the Major came to the point: he had heard that my uncle was putting it about that he, the Major, was indulging in a betting swindle.

Uncle Hector ordered Elsie to retire to the store-room, which she did, baffled but alert and all ears behind the flimsy partition. Aunt May, aroused by the raised voices in the shop, observed as best she could through the coloured glass door.

Uncle Hector told the Major that whoever had said such a thing had better come out into the open and say it again. The Major said he had every confidence in his informant and that Uncle Hector obviously was not aware of the law against slander. If Uncle Hector had an accusation to make, let him make it there and then and not spread his filthy rumours round the town by talking to anyone who was fool or rogue enough to listen to him.

"And what are these rumours I'm supposed to have been spreading?"

"You know very well what I'm talking about."

"I don't know what you're talking about. You come into my

shop with some cock-and-bull story about betting and expect me to know all about it. Well, I don't."

"I suggest you do."

"You can suggest what the hell you like. What you suggest and what you know are two different things. Now, Major, I'm a busy man. If you've got something worth-while to say, let's have it, shall we?"

The Major didn't answer at once, but he turned and pulled down the blue linen blind over the shop-door, thereby telling the shopping public that Uncle Hector's was CLOSED. Then he came back, leaned across the counter, took Uncle Hector by the lapels of his jacket and forcing him to bend forwards said. "You've been spreading it round that I've been swindling the Post Office and the Book-makers. I'm not going to argue the toss with you. You haven't a shred of evidence. Not a shred. But I'm going to tell you something. And don't you ever forget it. You say one word against my good name—you give as much as a hint—as much as a whisper of whatever it is you've been spreading about, and I'll hound you out of this shop and out of this town, and I'll see to it that wherever you go they'll hear the sort of man you are. And I'll tell you another thing: you don't play cricket here again, not on any ground that I've got anything to do with. Everyone knows how you let me down. I shan't give you a chance to do it again. And, by God, I'll see to it you don't give anyone else the same dirty treatment, either."

He threw Uncle Hector back against the drawers behind the counter, brushed the palms of his hands one against the other, and turning about released the blue linen blind before letting himself out with a crash and a jangling of the shop-bell.

Aunt May said that she couldn't get Uncle Hector to speak. She led him upstairs and took him up a strong cup of tea.

Willie and I, of course, knew nothing of this. We were probably just bursting out from the fir trees when it began. We knew where we were when we got out of the plantation, but it didn't diminish our determination to possess The Explorer's Friend. We had our three-and-sixpences with us: we must turn them into a postal-order.

When we got there the shop was still open. Aunt May was behind the wire mesh of the Post Office part. She had thumped down the date-stamp on one of our postal-orders when a heavy van drew up outside. "It's the man with the preserving-jars," she said. "Arthur, show him where to put them. In the shed." "I'll go," said Willie. "Don't forget the stamps."

I thought Aunt May seemed rather strange—surprising for me, because I never was one to notice that kind of thing off my own bat. She was destined to become stranger.

Willie came back into the shop. "Come quick," he said.

I followed him round to the store-shed at the back. The man with the crate of jars was just outside the open door pressing a red handkerchief over his mouth.

Uncle Hector was inside. He was holding his breath. His tongue was out. He was hanging by the neck. The cricket-ball in the sock lay on his chest. The sash-cord ran like an iron rod from his neck to the hook in the roof. Near his dangling feet was an overturned box.

XXII

AUNT MAY MOVED into our house that night. At first we were going to have Arnold, too; but he said he had a friend at the printing-works who would put him up. He did ask Aunt May if she would like him to stay with her, but Aunt May answered all questions with sobs, and it was felt that Arnold's presence might serve only to remind her of the tragedy. There was some talk of my being sent off to Grandfather's, both for my own peace of mind and so that Arnold could have my room; but Father said there wasn't much point: I'd seen the worst of it, and if Arnold could go somewhere else I might just as well stay at home.

So I stayed at home, or, rather, stayed at home when no one could find a reason for getting me out of the house, it being generally agreed that if I could possibly be sent off on some errand or some visit the better it would be for everybody.

For a few days we lived like shadows in a house of shadows. Aunt May wept quietly most of the time. Almost any remark, guarded or innocent, seemed in some macabre way to refer to deaths in general or Uncle Hector's in particular. Mother spent fewer day-time hours in bed, because, I suspect, lying there she could do little to help Aunt May, and Aunt May, unwittingly, was doing little to help her. Arnold looked in in the evenings, but he found almost nothing to say. His mother wouldn't go out with him, in fact she would not leave the house at all, so he got away into the calm summer evenings as quickly as he could.

There were, I gathered from hushed conversations, visits from The Authorities. Even I was subjected to one—that of P.C. Juniper. We sat in the best room for this, he, in bicycle clips, on the sofa with his helmet beside him, I on the plush chair usually reserved for Uncle Hector. He had a note-book on his knees and wrote with an indelible pencil which he dabbed to his tongue every time he told me I was going too fast. To be honest, P.C. Juniper

228

was very decent to me. Before he went into the kitchen for a cup of tea he showed me his handcuffs and mysteriously produced his shiny truncheon for my inspection.

We also had a visit from Mr. Benskin. I learned from this, though I was not present, that there was to be a memorial service 'later in the week'. (No funeral service?)

Later in the week was when I was going to hear about my scholarship. Saturday morning, Mr. Leaf had said. Eleven o'clock. I hadn't told anybody. I didn't want to set off with everyone knowing where I was going, only to have to come back and say it wasn't any good. And I was glad that the exam. had slipped quietly away. If I was going to fail, had failed, the hardest part was not going to be exclusion from the College but the admission of failure. And every morning my waking thoughts were that I hadn't got the scholarship. I don't know why. I don't remember my supposed failure being part of a dream; but wherever the idea came from it took a long time to get it out of my head. The sense of relief that came to me when I realised that it wasn't yet Saturday, that I hadn't yet seen Mr. Leaf, that I wasn't already doomed, came to me almost like a cleansing. So strong was this feeling that I found myself chanting bits of the psalms as I dressed. "Wash me thoroughly from my wickedness", I would render, or "Purge me with hyssop and I shall be clean". Perhaps, though I did not know it, I was offering prayers.

Whatever failure I was destined to suffer at the end of the week I certainly had to put up with one in the middle. To the surprise of everyone concerned, assuredly including myself, I was selected to play for the School 3rd XI on the Wednesday afternoon. The match was on our ground against a school called Wilton, known to us as Stilton—not because of the cheese, but as a reproach against them for including such lanky players in their junior team. I was so elated at being chosen that at the time I would not have cared if we were to play a race of giants, but on the day, when the others began to spin elaborate yarns of the terrible Stilton bowlers and their devastating batsmen, I began to have misgivings which bit by bit grew into sick panic.

By tea-time Wilton had scored nearly one hundred and fifty runs. Tea was an uneasy break in which we grudgingly passed halves of buttered buns to the Wilton fellows while searching for something to say to them. Our conversation did not reach great heights. "What's your headmaster like?" was a safe opening. "Have you

got any fast bowlers?" was more to the point, but far more dis-
quieting.

They declared their innings closed soon after tea, safe, no doubt,
in the knowledge that they did indeed have fast bowlers. When
my turn came to bat—and it came with sickening haste—we were
nearly a hundred behind. I had expected to be sent in last, and had
seen myself responsible for hitting a six off the last ball to win the
match. Mercifully no such task was imposed on me; there were
three batsmen to go in after me. The only thing was that although
most of our men made a brief stay at the wicket, Harold Witty,
one of our openers, had not only survived but had given Stilton
some of their own medicine. It was generally felt that if someone
could stay with Harold, even without scoring, the game might yet
be saved or even won. So it was that as I sat padded and gloved
miserably yawning in the gloom of the dressing-room our captain
earnestly impressed on me that, above all, once in I must not get
out. He didn't mind if I got no runs. All I had to do was to keep
my end up.

There came a shout from the field. It was my turn to go in. My
captain's last piece of advice, as with forced grim gaiety I left him,
remained with me all the way to the wicket—"Don't do anything
daft."

I squared up to my first ball. I saw it all the way from the
bowler's hand. I saw its stitches. I saw the faded gold stamped
upon it. I saw that I could hit it. It was made for hitting. It was
a chance for me. I advanced my left foot and swung my bat.

All the way back to the pavilion I experienced not a feeling of
shame but a hot anger at the unfairness of the game. The ball must
have hit a plantain, or kept low, or I must have caught my bat on
the straps of my pads. I couldn't have missed it otherwise. I was
so SURE of it, yet it had hit my wicket and I was out. It wasn't
fair.

Bell had been watching. She and Marcus Daveney faded away
into the trees behind the pavilion as, near tears, I made my stony
way back.

I suppose it was Bell and Marcus Daveney. Or perhaps it was
Bell with somebody else. When I asked her later on what she
thought of the game she said she hadn't seen it. I don't know
to this day if she did or not. But I did find out, years later,
that my inclusion in the 3rd XI was not in recognition of my
merits as a cricketer. Mr. Venables had arranged it with the master

who ran the school cricket so that I should be out of the way for the whole of the afternoon—the afternoon when the Coroner's Court sat on Uncle Hector.

Though I was not allowed in any way to participate in the proceedings of the inquest, nor in the conversation about it (I didn't know it had taken place until Willie told me, a week later), I was permitted to learn that Aunt May was to stay with us 'until she felt better', that Mr. Eustace had been down and 'put a man in' to run the Post Office until 'arrangements could be made' and that there was to be a memorial service for Uncle Hector on Saturday at eleven o'clock. It wasn't going to be funeral service; Uncle Hector wasn't going to be there 'because of certain difficulties' which I wouldn't understand. What I did understand was that eleven o'clock on Saturday morning was exactly the time when I was to see Mr. Leaf. I didn't know anything about memorial services. How long did they last? Supposing I was unable to keep my appointment?

It seems ridiculous to me now that I didn't go to Mr. Leaf and tell him of the difficulty I was in. That to do so never occurred to me at all shows either my simplicity or my respect for arrangements made by grown-ups. Aunt May showed little respect for the temporary help put in the Post Office by Mr. Eustace. She was obviously longing to go to inspect him, but could not bring herself to step outside, for, she said, she couldn't face her friends. She had heard that the replacement selected by Mr. Eustace was a mere youth, scarcely out of school. She thought it disgraceful that such an important post should be held by a schoolboy. Slippery Major Birkitt would, she knew very well, twist him round his little finger. Father tried to bring her round to talking about the rest of Uncle Hector's shop. Would it not be a good idea if Arnold took it on? It was a nice little business and Arnold knew the ropes. But Aunt May would have none of it, would not contemplate that part of her future at all. Arnold was a fine boy, she said. Arnold had a fine career in front of him. They had worked their fingers to the bone to see to it that Arnold should want for nothing, and he wasn't going to spend his days behind a counter, thank you very much.

Meanwhile, an undeclared war was waged between Aunt May and Bell as to who should be in charge of our kitchen. But in spite of the domestic rivalry, Bell seemed very happy again. Often I heard her singing lightly in her room. Her dresses were gay. She put flowers round the house. She gave me half-a-crown because I did all the washing-up one evening when she wanted to get away.

She seemed to want to get away on most evenings, and though I didn't have to stay in just because she was out, I did feel that I oughtn't to go far. They were lovely evenings, too, drenched in sun, spiced with flowers, tranquil in warmth. It did not seem to strike Aunt May that Bell was seldom at home. I think she would have gnawed upon it had not something else intruded upon her: news came that Major Birkitt had left Great Lodge.

There could not have been one single explanation about his departure left unexplored. Aunt May said he was ashamed of what he'd done and had slunk off like a cur who couldn't face the music; Mother considered that he'd gone to some race-meeting, like Ascot, which was only to be expected of him; Bell said he'd only done what a Gentleman ought to do; Father said that all he wanted to know was whether that Mrs. Chelvey had left Great Lodge too. It was generally agreed that the one person who could explain it all was Maidment; but when the chance came, no one thought of asking him, for when he did come to the house it was to bring a wreath and a card from the Major expressing 'Respect and Profound Sorrow'. This was such a surprise that when, after a glass of beer, Maidment had left, speculation began all over again.

I am ashamed to say that I avoided Aunt May. I didn't know what to say to her. I asked Mother about it and she said that Aunt May would like it if I talked about everyday things. But my everyday things were not Aunt May's, and while it seemed silly to tell her about cricket or about the way Willie could make a whistle out of a stalk of hedge-parsley or how a boy at school who had been smoking tea-leaves had been sick in Geography lesson, I couldn't think of anything at all that Aunt May did that I could talk about. And she was always on the edge of tears. When flowers came she said how kind people were and what a comfort it was to have good friends—and burst out crying.

I asked Mother about that, too. She said it was only natural. She said that when you weren't feeling very strong and someone was nice to you, then that would make you want to cry. She said I would understand one day and that I must be especially nice to Auntie May. Why didn't I show her my stamp collection?

I would never have thought of that. It seemed to me that the only thing my aunt and I had in common was her worry over

Uncle Hector and mine over the scholarship. I had wondered if I should tell her all about it and confide in her that on Saturday Mr. Leaf was going to tell me if I had passed or not, but now Friday had come, and with the service so near I didn't think that Aunt May could be interested in anything else. Besides, it didn't seem fair to tell her and not tell Mother. It would have to be the stamps.

I was surprised at her eagerness when I asked her. She would love to see my stamps. After tea would do very well. It was very nice of me to show my treasures to her. And she began to sob.

I wondered what stamps I should show her. None that might connect me with Major Birkitt, of course. Perhaps none that hinted of death and decay—I didn't want to bring out those tears that made me feel so helpless. Perhaps she would like animals. There were those Malay States tigers; the Tunis camels. Before tea I went through my Colonials to see what they could do for us. The album was dusty—I had been neglecting the colonies—but sure enough, its contents were full of colour. I had only to dust it and I should be ready for Aunt May. I held it before me, ready to blow it clean. An azure envelope slid into my lap. It bore the typed address, 'The Honourable M. Daveney. Mr. Annesley's House'. It was the note that Bell had asked me to deliver on the day when Uncle Hector had said that Bell was playing a hard game. It was crumpled; it looked as though it had been through a lot. It was still unopened and (I felt a spurt of guilt), it was, of course, undelivered. I couldn't remember whether at the time I had meant to hand it over. I was to leave it on the hall table or give it to Mr. Cater, Bell had said. I think I had kept it to see what would happen. I could not remember putting it where I found it.

On an impulse I forced my thumb under the flap and split the tough paper, at once ruling out the half-formed notion I had of giving it back to Bell with some story, not far from the truth, that, mysteriously, I had just come across it.

There was a typed sheet inside. It said 'To Typing. Top and two copies. 15/-'. At the foot of the leaf, in Bell's hand, a single word. 'Friday'.

I felt in a helpless kind of way that I should do something about it. But what was there to do? I hadn't done anything after Bell had entrusted me with it. What could I do now? All that was left was to get rid of the paper that smouldered in my hand. It crossed my mind that it was Friday. The note said 'Friday', but it was a Friday lost in the past. I wondered if it was as obsolete as it seemed. Suppose it wasn't! Suppose this very Friday was, for Bell, as good as the one I had impaired. I suddenly needed to know. I would . . . I would . . . What was there that I could do? I had to show my stamps to Aunt May; I had to go to Friday-night choir-practice. I could see no way of doing what I wanted to do; I wasn't even clear, I never had been, what it was that I wanted, unless it was to spy on Bell.

I told myself that it wasn't exactly spying. I just wanted to see for myself what Bell was doing. That was all. I would miss choir-practice. I would leave the house at the right time and follow Bell, or wait for Bell, or search for Bell. I wouldn't admit that I would look first behind the vestry; but I think I knew my feet would carry me there. And I think I knew that after that I would go to the little wood behind the cricket pavilion. What I didn't know was whether or not I really wanted to find her.

My conversazione with Aunt May wasn't really a success. After tea I took the most interesting sheets from the album and laid them on the kitchen table; I even prepared a little talk about them and found the ivory magnifying glass so that she could see with what care the engravers had worked. I was putting the finishing touches to my display when Bell called from the kitchen to say I was to help with the washing-up. It didn't take long. Bell sang away to herself giving the crockery a lick and a promise while I did the tea-pot and the knives and forks. It had been a 'choir-practice' tea for my benefit. I did not resent having to help with the washing-up; it lifted a little of the guilt I was already beginning to feel.

When I came out of the scullery Aunt May was standing by the kitchen table. She had collected together all my carefully-arranged sheets and laid the magnifying-glass on top of them. "Very nice, dear," she said. "How busy you've been." I tried to arouse her interest. I asked her if she'd seen this or noticed that; but she wouldn't be roused. All she would say was, "Yes, dear. Very nice." I meanly asked her what she thought of the stamps with the flags on. "Very nice, dear," she said. "Very interesting." There were no beflagged stamps on the table.

Bell passed through, humming. "I told you I'd be out this evening, Auntie, didn't I?" she said lightly. "Yes, dear," said Aunt May. And I half expected her to add, "Very nice."

I hung about miserable until six o'clock, my mind not completely made up. I had remembered that I must tell Willie that I wouldn't be coming to the practice. I wouldn't tell him everything, of course. That was one of the good things about Willie; he wasn't nosey. He wouldn't press me to say more than I wanted. But if I was going to tell him anything I must slip off and tell him at once. Faced with the reality of my scheme I was beginning to lose heart. But I would go through with it.

Father found me at the kitchen door. "Going out?"

"Yes. I'm going to see Willie."

"Oh, ah. Good. Tell him to let 'em know that you can't come to your what's-it tonight. Your aunt and I have got to see the solicitor. I want you to look after your mother till we get back."

He was dressed in his best suit.

At ten o'clock next morning I also was in my best suit. So was everyone else in the house. And there was that uneasy hush that people observe when they are going to assist in a solemn occasion. There were people I had never seen before, all to be explained to me and all to be shaken by the hand. Some, when they came in, seemed to be known by everyone, and their arrival was like a spurt of flame in a dull coal-fire. Sometimes the gathering found itself getting almost merry. Then, as if at a word of command, a hush would fall and a coughing and a nervous movement would begin. I felt as I felt at Major Birkitt's party. I was wondering if I could slip away to my room. I was sure no one would notice.

I was edging towards the door when Auntie Lucy, with Hatch close behind her, coming from nowhere, knelt down in front of me and took me in her arms and kissed me. Tears sprang to my eyes. I couldn't help it. It didn't matter that all those strangers were there. I couldn't help it. I think I was suddenly made aware why Auntie Lucy had come, and Hatch, and all the others. I think it was just the fact, for the first time becoming plain to me, that they had put aside whatever they would have been doing to come to unite for one purpose. It filled me with wonder and a kind of awe. And when Mother came, dressed for church, with Father's hand under her elbow, I ached with love and a kind of gratitude which choked me with humility and elation.

We all walked to the church except Mother and Father and Aunt May. Bell and I went with Auntie Lucy and Hatch. I don't know where Arnold was. With his mother, perhaps. Auntie Lucy said that Grandfather had given her a message for me. It was that he couldn't come because he had the Imperial Jim-Jams, but he

235

would be thinking of us all and was sending a little something to make up for his not coming. The little something was a gold sovereign. "Grandfather said I was to tell you to be sure not to put it in the collection-bag by mistake," Auntie Lucy told me. "Will there be a collection, Auntie?" I said. I had brought no money with me. Saturday was the day for pocket-money, but of course Father hadn't had time to think about it.

When Auntie Lucy mentioned the collection-bag I realised again that I had no idea what the Service was going to be like. Would we have to sing hymns? I wondered. Were there enough of us to make a go of a psalm? Would we sit in just four or five pews in an empty church?

Whatever I visualised, whatever ran through my mind as we gathered in the porch so that we could go into the church in the right order, I came nowhere near, not within touching distance, not within seeing distance, of reality.

The church was packed. Every pew, every seat was filled. A few heads turned and everyone stood as we were led down the aisle to the front. I think the organ was playing. It must have been. And as soon as we got up from our prayers there was a shuffling from the Lady Chapel and—I wanted to call out for joy—I wanted to shout—I wanted to cry—the full choir, swirling quietly behind the cross that Ernest Green carried high, processed to their stalls and quietly waited. I saw Mr. Webster and Jumping Jesus, Harold Witty and Jackie Dawes. They were all there. I didn't know they were coming. And there they were.

I couldn't have expressed my thoughts. I suppose, as I see it now, I wanted to say, 'Oh, dear God, Bless these wonderful friends for coming today!' I found myself thinking hard about Uncle Hector, and how I hadn't tried to get close to him.

We sang a hymn, *Abide with me*, and Mr. Gedge read the lesson about Death being swallowed up in Victory, and we sang *The Lord's my Shepherd*. There were prayers. Pretending to blow my nose, I half turned my head when everybody was settling as Mr. Benskin climbed up the pulpit steps. I saw our Headmaster and Mrs. Abrams with Mrs. Vosper, and Mr. Gentleman and Miss Partridge and Hughie Mynn and, I might have known that she would be there, Madge Ingles.

Mr. Benskin's address did not at first seem very respectful to the dead. He took as his text, 'The fool hath said, in his heart, there is no God', and he soon introduced the story of the Gadarene swine rushing to destruction, being filled with the Devil. My thoughts began to wander to Mr. Leaf and the scholarship. He would wonder why I was late. He might think I didn't care. Oh, but of course, he would know where I was. He would understand. Mr. Benskin found his way back to my vacant mind. God is always there, he said. You have only to look round you to see it. There may be times when you doubt, when, in your despair, in your foolishness, you say in your heart that indeed there is no God. But you must be comforted and have faith. (Aunt May was receiving no comfort. She was sitting with bowed head, dabbing her eyes.) We have all the proof we want, declared Mr. Benskin. Consider the sun, the moon, the stars. They tell us all we need to know. Only the fool doubts. There are greater works of God than we puny mortals. Let us lift our eyes unto the hills. Let us look to the Heavens.

I see now, what I didn't see then, that the closing hymn said in one language what Mr. Benskin had been saying in another. If it had been pointed out to me at the time, I think I would have understood, and I think I would have listened more attentively to the address. The hymn put Mr. Benskin from my mind. It filled my mind and it filled—I grope for words—my heart.

Mr. Benskin announced that we would for our closing hymn sing 'Addison's great perceptive song of praise,' 'The spacious firmament on high'. It was to the Tallis setting. You cannot call it tune, nor melody, nor song—for it is majestic, warming, touching music, a sublime utterance. It seemed that everyone was thankful to sing it, for the words and their music filled the church with great glory. It was when we came to the third verse, the one about the sun and the moon and the stars, I could find no voice to sing it—that I realised what Mr. Benskin had meant.

> ' What, though, in solemn silence, all
> Move round the dark terrestrial ball?
> What though no real voice nor sound
> Amid their radiant orbs are found?
> In reason's ear they all rejoice,
> And utter forth a glorious voice,
> For ever singing, as they shine,
> The Hand that made us is Divine.'

Afterwards, outside the church when Addison and Tallis had

slipped away, Mr. Benskin held court, shaking hands and having a jolly word with everyone. Even Aunt May managed to smile as he drew her aside and spoke quietly to her.

As I was waiting my turn I felt a light touch on my shoulder. "Come along as soon as you can, Arthur," said Mr. Leaf. "There ought to be something waiting for us."

Mr. Benskin was still talking to Aunt May. There seemed little point in my waiting. Mr. Benskin wouldn't want to shake hands with me. I moved away from our group—I could explain later. I was just slipping behind a tall tomb-stone when Bell caught me. "Where are you off to?" she said. I told the truth. "Mr. Leaf wants to see me for a minute".

She opened her handbag and took from it a blue envelope. "Then you can deliver this for me. There's a dear".

Taking the envelope I pushed it into my jacket pocket and ran for the Library as fast as I could.